Baby Love

CATHERINE ANDERSON

Baby Love

AVON BOOKS ◆ NEW YORK

This is a work of fiction. Names, characters, places, and incidents either are products of the author's imagination or are used fictitiously. Any resemblance to actual events, locales, organizations, or persons, living or dead, is entirely coincidental and beyond the intent of either the author or the publisher.

AVON BOOKS, INC.
1350 Avenue of the Americas
New York, New York 10019

Copyright © 1999 by Adeline Catherine Anderson
Author photo by Terry Day's Studio
Published by arrangement with the author

ISBN: 0-7394-0618-3

www.avonbooks.com/romance

To my dad, George S. Son, who taught me two of life's sweetest secrets: that the human heart has a limitless capacity for love and that the bond between father and daughter has nothing to do with genetics. You're living proof that the biggest and the best things truly do come from Texas.

 *Prologue*

An icy Idaho night wind whistled along the dark, deserted sidewalk, carrying with it the snow-crisp scents of mountain pine and fir. The gusts pushed at Maggie Stanley from behind, tossing her long dark hair over her eyes and cutting through her thin nylon jacket. Shuddering with the cold, she hugged her bundled baby close and forced herself to keep moving. Her feet felt as if they weighed a thousand pounds, and she worried that she might slip on the treacherous black ice that coated the cracked cement.

A flash of automobile headlights from somewhere behind made her heart do a flip. She flattened herself against a building, praying that the shadows cast by the eaves might hide her. The car moved on through the intersection. *Not Lonnie.* Going limp against the wet siding, Maggie gulped back a sob, the jolt of fear so numbing that she could no longer feel her legs. *Oh, God. Off the street. I have to get off the street.*

She lurched into a plodding run, clutching Jaimie protectively against her. With every step she took, the heavy diaper bag slammed into her bruised leg. As her fear moved away and feeling returned to her extremities, the pain of the blows became so excruciating that nausea rolled up her burning throat.

Up ahead, she saw an unlighted sign through the shadowy gloom. The boldly painted letters beckoned to her like a beacon. *Pacific Northern*. She'd done it. She was almost there. Only a few more steps now.

Breathless, she staggered to a stop when she reached the sign and stared incredulously at the chain-link fence. Beyond the sturdy wire mesh lay the railway yard where she hoped to hitch a ride.

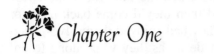 Chapter One

Drifting in the misty unreality of dreams, Rafe Kendrick surrendered himself to the images that moved softly through his mind. As he sank deeper into slumber, the details gained clarity and seemed more lifelike. He smiled drowsily. He was down on the lakeshore, he realized, not far from the main ranch house. Through the stands of evergreen trees, he could see the sprawling expanse of ivy-covered brick that was his family home, three of its fireplace chimneys silhouetted against the summer-blue sky. On the gentle breeze, he heard the whinny of a stallion coming from the north pasture behind the stables.

Home. On some level he knew this was only a dream, but it felt wonderfully real, a vivid recollection of all that he'd lost. Small, water-worn rocks shifted under his feet as he followed the sweep of shoreline. The soft lapping of the water soothed him. He took a deep breath, identifying the smells that had once been so commonplace he scarcely noticed them. Fir and pine. Sun-warmed grass and fertile earth. A crisp edge to the breeze, even on a summer day, because the high-elevation basin was ringed by snowcapped peaks.

His footsteps slowed as he crested a slight rise. Ahead of him in a shaded grove, he saw a sorrel mare and a buckskin gelding. They grazed contentedly, their reins loosely draped over the limbs of sapling oaks. Nearby two blanket-draped saddles rested on the green grass.

A sense of déjà vu filled Rafe. He remembered this day. He and Susan had taken the kids for a short ride through the forest, and then they'd come back here for a picnic by the lake. They had enjoyed themselves, singing silly songs they made up as they went along to entertain their three-year-old son, Keefer. It had been a near perfect outing, and they had ended it here because they loved spending time near the water.

He eagerly scanned the clearing, his yearning to catch a glimpse of his family so sharp that it made his breath hitch. Drawn by a red-checkered tea towel that fluttered in the breeze, his gaze came to rest on the wicker picnic basket first. The hinged lid was wedged partially open by the protruding neck of a wine bottle that their nanny-housekeeper, Becca, had slipped inside to accompany their meal.

Oh, yes . . . he remembered it all so clearly—Susan, in snug faded jeans and a pink cotton blouse, her golden hair caught at the crown with a clip to spill in a silky cascade to her shoulders. He could almost hear the sound of her laughter rippling around him—and smell the little-boy scent of his son, riding double in front of him on the buckskin. After coming here to eat, he had rocked his baby daughter to sleep while Susan set out the food, and he could recall exactly how his little girl's plump body had felt in his arms.

A slight frown pleated Rafe's brow. This was too real to be a dream. He could actually hear the water lapping and feel the breeze caressing his skin. With every step he took, the beach pebbles pressed sharply into the soles of his riding boots. Dreams weren't this vivid.

Oh, God. Could he dare to hope? Maybe a miracle had happened, and somehow he'd been hurtled back in time. Maybe, after all this time, his prayers had finally been answered and God was giving him a second chance.

Oh, yes, please . . . All he needed was just one more

chance. This time, he wouldn't blow it. He'd put his family first. Nothing had ever mattered more to him than his wife and kids. *Nothing*. He'd just gotten so caught up in the everyday responsibilities and obligations of being a husband and father that he'd lost sight of what was really important for a while.

He'd never make that mistake again.

Wanting, *needing* to believe that this was all actually real, he clenched his hands into throbbing fists and eagerly scanned the clearing. Susan and the kids lay only a short distance away from the picnic basket. The three of them were taking a nap on a Navajo blanket he'd spread on the grass for them. Their snuggled forms were dappled with sunlight that filtered through the fir boughs above them. Susan lay on her back with a child on each side of her, her sweet face relaxed in sleep, her lush mouth curved in a slight smile of contentment. His son Keefer had fallen asleep with his arms around her neck, and he still clung to her, his baby-soft cheek pressed to her breast. The six-month-old Chastity was cradled in Susan's other arm, her tawny curls glistening like drizzles of honey.

Rafe walked toward them, a sharp ache stabbing his chest. Dear God, how he loved them, and it had been so long—so very long—since he'd seen them. *Thank you, God.* He wanted to shout and run to cover the distance more quickly. But no. He couldn't shake the feeling that this scene from out of his past might exist only in his imagination. A loud sound or sudden movement might shatter it like fragile glass.

As he moved closer to the blanket, Susan's face grew less distinct. He squinted down at her, wanting to see her more clearly. But no matter how hard he tried, her features remained an elusive blur, framed by a nimbus of golden hair. He came to a stop, staring so hard that his eyes burned. It was like trying to see her through a plate of steam-fogged glass.

"Susan?" he called softly. *"Honey, wake up. It's me, Rafe."*

She didn't stir at the sound of his voice. He reached a hand toward her, his need to touch her a craving he couldn't deny. Just as his fingertips nearly grazed her cheek, the ground under his feet shifted and seemed to jerk. In a twinkling, his wife and children vanished, and he found himself surrounded by an endless and horribly empty darkness.

"Susan? Don't leave again! Susan?"

He felt a light touch on his arm, and as he turned, a dizzy feeling came over him. As the sensation subsided, he realized that his surroundings had changed. He was still on the lakeshore, only now it was late evening. Susan sat beside him on the grass, and once again, he couldn't see her clearly. She was only a shadowy presence, and he knew she would vanish again if he tried to touch her. The knowledge filled him with a sense of hopelessness and pain that ran so deep his bones ached.

Her face was a blurred, pale oval in the darkness as she turned to regard him. *"What are you doing, Rafe?"* she asked softly. *"You promised me you'd find someone else to love, that you wouldn't spend the rest of your life alone if something ever happened to me. Now, just look at you!"*

He clamped his arms around his knees to resist his urge to reach for her. *"I can't, Susan. I know I promised, but I can't. I'll never love anyone but you. Never."*

Her voice rang with sadness. *"Oh, Rafe, you can't go on like this. Life is such a precious gift, and you're wasting it."*

He closed his eyes. *"I don't have a life,"* he whispered raggedly. *"Without you and the kids, I'm just marking off the days. Why can't you understand that?"*

Silence settled between them, broken only by the gentle sound of lapping water and the night wind whispering in the evergreen trees. Those sounds had once seemed like music to him. Now hearing them only made him hurt, and he wanted to escape. Leaving right then was impossible, though. As long as Susan was there, even in this elusive, heartbreaking way, he couldn't leave her.

"*It's time, Rafe,*" she whispered gently, her voice seeming to fade in and out. "*You have to let me and the kids go now and move on.*"

Move on to what? He wanted to scream the question, only a lump had lodged in his throat, making it difficult for him to speak.

"*You keep praying for one more chance,*" she murmured. "*Well, dear heart, now you're getting one. Don't throw it away or mess it up because you're still clinging to ghosts.*"

"*Mess what up?*"

"*You'll see.*" He heard a smile in her voice. "*Just open your heart, Rafe. You'll see.*"

Rafe jerked awake in the middle of a snore. For an instant, he thought it was the bad dream that startled him, but as the grogginess cleared from his head, he decided it was something else. After two years of riding the rails, he had learned to sleep lightly even when drunk. Something wasn't right.

He heard nothing except the constant clank of the train wheels and the clatter of the boxcar. He nudged his Stetson back to regard his four traveling companions, who sat hunched along the rear wall of the boxcar just as they had been earlier, only now they all seemed to be staring at something to his left.

Shaking off the last trace of sleep and the haunting dream along with it, he flicked a glance in that direction and did a double take. A *girl?* He could scarcely credit his eyes. Pushing with the heel of one boot, he sat more erect and turned the full blast of his gaze on her.

A shaft of moonlight fell over her. He could see she was a beauty, slightly built with a wealth of dark hair and that rare milk-white skin you see in pictures but seldom run across in real life.

A fragile little flower.

Not likely. Fragile little flowers didn't hitch rides on boxcars. She probably had a switchblade in her hip pocket and was just waiting for some poor bastard to mess with her. Well, judging by the interest she was drawing from his fellow travel mates, she wouldn't have long to wait.

As if she sensed Rafe's gaze on her, she turned to look at him, and he found himself staring into the biggest, most vulnerable, and most frightened eyes he'd ever seen. He got the oddest feeling—a tight, achy sensation, dead in the center of his chest.

She ducked her head so fast he had little time to analyze his reaction. Not that it took a genius I.Q. to figure it out. He was drunk, for starters, and it had been a hell of a long time since he'd gazed into eyes that didn't seem shuttered and shrewd.

"Seem" was the keyword in that observation, he felt sure. First impressions were often deceiving, and women could be consummate actresses, especially the hard-as-nails variety who bummed the rails. The gentle caress of moonlight undoubtedly made her look prettier and more fragile than she actually was. She was probably about as vulnerable as a hedgehog and twice as ornery.

While she gazed fixedly down at the jacket she held clutched to her chest, Rafe studied her. An angelic countenance with delicate features. Long, thick eyelashes that cast shadows on her pale cheeks in the eerie illumination. A cute little turned-up nose and a chin that hinted at a stubborn streak.

Who in her right mind would hug her coat instead of wearing it when the temperature was registering close to zero? The boxcar door was jammed and wouldn't slide shut, making it far colder and draftier inside than usual. With no protection from the cold, she'd be dead by daylight. Not to mention that no young woman right in the head would climb on a boxcar with five sex-starved men. Correction: four sex-starved men and one uninterested, has-been rancher. Even at that, she was faced with some stiff odds.

Rafe snorted at the unintentional pun and curled his hand over the neck of his whiskey bottle. Thank God she wasn't his problem. He was too drunk to help her out if things got ugly, and he planned to get drunker yet before the night was finished. If there was a code that a man learned to live by while bumming the rails, it was to mind his own business. The little lady was on her own.

Glancing at the other men, who were still staring at her as if they'd never seen a female before, Rafe decided things were definitely going to turn nasty. He'd give it five minutes—ten at the outside.

Picking up the bottle, he gave a mental shrug. She looked on the high side of twenty-one. That was old enough to know better. Right? Damned straight. If you messed with the bull, you got the horn.

Well, she'd better be able to handle it. Those yo-yos weren't your street-corner-variety thugs; they were hard-core railroad trash, the kind who stayed in one town only as long as the welcome lasted and then freeloaded to the next small community before they got arrested and tossed in jail. They slept under bridges and highway overpasses, making a few dollars here and there for cheap wine by begging at traffic lights near shopping malls. They carried all their worldly goods from place to place in their knapsacks or backpacks, living by their wits and the whimsy of chance. When their luck ran out, they played rough and for keeps, surviving any way they could.

To men like them, a pretty, defenseless female was a rare delicacy.

Rafe unscrewed the bottle cap, intending to have a drink. But he burned with curiosity in spite of himself. What in the hell was she doing here? She was too old to be a runaway. He supposed it was possible she was fleeing from a husband, but if that was the case, why do it on a train? She should have just rolled the creep and bought herself a bus or plane ticket. Rafe sure as hell wouldn't have wanted any woman he cared about to put herself at risk like this.

Memories of Susan sifted through his mind. He tried to call up a picture of her face, but just like in his dream, her features remained a blur. Guilt swamped him. She'd been his whole life. Now, in only a little over two years, he couldn't recall her smile. His memories of his family were like color snapshots steadily fading with time.

The thought hurt so much he felt as if a knife were slicing at his guts.

He tipped back his head to swig the whiskey. The blessed burn promised oblivion, and he closed his eyes as the warmth spread through him, needing it—craving it—grabbing for it. Tomorrow he'd find an odd job and buy another bottle before this one went dry. At the bottom of a jug, he found sobriety, and for him, that was abhorrent. When he was drunk, at least he couldn't think.

A sudden wailing trailed to Rafe over the rhythmic clanking of the boxcar wheels. The sound startled him so much that he choked. A *baby?* Liquor backwash went up his nose. He strained to breathe, his eyeballs feeling as if they might pop from his skull. *Jesus Christ.*

He turned an appalled gaze back to the girl. The windbreaker she hugged to her chest was *wiggling.* Judging by the size of the bundle, the baby could be no more than a month or so old. She'd brought an infant on a freight train? He shot a concerned glance at the other four men. A baby put a whole new shine on things. He could look the other way when a woman angled for trouble and got some. But how could he do nothing when a kid was involved?

He immediately cut that thought short. She and her kid weren't his problem. *Nope.* He wanted nothing to do with her, period. And he really, really wished she'd make her kid shut up. The pathetic sound of the baby's wailing brought back painful memories of Keefer and Chastity.

Rafe shoved to his feet. He didn't miss the way the girl shrank away, as if she expected him to jump on her. *Sorry, sis. Not in the market.*

Staggering with each sway of the boxcar, he went to its opposite end, staking claim to the left front corner where he could slump and nurse his booze bottle in peace. Partly drowned out by the noise of the train, the baby's crying was a little less unsettling there. He took a long pull from the bottle, determined to consume enough liquor to pass out.

"Shut that kid up, lady!" one of the lowlifes yelled. "That cryin' is wearin' on my nerves!"

Amen to that. Rafe took another swig of booze and turned up his coat collar. *Chastity.* She'd been only six months old. Picture-clear, an image of her tiny, flower-draped coffin flashed through his head. He chased it away with another gulp of whiskey, wondering why he could remember the coffin so clearly and not her precious little face. The realization made him want to throw back his head and howl right along with the baby.

He had murdered his wife and kids—*murdered* them as surely as if he'd put a gun to their heads and pulled the trigger—and in less time than his three-year-old son had lived, he was already forgetting them. There was only one name for a man who could do that—a rotten, no-good son of a bitch.

"Either shut the kid up, or out it goes, lady!" another man yelled. "I'll throw it off, and don't think I won't! This ain't no place for a brat, anyhow."

Rafe froze with the whiskey bottle midway to his lips. Even in the poor light, the girl's face looked milk white, her eyes huge splashes of darkness and fear. Staring at the man who'd just threatened to toss her baby from the car, she drew the windbreaker over her shoulder and began to fumble beneath it.

Rafe clenched his teeth to bite back a curse. Of all

the things she might do to fix the problem, that ranked way low on the smart chart. Although, to be fair, he guessed she didn't have an option. If a baby was hungry, you had to feed it.

The other men snapped to attention like retrievers that had spotted a plump goose, their stares riveted to the activity going on under the girl's jacket. Her stiff movements spoke for themselves. Rafe found himself gaping right along with the others as she unbuttoned her blouse. Even with the nylon to block his view, he knew the exact instant when her breast popped free from her bra. As though plugged with a cork, the kid suddenly stopped screaming.

"Say now, honey. Whatcha got under that there coat?" one man asked.

The girl drew her knees higher and bent her head, her long, dark hair falling forward to further conceal her motherly undertaking. Rafe saw that she was shaking, whether from terror or the cold, he couldn't be sure. She looked so pathetic that his heart twisted.

The baby started to screech again. Her movements frantic, she jiggled the infant and cuddled it closer.

One of the bums laughed. "Say now, sweet thing, if the brat don't want it, I sure as hell won't turn it down."

Shit. Rafe really didn't want to mix it up with these lowlifes, but there were some things a man just couldn't walk away from. Four slimeballs raping a defenseless girl was one of them. Even more alarming, Rafe doubted it had been that long since she'd given birth.

He screwed the cap back on the whiskey bottle. The other men were undoubtedly packing switchblades. Just that morning, he had hocked his own knife to buy the booze.

He could think of better ways to die than with his guts spilled all over the filthy floor of a boxcar. But hey, better him than the girl. She might hemorrhage to death if those creeps got hold of her. Besides, it wasn't as if he honestly cared all that much if he died—or how he went. Quick and painless would be nice, but a man didn't always get his druthers.

One of the bums pushed to his feet and moved toward her. The other three rose to follow him.

This really isn't my problem, Rafe tried to tell himself one last time.

The man in the lead grabbed her roughly by her arm. She lost her hold on her baby, and the kid rolled from her lap onto the dirt-encrusted wooden floor. That cut it. Rafe could ignore a lot of things, but watching a baby get a raw deal wasn't on the list.

He was on his feet before he even realized he'd moved. He shifted his grip on the neck of the half-gallon jug and bent to set it on the floor, thankful for once that his taste ran to Early Times and not one of the cheaper brands bottled in plastic. Going to a knife fight with nothing but his fists had never been one of his aspirations. First though, he had to move the child out of harm's way.

After wrapping the infant in his coat and carrying it to the opposite end of the boxcar, Rafe retrieved his whiskey bottle and returned to help the child's mother. With the loud *clackety-clack* of the train to muffle the sound, he felt as if he were watching an eerie scene in a silent movie as he strode the length of the enclosure. The moonlight painted the men at the opposite end of the car in shades of white, gray, and black, and the shuddering of the train lent their movements the jerky rapidity common in dated films.

Only this was no scene being played out on a screen. It was real. Unless he intervened, that girl didn't have a prayer. With vague surprise, Rafe realized he was no longer staggering. Fury could be damned sobering.

He didn't bother to announce himself before he started busting up the party. He just gripped the glass bottle as though it were a club and waded in.

*   *   *

Maggie scrambled across the floor to get away from the men's feet, her breath coming in shallow pants. When she attempted to stand, her legs were so weak that she slid down the wall like a dribble of wet paint. Huddling with her back pressed into the corner, she twisted to and fro to avoid being stepped on, a fist shoved against her teeth to stifle her screams.

Watching the cowboy fight, she recalled her first impression of him when she'd gotten on this train, that he might be dangerous. She'd been right. The wild man in repose had come to life swinging, his chiseled features taut with feral rage. For a drunk, he moved with impressive speed and precision, his shoulder-length mane of tangled black hair whipping with every quick turn of his head. His big frame was oddly graceful, lean muscle and bone working together in a harmony of motion, the tendons in his thighs bunching under the loose legs of his faded jeans as he feinted and then pressed a vicious attack.

It seemed to Maggie that the fight was over almost before it started. Boots spread, knees slightly bent, the cowboy stood there, glancing at the human deadfall around him as he swiped glass from his shirt and pants. Then he moved toward her, his eyes glittering gunmetal blue in the moonlight.

To her frightened eyes, he looked a yard wide at the shoulders and twice that long in the legs. He walked with that loose-hipped, slightly bowed stride common to tall men who'd spent years in the saddle. Horribly aware that her blouse was partially unbuttoned, she tried to cross her arms over her chest, but for the life of her, she couldn't make the quivering muscles in her arms work properly.

He hunkered in front of her, the sheer breadth of his shoulders eclipsing the moonlight. Maggie shrank against the wall. Even in the shadows she could see the hard cast of his features. In contrast to his dark skin, his steel-blue eyes gleamed and seemed to miss nothing as he swept his gaze over her.

For an awful moment, she thought he meant her harm. Not that she considered herself to be any prize, but she doubted a man like him was any too particular.

She heard a strange whimpering sound. It took her a moment to realize the sound came from her. She tried to stop, to swallow it back, but it just kept erupting from her—awful and animal-like.

"Are you all right?" His large hands settled gently on her shoulders, his palms radiating warmth through the thin cotton of her blouse. "Don't be afraid, honey. I'm not going to hurt you."

Maggie had heard that line before. She expected his long fingers to tighten brutally on her flesh, but instead, he lightly caressed her arms, the touch so feathery and soothing that a sob of relief escaped from her.

"Well, hell."

He slipped an iron-hard arm around her waist, and the next thing she knew, she was drawn to her knees and trapped in his embrace, one of his hands cupped firmly over the back of her head. As he pressed her face against his shoulder, the musky male scent of him filled her senses. To her surprise, it wasn't an entirely unpleasant smell, as one might expect from a bum. Evidently he bathed occasionally, at least.

He swayed slightly from side to side with the rocking of the boxcar, one big hand gliding over her back. Even gentle pressure on her bruised flesh hurt, and she flinched when he touched a particularly tender place on her shoulder.

He went suddenly still, and she felt him stiffen. He drew his hand from her head and carefully separated the rent in her sleeve. After a moment of breathless waiting, Maggie thought she heard him curse, but the clack of the train was so loud, she couldn't be certain.

"You're all right now," he assured her in a louder voice. "And so is your baby. I checked him over good.

The bastards didn't hurt him, and they aren't going to. I promise you that.''

The gruff vibrancy of his voice curled around her like warm tendrils of smoke, and the gentle caress of his hands eased away some of her fear. As her panic subsided, Maggie's thoughts went instantly to Jaimie. She shifted to peer around his arm to where her baby lay at the opposite end of the boxcar. She kept remembering how Jaimie had rolled from her lap onto the floor, and despite the cowboy's reassurances, she couldn't help but worry. Oh, God. If her baby was hurt, she'd never forgive herself.

To her surprise, the cowboy seemed to understand how concerned she was and loosened his hold on her. Maggie drew back, fumbling with her blouse. She jumped with a start when he brushed her hands aside and made fast work of refastening the buttons for her.

He smiled slightly, his mouth tipping up at one corner. Even in the shadows, she could see the amused twinkle in his eyes.

''Better?''

Though she couldn't imagine why, she did feel better. And if that wasn't sheer madness . . . He was the kind of man you didn't want to meet in a dark alley.

He reached to smooth her hair back from her face. ''Go check on your baby while I get rid of these bastards before they start coming around.''

While he got rid of them? Maggie had forgotten all about the other men who lay around them. She cast a worried glance at them now. Surely the cowboy didn't mean to just toss them off the train? A hysterical urge to laugh struck her. Of course he didn't.

''It'll be all right,'' he said, gathering up her jacket and sweatshirt, then thrusting them into her arms. ''Go see to your baby. I'll handle it.''

Handle it? Maggie wasn't about to ask what he meant. Right now she had worries enough just watching out for herself and Jaimie. Besides, after what those men had tried to do to her, they deserved whatever they got.

Quivering with delayed reaction, she collected Jaimie, quickly checked to make sure he was all right, and then went to sit in the left front corner of the boxcar. Only seconds later, she heard the faint thud of the cowboy's boots over the sound of the train as he followed in her wake. He stooped to retrieve his hat and coat, then turned slightly to regard her.

"Here," he said as he extended the coat to her. When she hesitated, he dropped it in her lap. "That windbreaker and shirt won't keep your baby warm. Put it on," he ordered gruffly as he settled the Stetson on his head. "It's big enough for two men and a boy. It'll cover you both with room to spare."

The warmth of the sheepskin over Maggie's legs felt heavenly. She was freezing; there was no mistake about that. The thought of the thick wool all around her was tempting. But it seemed wrong for her to be warm while he suffered the cold with nothing.

He resumed his seat in the opposite corner, snorting with impatience as he settled his broad shoulders against the wall. "Do I have to come over there and stuff you into it?"

Maggie shook her head and laid Jaimie lengthwise in the cleavage of her upraised thighs as she drew on the coat. When she tucked her baby inside and pulled the woolly leather closed, warmth immediately surrounded her icy body.

"Thank you, mister."

He shifted to get more comfortable and tugged the hat down over his face. His voice gravelly and muffled, he said, "No problem. Just don't grow attached. I want it back when we part company at the next stop."

Maggie gnawed the inside of her cheek. "Not just for the coat. Thank you for—" Her voice trailed away like a talking toy that had wound down. She gulped and tried again. "Thank you for—for helping me. You risked getting badly hurt."

"Yeah, well . . ." He shifted again. "I didn't, so let's forget it happened."

Maggie's thoughts returned to the four men he'd tossed from the train. "Do you think those bums will be all right?"

He released a weary sigh. "I don't know," he admitted. "Sometimes circumstances don't allow you any choices."

She closed her eyes, thinking how very true that was. No choices. If not for that, she would never have climbed on this train in the first place. It had been a desperate move and a dangerous one. But the bottom line was, she'd run less risk of getting caught this way than if she'd hitched a ride on the highway. Once Lonnie raised an alarm, the cops might start looking for her. Standing alongside the interstate, she would have been a sitting duck.

With that thought, she found herself wondering what had led the cowboy to this pass. Had circumstances robbed him of a choice as well, or was he here simply because he wanted to be?

The faint smell of cow manure drifted to her nostrils, making her suspect this car had once been used to haul fertilizer. *Oh, God.* Just the possibility gave her the heebie-jeebies, and she cuddled Jaimie closer.

Who in his right mind would *choose* this mode of transportation? It was madness. Yet she had recently seen a television special about perfectly respectable individuals all across the nation who sought adventure by riding the rails with bums. A new craze, evidently, the appeal of which totally escaped her. One young man had been killed during his spring break from college last year when crates of heavy freight shifted and crushed him. Another had ended up dead of multiple stab wounds from an unknown transient's knife.

The grieving parents of both youths had gone on the air to warn viewers of the danger in riding the rails. But according to the television report, there were thrill seekers who ignored the statistics, risking not only arrest and conviction for breaking the law, but putting their lives in jeopardy as well. One of the men interviewed had been a heart surgeon, of all things. He claimed the excitement and danger provided a form of stress release he could find nowhere else.

Stress release? She guessed most people's everyday problems would seem less daunting after experiencing something like this. Sort of like curing the burn with a wildfire, in her estimation, but to each his own.

She opened her eyes to find that the cowboy had nudged up his hat to study her. Even with the shadows to cloak her, she felt as easy to read as large print.

"Don't tear yourself up feeling guilty about those men, if that's what's eating you. If I hadn't stopped them, they would have raped you and slit your throat. And that's not to mention what they would've done to your kid afterward." He shrugged. "I could've hauled ass before they came back around, but where would that have left you? You couldn't jump from the train. Not with a baby to worry about. Leaving you here alone to deal with the assholes didn't strike me as an option. You understand? It was them or you."

Maggie couldn't bear to even think about it.

He pushed more erect. After studying her for an interminably long while, he gently asked, "What are you doing here, anyway? Somehow you just don't strike me as the type to be riding the rails."

"What type of person does?" she asked, forcing herself to meet his gaze.

His mouth went hard, and even in the moonlight, she saw a sharp, measuring look enter his eyes. "Lots of types," he finally replied, "but most of them fall into two categories, crazy or desperate."

Hoping to keep the conversation centered on him, she retorted, "And which type are you?"

"The type who can take care of himself."

Maggie conceded the point by averting her gaze. Even though she owed him for saving her life, she didn't dare tell him her reasons for being there. Judging by his appearance, he probably had very little money, and it would be just like Lonnie to offer a reward for word of her whereabouts. After all, unless Lonnie managed to find her and got his hands on Jaimie, he'd have to return all that cash.

The cowboy sighed. "What's your name? Can you tell me that much?"

She weighed the possible consequences and decided sharing her first name couldn't hurt. "Maggie. How far is it to the next town, anyway?"

"I'm not sure of the distance. I think the next stop will probably be in Squire, and that'll take a few hours." He drew up his shoulders, which told her the cold was already starting to bother him. "That where you're headed?"

Maggie had no idea where she was going. She was just—going. "I don't know. It'll depend on how large a place Squire is, I guess."

Long silence. "You mean you don't know where you're headed?"

"Sure I do. I'm going where the train's going."

"Christ," he said, half under his breath. And then she could have sworn she heard him mutter, "Why me, God?"

"Is Squire a fairly big place?"

"It's not so little you'll miss it if you blink. It's just this side of the Washington state line."

Maggie needed to find a good-sized town—someplace where she could easily land a job, melt into the population, and not be traced.

"Who knocked you around?" he asked without preamble.

She stared at him. "Pardon?"

"I didn't stammer. I know damned well you didn't get all those bruises on your arm in that tussle tonight. Who beat the hell out of you?" He gave her a slow once-over, for all the world as if he could see through the sheepskin. "It's obvious someone did. And please, don't insult my intelligence by telling me that age-old story about running into a doorknob, unless, of course, you ran into it several dozen times."

If he hadn't been quizzing her about something so personal, Maggie might have smiled at his dry sense of humor. She was fresh out of smiles, though, and there were some things you didn't relate to strangers. "We have lots of doorknobs at our place."

"Who's we?"

She tried for a vacuous expression as she drew the coat closer.

"How bad are you hurt?"

"I'm fine."

"Looks to me like those ribs of yours are a little ticklish, and maybe other places as well."

Ticklish didn't say it by half. "I'm fine," she repeated.

He huffed, the sound disgruntled. "You nursed the kid since that legion of doorknobs worked you over? When you tried a few minutes ago, it appeared to me that you were having some problems."

She gaped at him. No man had ever asked her something so personal, and his saving her didn't give him the right to be the first. She averted her face.

The *clackety-clack* of the train seemed to grow louder. She could feel him studying her. She wished he'd just lower that filthy hat and go back to sleep.

"Appears to me you're down on your luck. If you're that banged up, how do you plan on feeding him? With your good looks?"

Through the sweep of her lowered lashes, Maggie stared at the cowboy's lean body, dread rising in her throat until it nearly suffocated her. His question rang in her ears. *How do you plan on feeding him? With your good looks?*

Maybe so, mister, she thought numbly. *Maybe so.*

 *Chapter Two*

Freezing his ass off was a great way to sober up. It beat drinking coffee all to hell, anyway. Rafe clamped his arms over his chest and drew his knees higher, his body swaying with the boxcar. From under the edge of his hat, he could see the pinkish light of dawn. The temperature wouldn't rise for about three more hours, but at least there was an end in sight.

He stared into the black void provided by the crown of his hat. Against the darkness, he kept seeing the girl's pale face and those gigantic, expressive eyes. He'd been a little rough on her. There was something indefinable about her that brought out his protective instincts, and it scared the hell out of him.

For two years, his sole focus had been on his own misery. Now, in the space of only a few hours, a half-pint girl had turned him inside out and tied his guts into knots. This wasn't like him. Usually he had no trouble at all in ignoring the rest of the world and all its injustices. In fact, he'd gotten so good at not giving a damn, he'd practically turned it into an art. So why was Maggie getting to him like this?

He remembered his dream and Susan's entreaties. *You'll see.* Was this the second chance she'd been telling him about?

He shoved the thought away, scoffing at himself. The booze must have pickled his brains for notions like that to find a foothold. Maggie with-no-last-name meant nothing to him. Here shortly, he'd say adios and never clap eyes on her again.

Despite his resolve, though, he couldn't stop thinking about those bruises on her arm. Was her entire body banged up? Where he hailed from, a man didn't strike a woman, period, not even with the flat of his hand.

Something heavy plopped on Rafe's legs. He shoved up his hat to see Maggie standing over him. She cradled her sleeping child in the crook of one arm. Pitching her voice to be heard over the train, she said, "You're freezing. You take the coat for a while." She cuddled the baby closer, her gaze reflecting gratitude mixed with wariness. "I was thinking maybe we could switch back and forth. Only after you get warm again, of course."

Settling the Stetson on his head, Rafe pushed himself to a sitting position. The fear of him that he read in her expression didn't bode well for the suggestion he was about to make. "Why don't we just share it?"

A frown pleated the skin between her delicately arched brows. "Share it?"

She sounded as scandalized as if he had suggested they have hot sex on a city sidewalk. Rafe felt a grin tug at the corner of his mouth. That surprised him. Smiling was a rare occurrence for him these days.

He lifted the heavy sheepskin with the crook of his finger. "I'll wear the coat, and you and the baby can slip inside with me. That way, we'll all stay warm."

She shook her head, the movement drawing his gaze to the fall of dark hair that lay over her shoulders. Against the white blouse, the silky curtains made him think of rich chocolate. Dressed in blue jeans and sneakers, she might have passed for a young teenager if not for the slight fullness of her hips and breasts. "I don't think that's a very good idea."

"For your baby's sake," he quickly added. "No matter how you circle it, switching back and forth with the coat won't be good. The baby will get cold, then warm.

I've always heard that causes colds. You want it to get sick?''

She dropped a worried gaze to the small bundle cradled against her. His stomach knotted. He was so cold his teeth were damned near clacking, but he wouldn't wear the coat while she and the child went without.

He nearly smiled again as he watched her struggle to reach a decision. Share the coat? God forbid.

''I have him wrapped in my jacket and sweatshirt. Do you really think he might get sick?''

Rafe was actually more worried about her than the baby. He cocked an eyebrow and lifted the coat higher. ''I think it's a risk you don't have to take.''

''I suppose it *is* more practical to share it than to switch back and forth.''

Amen. He watched her take a hesitant step toward him. Not that he faulted her wariness. After what those four bums had tried to do to her, any woman would want to run in the other direction.

He leaned forward to shove his arms down the coat sleeves. ''Come on,'' he coaxed. ''I don't know about you, but I'm about to freeze my ass off.''

She took another hesitant step. Then she stopped to stare down at him, looking very like a skittish doe, her lithe body tensed for flight.

Suddenly tense himself, Rafe spread his feet to make room between his bent knees. As he held the front of the coat open in invitation, he felt that odd, achy sensation in his chest again. It was that stubborn little chin of hers and those large, frightened eyes, he decided. The combination packed a wallop. ''Come on,'' he repeated huskily. ''I swear I won't try anything.''

When she knelt on one knee between his spread boots, she searched his face, her expression so dubious that he nearly chuckled. Instead he faked a shiver. ''Hurry, honey. I'm letting in cold air.''

She turned and sat with her back to him. The top of her dark head hit him just below the chin. As she cuddled the baby in her arms, his whiskers caught on her silky hair. He waited, expecting her to relax against him, but instead she kept her spine so straight it could have ruled paper.

Biting back another smile, he drew the front of the heavy coat closed over her and the child, his arms forming a loose circle around them. The chill of her body made him yearn to hug her closer to share his heat, but he didn't want to scare her.

"You say your name's Maggie?" he inquired softly next to her ear.

"Yes."

Maggie. It suited her perfectly somehow. Rafe breathed in the sweet scent of mother and child. "Is your baby a little boy?"

She bent her head and curled her fingers over the edge of blue nylon to reveal the child's tiny face. "Yes," she replied, her voice throbbing with love. "His name is Jaimie—with two I's. I named him after my father."

"That's a Celtic spelling, isn't it?"

"It may be. My father was a Scot."

He didn't miss the fact that she referred to her father in the past tense. Whoever had beaten her up, it hadn't been her dad.

She wore no wedding ring. He decided she was probably running from a boyfriend. "My name's Rafe Kendrick."

She turned to meet his gaze, her guarded expression making his heart ache. It had to be damned miserable, being trapped inside a coat with a man she didn't trust. Though she was trying to keep a safe distance between their bodies, he could feel her trembling, and he doubted it was from the cold now.

She lowered her lashes, the long dark spikes casting feathery shadows on her cheeks in the rosy light of dawn. An urge came over him to trace the shape of her mouth with his fingertips. He was relieved when she averted her face.

She continued to sit ramrod straight, which he knew couldn't be very comfortable, especially with aching ribs. Splaying a hand over the section of coat where he guessed the baby to be, he applied gentle pressure. "I don't bite, Maggie. At least not hard enough to break the skin. Go ahead and lean back."

"I'm fine," she insisted.

She looked exhausted. He suspected she was running on her last reserves of energy. He forced the issue by applying more pressure. Just as he anticipated, she relented instantly, which he doubted she would have done if he'd pressed his palm against her instead of the child.

Her body felt slight and wonderfully soft where it nestled against him. His breath froze in his chest. It had been so long since he'd held a woman that he'd nearly forgotten how good it felt. He wanted to bury his face in her beautiful hair and inhale its scent. And, oh, God, how he yearned to free his arms from the coat sleeves so he could slip his hands inside and explore her softness—the curve of her waist, the swell of her hips, the soft fullness of her bottom.

It had been too long since he'd had a drink, he decided. Without the constant infusion of booze into his system, the numbness was wearing off.

Normally he swept parking lots to get a new jug before the old one ran dry. Now that his most recently purchased bottle had been shattered, he'd have no choice but to go all day without a drink until he earned the money to buy more. What if he got the shakes and couldn't hold a broom? The thought made him feel frantic.

Rafe felt the girl flinch. He realized that in his agitation he'd increased the pressure of his hand on her and the baby. Concern for her chased away his sudden yearning for alcohol. Leaning around to regard her face, he saw that she was biting her bottom lip.

"What is it?" he asked.

"Your belt buckle. It's poking my back."

He relaxed his hold. As he reached a hand inside the coat to slide the silver buckle off to one side, she gave a startled jerk when he grazed his knuckles over her lower back.

"I'm not making a move on you, honey. I'm just shifting the buckle so it won't jab you."

"There's no need. I can just sit straight."

As the train rounded a curve in the tracks, she nearly toppled with the sway. He caught her from falling with the brace of his arm. A faint ray of rosy sunlight came in through the open doorway to illuminate her face. For the first time, Rafe could see her features in detail. What he saw scared the hell out of him. She wasn't just pale. Her skin had a white, bloodless cast to it, and dark smudges underscored her eyes.

Disturbed by the train's sudden motion, the baby chose that moment to awaken and emit a weak bleating sound. She murmured soft endearments, parting the windbreaker again. The infant's blue eyes blinked open, and small fists flailed the air, terry sleeper sleeves flashing yellow against the navy nylon.

An unpleasant odor drifted up to Rafe. He nearly groaned. Any man who'd once been a father knew that smell. Why was it that the odor of baby poop always seemed to drift upward and never sideways? But, oh, no. It was one of those smells that shot straight to a man's nose.

Rafe glanced around the cavernous boxcar, expecting to see a diaper bag. When one didn't appear, he scanned the enclosure again, convinced one would materialize. On a rational level, he realized kids weren't born with a diaper bag attached. But in his estimation, that was a major screwup on God's part. With a baby tossed into any equation, the absence of disposable diapers and Wet Ones equaled a major disaster.

"Where's the diaper bag?"

She didn't glance up as she replied. "I dropped it."

"You *what?*" Surely he couldn't have heard her

right. No diaper bag? "You're kidding. Right?"

She shook her head.

Visions of all the absolutely *vital* baby paraphernalia in a diaper bag went zigzagging through Rafe's head. Diapers and wipes were only the half of it. Raising his voice to be heard over the now screeching baby, who was thrashing his little legs and stirring up the odor, Rafe said, "You *dropped* it? Where at?"

"Back in Prior. It was an accident. I was trying to get on the train, and I couldn't run fast enough to keep up. I dropped both the bag and Jaimie's quilt. That's why I've got him wrapped in my sweatshirt and jacket."

Rafe leaned his head against the wall, racking his brain for a solution. The stink aside, somehow they had to change the kid's britches. Left as he was, Jaimie would get a sore bottom.

"I'll manage somehow."

Rafe couldn't imagine how. Then he felt her wiggling. The movements of her soft posterior against the crotch of his jeans brought about a reaction that brought his eyes wide open. His breath snagged, and he sat there for a full five seconds, staring at the back of her head.

Wonderful. Just frigging fantastic. He hadn't felt a stir in that region in over two years. Even worse than the piss-poor timing was the fact that Maggie might feel it.

He shoved a hand between her butt and his jeans, hoping to escape detection as well as protect himself from further stimulation. At the touch of his knuckles on her rump, she jumped again and jerked her head around to fix him with an accusing look.

"I'm not getting fresh," he hastened to assure her. "I'm just—"

His voice trailed off. He was just what? The baby's screams seemed to attain super-baby decibels. He was getting a real bitch of a headache. God, he needed a drink.

She squirmed to put some distance between his hand and her bottom, then resumed her activities. Watching her from the back, it looked to him as if she were un-fastening her top. *Red alert*.

"What are you doing?"

"I'll have to use my blouse and wear the wind-breaker."

Was it actually possible for a man's heart to leap from his chest cavity into his mouth? "Use your blouse for what?"

"A diaper."

"Say *what?*"

"I have to change him," she said in a shrill voice, "and my blouse is all I've got. I'll need the sweatshirt later to keep him warm, and the nylon jacket isn't ab-sorbent."

He quickly shrugged the coat from his shoulders. "Here, I'll lend you my T-shirt." *Lend?* As if he'd ever want it back. "Without your blouse, you'll be exposed to the cold. The nylon of that jacket will feel like ice against your bare skin every time the wind hits it."

He shucked his shirt in record time, then peeled off the T-shirt and handed it around to her. She took hold of it between thumb and forefinger, raising it up to the weak light of dawn. Shocked by the frigid air that washed over his naked upper torso, Rafe quickly slipped his shirt back on. He paused in the buttoning to stare at the undergarment she held up with such delicate but ap-parent distaste.

It looked—*gray*. Rafe leaned closer to peer at it, con-vinced his eyes must be deceiving him. The last time he'd looked, it had been white. Of course, he couldn't recall exactly when that had been—or how drunk he was at the time.

"It'll do for a baby diaper. It's just the light." At least he hoped it was only the light. "It isn't really dirty."

"How long since you washed it?"

"Not long." He thought back. "In South Dakota, I think it was."

"*South Dakota?*"

"Yeah. This big old gal who ran the mission there washed my clothes while I was sleeping one off. That was only—let's see . . ." Rafe peered at the shirt again. *Shit.* "What day is this?"

"The twenty-sixth of October. Or is it the twenty-seventh?"

"You mean it's damned near Halloween?"

She flashed him a slightly appalled look.

How time did fly when you never sobered up. "Really? I can't believe it's almost November."

She let the T-shirt puddle on the floor next to his leg and reached for the front of her blouse again. "I'm sorry, Mr. Kendrick, but I can't possibly put something that filthy on my baby. Better if I use my blouse and wear your shirt myself. Close your eyes, please," she said in a shaky voice that told him she felt none too sure he wouldn't attack her the instant he glimpsed bare skin. "I'll just slip your shirt on first. Then I'll change Jaimie. All right?"

"All right."

He leaned his head back and started to close his eyes. Only just as his lids were fluttering shut, he felt her lean forward to peel the blouse down her arms, and somehow, his upper and lower eyelashes never quite met.

After a two-year abstinence, it seemed to Rafe that he should enjoy stealing a peek at a partially clad female. Instead he felt as if a mule had kicked him in the guts. Her back was covered with bruises, all of them still an angry red, which he knew from experience would darken in another day or so to deep black-and-blue marks. Interspersed among the bruises were superficial cuts. There was no mistaking them for anything but the marks of a man's ring, for they were surrounded by knuckle prints.

Rafe ended up closing his eyes, all right, not to preserve her modesty, but in outrage. The *sick* son of a bitch! The pictures that exploded in his mind snapped him rigid with fury. To bruise a woman like that, a man would have to repeatedly drive his fists into her body, using all his strength.

It seemed like an eternity passed before she finished changing the diaper. As he once again enfolded her in the coat with him, he couldn't help but notice how the fussy baby eagerly nuzzled below her ear.

"I think he's hungry," he needlessly pointed out. "Don't you think you'd better try to feed him again?"

She glanced over her shoulder. "Would you mind closing your eyes again, please?"

In answer to that question, Rafe loosened his grip on the coat so she would have room to maneuver and let his eyes fall closed. Jaimie suddenly broke off in mid-screech, his eager little mouth making suckling sounds that seemed inordinately loud, considering the racket of the train.

No more than a second passed before he began to screech again. Rafe could tell by Maggie's movements that she was growing agitated. He heard her make a soft sound of distress. The infant quieted for a bit and then resumed crying.

Concern filled him. He didn't consciously make the decision to open his eyes. One moment, he was being a perfect gentleman, and the next he was getting an eyefull. To give himself credit where it was due, he had not a lascivious thought as he gazed over Maggie's thin shoulder at her breast. It was so swollen and bruised that he cringed. As hungry babies will, Jaimie latched eagerly onto her nipple each time it touched his lips, suckling none-too-gently on the tumid, discolored peak. Rafe knew it had to hurt like hell.

Leaning slightly to one side to see Maggie's face, he spied a tear slipping down her cheek. His heart caught at the resolute expression she wore. She clearly meant to feed her baby, no matter how much pain it caused her. He could almost feel every pull of the baby's mouth. A fragile flower? Not by anyone's standards. She was a delicately built woman, but hidden under all that fragility was a spine laced with steel.

In the end, her attempts to feed her child were a failure. Her milk refused to come down in either breast. Each wail from the baby cut through Rafe. A man never forgot being a father, he guessed. An almost overwhelming sense of helplessness came over him. When a baby was hungry, you fed it, bottom line.

Rafe estimated they would reach the next stop in about forty minutes. Every second of that time would seem like an eternity. He had to get away from this pair. They were unearthing feelings inside of him that he'd worked too damned hard to bury. He didn't need the hassle—or the heartache.

Jaimie cried only a short time before falling into an exhausted sleep, which Rafe counted a blessing until Maggie broached a concern he hadn't considered.

In a quavering voice, she said, "I think he's already losing his strength."

"How long has he gone without eating?"

"I started having some trouble nursing him late yesterday afternoon. He got a little to eat, I think, but maybe not that much. I was really upset, and—" Her voice trailed away. "Well, you know—things didn't go exactly right. I thought it was because I was so tense. In the book I have, it says nervousness can cause that."

Nervousness could be a cause. But then, so could severe bruising and swelling. After seeing what he had, he figured it was more than likely the latter.

"So he's missed only a few feedings?"

She nodded, looking worried and miserable. "He eats pretty often, though. About every two hours because he's still so small. Do you think he's losing his strength?"

His own babies had never missed a meal unless they were sick, so he was certainly no expert, but it seemed to him it should take longer than this for a kid to grow weak with hunger. On the other hand, though, Jaimie was tiny, as she said. Newborns didn't have the stores of fat older babies did.

"Nah," he assured her with more confidence than he felt. "Babies are tough little nuts."

"Are they?" she asked hopefully.

"Sure they are. We'll reach the next stop soon. He'll be fine for a half hour. There's bound to be a store where you can buy him a bottle and formula."

She shook her head.

Rafe didn't want to hear this. *Why me, God?*

"I don't have enough money. All I've got is eighteen cents in my pocket."

He really, really had to get away from her. Why was she telling him her problems? If she was entertaining the notion that he might help her, she had a shock coming. When he hit the next town, he would sweep a few parking lots to buy a bottle, all right. A *booze* bottle.

"Do you?" she asked.

"Do I what?"

"Have any money?" She turned those big brown eyes on him again. "Normally I'd never presume to ask. I'm sure I can find some sort of work in—what was the name of that town again?"

"Squire."

"Squire." She darted the tip of her tongue over her bottom lip. "Even if it's a small place, I can find something to do and earn some money. Only it would take hours. Jaimie is hungry now, and he shouldn't wait that long to eat." She squeezed her eyes closed, as if calling on all her reserves of strength. When she lifted her lashes, she said, "I can't just make him wait and risk him getting sick."

His throat closed off. *Christ.* Around this girl, he spent half his time oxygen-deprived.

Her mouth started to quiver even as she raised her chin in a futilely prideful way. Oh, God. He knew what she was about to say, and he was tempted to clamp a hand over those sweet lips before she could get it out.

"I won't lie and say I'll pay you back because we probably won't ever see each other again." Her eyes went dark with shame, but she didn't lower her gaze. Rafe could see this was the most difficult thing she'd ever done. "But I'll make you a trade if you'll give me the money for a baby bottle and formula."

"A trade?" Why he posed it as a question, he had no idea. It was blatantly obvious what she meant.

"My baby's hungry, Mr. Kendrick. I'll do anything I have to in order to feed him." Her white cheeks suddenly pulsed with pink. "Anything."

Rafe wanted to tell her he had no money and no way of getting his hands on any, but that wasn't entirely true. So instead he just gaped at her, the gold wedding ring he wore on a chain under his shirt burning a hole in his chest.

Her cheeks turned a deeper shade of pink. Then she averted her face, the very picture of humiliation. "I see," she said, her voice taut.

Only, of course, she didn't see. She was a beautiful young woman, and no unattached male in his right mind could fail to want her.

"Maggie, it's not what you're thinking."

Keeping her head bent so her hair hid her face, she raised a staying hand. "Don't," she said thinly. "Please."

Rafe tried to imagine how she must feel. It took a giant stretch of imagination. He'd never tried to sell his body and been turned down. He had, of course, been hit up more than a few times, but not by a young woman who had never sunk to such depths and was finding it to be the most humiliating experience of her life.

Though she had a child, there was a sweetness and innocence in her eyes he knew damned well wasn't feigned. He'd have bet every dollar he had in the bank that no man but the father of her baby had ever laid a hand on her.

"Honey, listen."

She shook her head, her hand still raised to silence him. "Please. Just forget I said it."

Rafe got a horrible urge to laugh. It wasn't the way she thought, and God help him, he wasn't sure how to set her straight without scaring her half to death. But neither did he want her to continue believing he didn't want her. Thinking that way could wound her in ways that wouldn't heal for years.

"Sweetheart, you're beautiful. So beautiful my eye-teeth ache when I look at you."

She threw him a startled look.

"Trust me. If I had a few bucks in my pocket, I'd be one happy man."

He slipped his arms around her and the baby, knowing even before his voice trailed away how sincerely he meant that. He *did* want to make love to her. The realization stymied him. What the hell was happening to him? He recalled his dream again, and an icy fear slithered through his belly. He couldn't seem to stop himself from caring more about this girl than was smart—or even rational. Was this what Susan had been trying to tell him, that he was about to meet someone very special and—

No. He swallowed, hard, and told himself not to be an idiot. He didn't believe in premonitions or fated encounters, and he sure as hell didn't believe he'd had a ghostly visitation from his late wife. It was just a dream. A stupid, whiskey-soaked dream that had meant absolutely nothing.

Marshaling his thoughts, Rafe forced his mind back to the moment. His voice sounded gruff and a little shaky when he said, "Please, Maggie, don't think for a second that I'm not interested in your offer. I'd take you up on it so fast it would make your head spin if I had a cent to give you. But I don't."

"You don't have any money on you at all?"

"Not a cent. I'm sorry."

"Oh."

For some reason, the way she said that made him smile again. "You can always get help from the mission. Most towns have one, and a woman with a baby will get red-carpet treatment."

She shook her head. "I can't go somewhere like that."

"Why? If you're feeling embarrassed, don't. Everyone needs help sometimes."

"It isn't that. I'm just—" She broke off and shook her head again. "There may be people looking for me."

He tightened his arms, wanting to hug her and the baby close to protect them. Who might be looking for her? *Jesus.* Was it the cops? He burned to ask, but two years of this kind of life had taught him not to ask too many questions. And since he doubted she'd answer anyway, why bother? Even if she was wanted by the cops, he couldn't believe it was for anything serious.

He drew her gently against him. "I'll tell you what. Why don't you get some rest? While you're sleeping, I'll think of some way for you to get help."

"I can't go around lots of people," she stressed.

"I understand that. I'll think of something. Trust me." He smiled slightly. "I'm an old hand at this lifestyle, remember. I know all the ropes."

To his surprise, she gave in to the slight pressure of his arms, twisting sideways to rest her cheek against his chest, the baby's tiny feet nudging his abdomen. Rafe wanted to think she followed his advice because she was beginning to trust him, but he suspected it was exhaustion getting the best of her.

Within seconds he felt the tension leave her body. He gazed down at her, thinking how sweet she looked with her relaxed mouth pushed slightly off center. He touched a fingertip to her pale cheek, testing the fragile curve of bone under her soft, silken flesh.

When he felt positive she was deeply asleep, he reached inside his shirt and drew out his wedding ring. The setting of large, fiery diamonds glinted at him in the thin morning light, a reminder of why he wore it hidden on a chain under his shirt. Flashing diamonds on a boxcar was a good way to get your throat slit.

Susan. Against all his objections, she'd worked in a hamburger joint to pay for this ring, insisting she had to buy him something as nice as he'd gotten her, and that she had to pay for it herself. The purchase price had been a little over four grand. It was anyone's guess what it might be worth now. Pawnshops were notorious for paying a fraction of an item's value. Still, he figured he could get several hundred dollars for it.

He made a fist around the ring and closed his eyes. He couldn't hock it. His wedding ring was his last link to Susan and his past, the one thing left to him that he treasured. In the two years since he'd been bumming the rails, he'd seen some mighty lean times, but never once had he considered hocking his ring.

Maggie and her baby weren't his problem. When they reached the next town, he'd give her his coat. That was the best he could do for her. Clenching his teeth, Rafe slipped the ring back inside his shirt where it could rest close to his heart. As it settled against his chest, he imagined he could hear Susan chiding him. *Oh, Rafe. It's just a ring. Can you really turn your back on a baby?*

As the imagined whisper grew clearer in his mind, Rafe could finally conjure a picture of his wife's face. It had been so long since he'd been able to remember exactly how she looked that he let his head rest against the wall and closed his eyes, smiling as he traced each of her features. Dear God, how very much he had loved her.

Susan. He knew if she were here, she'd hock that ring in a heartbeat to feed a hungry baby. In a way, Maggie reminded him a little of her. Not in looks or mannerisms, of course, but in the way she loved. If he lived to be a hundred, he'd never forget the look in her eyes when she'd offered him her body in trade for a bottle and formula. He had almost been able to taste her shame, yet she'd made the offer without a thought for herself.

He sighed and pressed his palm over his chest, the blunted edges of the ring digging into his flesh. If he wanted to be able to live with himself, he knew what he had to do.

But it wasn't going to be easy.

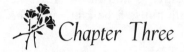

Chapter Three

Now that the train had stopped, the boxcar was eerily quiet. Maggie had no idea exactly what time it was, but judging by the brightness of the sunlight, she guessed it was at least eight-thirty or nine. The songs of birds drifted on the frigid morning air, the sounds faint and incongruously cheerful in such a drab, filthy place. Trying to block out the faint smell of cow, she concentrated instead on scents she caught on the breeze, a wintry blend of icy dampness laced with evergreen that was underscored by the acrid odor of engine fumes.

Huddled in the cowboy's warm coat with her back to the wall, she watched the open doorway, terrified that some bum might spy the empty car and climb inside with her. After her experience last night, she had no illusions. Most men were rats.

Oh, God, she was tired. She had a headache, an all-over sick feeling, and her back was killing her. All she wanted was to close her eyes and sleep for a while. But Jaimie would awaken soon, and when he did, he'd be hungry. She could only pray the cowboy kept his part of their bargain and returned with a baby bottle and formula.

She closed her eyes, picturing his tall, lean body. Hard strength emanated from him like the electrical charge in a high-voltage area. No matter. She simply wouldn't think about it, that was all. She'd just let him do his thing, blocking it out as best she could, and afterward, she'd pretend none of this ever happened.

Nausea rose in her throat. She gulped it back. She kept remembering how he had touched her cheek just before he left, his fingertips lightly caressing her skin. *I've thought of a way to get my hands on some cash. Stay right here. You'll be safe for the short time I'll be gone.* Maggie had yearned to add, *Until you come back, you mean?* Only she hadn't been able to work up the nerve.

That was just as well. She had made him the offer. Right? No one had forced her. And she should be glad he'd decided to take her up on it. What happened to her wasn't important. Nothing mattered but her baby. Nothing.

Rafe stood on the sidewalk outside the pawnshop, head bent, his shoulders shrugged against the cold as he gazed at the ring that lay on his palm. He wanted so badly to put it back on his neck chain and just keep walking. Who had elected him savior of the world?

But though he tried, he couldn't make himself move on down the sidewalk. He kept hearing Jaimie's cries of hunger. He lifted his head and hauled in a deep breath of air so icy it nearly choked him. Kitchen exhaust from a diner emitted the scent of grilled meat on the brisk breeze, the odor almost acrid. His eyes burned as he stared through the streaked front windows of the pawnshop at the jewelry and electric guitars and doodads on display. *Broken dreams.* Life had a way of dealing rotten hands, and the sad stories were as varied as the people who experienced them. Now one more broken dream would lie in there on that cheap red velvet.

Maggie's posterior nearly parted company with the floor when she heard footsteps outside the boxcar. The next instant, Kendrick appeared in the doorway, winter sunshine glancing off his black Stetson and tangled hair. He cast wary glances up and down the track, checking to be sure no one had seen him, a reminder that they both could be arrested if they were caught on this train.

A sick feeling settled in her stomach. Until now, she'd tried to be a model citizen, working hard, paying her bills, and never breaking the law, not even to cheat on her taxes. Now, here she was, miles from home, keeping company with a tramp and well on the way to looking like one herself.

As he braced a palm on the floor to vault inside, she couldn't fail to notice the play of muscle under the loose fit of his chambray shirt. He landed on both feet and straightened to his full height with a fluid strength. Maggie could easily picture him scaling a pasture fence with the same ease, grabbing hold of a post and leaping over as if no barrier existed. He was a tall man, and if the hardened bulges that padded his long frame were an indication, his body had been toned by years of physical labor. Though he'd evidently lost a lot of weight, the thick overlays of lean muscle still gave him impressive bulk.

For the second time since meeting him, she wondered what on earth had happened to make him choose this way of life. Was he wanted by the authorities? For reasons beyond her, he didn't strike her as the criminal type. But then, the same had been said by many people about the notorious Ted Bundy. Her throat tightened as he strode toward her. His every footfall rocked the boxcar and created a plodding tattoo that echoed all around her. His gunmetal gaze held hers, the visual contact making her feel stripped bare despite the sheepskin that enfolded her. With that heavy growth of black beard, he looked ruthless and determined; his strong jaw was set as if he found this situation almost as distasteful as she did. That made no sense at all. If he found their bargain disgusting, he wouldn't be here with the items she requested.

Tucked under one arm, he carried a paper sack, the

top folded over so the contents wouldn't spill. Judging by the large dimensions of the package, he'd purchased more than a baby bottle and formula.

A tremor of sheer dread coursed through her, for she knew she'd pay dearly for every dime he had spent. She wanted to huddle around Jaimie, let her head fall to her knees, and sob. But no. She'd struck this bargain with him, and she wouldn't let herself blubber and complain now that it was time to pay up.

"Do you feel like you can walk a couple of blocks?"

"Why?"

He arched one black eyebrow. She'd always envied people who could do that. "I'm taking you to a motel where you and Jaimie will be warm and can rest. Maybe get you something to eat. How long since you had a decent meal?"

Maggie had grabbed a piece of toast yesterday morning before she left the house with Jaimie. From that point on, everything had turned nightmarish. She was sort of hungry now—in an empty, nauseated way. But, oh, God, she didn't want this man to buy her anything to eat.

"Buying me a meal and renting a room wasn't part of our deal," she reminded him. "All I care about is feeding Jaimie."

He looked momentarily nonplussed. Then his eyes cleared and took on an amused glint, his firm mouth slanting into a grin that looked raffish. "Maybe I think you're worth more than a baby bottle and a can of formula." As he spoke, he bent to grasp her elbow. "Up you come. When a man wants to pay more than the asking price, a smart woman doesn't argue the point."

Oh, yes, she did. She was already in too deep. You got nothing for free, especially from a man. "I don't want to get into some big, drawn-out thing," she protested, even as he led her to the doorway. "I just want the bottle and formula for my baby, nothing more. If you're hoping for an all-nighter, forget it."

He released his hold on her arm and jumped from the boxcar with the same powerful grace he'd exhibited earlier, which did little to ease her mind. A motel? What did he have planned? A sexual marathon? *Oh, God*. Her legs felt as if they might buckle, and now that she was standing up, she had an awful, burning need to use the bathroom. It was also impossible for her to stand erect. The pain across her lower back became excruciating when she tried.

"Did you hear me?" she pressed. "I don't want to go to a motel."

He turned, set the package on the floor near her feet, and reached up for Jaimie. "I heard you, angel face," he said, still grinning slightly. "And I promise you, an 'all-nighter' would be far too taxing for an old guy like me."

She burned to tell him where he could stuff it. But she'd been on the receiving end of a man's anger enough times to know better than to ask for it. Besides, she still didn't have the baby bottle or formula in her possession. He might throw that sack in the next trash can he saw if she refused to cooperate.

For a moment, she stood there, clinging to Jaimie and glaring at him, but in the end, her physical condition forced her to relinquish her hold on the child. If he was absolutely bent on going to a motel, she had little choice but to go along with the idea. He who had the money called the shots.

After taking Jaimie, Rafe tucked him in the crook of one arm and reached up to take her hand. Pressing her other palm on her ribs, Maggie tensed to jump. The next instant, he gave a sharp tug, pulling her off balance. As she fell forward, he released her hand and caught her with his empty arm, clasping her firmly to his broad chest and sweeping her smoothly to the ground. The impact of her body against his made her throb from head to toe, and for an awful minute, she was afraid she might pass out.

"I'm sorry. I know that hurt, but you're so weak I was afraid you might fall, and it's quite a drop to the ground."

He held her against his hard length until she gained her feet, making her horribly aware of his greater strength. Then he collected the sack from the boxcar, his gaze lingering on her as he jostled the child and package to get a comfortable hold on both.

Glancing around the train yard, he asked, "Can you make it two blocks without help?"

Maggie shivered inside the coat, her attention darting to the bundled baby in his arms. "Yes," she said with more confidence than she felt. "Let me carry Jaimie, though. Either that, or you wear the coat so he won't get cold."

He glanced down at the sleeping baby. "He's fine with the jacket and sweatshirt around him. In five minutes, we'll be in the room."

He struck off, leaving Maggie to follow. Given the fact that he had her baby, he might as well have had her on a leash. She clamped a hand over her ribs and walked as swiftly as she could to keep up.

He set a brisk pace until they were out of the train yard. Once on the sidewalk, he paused to wait for her, his expression unreadable. "Sorry about the footrace. Coming and going in a railroad yard, it pays not to let any grass grow."

Maggie understood the need for caution. Huffing for breath and covering the remaining distance between them on legs that threatened to fold, she said, "No problem. I don't want to get tossed in jail any more than you do."

"I doubt we'd get arrested. Most times, the law looks the other way unless somebody causes trouble. Railroad employees are a slightly different ball game, though, and it's a lot less hassle if you can avoid them." His gaze searched hers. Maggie tried to slow her breathing, but

her lungs didn't seem to be inflating to full capacity.
"You okay?" he asked.

By way of response, all she could manage was a nod.

"I'm sorry, honey. I'd carry you if I could."

Coming to a stop, she yearned to lean against him and
rest for a moment. Then she remembered where they
were going and thought better of it. *A motel?* "I—I really haven't the time for this," she tried again, hoping
he might have a change of heart. "I've got to get where
I'm headed and find a job."

He thrust the sack into her hands. It was surprisingly
heavy, and not expecting the weight, Maggie nearly
dropped it. While she grappled to get a better hold, he
looped his arm around her back and drew her against
his side. "Lean into me. Maybe that'll help. It's only
two blocks. If we take it slow, maybe you can make it
that far." He bent his head and craned his neck to see
her face. "Is my arm hurting you?"

With the thick coat to provide cushion, the pressure
on her bruises was painful but not unbearably so. His
support also helped to ease the ache across her lower
back. Shaking her head, she said, "Did you hear me? I
have to find a job so I can send for my little sister. Will
another train leave here this morning?"

Without offering a reply, he set off, keeping a slower
pace this time and supporting her weight against him.
Finally he said, "You can leave tomorrow morning."
As he spoke, he drew her inexorably along the sidewalk.
Maggie felt like a condemned prisoner being dragged to
the execution chamber. "At the motel, you can eat a
little something and get some sleep. Right now, you
couldn't work to save your soul, and you know it. What
do you do, anyway?"

She blinked, wishing the air weren't so cold. It hurt
to breathe. She cast another worried glance at her baby.
"Is Jaimie's face covered?"

"He's bundled up like an Express Mail package."

He drew to a stop on a curb, puffs of vapor forming

with his breath as he glanced up and down the empty street. The building fronts were a blur to Maggie, but even so, she noted the absence of automobiles at the parking meters that lined the sidewalks. "Where is everyone?"

"When I walked into town earlier, I saw a sign that says the population inside the city limits is only a little over four thousand, and if that clock inside the bank is right, it's only nine-forty, which is still pretty early. This is largely a ranching community, and ranchers don't usually come to town until they've finished morning chores."

What bank? Maggie blinked again, feeling oddly separated from reality. "Do you do secretarial or assembly-line work?" he asked as he guided her across the icy asphalt to the opposite curb. "Prior's not that big a town. I can't imagine its being a hub of opportunity."

"Waitress," she managed to reply.

"Ah." He sounded none too impressed.

Maggie tried to straighten away from him, but the circle of his arm around her was as unyielding as forged steel. "I know it's a dead-end job, but I make—really good tips. A better monthly take-home than any secretary, that's for sure. Prestige takes a second seat when you have a family to feed and bills to pay."

He glanced down at her, the shadow cast by his hat brim concealing the expression in his eyes. "A family to feed, huh? Does that mean you're married and have other kids besides Jaimie?"

"No, I—" Maggie caught herself before she said too much. She angled him a look. "Fishing for information, Mr. Kendrick?"

He smiled. "And getting nowhere fast. Unfortunately for you, mysterious women have always fascinated me. So . . . you make good tips?" He nodded. "I can believe it."

She wondered what he meant by that, but she was too weary to pursue it. The sidewalk ahead of her seemed to stretch for a thousand miles. Her legs felt heavy and rubbery. "How much farther is it, anyhow?"

"Not very far." He drew to a stop, cradling her against him. "We'll just rest here a minute. There's no fire, right?"

His broad chest was there, offering a perfect spot to lay her cheek. Maggie tried to resist, but she couldn't. With numb arms, she hugged the package and nestled in beside Jaimie to lean against him. As if he understood how weak and woozy she felt, he supported nearly all her weight. "I'm sorry," she grated out. "I'm afraid you struck a poor bargain. I feel sort of sick."

"Sick?" he repeated sharply. "Where?"

"All over. Like I've been run over by a truck, and I'm kind of nauseated."

She felt the steamy warmth of his breath on the crown of her head. "If the pain in those ribs doesn't ease up, I'm taking you to the hospital."

"No." Maggie tried to push away from him, only to be foiled by his hold on her. "I told you, I can't go around a bunch of people. Besides, I can't afford a hospital. Do you know how expensive emergency-room treatment can be?"

"Calm down. It was just a thought."

"As bruised up as I am, I'm bound to be sore. I don't need a doctor."

"All right, all right," he said in a soothing tone. "Forget I suggested it. Maybe you'll feel better once you eat and get some rest."

With him footing the bill for both the food and the room? She wouldn't feel better until she saw the last of him. Oh, how she wanted to refuse his generosity, but her baby needed to be fed, and she couldn't gather her thoughts enough to think of an alternative. She just wanted to lean against him and keep her eyes closed forever.

He nudged her erect. "It's not much farther. You game? Or do you want me to get Jaimie settled in the room and come back for you? With nothing to carry, I can pack you the rest of the way if it's too hard to walk on your own.''

Maggie wasn't about to let her baby out of her sight. ''I can walk,'' she insisted, and somehow she managed to do just that, planting one foot in front of the other until he finally said, ''Here we are. You wait here for me, all right? I'll only be a minute.''

Maggie was grateful for the overhang post he propped her against. Clutching the bag to her chest, she rested her cheek against the wood and gazed after him. He stepped into a small, glass-fronted motel office. From where she stood, Maggie could see that a plump lady with gray hair manned the registration desk, which was little more than a scarred counter boasting a ratty potted fern and a display of brochures. Holding Jaimie in one arm, Rafe reached into his pants pocket for some money while the woman asked him questions and filled out some sort of form. Minutes later, he emerged holding a black plastic key ring with the number fourteen printed in faded white on its oval surface.

''I tried to get two beds,'' he explained as he helped her across the empty parking lot toward one of the cottages. ''But all she has is singles. It's a queen-size, though. That's a plus. Right?''

Maggie focused on the front of the cabin as he unlocked the door. White siding with red trim glared in the morning light, the lower horizontal panels spattered with flecks of mud by runoff from the eaves. Empty red window boxes, in sad need of paint, underscored the windows. The door creaked when he pushed it open. As he drew her into the room, she tripped on the threshold and might have fallen if not for the grip of his hand on her elbow.

The faint, closed-up smell of mildew blasted her in the face. Maggie stood just inside the door, numbly taking in her surroundings, which consisted of a dated dresser with a filmy mirror, a bed draped in white chenille, and an awful brown shag carpet that was so worn the nap lay flat. A rusty wall heater sat cold beneath a window covered by droopy short drapes that had once been white but were now yellow with age, one of the panels stained by a window leak.

"Well, it'll do in a pinch. At least it looks halfway clean."

Relieving Maggie of the paper sack, he turned on the heater and stepped around to the opposite side of the wide bed to lay Jaimie on the white chenille. As he drew away the coat and sweatshirt, the baby thrashed his legs and let out a plaintive whimper. "Right on cue for breakfast, hey, partner?" He glanced up at Maggie. "Shed the coat, honey, and lie down. I'll crack out the formula and bring His Nibs here a bottle in a minute."

Maggie tried to peel off the coat, but it was heavy and her arms hung at her sides like lengths of stiff garden hose. The wall heater made a monotonous humming noise that seemed to harmonize with the ringing in her ears. She watched Rafe disappear at the opposite end of the room into what she presumed was a bathroom.

His deep voice rang out from the enclosure. "Are we stylin' or what? We even have a coffeemaker."

She heard water run and then a squeak as he turned off the tap. Paper rustled as he opened the bag and sorted through his purchases—purchases she had yet to pay him for. During the silence that followed, she considered grabbing Jaimie and hightailing it out of there. Two things stopped her. The cowboy had the bottle and formula in the bathroom with him, and she could barely walk, let alone run.

She careened toward the bed, somehow managing to lift her feet enough to avoid falling flat. When the mattress nudged her knees, she sank gratefully onto the soft surface and buried her face in the pillow.

He'd come back in a minute and be all hot to do his thing. *Think, Maggie.* Unless she came up with a quick solution, he would expect her to pay him back as per the terms of their bargain. She trailed her fingertips over her bare left wrist, wishing she could offer him her watch in trade, but she'd broken the crystal at work last week, and water had gotten inside the casing.

Tears prickled behind her eyelids. That left her exactly nothing to barter with now—except her body.

Oh, how she hoped he really would let her sleep afterward. Then, perhaps, she'd feel better and would be able to leave. She just wouldn't think about what was in store for her. That was the trick. In fact, she was so tired, maybe she would be able to sleep through the ordeal. He could wake her up when he was done—or, even better, just let her go on sleeping.

From a long way off, Maggie heard Jaimie crying. She blinked to awareness, relieved that her need to use the bathroom seemed a little less urgent now that she was in a horizontal position. Pushing herself up on one elbow, she saw Rafe standing beside the bed. With the air of a man who'd done so many times, he dribbled formula from the bottle onto the inside of his wrist.

He glanced up and smiled. "I washed everything as best I could, and I got the chill off the formula by putting the bottle in scalding hot water from the coffeepot. This is premixed so we don't have to mess around measuring everything."

The frayed cuffs of his shirt looked wet, an indication that he had at least scrubbed his hands. But, even so, he still looked none too clean. She could only pray Jaimie wouldn't come in contact with some awful germ and get sick.

Rafe scooped the baby into his arm and offered him the bottle. Jaimie gummed the nipple, then pulled an awful face. Rafe chuckled and began walking, nudging the baby's mouth with the latex tip and jiggling him gently.

"I know it's not quite like what your mama has," she heard him say huskily, "but I don't come with the same equipment. Ah, there. See? It doesn't taste so bad." He gave another low laugh. "Whoa, son. Not that fast, or you'll get a bellyache." The nipple drew air when Rafe tugged it from Jaimie's mouth, the formula inside the bottle bubbling. He glanced at Maggie. "He's draining it like a little siphon hose."

Maggie yearned to get up and feed the baby herself, but the leaden heaviness of her body dictated otherwise. She watched longingly as Rafe held Jaimie over his shoulder and gently thumped his back to burp him.

"You're good at this," she observed hoarsely. "Have you been around lots of babies?"

A blank expression crossed his dark face as he resettled Jaimie in the bend of his arm and began feeding him again. "Yeah, I've been around a couple," he replied, his voice sounding oddly hollow. "Caring for them is kind of like riding a horse. You never forget how."

Maggie lowered her gaze, feeling as if she'd trespassed on forbidden ground. Glancing back up, she said, "I didn't mean to pry. I just—"

"No problem." His larynx bobbed as though he were swallowing a golf ball. When he spoke again, the sadness in his tone lay heavily on the air. "I had two kids, a boy and a girl."

Maggie couldn't help but note that he had referred to both children in the past tense. "Are you divorced?"

He kept his gaze fixed on the baby, his silence stretching out for so long she thought he meant to let the question go unanswered. But he finally said, "No," his voice gruff with emotion. "I, um—lost them in a car wreck."

Maggie's stomach clenched, and she wished with all her heart she had never asked. She started to say she was sorry, but the words seemed so trite that she chose to say nothing at all. Her gaze flew to Jaimie. She didn't think she could bear it if something happened to him.

"It's been over two years," he told her. "For a long time, I knew exactly how long ago, right down to the hour and minute. But then I hocked my watch." He laughed, softly and bitterly. "A good thing, I guess. Counting the minutes I'd been without them was kind of morbid. And it didn't do any good."

Maggie's mouth felt as dry as powder. She still didn't know what to say.

"But hey, life goes on," he said more brightly, his gaze still fixed on the baby. His mouth curved in a slight smile. "Right, little fella?"

He plucked the nipple from the baby's mouth and held up the nearly empty bottle. "You finished that off in nothing flat. Next time, I better fix you more."

He set the bottle on the nightstand and shifted the baby back to his shoulder. When Jaimie emitted a loud burp, Rafe grimaced. "Christ! Right down my collar!" He smiled and winked at Maggie. "I guess I don't remember everything about babies. Rule number one when you burp a kid: always wear protective gear."

He laid the baby on the bed and disappeared into the bathroom again. A moment later, he came back with a disposable diaper and wet washcloth.

"I'll change him," Maggie said, struggling to rise.

He glanced up. "I can handle this just fine. You see to yourself. You can get that coat off, for starters, before you melt. It's getting warm in here."

She pushed weakly to her feet and wrestled with the sheepskin, which felt as if it weighed a thousand pounds. Once she managed to shrug one shoulder free, the garment plopped heavily around her feet. Perspiration filming her body, she stared down at it, too exhausted to pick it up.

"I'll get the coat later," he assured her. "Jaimie's already nodding off to sleep, so it's not as if he needs you for anything. You just concentrate on shucking your clothes, all right?"

Her clothes? Maggie glanced from the coat to the dingy T-shirt she wore. Of course he expected her to undress. Why hadn't she thought of that? She imagined stripping off and standing before him naked. The very thought was so humiliating that she wanted to die. Oh, God. What was she doing here?

Don't think, she told herself firmly. *Just shut it all out. Concentrate on Jaimie. He's got food in his tummy, and he's warm and dry. No matter what it costs you, his needs are being met, and that's all that matters.*

She fixed her gaze on the opposite end of the room where the bathroom was located. *One foot in front of the other one. You can do it.* The walls seemed to lean inward as she circled the end of the bed. She glimpsed her reflection in the filmy mirror and thought she saw two of herself.

"Easy, honey. I've got you," a deep voice murmured next to her ear.

Not two of herself. Rafe was beside her. She felt his big hands clasping her elbows, and though she longed to pull away, she let him support her weight instead. *Oh, God.* This was so embarrassing.

"I'm sorry," she said in a voice that didn't sound like her own. Pathetic was how it sounded.

"No worries."

Once in the bathroom, he guided her to the toilet, then reached around her and quickly unsnapped her jeans. The sound of her zipper made alarm bells go off in her mind. "No. I can—by myself. Please."

"I know," he assured her. "I'm just getting you lined out here. Then I'll leave. Can you hold onto the vanity so you don't fall?"

Maggie grabbed the Formica edge of the countertop with both hands. "Yes," she said weakly. "Got it. Fine, now. I'm fine."

She heard him swear under his breath, and for a terrible moment, she feared he might insist on staying in there to help her. "Please, Mr. Kendrick. Go now, please."

"Are you sure you're all right?"

Maggie couldn't answer, so she just nodded. To her immeasurable relief, he left and closed the bathroom door. The small enclosure seemed to spin around her, but somehow she managed to maneuver. When she was finished, she got her jeans button fastened, but the zipper defied her rubbery fingertips.

"Maggie? Honey, are you done?"

She gave up on the zipper and let her arms dangle at her sides. What was wrong with her? Never had she felt so awful. She'd used the rest room, but she still had that burning ache. Did she have a bladder infection? She'd never had one, so she wasn't sure how they felt. Her boss Terry got them sometimes, and she said drinking lots of cranberry juice always helped.

The bathroom door cracked open. The next instant, her boxcar cowboy had a strong arm around her waist. "Jesus, honey. There's a time and place for modesty, and this ain't it." He helped her to the sink and washed her hands as if she were a child. It struck Maggie as odd that a tramp would bother. He grabbed a small towel from the rack and blotted her fingers dry. "There you go."

The next instant, the room turned upside down. Maggie gave a thin cry and clutched his neck, dimly realizing he had picked her up. "What're you—oh, God, don't drop me!"

She thought she detected laughter in his voice when he replied, "I doubt you'd tip the scales at a hundred and ten, fully clothed and soaking wet. I think I can manage. You need feeding up. How long since you ate?"

"Yesterday."

"What did you have?"

"Toast."

"Well, hell. No wonder you're thin."

He carried her back to the bed, depositing her gently on her feet beside it. Maggie tried to sink down onto the mattress next to Jaimie, but Rafe caught her by the elbows and drew her back up. His slate-blue eyes locked with hers for a long moment, and then he grasped the hem of the T-shirt. "Let me help you shuck your clothes. All right?"

She could tell by his tone of voice that he wasn't really requesting permission. It was more a warning of what was to come. When he started to tug the shirt up, she curled her fingers over his broad wrists, wanting to push his hands away. But she didn't have the strength. Instead, she simply rested her palms on his tattered cuffs, unable to tighten her grip. Tears filled her eyes again. Angry with herself, she tried to blink them away, but they kept coming.

He made fast work of peeling the shirt off over her head. Then, tossing it aside, he caught her under the chin with the crook of his finger. Lifting her tear-streaked face, he said, "What's this?"

"I'm—I'm sorry. I'm not very good at casual encounters."

"Casual encounters, huh? Is that what this is?"

She recalled all the public-awareness commercials she'd seen on television, and a new, extremely worrisome concern zigzagged through her head. "Mr. Kendrick? I do hope you thought to get a—" She gulped and blinked at a wave of dizziness. "A you-know-what."

He chuckled. "We don't need one."

"Yes." Her head cleared a bit, and she got his face into focus. Tangled hair, scruffy whiskers, and a shirt that looked as if it had been used to scour a pot . . . He was a walking, talking risk factor. "Please. Would you go get one? I'm not in the habit, and I'm afraid I'm not prepared."

"Yeah, well . . . I figured as much." Sandpapery fingertips brushed the tears from her cheeks. "You're also a rotten judge of character. Do you really think I brought you here for a tumble in the hay?"

Maggie gazed up at him through a swimming blur. "That was our bargain. I owe you for the stuff you bought."

He rubbed at her cheeks again. "Hell's bells, girl." He gave a throaty laugh. "Would you stop looking at me like that? I'm not expecting paybacks. All right? If you insist on keeping it even, you'll have to give me a rain check. Red and purple not being my favorite colors, I can't get excited about collecting on the debt until those bruises are gone."

"I can't stay here until then. I told you, I have to get where I'm going and find a job. My little sister is waiting for me to send for her, and I—"

He cut her off by pushing her down to sit on the edge of the bed. "And you're not interested in a big, drawn-out thing," he finished for her. "I read you, loud and clear. So I guess you'll just have to owe me."

"But I won't be able to pay you back. I told you, remember?"

Hunkering before her, he lifted one of her feet onto his knee and began untying her sneaker. "I remember." He drew off the shoe and sock, the grip of his warm fingers sending jolts up her calf. After lowering her bare foot to the rug, he lifted her other leg. "I kind of like the idea of a pretty lady being forever in my debt. On Judgment Day, maybe it'll count as a point in my favor. You reckon?"

Maggie stared down at the top of his dark head, just now registering that he had shed his hat. "You mean you really don't want to—well, you know—like we talked about?"

"Like *you* talked about," he corrected. He tossed aside the second shoe and sock, then rose, grasping her carefully by the shoulders to draw her erect. "You know what your problem is? You assume every man you meet is a low-down skunk who'll take advantage of you if he gets half a chance."

Too late, Maggie realized that he had unfastened the button of her jeans as he spoke. She gave a startled gasp when he bent to tug the denim over her hips. Her panties were full-cut, but the white nylon was semitransparent.

He swore under his breath when he saw the bruises on her thighs. "That son of a bitch. If I ever run into him, he's a dead man."

Maggie's attempt to cover the apex of her legs with the splay of her hands was abruptly aborted when he pressed her back down to sit on the mattress. He gently drew her jeans down to her ankles, taking care not to graze her shins.

"Damn," he whispered. "You're just one big bruise, sweetheart." He tugged the denim over her feet and dropped the pants on the floor. "I'm amazed you can even walk."

He reached behind her to turn back the covers, then stood to gaze down at her. A flush of embarrassment warmed Maggie's skin.

"Mr. Kendrick, if you have no intention of—why are you taking all my clothes off?" she asked, her distrust lending a shrill sharpness to the question.

"So I can disinfect those cuts. Someone has to do it. Even if you were strong enough to take care of it yourself, you can't reach two-thirds of them. You don't want infection to set in, do you?"

Maggie had dreaded living up to her side of their bargain, but this latest development seemed even worse. She had cuts everywhere, some in places she would die of humiliation if he touched. She imagined lying naked while he examined every bare inch of her, and the prospect was so alarming, she found it difficult to breathe.

"But I'm nearly naked," she observed, her voice quaking.

"I'll do my best to make this easy for you. Haul out my manners. Be a complete gentleman. I promise not to uncover all of you at once. How's that sound?"

Maggie could only think of the parts he *would* uncover.

"You'd be more exposed in a bikini," he pointed out, as though that should make her feel better. "I can't really see much."

She was clinging to that thought and trying to convince herself she wasn't really indecently clad when he slipped his hands around to her back and tried to unfasten her bra. After tugging at it several times, he said, "Shit," and leaned around so he could see. "A woman invented these damned things. I'd bet money on it. I've never pulled off a sneaky bra maneuver in my life." He finally conquered the clasp with a clumsy tug and jerk. "When I was seventeen, I even swiped one of my mom's bras to practice my technique."

She gave him a startled look that he met with a wink and lazy grin. She had a feeling he was making this story up, trying to keep her mind occupied so she wouldn't feel self-conscious.

"It's a guy thing. If you don't pass Bra Clasps 101, you're flat out of luck with the girls. I practiced every night, no lie, and I still never got the hang of it. One day Mom found the bra under my mattress and told my dad. He confessed to me later he was worried sick for over a year that I was a cross-dresser."

"A cross what?"

He chuckled. "Never mind."

To her immense relief, he didn't draw the bra cups from her breasts, which at least gave her some covering. Instead, he gave her a gentle push, and she found herself flat on her back. Before she had time to protest or feel alarmed, he drew the bedcovers over her and tucked them around her shoulders.

"There. Completely hidden again. Now that wasn't so bad. Was it?"

His tone reminded her of the one he'd used to cajole Jaimie into nursing from the bottle—his voice pitched low, the vibrant timber seeming to surround her with warmth. Only she wasn't quite as trusting as her son. Her bra was undone, which had to mean he planned to relieve her of it soon.

He left her to chew on that worry while he returned to the bathroom. She heard him rustling the paper bag and clanking around, and she closed her eyes in dread. A moment later, the muted tread of his boots on the carpet reached her, the sounds moving closer. She didn't need to lift her lashes to know when he came to stand over her. She felt his nearness in every pore of her skin. A glass bottle made a *chink* on the nightstand. Then the mattress sank sharply at the outer edge as he sat down.

She could only guess what might come next, the one certainty being that it wouldn't be pleasant. Panic welled. She knotted her hands into fists at her sides and forced herself to be calm. *Pride*. Maybe to some people it was only a word, but aside from her son, it was all she had left. After everything she had endured to come this far, she'd be damned if she would let a small dose of humiliation get the best of her. So far, at least, Rafe Kendrick didn't strike her as being a cruel man. Not that you could tell much about a man's nature on such short acquaintance.

Oh, yes, she'd learned the hard way just how treacherous men could be, being kind one moment and acting like barbarians the next. Recalling those experiences now, her instincts warned her not to trust him.

Only if he meant her harm, what was he waiting for? They were alone in a seedy motel room behind a locked door. There was no one to intervene. In short, there was nothing to stop him from being a jerk.

"I can stack the pillows behind you so you don't have to actually sit up by yourself," he offered. "You think that might help?"

Maggie merely nodded. Speaking was beyond her. Afraid that her bra straps might slip off her shoulders, she clutched the covers to her chest when he slipped an arm behind her. She needn't have bothered. Once she gained a sitting posture and he released her to plump the pillows, she saw that he had been holding the bedspread over her front.

He caught her look of surprise and gave a dry laugh. "This isn't exactly what you were expecting, I take it."

He shrugged. "Think about it. Is there a spot on you that I could touch without hurting you?"

Some men wouldn't care. Maggie knew that. Oh, God, she was going to bawl and make a total fool of herself. He was bound to think she was crazy, and she wouldn't blame him.

It was just—so unexpected. A dirty drunkard in tattered cowboy garb, turning out to be the kindest man she had encountered since her father died? It made no sense. Everyone knew that practically all railroad bums were lowlifes who'd steal from a blind man if the opportunity arose. How had she been so lucky as to meet one of the few nice ones? Maybe God actually had heard her prayers, after all, and He'd answered by sending her this man.

He handed her the bottle of medication and a cotton ball. A strong antiseptic smell seared her nostrils. "I'll hold the spread up close, so don't worry about me looking over the top. You just get the bra off and concentrate on doctoring your chest."

With shaking hands, Maggie drew the straps down her arms, laid the bra aside, and tipped the bottle to moisten the cotton. As she began dabbing at the cuts, the alcohol in the antiseptic smarted so badly she gasped and blew to ease the sting.

"Christ. I should have read the labels, I guess. I might have bought something that wouldn't burn."

"It's f-fine. I appreciate that you even bothered. It wasn't part of our deal, you buying stuff for me."

"Our deal. You sound like one of my dad's scratched records. I wish you'd get that bargain you made with me out of your head."

Feeling strangely vague and detached from reality, she glanced up. "You really have a dad?"

He narrowed an eye. "No, a stork dropped me on my mother's doorstep."

"Well, of course you have a dad. What I meant was—" She broke off, not entirely sure what she meant. Her mind didn't seem to be tracking right, which left her mouth to operate solo. "It's just that you—well, looking at you, one doesn't picture you with a family. Parents, brothers and sisters, and all of that."

"I assure you that I'm normal in that respect, with a mom, a dad, and a brother." He loosened his hold on the spread with one hand to rub his bewhiskered jaw. "God, do I look that bad?"

Maggie's thinking was so hazy it took her a moment to realize he'd turned loose of one side of the bedspread. She grabbed for the drooping section.

"Oops! Sorry." He jerked the chenille back up. "I didn't see a thing. Honest."

Above the scraggly growth of beard, the skin over his high cheekbones turned a ruddy red. She knew he was lying through his teeth. At least he had the good grace to blush.

"All done?" At her nod, he relinquished the spread into her keeping while he helped her lie back down. "It hurts like hell, doesn't it? I got sandwiched between a corral rail and a bull once. Cracked two ribs, so I can sympathize."

"So the cowboy apparel isn't just for looks?" she asked, her breath snagging with a catch in her side.

He tucked the covers over her. "For looks? You're joking, right? Even back when I was a rancher, I never dressed to make a fashion statement, and I've gone downhill on greased runners since."

Maggie studied his chiseled features, trying to imagine what he'd look like cleaned up. His blue eyes were the kind to make a woman's heartbeat skitter, and his large, sharply bridged nose was attractive on him, but she could see little of his lower face with the whiskers covering so much. He had a strong, square jaw and chin. She could discern that. And a full, sensual mouth when he wasn't grim-lipped and scowling.

He distracted her from her perusal of him by thrusting

one of the towels at her. "Cover the goods. Now it's my turn."

Tugging the towel under the bedding, she fumbled to spread it over her chest. When she went still, he drew the covers down to her waist. Maggie crossed her arms over the terry cloth so it wouldn't shift.

He soaked a sterile cotton ball with medication, then started dabbing at her closest shoulder and arm. She felt so uncomfortable she closed her eyes. An instant later when she felt him blowing on her bare skin, her lids popped back open. He flicked her one of those whiskey-and-smoke looks that unsettled her so, but he didn't stop puffing.

"Sorry, but I know how it must sting." He returned his gaze to her shoulder. "The asshole wears a ring, doesn't he?"

A picture of Lonnie's diamond flashed in Maggie's mind. Oh, how she detested that ring, knowing he'd bought it with some of her dad's life insurance.

"You know, I've changed my mind about asking nothing of you as payback for the money I spent," Rafe suddenly told her.

Her heart leaped and then sank with crushing disappointment.

"As payback, answer me this. You're covered with bruises from the neck down. How come there isn't so much as a mark on your face?"

Maggie swallowed, the walls of her throat feeling as if they were coated with fast-drying glue. "That's it? All you want is the answer to one question?"

"Maybe two or three." His eyes glinted with laughter. "Let's agree on three. That way, I'm leaving myself some room to be nosy again if the urge hits."

Maggie nearly smiled. "You're selling out cheap."

"Yeah, well, I'm letting you off easy. Usually I'm more shrewd at dickering." He dabbed at a scrape above her elbow and blew softly on the moistened patch of raw skin, making her stomach flutter.

"Well? You gonna pay up? Or do I have to take my money's worth out in trade?" When he met her gaze, the glint of laughter in his eyes had turned unmistakably mischievous. "Don't press your luck too far, Maggie girl. You come nicely packaged, even if you are a little too colorfully spotted with red and purple blue to suit my tastes."

"Bruises on my face would have been a dead give-away that he'd beaten me up," she hastened to reveal.

"Ah." He nodded. "Makes sense. Can I take that to mean there's someone else in your life who might take exception to his working you over?"

"Is that your second question?"

"Always on your toes, aren't you?" He nodded. "We can count it as my second question if you're forthcoming with the right answers. Not only who that person is, but why in the hell he hasn't stomped the snot out of the bastard."

" 'He' is a she. My mom. And she's a dear heart who would never dream he might hurt me unless she saw evidence of it. I've kept it from her. She's in fragile health and shouldn't get upset."

"She can't be much of a mother if she never noticed you gimping around."

"She's as good a mother as she can be, and that's all the information you're getting unless you want to use up all three questions."

Rafe leaned closer to work on her arm, taking care not to let his chest graze hers. She lay rigid, her small chin lifted a notch, as if it took all of her self-control not to shove his hands away. His heart broke for her. It was horrible enough that she'd been so badly abused. But to be placed in this position, on top of it all, having to endure the indignity of a stranger touching her . . . Sometimes there was simply no justice in the world.

He yearned to gather her close and promise her no one would ever lay a hand on her again. But even as the thought took shape, he shoved it away. He'd been around this girl one night and part of a morning. He had no business caring about her like this. The rush of feelings he was experiencing didn't even make sense.

When he was finished cleaning her cuts, he drew the sheet over her back, positioning the top hem well above her shoulder blades as he pushed to his feet. Regarding the back of her dark head, he said, "I have to go out for a while. Jaimie is sleeping right next to you. If he cries, do you think you'll wake up?"

Clutching the sheet close, she eased painfully onto her side, her face so pale it was nearly as white as the pillowcase. Her long, dark eyelashes fluttered, and she fixed him with a befuddled gaze that told him she was mere inches away from flickering out like a candle flame.

"He can't roll off the mattress?"

"I rolled up a towel as a bolster pad. He'll be fine." Rafe raked a hand through his hair, wincing at the tug when he hit a tangle. "I'll be back soon."

"Where are you going?" she asked faintly.

"To get some food, for one thing."

She searched his face, her expression conveying resigned hopelessness. "You're not coming back, are you?"

The thought had occurred to him a couple of times. He couldn't deny it. Only he couldn't bring himself to be quite that rotten. The edge of fear he heard in her voice made him wonder what in God's name had happened in her young life to make her trust so little. Did she really think he would just walk out and leave her like this? She was too weak to take care of herself, let alone that baby.

"I'll be back."

"I know it's not your problem, but if you don't, I'm afraid I won't hear Jaimie if he cries." She gestured limply with her hand. "If I can just rest for a little bit, I'll be better and . . ." Her voice trailed away, and she blinked.

A part of Rafe felt glad that she had at least come to trust him enough to want him to come back, but another part of him sensed the trap and yearned to run. He bent to collect his coat from the floor where she had dropped it. "I'll be back, Maggie. I promise," he said hoarsely.

As though that was all she'd needed to hear, she let her eyes fall closed. He drew on the coat and stood there for a moment, his gaze tracing the lines of her face. He couldn't recall ever having seen a sweeter countenance. Even in that, he found cause for alarm, for until now, he had never entertained such thoughts about any woman but Susan.

After checking to make sure he had the room key, Rafe retrieved his hat and quietly let himself out. Once on the porch, he double-checked the lock to make sure no one could get inside. Then he stood and grabbed deeply for breath, his lungs aching at the influx of icy air.

As he struck off across the empty parking lot, he kept hearing the echo of her voice. His guts knotted, and he clenched his back teeth. Never in his life had he broken his word. It shamed him to realize that he yearned to now.

Chapter Four

Wind buffeted Rafe as he strode along the sidewalk toward the restaurant at the corner of the block. He shoved his hands deep into the lined pockets of his overcoat and hunched his shoulders. When he came upon a drugstore with colorful Halloween displays in the windows, seeing the jack-o'-lantern made his heart catch.

He drew to a stop and stared, waiting for the pain to strike as it always did when something reminded him unexpectedly of his family. Only the pain was no longer there. A sad acceptance had taken its place. He closed his eyes, searching within himself almost frantically for the grief that had been a part of him for so long. Its gradual lessening was one of the reasons he'd been drinking so heavily these last few months. He was starting to get over losing his family. How could that be? What kind of man was he, to forget them so quickly?

Forcing himself to move, he made his way almost blindly along the sidewalk. *Damn.* He needed a swig of whiskey. Strike that. He needed an entire bottle. *Oblivion.* That was what he wanted. So he wouldn't have to deal with the fact that he no longer wanted to curl up somewhere and die when he remembered his family.

As though in answer to a prayer, an overhead sign loomed in his blurred vision. *Liquor Store.* Rafe's stride faltered, and the money in his front trouser pocket seemed to sear his left thigh. He'd gotten seven hundred dollars for his wedding ring. Why shouldn't he buy something for himself with some of it?

A bell tinkled as he pushed open the door. His hands began to shake. Vaguely aware of a tall, thin woman watching him from behind the cash register, he headed straight for the ceiling-high shelves of booze that lined the right wall, his familiarity with the labels leading him unerringly to the whiskey section. Early Times. Rafe curled his hand around the neck of a half-gallon bottle, his mouth cottony with a raging thirst.

"That'll be twenty-three fifty," the woman said when Rafe approached the counter. "Plastic or paper?"

For a moment, he wasn't sure what she meant. Then he realized she was asking about his preference in sacks. "Paper."

He set the bottle on the counter, then drew back the tail of his coat and shoved up the sleeve to dive his hand into his jeans pocket. As he pulled out the wad of money and started sorting through the bills, his gaze snagged on the inside of his left wrist. A shade lighter than the rest of him, squiggly little lines marbled his skin. It looked as if he'd trickled bleach on himself.

Flashing back to the motel room, Rafe remembered dribbling baby formula on the inside of his wrist. He stared at the irregular lines, realizing that their paler brown color was his skin showing through the gray-brown buildup of grime. *Jesus*. Was he that filthy? It hadn't been that long since he'd had a shower. He shifted his gaze to his shirt cuff. Not only was it badly frayed at the edge, but it was nearly black in places with ground-in dirt. He could remember a time when he had showered and changed clothes from the skin out twice a day.

Uncertain how long he'd been standing there staring at his wrist, Rafe jerked his gaze back to the clerk. She peered at him from behind a pair of rhinestone glasses, her brown hair tidily styled to frame an aging face. She looked like the type who used a magnifying glass to pluck her eyebrows. Fiery heat crawled up his neck.

"That'll be twenty-three fifty," she repeated, clearly ill at ease.

He looked at the bottle of whiskey. For well over a year, he'd been aware he was hooked on alcohol, but he'd laughingly told himself he couldn't be classified as a problem drinker until he decided to quit and couldn't. Since he had no intention of quitting, wherein lay the problem?

Now that he was sober, he couldn't quite see the humor in that way of thinking. He was a bum—a filthy bum. He lived from one moment to the next wondering how he would get his hands on the next bottle. Less than an hour ago, he'd mixed formula, handling the nipple of Jaimie's baby bottle. He had washed his hands first, but gazing down at them now, he saw the black under his fingernails and on his knuckles. Clean? Not by a long shot. And he sure as hell couldn't claim to be germ-free.

"Mister? You gonna buy this whiskey, or stand there while it ages?"

Rafe closed his fist over the money. "I've, um . . ." He retreated a step from the counter, his gaze locked on the bottle. "I've changed my mind."

"I already rang it up."

Rafe kept backing away. Just looking at the whiskey made him shake. But the yearning would have to keep until he parted company with Maggie and Jaimie. He had to think of that baby, damn it. Maggie couldn't care for him by herself right now, and if Rafe meant to assume her responsibilities while she got a few hours' rest, he'd be damned if he'd do it drunk.

Maggie surfaced from a deep sleep to the sound of water running. She strained to open her eyes. The ceiling looked unfamiliar. Bleary-eyed, she scanned her surroundings, remembered Rafe Kendrick bringing her to a motel room, and turned her head to check on Jaimie.

The baby no longer lay beside her. Alarm registered in her foggy mind. Gone? Oh, God.

Pain exploded the length of her body as she started to sit up. She gasped and grabbed her side, scarcely able to breathe. Then she heard a deep, resonant voice coming from the bathroom.

"Aren't you a pistol? Look at those fists and feet go. You like getting a bath, I can tell that much." Water splashed. "Well, you're not alone, little guy. I kind of enjoyed my shower, too. It feels good to be clean, doesn't it?"

Rafe. He was giving Jaimie a bath? Maggie sank back against the pillows and drew the blankets to her chin, relieved beyond measure that she needn't move. Everything hurt, even her butt. She let her eyes drift closed, listening to the rich timber of his voice and wondering yet again if the man was heaven-sent. How strange that her savior should be a ragged drunk in a sheepskin coat and droopy Stetson. Maybe, she decided drowsily, he was her guardian angel in disguise. Or a frog who was actually a handsome prince who had come to carry them off into the sunset on his prancing steed.

The thought made Maggie smile slightly, for she'd long since stopped believing in fairy tales. That was for little girls her sister Heidi's age, and, sadly, even for them, happy endings were few and far between.

Weighted with exhaustion, Maggie drifted in a sleepy haze. She felt as if she'd been rolled up in a heavy rug. She wasn't sure how much time passed. It might have been a minute or an hour. When she heard the bathroom door open, she struggled to lift her eyelashes.

As the man standing at the foot of the bed came into focus, Maggie blinked, convinced she must be imagining him. He resembled Rafe Kendrick. His hair was jet black, at any rate, and he had the same dark skin, smoky blue eyes, and sharply bridged nose, but there all similarity ended. Not only was this man beardless, but he had short hair, looked well-scrubbed, and wore clothes so spanking new they still bore package creases. He was also one of the handsomest men Maggie had ever clapped eyes on, the very epitome of tall, dark, and dangerous. His new blue chambray shirt was open at the collar, revealing a V of bronze, muscular chest, lightly dusted with black hair.

No question about it: she was dreaming.

Cradling Jaimie in one arm, he glanced down. "I can't look *that* different. Except for the clothes, all I did was get a haircut, and shower and shave."

Where had her drunken bum gone? Only a bit ago, she'd been likening this man to a frog, and now, as though she'd conjured him up, the handsome prince had materialized.

He brushed at a horizontal crease in the new jeans, which, unlike his old pair, fit him properly, revealing the powerful contours of his legs. "I thought I ought to clean up." When he met her gaze again, she glimpsed a ruddy flush creeping up his tanned throat. "Handling the baby and all that, I didn't want to—" He shrugged and thrust his fingers through his hair, which fell across his forehead in glistening, unruly waves the instant he released it. "I just thought I should clean up is all."

"Clean up" didn't describe the transformation. And since when did dream princes blush? A deep crease appeared in his lean cheek as his firm lips tipped into a crooked grin. Oh, God. He was drop-dead gorgeous.

Maggie closed her eyes, too exhausted to deal with this right now. With all the hair and baggy clothes, he'd looked older. Now he didn't look a day over thirty. Remembering how she'd let him doctor her cuts, her heart flip-flopped. He'd seen her in the nude—close to it, anyway. And he'd touched her practically *everywhere*. That had been embarrassing enough before; now it was mortifying.

"Maggie?" he said softly.

She kept her eyes closed, pretending to be asleep. It wasn't a difficult ruse to pull off. Right now her throbbing body craved rest, the need overriding all else. Later. She would worry about everything later.

As that thought sifted through her mind, Maggie let the warm, fuzzy blackness settle over her again. She was only distantly aware of the sounds Rafe made as he cared for Jaimie—his deep voice murmuring nonsensical phrases, paper sacks rustling, the clank of something metal in the bathroom, and then water running. In her sleepy mind's eye, she pictured him as the ragged cowboy again, far more comfortable with that image than with the tall, ebon-haired man who'd taken his place.

Sometime later, she felt the grasp of his hand on her shoulder. "Hey, sunshine, you think you can wake up enough to swallow? You need to eat."

The tantalizing smell of food wafted to her nose, and her stomach rumbled loudly in response. "I guess that answers my question. Here, let me help you roll over."

Maggie surrendered herself to the gentle strength of his hands. His dark face swam before her. When she felt him tuck the blankets over her chest, she wanted to thank him, but even as she groped for the words, she forgot exactly what it was she wanted to say.

"Don't try to talk. Just let me get some soup down you. Then you can go back to sleep."

A spoon touched her mouth. The wonderful taste of vegetable soup flowed over her tongue. She swallowed without even attempting to chew. The heat of the liquid made her stomach clench with urgent hunger.

"I didn't know what kind of soup you like. I settled for vegetable beef." A paper napkin grazed her chin. "Sorry. It's hard not to spill with you lying down."

Maggie tensed to sit up, but he immediately pressed her back. "Don't move. We can manage well enough this way." Another spoonful of soup filled her mouth. "I gave His Nibs a bath. Then I fed him two ounces of formula, just to tide him over."

She struggled to make sense of what he was saying, but try as she might, his words darted in and out of her mind. Strangely, it didn't matter. In her present state, she couldn't work up the energy to worry about much. She relaxed against the pillows. His voice reassured her, and she drifted back into the blackness, trusting him to take care of her.

Rafe lightly touched a hand to Maggie's forehead. He could detect no sign of fever, but even so, he couldn't help worrying. He'd never seen anyone sleep this deeply.

"Maggie? You have to wake up now and try to feed Jaimie."

Her long dark eyelashes fluttered. The next instant, Rafe found himself looking into confused brown eyes. He'd never been the sappy type, but in that moment, if he'd been asked to describe the feeling that swept over him, he would have said he felt as if he were drowning.

"Jaimie?" she repeated in a sleepy whisper. "Is he all right?"

Rafe slipped an arm behind her back to plump the pillows and prop her up. He smiled slightly, for even half-awake, she clutched the covers protectively to her chest. "He's fine. Just hungry."

He went to fetch the baby. When he swung back toward the bed, he saw that Maggie's head was already nodding. He gave her a light shake to wake her. "Honey, maybe we should take you to the emergency room."

"No!" she croaked, her eyes opening wide. "I'm not sick or anything. Just tired. All I need is a little more sleep. That's all."

She winced as she struggled to sit straighter. Rafe couldn't determine if her breasts or ribs were causing the most pain, or if it was something else. Judging by the vicious marks he'd seen on her shins, he felt fairly certain she'd been kicked with heavy boots. What if she had internal injuries?

At least she didn't have a fever. That was a good sign.

And she'd kept the soup down. "All right," he agreed reluctantly. "I'll give it until morning. But if you're not better by then, I'm taking you to a doctor. Do we have a deal?"

She blinked, making an obvious effort to wake up. "Yes, a deal," she replied, slurring her words slightly. She held out her arms for the baby. "Hi, sweetkins," she said softly as he gave her the infant. "How's my boy?"

Rafe handed her a bathroom towel to drape over her shoulder while she nursed the child. After taking the rectangle of terry, she gazed bewilderedly at it.

"It's to cover yourself."

A flush flagged her cheeks. "Oh."

Rafe turned away. He found himself staring at a bare wall. *Damn*. He felt trapped. Being locked up in this small room with her was sheer hell. What was he supposed to do, count the hairs on his arms? He went to the window and drew back one of the sagging drapes. Leaning his shoulder against the frame, he gazed through the steamy pane at the dark, nearly empty parking lot.

He could hear the sucking sounds that Jaimie made as he latched onto a nipple. His stomach clenched. He hoped like hell Maggie did feel better in the morning. If he was around her much longer, he couldn't guarantee he'd be able to keep a lid on these feelings she was stirring within him.

He sighed and rubbed the back of his neck, taking heart when he didn't hear Jaimie start to fuss. That had to mean her milk was coming down, and that could only be a good sign.

He closed his eyes, trying to blank out his thoughts. While caring for her, he'd gotten an eyeful a few times. He felt guilty about that, but in all fairness to himself, he hadn't been able to help it. He'd tried not to look, but not seeing what was right in front of his nose was damned near impossible.

All afternoon and evening, one question had been circling in his mind. Who? While her guard had been
down, he'd been so tempted to ask her questions, specifically who had beaten her up. His sense of fair play
had forced him to bite his tongue.

Rafe pinched the bridge of his nose. Why pry into her
personal life when he had no intention of hanging
around? Come morning, he was out of here. He'd take
twenty-five bucks from the money he'd gotten for his
ring, give Maggie the rest, and hit the road, his first stop
the liquor store. He wanted no part of a woman and
baby. Didn't want to care about them, and damned well
wouldn't.

The soft suckling sounds continued. He wished he had
turned on the radio. Anything to drown it out. He knew
every tug of the baby's mouth had to cause Maggie pain,
that if he turned and looked, he'd see tears trailing down
her pale cheeks.

He rubbed a hand over his face and blinked, trying
not to think about how it must be hurting her. He took
a deep breath. "Given the lack of complaint from the
diaper section, I take it your milk is coming down?"

After a moment's silence, she replied in a thin voice.
"Yes."

Rafe swallowed, his throat closing around a pocket of
air like a tight fist. "I know it must hurt like the very
devil to nurse him. As soon as he's done, I'll bring you
a cup of instant soup. I've got water heating on the hot
plate."

"A hot plate? Did it come with the room?"

"No, I bought a few things while I was out. I needed
a way to heat water and do a little cooking. Nothing
fancy. Soup and stuff like that."

"You bought a hot plate?" There was a ring of what
sounded like panic in her voice. "Oh, Mr. Kendrick,
you've spent enough on us as it is. I've told you and
told you, there's no way I can pay you back."

Evidently her life experience had taught her that men

couldn't be trusted not to feel proprietary if a woman accepted help. In fact, judging by the edge of panic in her tone, he suspected some man had gotten ugly with her about it.

"I don't expect you to pay me back, Maggie."

"A hot plate must have been expensive."

For some reason, that made him want to laugh. He could remember a time when a fifty-dollar bill had been small change to him. "It's just a cheap one, and we needed it. What choice did I have?"

"How much was it, exactly?"

Rafe worked his throat to swallow again. "Forty something. Don't worry about it. I've got plenty of money left."

"Where'd you get that much money? You didn't steal it, did you?"

Rafe smiled in spite of himself. He could see how she might think that. "No, I didn't steal it. I hocked a ring."

"A ring? It must have been quite some ring."

"Yeah," he replied huskily, "it was quite some ring."

"Jaimie's done," she said softly.

As he came about, he found himself impaled by those beautiful brown eyes. His heart caught at the shimmer of tears he saw in them.

Her mouth quivered as she searched his face. "Have you ever been so indebted to someone you couldn't even think how to thank him?" she asked in a shaky voice. "I know it irritates you. But I can't help but worry. I'm in the habit of making my own way, and I'll never be able to repay you for all this."

The lump was back in Rafe's throat. Making her own way? She could barely walk.

"No paybacks. Remember? Just knowing I've helped a little is all the thanks I need."

He approached the bed, intending to take the baby from her and put him back in his makeshift bed. But once there, he sat beside her, his gaze locked on her sweet face. Dark smudges underlined her eyes, and her soft mouth was almost colorless. He cupped her cheek, trailing his thumb along her cheekbone, which felt frighteningly fragile.

Noting the prideful way she held her head and the stubborn thrust of her small chin, he struggled to sort his emotions. Down for the count, flat broke, and fresh out of luck—that was Maggie. Yet she still clung to her pride. He couldn't help but admire that about her. On the other hand, though, it made for rough going when a man was trying to help her.

"Maggie, I know you feel uncomfortable about telling me too much, but I've got to ask. Who beat you up? And why?"

She lowered her gaze, a sign to Rafe that she didn't intend to answer him.

"Was it Jaimie's father?" He lightly touched her tousled hair. The sable tendrils were as soft as silk, an incongruous contrast to her mutinous expression, which, for reasons beyond him, made him want to smile. "Surely you can tell me that much."

She raised her chin higher. "Jaimie has no father."

Rafe's heart caught, for there was a wealth of pain in those four words. "Everyone has a father, honey."

"No."

Just that one word: no. The way she said it, her voice laced with stubborn denial, made him yearn to hug her. Though he knew she had to be in her early twenties, she seemed so very young right then and so horribly alone.

"Jaimie is my baby," she whispered. "Nobody's but mine. On his birth certificate, I listed his father as 'unknown,' and that's the way it's going to stay."

Rafe sighed. "Someday he'll ask about his dad, you know. Is that what you're going to tell him, that his father is unknown?"

"Yes."

"That won't reflect very well on you," he pointed out.

"Better that he believe his mother was promiscuous than to learn the truth about—" She gulped and closed her eyes. "He has no father, end of subject. Please don't ask me about it again."

Of all the women he had ever met, she was the least likely to have been promiscuous. Rafe had a host of flaws, but being a poor judge of character wasn't one of them. The first time he'd ever looked into Maggie's eyes, he'd sensed her innocence, and discovering that she'd given birth to an illegitimate child hadn't altered that impression. He didn't know how she'd wound up pregnant, or why she so vehemently denied Jaimie's father's existence. But he would have bet his life on the fact that she hadn't slept around.

Realizing that there was little point in pursuing the subject further, Rafe took the sleeping baby from her arms and pushed to his feet. As he stood there gazing down at her, he once again noted how very young and defenseless she looked. Her narrow shoulders barely took up half the pillow behind her, and above the blankets she clutched to her bare chest, he could see the delicate structure of her breast and collarbone. For an instant, his gaze locked on the ugly purple bruises that marred her ivory skin.

Whether she wanted to admit it or not, she desperately needed someone to take care of her. En route to the dresser drawer he'd fashioned into a bed for the baby, he found himself entertaining the thought of filling that role himself. And if that wasn't a damn-fool notion, he didn't know what was.

As he laid Jaimie in the cocoon of downy receiving blankets he'd bought, Rafe gave himself a hard mental shake. Like he was in any position to help someone else? Get real. His life was a mess. Even now, his hands trembled in need of a drink. No question about it; she needed help. But not from a hapless drifter whose one goal in life was to buy the next bottle.

Come morning, he'd do them both a favor and get the

hell out of here. She wouldn't be alone for long, he assured himself. With those eyes and that sweet face of hers, some other man would take one look at her and be putty in her hands.

 Chapter Five

Sometime around midnight, people rented the cottage next to theirs, and the commotion of slamming doors, raised voices, and thumping luggage startled Maggie awake. Gasping at the pain in her ribs, she shot upright in bed and grabbed the first thing at hand to defend herself, one of the pillows.

Rafe glanced up from tending Jaimie to see her clutching the sheet to her chest, her terrified gaze fixed on the door, the pillow raised as if she meant to clobber the first thing that moved. Given the fact that in her befuddled state she'd chosen what could only be considered a pitifully ineffectual weapon, he nearly smiled.

"You expecting company?" he asked.

"Maybe."

The moment she spoke, she winced, as if regretting her candor.

"I see. And what's the plan, to smother him or bludgeon him to death?"

She rubbed at her eyes. "Very funny."

As he applied himself to the task of snapping Jaimie's sleeper, he said, "There's no need to be jumpy, Maggie. If anyone tries to come in, he'll have to go through me to get to you, and I'm not going to let that happen."

"I know," she said softly.

The response caught him by surprise, and it meant more to him than he could say.

She cast him a shamefaced look and lay the pillow aside. "Reflex reaction. I was dreaming, and the noise startled me."

Rafe could see by the taut set of her mouth that the dream still held her in its grip. Still crouched by the dresser drawer he had commandeered to serve as Jaimie's bed, he tossed a soiled wipe in the wastebasket, then rested his loosely crossed arms on an upraised knee. "A nightmare, I take it?"

She nodded.

"Care to talk about it?"

Her response to that was a negative shake of her head.

Seeing how upset she was, Rafe wished he could comfort her. But how? Even though she seemed to be starting to trust him a little, he'd still never met anyone who so stubbornly resisted accepting help. When left with no choice, she acquiesced, but he had a feeling she wouldn't, even then, if not for the sake of her baby.

"I have more than my fair share of bad dreams myself," he admitted, "so if you're feeling embarrassed about it, don't."

"You have bad dreams?" She fixed him with that lovely, brown-eyed gaze, her expression conveying relief that the conversation had shifted from her to him. "What do you dream about?"

Rafe's throat went tight. "My family, mostly."

She bent her head and tugged at the corner of the pillowcase. "The car wreck?"

He'd never talked with anyone about that night, but there was something about Maggie—an indefinable something—that made him consider doing so now. *Kindred souls.* On the surface, it might appear that her wounds were mostly physical, but one look into her beautiful eyes told him she'd been emotionally battered as well. Shadows lurked there. Dark, shifting shadows—and a wariness of him that tugged at his heart. It didn't take a mind reader to determine that she had suffered, in her own way, nearly as much as he had.

She needed a friend, perhaps desperately, and, he supposed, so did he. But before either of them could reach that point, they had to lower their guards. How could he expect her to trust him enough to reveal her secrets if he didn't have the guts to share some of his own?

"Yeah," he said, his voice reminding him of a whetstone rubbing over a knife blade. "I dream about the wreck. It was my fault, and ever since, I've had to live with that knowledge. During the day, I can hold the thoughts at bay, but when I'm sleeping, the memories haunt me."

In the amber glow of the bedside lamp, her eyes were luminous, and a golden nimbus shimmered around her tousled dark curls, making her look for all the world like an angel perched there. "Were you drinking when it happened?" she asked tremulously.

Rafe gave a humorless huff of laughter. He could see how she might think that. "I didn't start drinking a lot until after the accident. Booze, my panacea." He felt suddenly embarrassed and ran a hand over his face. "No, I wasn't drinking. I almost wish I had been. Then maybe I could live with the decisions I made that night." Blinking to bring the room back into focus, he said, "It happened the first part of October, just a little over two years ago."

She curled her legs beneath her, leaned more heavily against the headboard, and tugged the sheet higher. The droop of her thick eyelashes was a telltale sign of fatigue, yet he could still detect a certain tension in her posture that told him she wasn't ready to fall asleep just yet.

"Is that why you looked so sad last night when you realized it's almost Halloween?"

"Yeah," he said gruffly. "Right before he died, my little boy Keefer got his first pumpkin. Susan helped him carve it. This time of year—it's tough."

He batted at the open lid of the disposable diaper box that sat on the rug next to Jaimie's bed. When he realized what he was doing, he pressed the flaps closed.

"Were you the one driving?" she asked.

"No. God, how I wish I had been." He raked his hand over the nap of the rug, watching the limp tufts of yarn stand and then fall. "In my other life, I was a rancher in eastern Oregon." He forced a stiff smile. "Shaved and showered every day. Went to council meetings, five-star restaurants, and church on Sunday. Looking at me now, I guess it's probably hard for you to believe I was respectable once."

A ghost of a smile touched her mouth. As it faded, she rubbed her temple as if her head were aching. "Not all that hard. Was it a cattle ranch you owned?"

He nodded. "We raised and trained quarter horses on the side, but cattle were our main stock in trade. That fall, my brother and I had arranged to buy another stud and a brood mare, and we were scheduled to make a trip up north to pick them up. We'd been gone a lot that spring and summer, riding the rodeo circuit, and I hadn't been able to spend much time with Susan and the kids, so I decided to take them with us."

"Susan . . ." she echoed softly. "When you say her name—well, I can tell you really loved her a lot."

"She was an extraordinary person. Smart, witty, fun to be with, and so beautiful she took my breath away." Rafe shrugged. "I've never seen a better mother, and, oh, God, I loved it when she laughed. She was an incurable optimist, and she always put other people first. She understood me—sometimes better than I understood myself. When she died, I felt as if my heart had been cut out. We fell in love in high school. She was so much a part of me, I didn't know how to go on without her."

Rafe fell silent, letting his mind drift back to that fateful autumn night.

"We had a great time that weekend. Perfect weather, perfect everything. But as we headed home, we ran into a bad storm. Freezing rain that turned to hail the size of marbles."

"Eastern Oregon must be a bit like northern Idaho, unpredictable when it comes to the weather."

"You've got that right. We weren't expecting any hail, that's for sure, or we would have laid over until morning. I was in the station wagon with Susan and the kids. My brother and a hired hand were in the truck ahead of us, pulling the horse trailer. The sound of the hail hitting the roof of the trailer frightened the stallion, and I could see him rearing up. I was afraid he might bust a leg."

She shifted lower in the bed to rest her cheek on the double stack of pillows. Watching her, Rafe couldn't help but note her pallor.

"You're exhausted. I should let you go back to sleep."

"No, please. I want to hear this." She rubbed her eyes again. "I doubt I could go back to sleep right now, anyway. Listening to you talk is helping me to relax."

Rafe couldn't remember what he'd been about to say. "Where was I?"

"The stallion was rearing, and you were worried about it getting hurt. Was it a really expensive horse?"

"Yeah, but that wasn't my main concern. Plain and simple, I loved horses. They were a passion of mine back then, always had been. I couldn't bear the thought of the stallion breaking a leg and possibly having to be put down. So I got on the radio and suggested to my brother Ryan that we ride in the trailer to keep the animals calm. Susan was an excellent driver, and she'd been raised in eastern Oregon, so she was used to snow and ice. It never occurred to me that she—" He broke off and swallowed. "About two miles up the road, she lost control in a curve. The car plunged off a hundred-and-fifty-foot embankment. She and the kids were killed instantly." He had to force out the next words. "I placed more importance on the safety of a horse than I did my own family. I've had to live with that ever since."

"Oh, Mr. Kendrick, I'm so sorry."

Her voice rang with sincerity. That helped, somehow. For once, he didn't feel so horribly alone with the pain of remembering.

"Anyway, that's what I dream about," he said hollowly. "I saw it all happen from the back of the trailer. The car suddenly fishtailing, then skidding sideways on the ice. The way it hung there for a moment at the edge of the cliff before it went over." A burning sensation washed over his eyes. "I swear to God, to this day I think Susan turned to look at me. Just for a split second, you know? But in my nightmares, that split second lasts an eternity. All I can see is the terror on her face and that pleading look in her eyes. And in every dream, I try to reach them, only I feel as if I'm running through hip-deep molasses, and I never get there in time."

"How awful for you. And then to relive it, over and over, in your dreams."

Rafe ran his fingertips along the edge of the drawer. When he touched the corner of a new receiving blanket poking up over the side, he fingered the downy softness and closed his eyes. "You know the worst part? Over the last few months, even in my dreams, it's gotten so I can no longer see her face clearly, or the kids' either. I try my best to remember how each of them looked, and I can't. My memories of them—they're all I have left—and now I'm even losing those."

"Has it occurred to you that maybe you're finally healing? I know you may not want to believe that. But grief does pass after a time, and we have to get on with the business of living. Once you do that, I think you'll be able to remember their faces again. Not in nightmares anymore. Your memories will be of all the wonderful times you had together."

Rafe recalled his recent dream about Susan. In some ways, that had been a good dream. Remembering the fun they'd had down by the lake. Believing, if only briefly, that he was actually back there with them.

"Deep down, do you still blame yourself as much as

you did right after the wreck?'' she asked.

He took a moment to consider the question. ''Truthfully? Sometimes traitorous thoughts creep in.'' Even to admit that made him feel guilty. ''I'm not even sure where they come from. I get to thinking how I never meant for it to happen. That I loved them more than life itself, and that it's stupid to go on blaming myself when I know damned well that Susan wouldn't want me to.''

''And thinking that way makes you feel terrible,'' she inserted.

He focused on her face. ''You sound as if you've been through this.''

She nodded. For a second, Rafe thought she meant to say nothing more, but then she gestured limply with her hand and said, ''My dad. He, um . . . he was killed in a logging accident.''

''And you blame yourself for that?''

''Not now, but I did for a long time. And when I finally started to turn loose of the guilt, I felt like a worm.''

The description caught him by surprise, and with a low laugh, he nodded. ''That describes it perfectly, a worm. Only I feel like a worm that's being fought over by two birds and torn apart.''

She nodded as well, indicating that she understood exactly what he meant. ''In time, the torn feeling goes away, and you just feel lower than low. And soon after, even that feeling passes. Losing a parent doesn't compare to what happened to you. I know that. But I think the stages of grief must be pretty much the same for everyone, regardless. It seems that way, anyhow.''

Watching the expressions that crossed her face, Rafe said, ''You loved your dad a lot. Didn't you?''

''We were especially close. I was devastated when he was killed, and in the ten years since, my life has never been the same. But nothing will bring him back.'' She regarded the ceiling for a moment. ''Now I think of all the good times we had, and I'm thankful to have so many wonderful memories.''

"How old were you when he died?''

"Fourteen.''

"So now you're, what, twenty-four?''

She shot him a startled look. He winked and smiled. "Gotcha. I'm relentless. I'll keep digging for information until my curiosity is satisfied.''

"Oh, well. It's not as if my age is critical information.''

Critical information? Just the fact that she'd used that term told Rafe he hadn't misread this situation. Given her determination to reveal so little about herself, he had to accept the fact that she might be evading the police.

Normally Rafe would have disassociated himself from anyone he believed was in trouble with the authorities, but gazing at Maggie's sweet countenance, he couldn't quite fathom her committing a crime. No, if she was in that kind of trouble, there had to be some kind of mistake or circumstances that had been beyond her control.

He fleetingly found himself wondering if she had accidentally killed the man who beat her up. He was tempted to ask. No court in the land would hold her accountable for it, if that were the case. Hell, given what the bastard had done to her, they'd probably let her off even if it had been premeditated murder.

Gently, he steered the conversation back to her by saying, "You say your dad died in a logging accident? It seems like a stretch for a young girl to blame herself for that.''

"Mmmm,'' she responded softly. "I suppose it does. But then, it seems like quite a stretch to me that you blame yourself for that car accident. We play nasty head games with ourselves when we're grieving.'' She passed a hand over her eyes, then let her arm settle limply on the pillow again. "There were extenuating circumstances. My mom had been really sick. Daddy was exhausted from all the extra workload at home, and he wasn't paying close enough attention in the woods. A log rolled and crushed him. I couldn't help but think that it might not have happened if I'd only done more of the chores to lighten his load.'' She stared off at nothing for a moment. When she looked back at him, her eyes gleamed with curiosity. ''So . . . that's the story of how you came to be bumming the rails?''

''Pretty much. After they died, I despised the ranch and everything it represented. One morning, when I couldn't bear being there with all the memories any longer, I left my brother a note on the kitchen table and just walked out.''

''And you never went back?''

''Nope. I've never even called home to tell my mom I'm okay. Bad of me, I know. I tried a few times, but I always hung up before anyone answered. I just couldn't face hearing her voice, or listening to her plead with me to come back. I severed all ties the morning I left. I suppose it makes me sound weak, admitting that I ran away and tried to drown my sorrow in a bottle, but that's what I did. I haven't been sober since.''

''You're sober now,'' she reminded him.

Rafe gazed down at the baby. After a long moment, he slipped a finger under the infant's loosely curled fingers, the pad of his thumb tracing the pointy little knuckles. ''Yeah, I'm sober now. Since meeting you and Jaimie, I've had a reason to be. You want to hear something strange? I never thought I could bring myself to touch another baby, let alone let myself care about one. But the instant I held him, I started to feel—I don't know—protective, I guess. He sure is a cute little tyke.''

He looked up and saw that her eyes were sparkling with unshed tears. The corners of her mouth quivered slightly as she said, ''Thank you for helping us, Mr. Kendrick. Until now, I didn't realize just how painful this must be for you.'' She hugged the sheet to her chest with one arm as she swiped at her cheeks. ''We'll be on our way in the morning. No more unpleasant reminders.''

''Unpleasant reminders?'' He smiled and shook his head. ''I've had a couple of rough moments. I admit that, but overall, tying up with the two of you has been a godsend.''

''A godsend?'' she echoed incredulously.

''Hell, yes.'' He stroked his clean-shaven jaw. ''For the first time in months, I'm not drunk on my ass. And you know why? Because I couldn't take care of Jaimie in that condition. Do you have any idea how long it's been since anyone needed me?'' He cupped a hand over the baby's dark head. ''If anyone should say thank you, honey, it's me. I just wish—''

He broke off and fell silent. Watching him, Maggie guessed what he'd left unsaid, that he wished this time with them didn't have to end. Her heart caught at the look of naked yearning on his face as he gazed down at her son. Even worse, she could understand it. He'd lost his own children, and there'd been a void in his life ever since. Now, in a twinkling, that void had been filled, and deep inside, where reason held no sway, he couldn't help but wish that Jaimie were his child. That he need never go back to his lonely existence of riding the rails, his life a one-way ticket to nowhere.

Oh, yes, she understood. But as sorry as she felt for him, it scared the sand out of her as well. The last thing she needed right now were complications with another man.

All the more reason for her to make fast tracks in the morning, she told herself. The quicker she and Jaimie got away from him, the better it would be for all concerned.

When morning came, Maggie wasn't much stronger, and Rafe's determination to leave was a whole lot weaker. She was such a curious blend of indomitable spirit and vulnerability that he found her almost irresistible.

Yawning awake, he twisted around in the puke-green vinyl chair where he'd spent the remainder of the night, trying to work the kinks out of his spine while he considered the sleeping cherub in the drawer next to his feet. The rumpled collar of his new shirt grazed his chin. It smelled faintly of baby burp. It was a leg up on soured whiskey, at any rate.

A man could bond pretty quickly with a baby when he cared for it all night. It was also difficult to keep his emotional distance from a young woman who loved her child so selflessly. Each time Rafe had taken Jaimie to Maggie during the night, she'd put him to her breast without complaint. Rafe knew that every tug of the baby's mouth had to hurt like the very devil. But she had endured the pain in stoic silence, the tears gliding down her cheeks the only indication she gave that she was hurting, and she'd done her best to hide those.

Watching the gentleness and love in her expression as she took Jaimie into her arms, he'd invariably felt a wave of fierce protectiveness, and crazy thoughts went spiraling through his mind. That maybe he should stay here and take care of her for a while.

She had dreamed again during the night, talking out in her sleep. Rafe had been able to make little sense of anything she said, but one thing had been absolutely clear. She was terrified of someone named Lonnie.

Was he the man who'd beaten her? If so, and the son of a bitch found her, she would need someone to defend her. He'd sure as hell get a nasty surprise if Rafe was still around. Any man who mistreated a woman like that deserved a good ass-kicking.

God, he was in over his head and sinking fast. These protective feelings he was developing for Maggie were crazy, just plain crazy. Only he couldn't seem to stop himself.

Where was his head, up his ass? As if he was in any position to take care of her. He'd vowed to love Susan until he no longer had breath left in his body, and he couldn't possibly make room in his heart for someone new. He wouldn't be able to live with himself if he did.

As he dialed the local restaurant to order takeout for breakfast, his hands shook so badly that he had trouble punching in the correct numbers. He needed a drink. His yearning from yesterday had become a burning, desperate need.

While walking to the restaurant to pick up the food he'd ordered, the winter morning sun, as sharp as a straight razor, lanced his eyes. Rafe tried deep breathing to relieve his need for alcohol. The bracing intakes of cold air only made his chest hurt. He nearly rectified the problem by stopping at the liquor shop. Only thoughts of Jaimie forestalled him. He couldn't care for an infant if he was drunk. Instead he went to the department store again, where he bought Maggie a new blouse and warm parka, and Jaimie some sleepers, a few undershirts, and a little snowsuit. It was the least he could do, he assured himself. When he left them, he'd know they would be warm, anyway.

When Rafe returned to the motel room, he found Maggie dressed and sitting on the bed, struggling to put on her sneakers. With one glimpse of her pale face, he felt his legs go watery. He quickly closed the door to keep cold air from rushing inside and then deposited all his purchases, including the food, on the small round table near the window.

"Maggie, honey, what are you doing?"

Why he asked, he hadn't a clue. She was obviously preparing to leave. It scared the ever-loving hell out of Rafe to realize there wasn't one damned thing he could do to stop her. In that moment, he wished he did have that authority—that he could tell her to get her little butt back in bed, pronto.

"I have to leave today," she told him in a thready voice. "I've got to get where I'm going, find a job, and send for Heidi."

Rafe had the feeling Maggie was talking more to herself than to him, as if by saying the words, she might force her body to obey the commands from her brain.

He couldn't bear to watch her struggle with her shoes. Even though letting her leave was the last thing he wanted, he found himself shedding his coat and hat, then hurrying over to help her. Her brown eyes shiny bright, she sighed and hugged her ribs, allowing him to work the sneaker onto her narrow foot and tie the laces.

"Thank you." She eyed the white bag that contained the coffee and breakfast. The warm scents were hard to ignore, but he knew she'd rather starve than ask him for some of the food.

"Maggie, if you can't even get your shoes on, how can you work?"

"I have to," she said simply. "Heidi's counting on me."

"Heidi? Your little sister?"

"Yes. She's staying with a friend until I can send for her. I can't leave her there for very long." She loosened one arm from around herself to brace a hand on the bed. "Do you know what time the trains come through here?"

She would get on another boxcar over his dead body. Rafe bent to put on her other shoe. As he tied the strings, he made a vain attempt to remember all the reasons he shouldn't become any more involved with this girl. But somehow, the vague image of Susan's face did little to set his feelings back on course. Susan no longer needed him. Maggie did.

"You know, I've been thinking." His voice sounded hoarse and thick even to him. He raised his gaze to meet hers. "What's to say that you and I can't stay together for a while?"

"What do you mean?"

That was a damned good question. What the hell was he thinking? "I don't mean—well, you know—that kind of together. Just as friends. Nothing permanent. For a while. Until you're stronger and can manage on your own. Remember, I told you I hocked a ring? I've got some of the money left. We can hang out here at the motel for a while, and I can take care of you and Jaimie for a week or so. Until you're well.''

Her eyes reflected her incredulity. ''Why? You've already helped us more than—'' She shook her head and pushed to her feet, putting him at an eye level with her hips. ''No. I don't think that'd be a good idea.''

She sounded almost frightened. He recalled the panic he'd heard in her voice when she learned he'd bought a hot plate. *Damn*. He didn't want to buy her. He just wanted to help her.

''Just look at yourself. How can you possibly work?'' He caught the hem of the T-shirt to prevent her from moving away. ''Hey, listen to me. We'll work out some kind of arrangement. How's that sound? Some way for you to pay me back—or work off the debt.''

She flashed him a scathing look.

''Nothing like *that!*'' he assured her.

''How then?'' She sighed and rolled her eyes. ''I'm fairly accomplished at only three things: bookkeeping, waiting tables, and cleaning house. As near as I can tell, you aren't exactly up to your eyebrows in daily receipts these days, you don't own a table, and if you did, you have no house to put it in.''

Rafe nearly set her straight on that, but he bit back the words. What he did or didn't own wasn't the point.

''I care about what happens to you and that baby. You need a friend, and I'm willing to be that for you.''

''No,'' she said softly. ''I appreciate the offer. Truly I do. But I already owe you too much.''

''Who's keeping a tally? I'm sure as hell not.''

She pulled from his grasp. Rafe couldn't be sure, but it looked to him as if she swayed slightly as she stepped away, and she seemed to be breathing a little rapidly. ''You say that now. Been there, done that.''

He stood up. ''What's that supposed to mean?''

''There aren't any free rides,'' she said as she bent

with painful slowness to collect her jacket and sweatshirt from the corner where he had tossed them. "What are you hoping to get out of it? A temporary ready-made family to replace the one you lost?"

That stung, possibly because it struck so close to the truth.

She sighed and passed a tremulous hand over her eyes. "I'm sorry. I didn't mean that. It's just that I'm already in so deep I'll never be able to repay you. By your own admission, you're growing attached to Jaimie. The longer you're around him, the more wrenching it will be for you when we leave."

Rafe couldn't argue the point. He felt a little frantic when he thought of them going their separate ways. He'd head straight for the liquor store, and within an hour, he'd be drunk.

"Nobody helps someone, expecting nothing," she said. "Everyone eventually wants a payback of some kind. I learned that the hard way."

Judging by her expression, she obviously had learned a bitter lesson from someone. "Are we talking about people in general, or men, more specifically?" He knew the answer to that question. It was written all over her face.

"I've worked in a truck stop for ten years. Need I say more?"

She laid out the sweatshirt and jacket on the bed, preparing to wrap Jaimie in them before she left. Now probably wasn't the best time to tell her that the makeshift blanket was no longer necessary, but he couldn't see a way around it.

"You can use the blankets in the drawer, and I bought him a snowsuit." He stepped over to open a sack. "I picked up a parka for you as well. I need my coat, and you can't be running around out there in nothing but a T-shirt."

She fixed wide, staring eyes on the winter outerwear.

The panic in that look was impossible to miss. "You shouldn't have. We're not your worry."

Rafe knew he shouldn't get angry. It was just so frustrating. "Maybe I'm making you my worry."

"Look, it was very thoughtful to buy us warm things. Truly, and I appreciate the gesture. But I wish you hadn't, and I'd like you to return them."

Gazing at her, Rafe thought of his home, a place he hadn't been in quite some time, and all the advantages he could provide for her there. In that moment, he knew he couldn't let her walk out. If he did, he'd spend the rest of his life regretting it and wondering what had happened to her. It was as simple and as complicated as that.

It's time, Susan had told him in his dream. He didn't know if she'd actually come to him. Rationally, he knew it was far more likely that the dream had been a product of wishful thinking. But what did it really matter? What did was that he'd actually had a similar conversation with Susan shortly before she died, and she'd extracted a promise from him that he wouldn't spend the rest of his life alone if anything ever happened to her. Bless her heart, she'd done everything in her power that night to set him free—to let him know she wanted him to be happy.

Looking back on that night, Rafe had reason to wonder now if Susan had had some kind of premonition. *Promise me, Rafe. I want your word that you'll find someone else to love.* At the time, he'd thought she was being silly. They'd both been young and in excellent health. He had laughed and tousled her hair, pointing out the possibility that he might marry unwisely on the rebound. Susan had given him a scolding look. *You made a good choice the first time around*, she'd reminded him. *You will again. When you meet the right person, Rafe, you'll know. You'll look into her eyes, something magical will happen, and you'll just know it's right.*

From the first moment he'd clapped eyes on Maggie, something had stirred back to life within him, and his feelings had been in a hopeless tangle ever since. Was he going to ignore that and keep walking?

A man found magic so rarely. When it came along, you either had the courage to throw caution to the wind and grab hold of it—or you forever lost the chance.

So what if his feelings for Maggie and Jaimie made no sense and didn't conform to a timetable? For the first time in a very long while, he had a *reason*. She and the baby gave him something to care about, something to fight for, something to grab hold of that was solid. He couldn't just turn loose of that now and say, *Nice knowing you.*

God help him, he needed her every bit as much as she needed him.

Maggie had worked as a waitress too many years not to recognize possessiveness in a man's eyes, and she saw it in Rafe's. She took a wobbly step in retreat and held up a shaky hand.

"I—I really have to go."

"Name me one reason why." He moved toward her, his long legs taking unhurried strides that seemed to eat up the distance at an alarmingly fast pace. "I haven't always bummed the rails. Like I told you last night, I used to be a rancher. If we run out of money, I can call my brother and have him wire me some more. When I walked out, Maggie, it wasn't just the ranch I left behind. I had a substantial amount of money in the bank as well. It's just sitting there now, being put to no good use."

Her heart caught, just at the suggestion. "You haven't called home in two years. Now, suddenly, you're ready to pick up the phone? No. Do it for yourself if you're going to, but not for Jaimie and me. That's a decision of the heart, one you need to make because it feels right."

"Maybe I've just been waiting for a reason. Now I have one."

"No," she insisted. "I won't have you doing that, not for us."

"It's a moot point. I've still got some cash. If we watch the expenditures, we won't need more money. The rate on this room isn't that steep. I can cover the expenses while you recuperate." He drew to a halt in front of her, his smoky gaze holding hers relentlessly. "After that, we'll just play it by ear, see what happens."

Maggie backed away another step and shook her aching head. She had only just escaped the autocratic rule of one man; she had no intention of indenturing herself to another. Rafe had been kindness itself so far, and she was grateful. But she wasn't dumb enough to believe the situation would remain status quo if she stayed with him. Sooner or later, he'd begin to feel his helping her gave him certain rights, and in all fairness, she couldn't argue the point. If she accepted what he was offering, she would owe him, and with each passing day, the size of the debt would increase until there would be no way out.

"I can't."

He rubbed a hand over his face and blinked, his expression conveying that he found her refusal to accept his offer not only irrational but unacceptable. "Is it your sister? I'll send her the money for a bus ticket right now." He shrugged his shoulders, which were looking broader with every passing second. "I like kids. I've proven that with Jaimie. How old did you say she is?"

"I didn't." Shivering with a sudden chill, Maggie realized she felt light-headed and wished for something, anything to lean against.

He studied her for a moment. "Is that your answer? For God's sake, surely your sister's age isn't a state secret. Why is it so imperative that you send for her, anyway? You said your dad's dead, and you mentioned your mom, so I know the kid has someone to take care of her. Is there a mean stepfather lurking in the background or something?'' He narrowed an eye. ''Who is Lonnie?''

Maggie's heart skipped a beat. She stared up at him, wondering how on earth he'd learned her stepfather's first name.

''You cried out in your sleep. You said the name several times.'' He held her gaze, making her feel he was reading answers in her eyes that she didn't dare reveal. ''You're afraid of him, aren't you? He's the one who beat you up, the one you're afraid may come after you.''

That he had so easily guessed the truth made Maggie feel frantic. She no longer thought Rafe might turn her in for a reward. He'd been too kind and caring for her to believe that. But experience had taught her to trust no man completely. Rafe wanted her and Jaimie to stay with him. What if he learned too much and decided to use it as leverage against her? She instantly felt a stab of guilt for entertaining such thoughts about him. He'd been so good to them.

''Honey, please,'' he whispered. ''Take a chance on me. Trust me. Let me take care of you for a while.''

Oh, how she wished she *could*. There was nothing she wanted more than to go back to bed, have a sip of coffee, and then sleep. It would be so wonderful to know that Rafe would take care of her and Jaimie for a while, that he would be there if she needed him and would send for Heidi.

Maggie aborted the fantasy. Taking the easy way out wasn't always best. She'd pay for it, perhaps dearly, and even worse, she'd end up hurting this man in the process. Better to sever the ties right now than to risk breaking his heart. He had suffered enough grief already.

Her dizziness increasing, she groped behind her for the wall. It wasn't there. The only solid thing within reach was Rafe. She longed to step close and prop herself against his strong body as she had yesterday. The very fact that she wanted that so badly prodded her to move farther away.

"I have to use the bathroom," she told him.

It wasn't a lie. As she flipped on the light switch and locked the door, the small enclosure went even darker, casting everything in gray black. *Too weird.* Even the faint light coming through the tiny window grew dimmer. Maggie blinked and tried to hit the wall switch again, thinking she'd flipped it down instead of up. But her arm suddenly felt as if it weighed a couple hundred pounds, and she couldn't raise her hand.

She staggered and tried to grab the vanity. The next instant she hit the floor. She lay there, feeling like a tiny, translucent flake in a swirling, gray-black kaleidoscope. From a long way off, she heard Rafe calling her. She couldn't make out the words. Then more loudly, he said her name. *Maggie! Maggie, answer me!* She blinked, trying to see through the dizzying rush of shadows.

Then—blackness.

Rafe tried the doorknob, knowing before he touched it that Maggie had turned the lock. The loud thud he'd heard echoed in his mind. Oh, God. She'd fainted. He imagined her lying on the other side of the door with her head split open. If she didn't answer him in a second, he'd have to kick down the door.

"Maggie? Maggie, answer me, damn it!"

No response.

Rafe saw no way around it. He had to reach her. Not allowing himself to consider the possible consequences, he reared back and planted his boot just below the doorknob. Wood splintered, but the lock didn't give. *Son of a bitch.* Grabbing the knob, Rafe put his shoulder into it, hitting the door with all his weight. Once. Twice. The framing broke, and the door crashed open.

Maggie lay on the worn linoleum. In the harsh light, her face was so pale she looked dead. His pulse stuttered as he dropped to one knee beside her.

"Maggie?"

He cupped her face between his hands. The second

he touched her, he realized she was burning up with fever. He lightly tapped her cheeks but got no response. He gathered her into his arms. Her slight body was completely limp. Over the crook of his arm, her head lolled like a rag doll's.

"Maggie, talk to me." He strode into the other room and laid her gently on the bed. She reacted to his voice by moaning, but that was as close as she came to regaining consciousness. Rafe grabbed her wrist to check her pulse, then swore and dropped her arm. Like he knew what he was doing? Without a watch, he couldn't even check the beats per minute. Launching himself across her inert form, he grabbed the phone, jabbed out 911, and felt as if he would explode with pent-up fear while he waited for someone to answer.

"I need an ambulance!" he barked when a female dispatcher answered.

"May I have your name, sir?"

His name? "Lady, I've got an emergency here. I need an ambulance!"

"I understand that, sir, but you need to remain calm. Can you tell me the nature of the emergency? Has there been an accident?"

Bracing his elbows on the mattress to keep his weight off Maggie, Rafe stared down at her lifeless face. "No, not an accident. I've got a very sick young woman here. She just collapsed. High fever. I need an ambulance, damn it!"

"Where are you, sir?"

Rafe couldn't remember the name of the motel. He vaulted off the bed to peer out the window. Forgetting he held the phone receiver, he jerked the base off the nightstand. The resultant crash and ringing sound were deafening. "The Traveler's Rest." The sickening smell of bacon and eggs wafted to his nose from the sacks on the table. "Over by the train tracks. I don't know the address."

Seconds of silence ticked by. "May I have your name now, sir?"

Rafe exploded. "Rafe Kendrick's my name, and you'll wish you'd never heard it if you don't get a damned ambulance over here, lady! Stop asking stupid questions and do your job!"

"I just dispatched the ambulance, Mr. Kendrick. It will be en route momentarily. Please, calm down. It's my job to keep you on the phone and assist you until help arrives."

Rafe struggled to stifle what could only be an hysterical urge to laugh. All his life, he'd been levelheaded and calm in emergencies. The only other time he'd ever lost his cool like this had been the night his family was killed. "I'm sorry. For yelling, I mean." He threw a frightened glance at Maggie. "What should I do? I don't know what to do. She's unconscious, and she's burning up with fever. Really sick. She's really sick."

"Just stay calm. That's why I'm here, Mr. Kendrick, to help you and tell you what to do. First of all, is the woman in the motel room?"

"Yes, I laid her on the bed."

"Can you reach her and still remain on the phone with me?"

"Yes." He moved back to Maggie. "I'm with her now."

The dispatcher asked Rafe questions about Maggie's condition, but he listened with only one ear. With the other he listened for a siren. This was like revisiting a nightmare. Pictures flashed in his head. Susan and his children, the icy hail lashing him as he frantically tried to help them, knowing even as he did that they were beyond help. *Oh, please, God, not again.*

"The ambulance will be there in just a minute," the dispatcher promised.

Rafe cocked an ear. "I can hear the sirens now, I think," he said, thankfulness ringing in his voice.

"They're coming. Damn. What'd they do, give the rig a lube job before they took off?"

She laughed softly. "Trust me, it seems to take a lot longer than it actually does. It's been only four minutes since you called."

"It's been the *longest* four minutes in history."

"Yes, I know. Is your baby all right, Mr. Kendrick? I can hear it crying."

Rafe glanced toward the drawer where Jaimie lay snuggly enfolded in receiving blankets. "He's fine. Just hungry, probably."

"Good strong lungs. What's his name?"

Rafe was about to reply when he remembered how secretive Maggie had been. So much for her attempt to stay away from people. This had blown that plan all to hell. "He definitely has a good set of lungs," he agreed, ignoring the question. The sirens came closer. "I think the ambulance is pulling in here."

"I'll stay on the phone. You go flag them down. All right? If they should miss seeing you, simply come back and tell me so I can pinpoint your location for them. Will you do that, please?"

"Of course."

"And then you'd better take care of your baby. In all the confusion, don't forget you've got him."

Forget? In the last two days, Rafe had come to feel as if he and Jaimie were connected by an umbilical cord.

The ER waiting room at Squire Community General looked pretty much like every other ER waiting room Rafe had ever seen. Blue vinyl chairs and sofas lined the off-white walls. The beige floor tiles had the usual smatterings of color, variegated swirls of white and pastels. It made Rafe wonder if there was a worldwide order of interior decorators who specialized in medical facilities.

The only notable difference Rafe could see between this waiting room and others was that he was the only person there. Strike that. Jaimie counted as one more head.

Settling back on the sofa next to his coat, he gazed down at the baby's face resting on the bend of his arm. He'd already removed the snowsuit. Now he peeled away one of the blankets, afraid the child might be too warm. Since racing here in the taxi, they'd been waiting for over an hour, and typical of a hospital, the heat was kept at one temperature—stuffy. But then, maybe it only seemed that way to him because he was so tense.

How long did it take to examine someone and decide what the hell was wrong, anyway? Had they forgotten he was out here? Hell, she had a baby out here, too. Or had they simply written her off as unimportant?

Given Maggie's unconsciousness, it had been left to Rafe to answer the admitting receptionist's questions. He'd been able to provide no last name, and when he'd been asked Maggie's address, he'd answered, ''Homeless.'' He suspected Maggie was from Prior, but recalling her secretiveness, he'd hesitated to reveal even that much information. As briefly as possible, he'd explained how he'd met Maggie and taken her to a motel when it became apparent she was ill.

A few minutes later, he'd overheard the women at the front desk discussing Maggie, and one of them had said, ''Some guy brought her in. I seriously doubt she has insurance. Collections will be so thrilled.''

As if it mattered if she could pay? One human being was no less important than another. What did one's financial situation have to do with it?

He got up and began pacing again. Maggie lay just beyond those double doors. A suffocating sensation squeezed his chest when he remembered how white her face had been. If only he'd insisted she see a doctor.

He wasn't even certain there was a qualified doctor on duty in this place. This hospital was a small-town, rinky-dink facility. Had anyone examined Maggie yet? She'd better be receiving first-rate care, or heads were going to roll. He'd have their asses in court so fast they wouldn't know what hit them.

The thought made Rafe break stride. What did he plan to use for money to hire a lawyer? His irresistible charm? He wasn't back home in Oregon where his last name meant something. This was Podunk, Idaho, and the people here had never even heard of the Kendrick family. He could threaten them all he liked, but he doubted he'd get any results. They'd figure he was just a vagrant with an attitude. Or a mental condition.

Well, that could be rectified, he promised himself. And damned quick. It might be true that he hadn't contacted his parents or brother in two years. But they would rally around him if he suddenly decided to call. Rafe could almost see his father bursting into this small hospital, voice booming and blue eyes flashing. Those holier-than-thou secretaries would quake on their caster chairs.

"Mr. Kendrick?"

Rafe whirled to see a slender redhead in a white lab coat walking toward him. The stethoscope in her pocket flashed in the fluorescent light. When she drew up, she tucked a clipboard under her arm, her kindly green eyes settling on his face as she extended her hand. "I'm Dr. Hammish. I understand you're the gentleman who called the ambulance for our Maggie Doe?"

Rafe shifted Jaimie to free his right arm. As he shook hands with the doctor, he took quick stock of her and liked what he saw, especially the worried frown that pleated her forehead. Seeing that, he felt a little better and a whole lot sheepish for imagining that Maggie might not be getting good care.

"How is she? Is she going to be all right?"

The doctor gestured for him to take a seat on the sofa and then followed suit, setting aside the clipboard and then turning so she could search his gaze. Rafe realized she was looking him over as carefully as he had her. "Our Maggie Doe has had a rough time of it," she said softly. "She's been badly beaten. I assume you're aware of that?"

"Yes." Judging by the doctor's expression, Rafe guessed he ranked high on her list of suspects. "I've been taking care of her for two days. Bruises like that are pretty hard to overlook." He met her gaze. "I didn't do it, if that's what you're thinking. I met her two nights ago, and she was already in that condition."

The doctor inclined her head, the gesture indicating that she found his explanation credible, but that she still wasn't totally convinced he was innocent of any wrongdoing. She smiled slightly. "How did the two of you meet?"

Rafe bit down hard on his back teeth in an effort to control his temper. After taking three deep breaths, he said, "Doctor, do you mind? I'm very worried about her, and you still haven't told me how she is."

The physician gave a soft, humorless laugh. "I'm sorry. I'm rather one-track–minded when it comes to an abused woman." She folded her hands on her lap. "Maggie has regained consciousness, and I'm hopeful she'll recover nicely."

"Thank God."

"Nevertheless, she's very ill. She's postnatal, which can cause a host of problems if a woman receives no medical care, and I'd venture a guess she hasn't seen a physician since she gave birth. She has a kidney infection that has gone untreated. I believe she has a condition called septicemia. I can't be positive until I get the lab reports, of course, but that's my preliminary diagnosis."

"Septicemia? That's really dangerous, isn't it?"

"It's serious, yes. Bacteria escape from the focal point of the infection into the bloodstream, multiply rapidly, and spread throughout the body. If left untreated, it can cause septic shock and be life-threatening."

Rafe realized he was shaking and cuddled Jaimie closer.

"I've got her on an intravenous infusion of heavy-hitting antibiotic and a saline solution. We'll continue that treatment and keep a close eye on her for at least three days. After that, I believe she will do well enough on oral medications to be released—if she has anywhere suitable to go and I can be assured she'll get follow-up exams and complete bed rest for another seven to ten days. If not, despite her apparent concerns about the cost, I'll have no alternative but to keep her in the hospital."

Rafe closed his eyes for a moment, so relieved he felt almost boneless. "But she'll be all right?"

The doctor sighed. "I can't give you an absolute guarantee. Whether or not she'll be all right will depend entirely upon how she responds to treatment. However, I can say that I see no reason at this point to anticipate problems." She studied her folded hands for a moment. When she glanced back up, her gaze was direct and searching. "Maggie has been severely beaten, Mr. Kendrick. I believe the blows to her kidneys worsened her condition immeasurably, bruising the already inflamed organs and the surrounding tissue. To be quite honest, I'm not as concerned about her responding to the antibiotics as I am about what may happen to her when she leaves here. In my estimation, she's very fortunate her spleen wasn't ruptured and she sustained no other internal injuries."

"She won't be beaten again." Rafe nearly snarled the promise. "If the bastard comes anywhere near her, I'll—" He broke off and swallowed. "He won't lay a hand on her, guaranteed."

The doctor searched Rafe's gaze, and then she nodded. "I don't generally make snap judgments. But I tend to believe you. You truly aren't the man who did it, are you?"

"I'd like to beat the son of bitch to within an inch of his life. I've never seen bruises like that on anyone, including myself, and I've gotten pretty busted up a few times in rodeo competition.'' He thrust a hand through his hair. "I can't believe a man deserving of the name would do that to any woman, let alone a slip of a girl who just had a baby."

The doctor sighed again, obviously in complete agreement. Then, leaning toward him, she whispered, "If you get a chance to beat the hell out of him, don't hog all the fun. If you'll hold him, I'd dearly love to let him have it at least once myself."

Of all the things Rafe had expected her to say, that was the last. He gave a startled laugh. "Dr. Hammish, you've got yourself a deal."

She chuckled. "I'll hold you to it." She craned her neck to peek at the baby. "This must be the little fellow I've been hearing about—the most wonderful, perfect, precious, and handsome baby in the whole world. Jaimie, if I remember right?"

"She told you his name?" Rafe raised an eyebrow. "What did you do, twist her arm? It took some doing for me to worm that out of her."

"I cited doctor-patient confidentiality. And then I swore on threat of death not to repeat anything she told me. At that, it was slim pickings as far as information went. She's quite sick, of course, and doesn't feel like talking, which may account for some of her reticence. But it's still a bit odd that she refused to give us her last name or say where she's from."

"I think she's running," Rafe told her.

The doctor nodded. "And judging by those bruises, who can blame her? You never said how the two of you met."

"What's the scoop on that doctor-patient confidentiality?" he asked.

"I won't break Maggie's confidence, or yours," she assured him. "My first responsibility is to my patient."

Rafe told her the story of how he met Maggie. "I tried to get her to see a doctor, but she refused. To be honest—" He searched the physician's gaze again. "I want your word you won't repeat any of this, Doc.''

She nodded. ''You have my word. I believe that young woman needs protection, and I won't jeopardize her safety.''

Rafe wasn't certain why, but he believed her. He just hoped he wasn't making a mistake. ''I think maybe Maggie's afraid the cops are looking for her.''

The doctor lifted an eyebrow. ''The cops? Why, I wonder?''

''Your guess is as good as mine. She doesn't strike me as the criminal type.''

''No,'' the doctor agreed thoughtfully. ''Do you think she may be fleeing from an abusive husband?'' She glanced pointedly at Jaimie. ''Perhaps she's embroiled in a nasty divorce and child custody suit, and she's made off with the baby.''

''I don't think so. She wears no ring, and there's no sign she did recently. Not every woman wears a ring these days, of course. But she said other things that lead me to believe she's unmarried.'' He quickly recounted Maggie's insistence that Jaimie had no father. ''That doesn't sound like something a married or recently divorced woman might say.''

''No, it doesn't.'' The doctor sighed and settled her gaze on Jaimie again. ''It would seem that you've bitten off a large chunk of responsibility, Mr. Kendrick. I imagine you'll be relieved to get that little fellow off your hands.''

Rafe's heart caught. ''Off my hands?''

''Well, yes,'' she said, smiling kindly. ''Maggie and her baby aren't your responsibility, after all. Until she can care for him herself again, Jaimie should be placed with the county. The temporary care is quite good, I assure you.''

''No.'' The refusal was out of Rafe's mouth before he could even contemplate his reasons. He couldn't hand Jaimie over to strangers.

"As I already pointed out, Maggie and her baby aren't your responsibility."

"Responsibility can be assumed."

"Well, yes, I suppose it can."

"Well, then? I'm assuming it."

The doctor tapped her chin, regarding Rafe with concern. "I know you mean well, Mr. Kendrick. And please, don't be offended. But are you certain you're in a position to assume that responsibility? It isn't only Jaimie you must consider, but Maggie. She'll need care when she leaves here, and I'm not—"

"I'll see that they're both taken care of."

"How? When Maggie is released, she'll be unable to look after the baby. She'll need constant care herself for at least seven days, and she can't receive the quality care she needs in an econo-rate motel room. How can you care for her if you have to get a job to foot the bills, which may be substantial? She's going to need one or two rounds of very expensive medication, for starters. And nourishing, well-balanced meals, not fast food or the greasy fare available in our local restaurants." She shook her head. "By your own admission, you're presently unemployed, low on funds, and have no home where you might take her." She held out her arms. "Jaimie will be better off in temporary foster care. Please, let me—"

Rafe cut her short by pushing to his feet. A feeling of impending doom filled him as he gazed down at the infant in his arms and thought about handing him over. He met the doctor's worried gaze.

"Looks can be deceiving, Doc," he informed her gruffly. "I own a home where I can take Maggie to convalesce. The place is damned near as big as this backwoods hospital, and there's a full-time housekeeper to do the cooking. As for money, I guarantee I have a hell of a lot more in the bank than you do."

The doctor's expression conveyed more clearly than

words that she sympathized with his feelings, but that she didn't believe a word he had said.

Rafe glanced up the hall at a bank of pay phones. "By the time Maggie is released, I'll have the Kendrick family Cessna flown in from Oregon and waiting here to pick her up." He returned his gaze to hers. "Assuming, of course, that this one-horse Idaho town even has an airport where it can land."

Her expression reflecting startled amazement, she nodded. "Yes, we have a small municipal airport here." She raked him with an incredulous look. "If you're about to tell me you're an eccentric millionaire, I'm not inclined to believe you without some kind of proof, and I won't allow you to remove Maggie from this hospital until I get it."

"Multi, and I'm not eccentric. As for proof, what do you have in mind? Will verification from my bank convince you?"

"I, um . . . well, yes, I suppose that would suffice."

He plucked her clipboard from the sofa and jotted the name and branch of his bank in the upper right-hand corner of Maggie's chart. Below it, he underlined his Social Security number. "Go ahead and call. I can't remember the account number, but they'll know the name. Tell them I'm about to write you a check for whatever amount you like and that you want to verify funds before you accept it. They won't tell you my exact balance, but they will tell you if I can cover the draft."

He handed her the clipboard. Then he headed for the pay phones, never looking back to see the stunned expression that crossed her face.

 Chapter Six

Rafe stood in the hospital hall and stared at the phone for several long seconds before he lifted the receiver. Tucking it under his chin to use his free hand, he dialed the operator and placed a collect call to Oregon. While the phone rang, he fixed his gaze on Jaimie's small face. Finally he heard his brother Ryan's voice.

In a voice gone stony and suspicious, he said, "Yeah, sure, I'll accept the charges."

"Go ahead, sir," the operator told Rafe.

"Rye?" Rafe heard the quaver in his voice. He closed his eyes and swallowed, scarcely able to believe he was doing this. "It's me, Rafe."

"My God, it really *is* you. I figured it was another crank call."

"Crank call?"

"Long story. Rafe, where the hell are you? Are you all right?" His voice sounded the same but a little older, a little rough-edged.

"I'm fine." As Rafe said the words, he knew they were true. Since meeting up with Maggie, he actually was all right again. "I, um . . . don't know exactly what to say. Hello, I guess."

"Hello?" Ryan swore, and the line crackled. "You rotten son of a bitch, we thought you were dead! Where the hell have you been?"

Rafe was about to answer when he heard his brother

sob—one of those dry, straight-from-the-gut sobs that come only from strong men who never break down. "Rye? Hey, bro. Don't."

"Don't? How could you do this? You've got a family who loves you, damn it. Have you any idea the heartache you've caused our mother?"

Rafe leaned a shoulder against the metal phone partition. When he spoke, his voice grated. "I'm sorry, Ryan. I just—couldn't call. I tried several times. I'm—sorry."

"You're sorry? She couldn't eat, couldn't sleep! She lost over thirty pounds, for God's sake. Where are you? When I get there, the first thing I'm going to do is hug you. Then I'm going to stomp the holy hell out of you."

Rafe smiled slightly, his eyes blurry with tears. "Right now you could probably do it with one hand tied behind your back."

"Oh, Christ! Are you sick?"

Rafe made a fist around the metal-sheathed phone cord. "I'm okay now. It's, um, sort of a long story."

"Like I can't afford the phone bill?"

Rafe chuckled, if a little wetly. "Damn, it's so good to hear your voice. I've missed you, Ryan." Slowly he filled his brother in on what he'd been doing since that fateful morning when he'd left a note on the kitchen table and walked out.

"I can't believe I'm hearing this. You've been bumming the rails?"

"Yes."

"I haven't heard of anyone doing that in years."

Rafe smiled slightly. "We have more homeless people in this country now than ever before. Do you think they all live in large cities?"

"Of course not. I just—" Ryan made an exasperated sound. "My brother, a tramp? What do you mean, you have a drinking problem?"

"Just that I do. I sobered up two days ago. I didn't

have much choice. I tied up with a lady who needed my help more than I needed another bottle.''

''A *lady?* Where the hell does a bum meet a lady? In a boxcar?''

''Yeah, as a matter of fact, it was in a boxcar.''

''I don't want to hear this. A boxcar? I've heard of men picking up women in bars. I thought that was bad. But a boxcar? Have you lost your mind?''

''She's beautiful, Rye. I know it sounds nuts, especially in just two days, but I think I'm falling in love with her. She's one of those people you just can't help but care about. You know?''

''Oh, shit.'' Long silence. ''Rafe, where are you?''

''At a hospital in Podunk, Idaho.''

''You said you weren't sick.''

''I'm not sick. It's Maggie. I know it's a lot to ask, but can you fly over and pick us up, Rye? I need you to be here in three days. What is today, anyway?''

''It's Thursday, the twenty-eighth. And what do you mean, pick 'us' up? You're bringing her home with you? Rafe, are you even thinking straight?''

''Straight as an arrow,'' Rafe assured him. ''Meeting her saved my life, Ryan. I promise you'll love her. And hey, just wait until you see Jaimie.''

''Jaimie?''

''Her baby boy. He's cute as a speckled pup.''

''She has a *baby?* Rafe, where exactly are you?''

''Squire, just across the Idaho border.''

''I've never heard of it.''

''Well, it's not exactly a metropolis. It's up north. Colder than a well digger's ass up here, too. Your lungs damn near freeze when you breathe.''

''I'll be there tomorrow morning,'' Ryan promised. ''I'd be there tonight, but it's been a while since I've taken the Cessna up. It'll need a preflight, and I've got to map a flight plan. Rafe? Don't do anything dumb before I get there.''

''Like what?''

"Like—well, hell, I don't know. Marry her or something stupid like that, I guess. Let's you and me have a long talk first. All right, brother?"

"Actually I hadn't thought far enough ahead yet to consider marriage. Not a bad idea, though. If ever a woman needed a husband, it's Maggie."

"You're kidding, right?"

Rafe was, and yet he wasn't. "We'll have to see what happens, I guess. She's a little skittish about tying up with me."

"Well, at least one of you is thinking straight. I may be able to get there sometime late tonight. Sounds to me like you need a caretaker."

Rafe threw back his head and barked with laughter. The rumble wakened Jaimie, and he let out a thin cry.

"Damn, there really is a baby."

"Yeah," Rafe said, jiggling the infant to lull him back to sleep. "And there's no need to break a leg getting here, Rye. There's nothing you can say or do to change this. I already swallowed the hook."

Ryan sighed. "You're a grown man. I guess you know what you're doing. All I care about is that you come home to do it."

Home. The word moved softly through Rafe's mind, rekindling memories that he had been trying to escape. Now he no longer felt the need. He was going back, and unless Maggie came up with a damned good argument against it, he was taking her with him. There was a great college there and plenty of employment opportunities. It'd be the perfect place for her to start over, with the added benefit that he'd be nearby to look after her.

Fleetingly, Rafe thought of Susan. One corner of his heart would always belong to her and his children. But he was finished with punishing himself for something he'd never meant to happen and couldn't change.

"Will you call Mom and Dad for me?" Rafe asked gruffly. "I don't want it to be a shock when they see me."

"They're in Florida. But I'll call them. They'll want to fly back to see you. Dad's been having chest pains, though. I think he has an appointment scheduled with a heart specialist, so it may be a few weeks. Mom probably won't let him fly until the doc says it's all right. That'll give them both some time to talk to you on the phone and absorb the news before they actually see you."

Rafe pictured his tall, robust father. "A heart doctor? Is he all right?"

"Nothing out of the ordinary for a man who's sixty. Frequent angina attacks, Mom says. You know how that goes, though. The RN in her can't resist diagnosing stuff, and a fourth of the time, she's wrong."

Rafe frowned. "It seems odd that he'd get heart trouble all of a sudden."

"I think it's the food," Ryan said. "They've been into Creole lately. And you know how he is about grease. Put the two together, and you've got chronic indigestion. He's still sneaking smokes behind her back, too. Ornery old cuss."

The thought of losing his dad before he had a chance to see him again made Rafe's blood run cold. "I'm glad Mom's on top of it. He'd say, 'Screw the chest pain' and climb on a plane."

Ryan chuckled. "Damn, it's good talking to you again."

"It's good talking to you, too." It felt so good Rafe wondered why he'd waited so long.

"We're getting Christmas early this year. We've combed the whole country, looking for you. Offered rewards. We'd damned near given you up for dead."

"So had I," Rafe admitted softly. "For a long time, I wanted to die and spent a lot of time wishing I would." He took a cleansing breath and smiled. "Sounds pretty stupid, saying it aloud. But I was pretty messed up, Rye."

"You had a right." Another silence came over the

line. "I wish you had stayed here and gotten counseling like I suggested. They have all kinds of help for people to get through the grieving process."

The grieving process. Rafe could remember Ryan's using that phrase before and how it had infuriated him. Now he knew that there was a grieving process. It was called hell, only you didn't have to die to go there.

"I found my own cure."

"Do you know how lucky you are to still be alive, you blockhead?"

Rafe chuckled. "Damned lucky," he said, and sincerely meant it.

"How are you fixed for money?"

"I have some business to settle up here in town that'll set me back a little over seven hundred, so I'll need some cash. Bring me a little extra, hey, bro? Speaking of which, is my checking account still active? I have a woman calling the bank to verify funds."

"Of course it's still active." Long silence. "I, um . . . couldn't quite bring myself to close it out. It felt so final. Rationally, I figured there wasn't much hope that you'd ever come back, but a part of me just couldn't—" Ryan cursed under his breath. "Yeah, it's still active." He sighed. "What makes you think I haven't managed to go bust, trying to run this place by myself?"

Rafe laughed. "Because you're a Kendrick. You teethed on saddle leather and cowhide. I'm probably worth more now than I was when I left."

"Yes, and you owe me a two-year vacation."

"Give me a month to get buffed out, and it's yours to take, if you want to. Now that I've made the decision, I'm anxious to smell cow manure again."

"That's good. I may rub your nose in it."

Rafe was still chuckling when he hung up the phone. The smile was short-lived. As he turned toward the waiting area, he saw Dr. Hammish walking down the hall, and her expression conveyed that something was wrong.

Rafe's heart bounced in his chest like a tennis ball, and he picked up his pace to reach her. "Is Maggie all right?"

She nodded, but her pallor told him otherwise. "We have a wrinkle." She lifted her hands, flashing him a stricken look. "One of our aides found Maggie's driver's license in the pocket of her jeans. Because she'd been brought in unconscious, he took the license to the admittance desk. Technically, he was following procedure. He had no idea Maggie didn't want her family contacted."

"Oh, damn."

The doctor gave him a commiserating look. "I never meant for this to happen, but one of the receptionists called the police, and they contacted her family. The officer spoke with her stepfather, a man named Lonnie Boyle."

Rafe groaned and passed a hand over his eyes. "Fantastic."

"Do you think this Boyle is the man who beat her up?"

Rafe considered the question. "I think it's a damned good possibility."

"I feel terrible about this. The policeman said Mr. Boyle sounded very concerned and plans to drive straight here. If he's the man who hurt her—well, normally I'd apprise the police of my suspicions. Her name didn't seem to set off any red lights with them, but I imagine a lot of names go across an officer's desk in a day's time. What if she *is* in some kind of trouble? I'm afraid to call back about Boyle for fear I'll only complicate matters."

The doctor had a point. Until he could pry more information out of Maggie, Rafe was reluctant to involve the police any further as well. "If her stepfather is the one who beat her up, there's nothing he can do to her here."

"That's true."

"Let's play it by ear. If he causes trouble and things get out of hand, we'll have no choice but to call the police. Until then, though, I'd rather hold off."

The doctor gnawed her lower lip. She glanced at the baby in Rafe's arms. "Mr. Boyle may insist that Jaimie be turned over into his care."

Rafe stared down the hall for a long moment. "That'll be up to Maggie. If she trusts the man, then I will. If she doesn't—" He broke off and shook his head. "He'll play hell laying a finger on this child, I can tell you that."

Dr. Hammish gave him a thoughtful look and smiled. "I called your bank, by the way."

"And?"

"The teller said the check was well covered." She arched an eyebrow. "I told her we were negotiating a real estate transaction and that the check was for three hundred and fifty thousand."

"Satisfied?"

She nodded bemusedly. "I know it's a bold question, but how much money do you have, exactly?"

"Enough. As long as you're assured I have the means to take care of Maggie and Jaimie, the amount doesn't really matter, does it?"

"No," she admitted. "Do you think Maggie knows how lucky she is that you're in her corner?"

Rafe gave the doctor a wink and slow grin. "Not yet."

"Have you told her you're a man of considerable means?"

His grin broadened. "Not in so many words."

"Hmmm." She narrowed an eye. "This should be interesting."

At that, Rafe chuckled, waking Jaimie a second time. The baby refused to go back to sleep until he was fed and changed. The doctor left Rafe to handle it when she got a whiff of the odor emanating from Jaimie's sleeper.

"You did say you were assuming responsibility," she reminded him.

Angling his head off to one side, Rafe did his best to keep his mouth closed as he replied. "I did say that, didn't I?"

Rafe Kendrick was a man of his word, messy diapers notwithstanding.

Maggie had been moved to a private room. She lay staring at the ceiling, the muted ticking of the wall clock marking off the seconds. Considering the daily rates for a hospital stay, she wondered how much this was costing her per minute. The IV shunt in the back of her right hand made her feel as if she were on a leash. If not for that, she would have asked the doctor to write her a prescription, located her clothes, and walked out of here.

She couldn't believe she'd fainted. She might have laughed if it hadn't been so awful. Why now, of all times? She needed to be on her way. She had to send for Heidi, and she needed to get settled to take care of Jaimie. Now, to top everything off, she'd have hospital bills up to her eyebrows.

No matter, she assured herself. She'd manage somehow. The doctor said she was really sick, so she didn't have much of a choice about staying here until she got back on her feet. Once she was released, she'd have to work two jobs for a while. That was all. She'd done it before; she could do it again. Child care might prove to be a problem, but she'd find someone trustworthy to watch after Jaimie. Everything would work out. She had to believe that.

Maybe if she really concentrated, she could conjure up a fairy godmother who'd wave her wand and make all her troubles go away.

She closed her eyes, so sick and exhausted that contemplation of anything beyond the moment was too taxing. So, instead, she surrendered her mind to the whimsical. If there really were such a thing as magic and fairy godmothers, what would she wish for? Nothing so silly as a pumpkin coach and a glass slipper, that was for sure. No, if she were going to wish for anything, she'd set her sights on more practical things, like a really good job and a chance to get a better education. She didn't need anyone to take care of her. She could do a fine job of that by herself. More earning power would definitely be nice, though . . .

Rafe tapped the toe of his boot on the lobby carpet, his gaze flickering to the information desk where an elderly female volunteer commandeered the telephone and gave visitors directions. Shrunken with age, she put him in mind of a cheerful elf with her silvery white hair and jolly pink uniform. She had promised to let him know the moment Maggie was settled in her room. It seemed as if he'd been waiting an eternity.

A man stepped up to the counter and muttered a question to the woman. After giving the fellow a quick once-over, Rafe lost interest. Guys just like him were a dime a dozen in the Western states. Classic small-town redneck, the kind who swilled cheap beer, believed pro wrestling was on the up-and-up, and considered himself well-read because he stumbled through a pulp-fiction paperback once a year. Scraggly, sandy-colored hair hung in oily strands to his shoulders. He wore faded jeans and a dingy white T-shirt, one sleeve rolled up over a half-smoked pack of Camel straights.

When the man suddenly turned and looked directly at Rafe, all his senses went on alert. *Lonnie Boyle?* Why he felt surprised, he didn't know. He hadn't been expecting an upstanding citizen, after all.

As Boyle strode toward him, Rafe took more careful inventory, noting the gold hoop he wore in his right ear. His stringy biceps sported tatoos, the one on his right arm of a naked woman with a fanged serpent coiled around her. Instinctively, Rafe held Jaimie a little closer.

Preceded by a beer belly that protruded over the

waistband of his low-slung Levi's, Boyle swaggered cockily. As he drew up in front of the sofa, Rafe saw that he clutched some folded papers in his left hand. The man puffed out his chest, his shifty gray eyes taking Rafe's measure and then settling on Jaimie. He had "bully" written all over him.

"You Kendrick?"

Rafe nodded.

"Name's Boyle, Lonnie Boyle. I'm Maggie's father."

He extended his right hand, a large diamond ring flashing on his finger. Rafe stared at that ring for a long moment, took measure of the jutting prongs that secured the stones, and immediately wanted to kill the son of a bitch. Since they were inside a hospital, he settled for declining his handshake.

Boyle lowered his arm, rubbing his palm on his jeans. Rafe's gaze followed that ring.

"I'm Jaimie's grandpa." He gestured at the baby. "The doc says you been takin' care of him. I sure appreciate that. Now I'm here, though, you're off the hook. What do I owe you for your trouble?"

All Rafe wanted was to catch him outside. "You owe me nothing. As for Jaimie, I'll continue to care for him until Maggie tells me differently."

Boyle thrust out the papers. "Well, Mr. Kendrick, you best be readin' these then before you get yourself neck-deep in hot water. These here are adoption papers. A private arrangement. The folks who adopted the baby paid Maggie a pretty penny to cover her medical expenses, plus a handsome sum to put her through college. Maggie took the money, but then she got all motherly and ran off with the baby. Too late for that. She's got no rights now, and I've come to take the kid back to his new mama and daddy."

"Nobody is taking Jaimie anywhere until Maggie gives her authorization."

Boyle's face flushed. "Look, buster. You're inter-ferin' where you got no business. That kid ain't hers no more, and she's got no say-so.'' He tossed the papers on the sofa. ''Read 'em. She signed the goddamned things of her own free will, and I'm takin' that baby, whether you like it or not.''

Rafe unfolded the document and quickly scanned it. The signature that was supposedly Maggie's looked as if it had been written by an unsteady hand. There were also some dirt smudges and faint, reddish-brown smears on the papers. The notary seal looked genuine. He ran his thumb over the raised dots.

''Were these papers even signed in an office? They're dirty, and these stains look like blood.''

Boyle never missed a beat. ''They *are* blood. Maggie poked her finger with one of the staple prongs. As for the dirt?'' He glanced down at his hands. ''I got me a flat tire drivin' down here. My hands was a mess. I just washed up in the men's room a few minutes ago.''

A poked finger and dirty hands, huh? The story was credible enough. Only something told Rafe that Boyle's delivery was a little too well practiced.

As he returned the papers to the man, he said, ''No one's touching this child until Maggie gives me the go-ahead. Clear? If you mean to take this baby anywhere, she has to authorize it.''

Boyle's face turned an even darker shade of red. He snatched the document from Rafe's hand and slapped it against his thigh. ''I'll get her authorization in damned short order then! To hell with this bullshit.''

With that, he turned and struck off across the lobby, heading for the east wing. Rafe tried to resist his urge to follow the man. He had no business interfering between Maggie and her stepfather. She was in a room near the nurses' station. She was bound to have an emergency buzzer to press if she needed help. There was no reason for him to get in the middle of this.

The smell jerked Maggie awake. *Cigarettes and beer.* Thinking it was only a bad dream, she opened her eyes. A face swam in her bleary vision.

"Lonnie?" Her heart gave a violent leap.

"Who else? Nobody skips out on me and gets away with it. You had to know I'd find you."

Struggling not to panic, Maggie groped for her buzzer. When her fingertips didn't connect with the plastic casing, she cast a wild glance at the bed rail, searching for the thick gray cord.

"Oops." Lonnie braced his hands on the metal bars, effecting a trap with his arms, and leaned closer so their noses nearly touched. "Looks like it fell off the bed. Ain't that a shame? Though I gotta say it works out real nice for me. This way, we can get this settled without nobody bargin' in and pokin' their nose where it don't belong."

A cold resolve settled in the pit of Maggie's stomach. He'd closed the door. If she screamed for help, she had no idea if anyone would hear her, and she'd only get one chance before he covered her mouth. She forced herself to meet his gaze, trying not to show any fear.

"There's nothing to settle. You forced me to sign those papers. I've got bruises all over me to prove it. Big mistake. You didn't keep me home this time until the evidence faded. Give back the money, Lonnie, and cut your losses. I'm not going to give up my child."

He laughed, the sound oily and horrible. "Them bruises don't got my name on 'em. You can't prove nothin'. Far as anybody else knows, you got yourself a nasty-tempered boyfriend." He traced a fingertip along her cheekbone. Maggie tried to jerk her face away, but pain and weakness made her movements sluggish. "Here's how it stands, sweetness. I got signed, notarized papers sayin' you gave up your kid for adoption and that you took the money. All legal and tidy. If you try to fight me, there ain't a judge anywhere that'll rule in your favor, especially not when your own stepdaddy speaks out against you, testifyin' that you ain't a fit mother."

"Unfit?" Using the hand unhampered by the IV, she shoved his arm away. "Get out of here. You've got no hold over me now. Heidi's safe. I've seen to that, and she's prepared to tell a judge what a creep you are so she can live with me. You'll never get within a mile of her again. I'm warning you, Lonnie. Back me into a corner on this, and even though it may upset Mama, I'll come out fighting. You'll be the one who lives to regret it. Do you understand? I'll file charges against you for assault. The doctor here will back me up. She's seen what you did to me. They'll toss you in a cell and throw away the key.''

His grin only broadened. ''So Heidi's safe, is she? You sure about that, little girl?''

Maggie's heart caught. She'd seen that gleam in Lonnie's eyes before.

''I figured out where you took her,'' he whispered.

He was lying. He had to be lying, Maggie thought frantically. Her boss's sister had offered to let Heidi stay with her until Maggie could send for her. The woman had a different married name than Terry and lived in another town. There was no way Lonnie could have tracked Heidi down.

''You're lying.''

''Am I? Well, now, sweetness, you best be damned sure.'' As he spoke, he curled his fingers over her hand and started bending her wrist back. ''You see, it went like this. Heidi, she got to worryin' about your mama frettin' over her, so she telephoned home to tell her she was all right.'' He laughed. ''I always knew that caller ID would come in handy someday. Heidi bein' only ten, I guess she didn't stop to think about me tracin' the call. I wrote down the name and phone number, went to the sheriff's office, and me and a county deputy drove over to Tillard to fetch her back.'' He smiled evilly. ''If you don't come home, fine by me. Me and Heidi will get along right fine.''

A wave of dizziness made Maggie blink. Pain lanced up from her twisted wrist. Through clenched teeth, she whispered, ''You *monster!*''

Lonnie wrenched harder on her hand. "Say now, let's not call names. Start gettin' mouthy and disrespectful, and I'm liable to get mad. What happens to Heidi then?" He pressed his face so close that the rancid smell of his breath nearly gagged her. He arched his brows in question. "Hey, sweetness, what's wrong with your screamer? It broke or somethin'? All of a sudden, like, you're bein' a model of good behavior!"

Through the closed door of Maggie's room, Rafe could hear the growl of Boyle's voice, interspersed with Maggie's faint responses. Settling Jaimie in the bend of his right arm, Rafe inched the door open. Through the crack, he could see Maggie on the raised hospital bed. Boyle leaned over her, twisting on her wrist and laughing softly. Rafe's gaze shot to the side of her bed where the emergency buzzer dangled at the end of its cord.

"You're gonna tell that asshole to let me have that kid, or you'll be sorry. You understand me?"

Maggie arched her spine and tried to grab his wrist with both hands, but her IV tube snagged on the bed rail.

Helpless to intervene with a baby in his arms, Rafe turned to catch a nurse who was hurrying down the hallway. Ignoring her startled expression, he thrust the infant into her arms. "Take this child to the nurses' station and see to it he's kept safe. No one but me is to take him. You understand?"

Wide-eyed, the young nurse nodded mutely.

"Then get on the horn to page Dr. Hammish and security. There's a disorderly visitor in 122. He's roughing up a patient. There's going to be trouble, and I may need help."

As the nurse scurried back toward the nurses' station with Jaimie, Rafe turned to face the door, trying with everything he had to get his temper under control. It was a no go. He'd never been so mad.

When he pushed the door back open, he grew even

more furious. Face averted from her stepfather, Maggie struggled while Boyle continued to bend her wrist to the breaking point. The tendons at each side of her throat were distended as she strained to free her twisted arm.

Rafe didn't feel his feet move. Between one breath and the next, he was across the room. Not bothering to speak, he swung at Boyle with all his strength, knocking him off Maggie and backward. Maggie screamed as Boyle spun with the force of the blow. After doing a full turn, the heartless bastard grabbed for the privacy drape to break his fall. He pulled the drape down with him, sending the curtain hooks flying in all directions, and landed flat on his ass.

Rafe was on him again before he could move, grabbing him by the front of his shirt. At the edge of his mind, he knew this wasn't the time or place for it, but he couldn't resist planting his fist squarely on the bastard's nose. Just once. Boyle howled and clamped a hand over his face.

"You broke my *nose*!"

"That's not all I wanna break, you worm!" Seizing the man's bent arm, Rafe twisted it behind his back, flipped him over onto his belly, and straddled his hips. For good measure, he smacked the back of Boyle's head with the heel of his hand to make damn sure he did a face plant on the tile. "You ever lay so much as a finger on her again, and I'll kill you. You read me loud and clear, you rotten son of a bitch?"

Boyle grunted and gasped out, "My arm! God*damn!* Let up before you break my wrist."

"How's it feel to get some of your own medicine?" Rafe twisted harder. "Oh, Jesus, God!" Boyle cried. "Maggie, make him let me go! Maggie!"

"Rafe, please! Let him up. This will only make it worse!"

Amazement coursed through Rafe. He'd seen the look on her face. She hated and feared this man, and there wasn't a doubt in Rafe's mind that it had been Boyle

who'd beaten the hell out of her. Yet she was pleading
with Rafe to release him? Not a chance.

"Rafe, *please!*" she begged. "Oh, God! You don't
understand. You've no idea what he'll do. *Please!* Oh,
please."

Rafe reluctantly eased the pressure. "Are you all
right?"

Sitting up in bed, she was shaking violently, one arm
curled around her ribs. Her brown eyes swimming with
unshed tears, she glanced fearfully around the room.
"Jaimie. Oh, God, my baby! What did you do with
him?"

"The nurses have him, and they've been warned to
turn him over only to me," Rafe hastened to assure her.
"He's fine, Maggie."

Her shoulders slumped with relief.

"Dr. Hammish and security are on the way here,"
Rafe told her. Then, leaning forward, he met Boyle's
gaze and added, "You're going to jail. You may get
away with this where you come from, but you can't walk
into a hospital and manhandle a woman. I hope they toss
you in a cell and throw away the key."

"What's going on in here?"

Rafe reared back to see around the bed. He recognized
the flash of Dr. Hammish's red hair as she ran to Maggie's side. Over the top of the mattress, Rafe saw her
quickly check the IV shunt in the back of her patient's
hand. Then she pressed Maggie against the pillows and
sent Rafe an inquiring look. He nodded at the man beneath him.

"Meet Mr. Boyle. I caught him trying to strong-arm
your patient. It seems he forced her to sign adoption
papers. I think we both know what kind of coercion he
used. Now he's demanding she relinquish custody of the
baby. He claims the adoptive parents paid her hand-
somely to give Jaimie up—all her medical bills and
money to go to college."

"I never got a cent!" Maggie insisted. "I *wouldn't*

sell my baby! It's a lie, a horrible lie. Lonnie took the money. All of it. He arranged everything behind my back and then forced me to sign the papers."

The doctor slipped an arm around Maggie's shoulders and drew her close. "Shhh, Maggie. Calm down," she soothed. "He won't take your baby. In most cases, even if a woman does sign the papers, a judge will rule in favor of the natural mother if she changes her mind."

"Wanna bet?" Boyle cried. "How about if the natural mother's unfit? I'll testify against her. See if I don't. How will that look? Huh? Her own stepfather speaking out against her! After I get done talkin', the judge will think twice about ruling in her favor, mark my words."

"Don't believe him, Maggie," Dr. Hammish interjected.

"Doesn't make no difference what she believes!" Boyle retorted. "Only what a judge thinks will matter. He'll want that kid to have a good home, and the folks adoptin' him are rich. Big, fancy house. Uppity-up neighborhood. They'll send him to the best schools! No contest! They'll already have that baby, and no judge in his right mind will make them give a child back to a two-bit little tramp who sold him to support her drug habit!"

Maggie made a tortured sound. "Drug habit? I don't take drugs!"

Boyle sneered. "Oh, yeah? Prove it! I'll swear you did! And so will the attorney. We'll say you only stopped using long enough to get your kid back."

The physician's green eyes darted to Rafe. The security guards rushed into the room just then. After taking quick stock of the situation, one of the uniformed men turned to the doctor. "Should we call the police?"

"Yes! Call the goddamned police!" Boyle yelled, straining against Rafe's hold. "She signed them papers of her own free will and took *money*. Sold her own baby. Some mother! The adoption attorney notarized the papers himself. They're on the bed. Look and see for yourself. She's got no claim to that kid anymore, and I'm takin' him to his new parents. None of you can stop me. I got the law on my side! It'll take months before the case goes to court. By then the kid'll love his adopted parents, and she'll play hell gettin' him back.''

Rafe didn't doubt for an instant that money had changed hands. He was also convinced it had gone straight into Boyle's. Maggie had gotten nothing out of the deal but a beating that had damned near killed her. Evidently, after being forced to sign the papers, she had somehow managed to flee with the baby before her stepfather could turn him over to the adoptive parents.

Any attorney who had been present to authenticate those adoption papers when Maggie was being physically forced to sign them had to be as slimy a worm as Boyle was.

A crooked adoption attorney who dealt in human flesh. A son of a bitch for a stepfather. *Dear God.*

Searching Maggie's terrified gaze, Rafe knew she was in way over her head. Boyle was right. It would look bad for Maggie if her own stepfather testified against her at a hearing, and in the ensuing months until the case was reviewed by a judge, Jaimie would become attached to his adoptive parents. The court would definitely take into account that Maggie was a virtual stranger to him. Unless she could prove she'd been muscled into signing those papers, she could lose her baby, and as Boyle had already pointed out, none of those bruises on her body had his name on them.

It would nearly kill Maggie if she lost her child.

Seeing no alternative, Rafe released Boyle's arm and swung off him, signaling the guards to take over. Boyle rolled onto his side, rubbing his wrist. He sneered as the two security guards pulled him to his feet, then shook their hands away as he gained his balance. He swiped furiously at the blood under his nose, grabbed the adoption papers off the bed, and staggered to the door.

Before storming from the room, he turned and leveled

a finger at Maggie. ''You made a bad mistake when you decided to mess with me, little lady. That baby ain't all you're gonna lose. What about your sweet mama and that cute little sister of yours? I'll wait in the lobby and give you an hour to think about it. If you don't change your mind and hand over the kid in that time, I'm callin' the cops.'' He waved the papers and shot Rafe a smoldering look. ''You won't be such a hotshot then, hey, boy? Refuse to give *them* that kid and see what happens! They'll throw your ass in jail so fast, it'll make you dizzy.''

 Chapter Seven

After Boyle made his exit, the hospital room went deathly quiet. Rafe wasn't sure how he expected Maggie to react. He only knew any reaction would have been less alarming than nothing at all. She lay motionless, staring straight ahead, her face so pale and her eyes so lusterless she might have been a corpse.

Dr. Hammish flashed Rafe a worried look, then stepped to the bed and retrieved the emergency buzzer. After ringing for a nurse, she rewound the cord on the bed rail. "It's going to be all right, Maggie. You have a friend in me and in Mr. Kendrick. We'll help in any way we can."

A nurse in pink scrubs rushed into the room. Her rubber-soled shoes squeaked on the tile. Dr. Hammish turned to softly issue orders for medication.

During their exchange, Rafe had eyes only for Maggie's drawn face. God only knew what she had endured at Boyle's hands, the only certainty being that she couldn't take much more. "Maggie?" he said softly. "Honey, can you talk to me? I want to help you, but I need to know exactly what I'm up against here."

"You can't help me," she said stonily, and then, before Rafe realized what she meant to do, she sat up, jerked the IV shunt from the back of her hand, and swung her legs over the edge of the bed. "Where are my clothes?"

The doctor gasped and grabbed for her patient's bleeding hand. "Dear God, what are you doing?"

"Leaving." Applying pressure to her hand to stop the bleeding, Maggie stepped down off the stool and headed for the wall locker, the back of her hospital gown flapping. As she threw open the locker and grabbed her jeans, she cast Rafe a determined glance. "Could you go and get Jaimie for me, please?"

Even as she spoke, she swayed with weakness. Dr. Hammish scurried across the room. "You can't do this!" she cried.

Maggie shook her off. "I *am* doing it." She braced a hand on the locker to support herself as she bent to thrust a foot down one pant leg. At the effort, her face lost even more color. "I have to get back to Prior before Lonnie does so I can get my sister out of there."

Rafe couldn't move. He had the oddest sensation, as if the tile beneath his feet had turned to water, and he was about to sink. Over the last two days, he'd been assaulted by one inexplicable feeling after another about this young woman, and now, in a heartbeat, they were all hitting him at once.

"I'm sure your sister will be fine for a day or so," Hammish insisted. "You're very ill, Maggie. You can't leave here without receiving treatment."

"Write a prescription for pills," Maggie retorted as she worked the jeans up over her slender hips. "If I don't get my sister out of there, Lonnie may hurt her to get back at me. That's the way he operates."

The doctor seized Maggie's elbow to help steady her. "Let's not overreact. We've other options. Calling the police is one of them. And isn't your mother living in the home? Surely she'll look after your sister until we can work through appropriate channels to get the child out of there."

Her movements jerky with urgency, Maggie snapped her jeans and bent to collect her socks and shoes. "I can't call the police. They might take one look at that adoption agreement and hand Jaimie over to my step-father.'' She tugged on a sock and shoved her slender foot into a sneaker. ''Then it'd take months, maybe even years, for me to get my baby back.''

''I admit there may be an element of risk,'' the doctor conceded, ''but calling the authorities is still your best bet. I'll intercede on your behalf. It's obvious you've been physically abused. They'll see that and take steps to help you.'' Tightening her grip on Maggie's elbow, Dr. Hammish added, ''Don't put me in this position. If you persist in trying to leave, I'll have no choice but to sedate you, and I really hate to have to do that.''

Maggie hesitated in putting on her second shoe to glance up, the haunted, hopeless look in her eyes nearly breaking Rafe's heart. ''So, you're going to save me from myself? And what about Heidi, Dr. Hammish?'' she asked in a quivering voice. ''Can you intercede on her behalf as well?''

The doctor's lips parted as if to speak, but then she simply stood there, saying nothing.

''You see?'' Maggie said softly. ''It's not just me and my baby. If not for that, don't you think I would have left a long time ago?''

''What pushed you into leaving this time?'' Dr. Hammish asked.

''Things came to a head, and I didn't have a choice. It was that or lose Jaimie. I thought Heidi would be safe, that there was absolutely no way Lonnie could find her. But he did!''

Rafe took a hesitant step toward her, not entirely sure what he could do to help her, but convinced he had to do something. She squeezed her eyes closed, her face twisting with anguish.

''I wanted to bring Heidi with me, but Lonnie isn't stupid. He knew I might try to leave, so he took all my money and charge cards before he went to bed that night and locked them in his nightstand drawer.

''My boss floated me a loan, but she's only the truck

stop manager, not the owner. She gave me all that she could, but it still wasn't enough for me to get settled someplace. Rent, deposits, food. I had no choice but to take Jaimie, but unless I absolutely had to, I couldn't go dragging a ten-year-old all over God's creation in the dead of winter, not knowing if I could even provide adequate shelter for her. I decided she'd be better off staying with Terry's sister where she'd be safe until I could find a job and send for her. With the money Terry gave me, all I needed was one week's pay.''

She lifted her hands in a gesture of futility. "It wouldn't have been for very long. Only nothing went right! While I was trying to get on the train, it started to move. Jaimie was already on board, and I was running to catch up. I slipped on the ice and dropped his quilt and the diaper bag. *Everything* was in it. Stuff for Jaimie, the money, *everything*. And then I got sick. Now Heidi's back home. I *can't* just leave her there. Please, try to understand that.''

"If we call the authorities, I'm certain there's something that can be done," Dr. Hammish insisted.

With shaking hands, Maggie tied her laces and shook her head. "Not without proof that she's being mistreated, and trust me, there is none. Lonnie's far too clever for that. Oh, no. So far, he's kept his hands off Heidi. She's his ace in the hole. He uses the threat to her safety as leverage to keep me in line.'' She straightened, keeping one hand pressed against the locker for support as she gave the older woman an imploring look. "I know you mean well, Doctor, but you don't have the whole picture. Do you think I've never gone to the police for help? Or to legal aid or children's services? Think again. I've gone so many times, they know me by name.''

"What did they do?''

"Nothing. That's the whole point.'' She pulled her arm from the doctor's grasp and jerked her blouse and bra off the locker hook. "Without proof that Lonnie abuses my sister, there's nothing they can do. They couldn't take a child away from her mother without a good reason. Something had to actually happen to her first.''

''And your mother? She won't help?''

''My mother is . . .'' Maggie's voice faded, and she slumped against the locker frame, her lashes fluttering as if she were about to faint. After several seconds, she took a bracing breath. ''When my dad was killed, she had a heart attack. Oxygen deprivation left her brain-damaged. She's very childlike now and her health is fragile. She's a dear heart and she loves Heidi, but as a protector, she's useless.''

Rafe remembered the sadness in Maggie's eyes last night when she told him that her life had never been the same after her father's death. Now he could understand why. To all intents and purposes, she'd actually lost both of her parents the same day.

Looking at her now, Rafe recalled all the times he had wondered what had happened in her life to make her so distrusting. Now the mystery was solved. At fourteen, she'd been left with a childlike mother and a baby sister to look after. Toss a creep like Lonnie Boyle into that equation, and you had a nightmare. *Dear God*. Sudden nausea made his stomach roil.

''Lonnie is clever and manipulative,'' Maggie continued shakily. ''He took one look at my mother and saw a life on easy street. A not very bright widow with her own home and a little money in the bank. He has Mama wrapped around his little finger now and convinced he's wonderful.'' She pressed the back of her wrist to her forehead. ''You saw him. He's a creep.'' She lowered her arm and blinked. ''I won't let him do to Heidi what he's done to me. I *won't!*''

''I'm not suggesting that you should,'' the doctor assured her. ''Only that your leaving the hospital isn't the best answer.''

Maggie shot Rafe a querulous look. ''Please, Mr.

Kendrick, don't just stand there. Go get Jaimie while I finish dressing. I don't have much time.''

With a vague sense of disgust, Rafe realized he *was* just standing there, and in that moment, he knew he had to do something, even if it was wrong. *Don't do anything dumb*, Ryan had cautioned him on the phone. Only would it be dumb? He could help this girl. And damn it, whether his feelings made sense or not, he cared about her.

He hadn't been able to help his own family. A perverse twist of fate had stolen them from him so quickly there had been nothing he could do. But that wasn't the case this time.

Rafe barely felt his feet moving as he crossed the room. ''You don't need to leave, Maggie,'' he said firmly. ''The cavalry has just arrived.''

''The what?''

''The cavalry,'' he repeated. ''In this case, only a one-man army, but I've got clout. Marry me. If I get my name on Jaimie's birth certificate and claim to be his father, there's nobody on God's green earth who'll be able to take him away from me. Boyle can't prove differently without a blood test, which he'll play hell getting with all the interstate red tape. Meanwhile, I'll make Boyle an offer he can't refuse to hold him at bay. Heidi won't be harmed. I promise.''

''Marry you?''

''It's the perfect solution. Think about it. A precedent has already been set in the courts. These days, a father has rights. If I say Jaimie is mine, and you marry me to strengthen my legal claim, that adoption agreement won't be worth the paper it's written on without my signature.''

She shook her head.

''Listen to him, Maggie,'' the doctor encouraged. ''Don't reject this offer out of hand. I know you haven't known him for long, but I believe he can be trusted and has your best interests at heart.''

"I can hire top-notch lawyers and fight it out with Lonnie in court if I have to," Rafe rushed to assure her. "You won't lose your son. I guarantee it."

She stared up at him with a blank look on her pale face. "Hire top-notch lawyers? With what?"

"I told you this morning, remember? That when I left home, I left a substantial amount of money behind."

"A court battle would cost a *lot* of money."

Rafe glanced at the doctor. "You called my bank. It'll be more believable coming from you. Tell her."

"He's rich," Dr. Hammish told her. "It's true, Maggie. I'm not sure exactly how rich, but I think it's fair to say he's got a bundle."

"Rich?" Maggie repeated, her expression incredulous. "A rich boxcar bum?"

"Not a bum, a rancher. I still own half of a huge spread in eastern Oregon. Three years ago, there was a forest fire. The ranch was left financially strapped. To recover, my brother and I parceled off five thousand acres and sold lots to developers. We split the proceeds between us and our folks. My third was around fifty million, most of which is invested. I've got a lot of money, Maggie. Enough to buy off dozens of Lonnie Boyles and still make change. You understand? Money means power. Marry me, and that power will be in your corner."

"*Marry* you? But that's crazy."

It *was* crazy. Rationally, Rafe knew that. But it was a wonderful kind of crazy. For the first time in so long, he felt alive again.

"Really think about this, Maggie," Dr. Hammish urged. "I know it sounds a little archaic, but just imagine all the advantages. I don't know all the details, and it's not my business to pry, but you're obviously in one hell of a mess, and evidently your little sister will be as well if you don't do something. Is running away the answer?

"You've tried that, and look what's happened. Boyle

is here, breathing down your neck. You can run again if that's your only option. But whenever possible, it's always best to make a stand and fight back. Mr. Kendrick is not only offering you his protection, but the means to fight this battle and win.''

Maggie felt as if the world had suddenly tipped off its axis. Her boxcar cowboy was actually a multimillionaire? And he was offering to marry her and use his money to fight her battles? It was like going to sleep and waking up, smack-dab in the middle of a fairy tale—with her cast in the role of damsel in distress and Rafe Kendrick playing the handsome prince.

She leaned more of her weight against the locker, not entirely sure her legs would continue to hold her up. She was dreaming, she decided. The doctor had given her a sedative, after all, and she was actually in bed, doped to the gills and having a crazy dream. It was the only explanation.

''Why?'' she asked dizzily.

''Why what?'' her handsome prince asked.

''Why are you offering to marry me? I can see the benefits for me. But what will you get out of it?''

He flashed her a crooked grin. ''You.''

Maggie groaned. ''You barely know me. I've got an illegitimate baby and a ten-year-old sister I'm responsible for. You'd be taking on a ready-made family.''

The instant she spoke, Maggie realized that was exactly it. Rafe Kendrick had lost his wife and children in a car wreck, and he was still grieving. She recalled the expression of yearning she'd seen on his face last night when he looked down at Jaimie. Now he saw a way to keep her and the baby with him, a way to make Jaimie his very own. Convenient replacements, that's what they would be.

It was an insane idea. Maggie could scarcely believe she was actually considering it. Who in her right mind would agree to such a thing? On the other hand, given her situation, who in her right mind would pass on the offer? Fifty million? With that much money, he could hire a legion of clever lawyers. Lonnie wouldn't stand a chance. And it wasn't as if Rafe would be getting nothing out of the deal. He'd be getting a son—someone to make him feel needed and necessary again.

There was just one hitch: by accepting such an offer, she'd be selling herself, body and soul. Unless Rafe co-operated, there might be no way to call this off later. No walking out. She'd be his wife. Even worse, he would have the ultimate leverage over her, joint custody of her son. She also had Heidi to think about. Where, exactly, did she fit into this puzzle?

"I can't," Maggie said, her voice so faint it seemed to come from a great distance. "It's a wonderful offer, and it would solve most of my problems. But it wouldn't solve all of them, and I just can't."

"Name me one reason," Rafe argued. "You've got nothing to lose and everything to gain."

"I told you, I have to go get my sister." The room seemed to spin. Maggie grasped the open locker door to stay on her feet. Her words seemed to echo inside her head. "Please, go get my son so I can finish getting dressed and leave."

"How will you get to Prior?" he asked.

"I'll hitchhike."

"And if you can't catch a ride right away? You're too sick to stand along the highway, especially with a baby to hold. You might pass out. What will happen to Jaimie then?"

Her legs felt like overcooked spaghetti. She was afraid they might buckle. Oh, God, he was right. She was too sick. If she left the hospital, she might never make it to Prior, and where would that leave Heidi?

"I have to go get her," she cried. "I can't leave her there."

"I have no intention of leaving her there." His voice seemed to surround her, deep and warm—and so wonderfully strong. "We'll get custody of her and bring her to live with us, Maggie. You've got my word on it. We'll make that part of our bargain. And meanwhile, I swear to you on everything that's holy, Boyle won't hurt her. I'll make damned sure that she's safe.''

''How? You don't know Lonnie. He's a snake. You can't trust anything he says.''

As if he sensed she was about to fall, Rafe gently encircled her waist and drew her against his chest. For the second time since meeting him, Maggie leaned into him, too weak to stand alone. ''Honey, trust me just a little. I swear to you that Heidi will be safe. Just say yes. You'll have no more worries.''

No more worries. That sounded so wonderful, so absolutely wonderful. She was so awfully, horribly tired, and he was offering her a solution to all of her troubles. All she wanted was to close her eyes and let him take care of everything.

''But at what cost?'' she murmured aloud.

''What do you mean?''

''I'll be so indebted to you, how will I ever pay you back?''

''You don't have to. I'll never miss the money.''

''Yes,'' she insisted. ''No free rides. I pay my own way. I've told you that.''

Oh, God. What was she doing? Was she actually about to accept this offer? *Yes, God help her, yes.* Heidi would be safe. She and Jaimie would be safe. It wasn't as if she had a host of choices. This was it.

''If I do this, I have to know you'll keep track of every penny you spend.'' Trying frantically to clear her head, she said, ''And I want you to agree to it in writing.''

''You want a prenup agreement?''

''Is that what it's called?''

''Yes.''

''Then that's what I want, a prenup agreement, stating that if this doesn't work out, we can go our separate ways, with the understanding that I'll reimburse you for all you've spent and that you won't make things difficult for me about leaving.'' She managed to lift her head and look up at him. "That's the only way I'll agree to such a thing—if I know I'm going to be paying my own way."

"Done."

Maggie hadn't expected him to agree so easily. "You're sure?"

"It's fine by me."

She had a bad feeling he was only saying that so she would say yes, that he had no intention of letting her work to pay her own expenses. "I'm dead serious about this. Until I'm able to wait tables again, is there anything at your ranch that I can do to earn a wage?"

He muttered something under his breath and then shrugged. "You said you're good at bookkeeping. I hate paperwork. You can be my in-house accountant."

It sounded like a job he had dreamed up just to keep her happy. "Someone else has been keeping your books, obviously. It has to be something extra that I can do—something that's a real contribution, not just a pat on my head to make me feel useful." Dizzily, she tried to think of an alternative. "I'm a good housekeeper."

"That position's filled." He searched her gaze, his eyes delving deeply. "It's true that Ryan and I have always kept the books, but neither of us are fond of the job or very good at it. It'd be great to have someone really keep on top of it for us, especially if you can learn the cattle business and chart information so we can see how we're doing at a glance. I always just dumped the receipts in a drawer and tried to make sense of them later. Ryan didn't bother to do that half the time, so our records were never very accurate."

"And if I do a good job, you'll pay me the going rate? All on paper, of course, to apply it against my debt. You'll call around to see what a good accountant usually gets and be agreeable about paying that?"

"Jesus Christ. Are we going to negotiate wages right

now?'' He stared down at her. "All right. Sure. The going rate.''

"I can learn the cattle business,'' she assured him. ''I'm quick to pick up on things.''

"Then pick up on this,'' he said, lowering his voice for her ears alone. ''I get a wife and child in this bargain. And if you think I won't do everything in my power to make sure you want to remain my wife, think again. I don't make a commitment like this lightly, Maggie.''

She could tell by his expression that he meant it. ''No, of course not. Neither do I. But I'm not willing to make a lifelong commitment until I'm certain we can make it work, either. We barely know each other. In the event that we separate, I need to know I've brought as much into this as you did, and that you won't be blowing a bunch of money, with nothing to show for it in the end.''

"I'll be giving Jaimie my name,'' he reminded her. ''The moment I do that, he'll be my son in every way that matters, and prenuptial agreement or no, he'll always be my son, even if you decide to leave me. In my estimation, a child is a bona fide contribution, and I'll be more than adequately reimbursed for my expenditures. There's also the possibility we'll have a baby of our own. How can you worry that you're not bringing anything worthwhile into the relationship?''

Until that moment, Maggie had been thinking that this would be a platonic arrangement. ''You mean you want this to be—a *real* marriage?''

Rafe glanced at the doctor. ''Can you step outside for just a moment? When I get her back into bed, I'll holler for you.'' He watched until the doctor had exited and closed the door. His steely blue eyes gleamed with determination when he looked back down at Maggie. ''Yes, a real marriage. I don't do things halfway, especially not something like this, and I'll explain why. It may take months for all the legalities to be finalized. In that time, Jaimie and I will start to bond. Even little guys can form strong attachments. I don't think it's fair to let him be around me and start to love me unless we're both going to put a hundred percent of our efforts into making this work.

"If it doesn't," he went on, "then, sure, we'll have no choice but to call it quits, and I'll have to settle for visitation privileges. But we owe it to him and ourselves not to go into this with the thought that it's a stopgap measure. Don't you agree?"

Maggie did agree. She was just so swimmy-headed that she hadn't thought about how all of this might affect Jaimie emotionally. "I, um . . . I'm just not real comfortable with—well, you know."

"Sex, you mean?" He smoothed his hand over her hair. "Honey, if you do this, you'll be trusting me with so much. Don't you think you can trust me about that as well?"

He was right; she'd be trusting him with everything. Held so gently against him, she was beginning to feel like a pat of butter melting over a flapjack. She didn't know how much longer she'd be able to stand. Her body felt disconnected from her brain, and she was afraid she might pass out. Before that happened, she had far greater concerns than her own well-being to consider.

"Promise me again that you'll get Heidi out of there as fast as you possibly can," she whispered. "Promise me, or there's no deal."

"I promise. Hell, I'd go get her now if I could, but snatching a child and transporting her over the state line is a serious offense."

"I have to know she'll be safe. She's only ten years old, and she never asked for any of this."

"She'll be safe. That I can guarantee. And before you know it, she'll be with us, Maggie. Consider it done."

Maggie could only pray it would prove to be that simple, but a part of her feared that Lonnie couldn't be so easily handled.

"How do you plan to do it?"

He swept her into his arms. Maggie gasped and clung

weakly to his shoulders. As he carried her toward the bed, he said, "I'm just going to jump in with both feet and follow my instincts. I've been out of circulation for a while, but I'm an effective negotiator. I can handle Boyle. You concentrate on getting well. I'll take care of everything else."

As he carefully deposited her on the mattress, Maggie searched his dark face, a part of her fearing that she'd just struck a bargain with a madman. What other explanation was there? She'd known him only two days, and he wanted to marry her? Oh, God. What had she done?

"I'm not Susan," she whispered, fighting to keep her eyes open so she could hold his gaze. "Take a long hard look at me and know what you're doing, Mr. Kendrick. Susan's dead, and so are your children. Jaimie and I will never be able to replace them, and it isn't fair to ask that we try."

Using the bed rail, he braced his weight with one arm to cup her chin in his hand. His hard, leathery fingers felt featherlight and cool on her skin, yet vibrant with latent strength. "I know exactly what I'm doing, Maggie, and I don't for a moment have you confused with Susan."

Maggie wished she felt as certain of that as he seemed to be. "I can't pretend to be someone else. That's all. I want to be sure you understand that. I'm me, and I'll never be able to fill her shoes."

"I don't expect you to try," he assured her. "You're sweet and beautiful, Maggie. No man in his right mind would want you to be anyone but exactly who you are, and I'm definitely not out of my mind."

 *Chapter Eight*

Nightmares plagued Maggie as she drifted in a sedative-induced sleep. In each dream, her mother, Heidi, or Jaimie was in terrible peril, and Lonnie played the villain with Rafe Kendrick as his sidekick. Frantically Maggie tried to protect the people she loved, but at every turn she met with insurmountable opposition.

In the last nightmare, she was lost in a graveyard after dark, and she knew Lonnie was lurking in the blackness with a huge knife, intent on killing Jaimie. She could hear her baby crying, only no matter where she looked, she couldn't find him. Instead she continually ran into a tall, steel fence with spikes at the top. Rafe was always standing just outside the enclosure, grinning at her in that lazy way of his. *"Marry me, Maggie. No more worries. I'll take care of everything."*

She awoke confused and drenched in sweat to find herself back in her hospital room with a nurse at her bedside. When Maggie saw the face hovering over hers, she cried out and tried to jerk away.

"Now, now. It's all right," the nurse said in a soothing voice. "I didn't mean to startle you, but it's time to wake up now."

Maggie blinked. Her heart felt as if it were leaping from her chest. The nurse held up a strange-looking plastic contraption.

"Why do I have a feeling that's for me?"

The nurse nodded. "You guessed it. You can't nurse your baby until your infection is gone and you're off the strong medication."

With the nurse's help, Maggie managed to sit up. The woman unfastened the back of her gown. "I'll shut the door and put up the 'Do Not Disturb' sign. When you're finished, buzz for help, and one of us will come in to refasten this."

After the nurse left, Maggie applied herself to the task at hand. The clock on the wall said it was nearly eight o'clock by the time she finished and another nurse looked in on her. Exhausted, she lay against the pillows, her gaze fixed on the venetian blind over the window. Between the slats, she could see the darkness of night beyond the glass, which told her she'd been asleep for hours.

I'll take care of everything, Rafe had promised her. Now that her head was a bit clearer, Maggie thought of all the things that could have gone wrong, and her heart squeezed with fear. Lonnie was so unpredictable.

Stop it, Maggie. Rafe said he would take care of it, you agreed to let him, and now, all you can do is pray he does. It's not as if you have another option.

He had probably looked in on her while she was sleeping and decided not to disturb her. Yes, that was it. He had come to give her an update on the situation, but she'd been resting, so he'd left, planning to come back later.

So . . . it was later. Where was he?

Trying to shove all negative thoughts aside, she focused on the positive. Everything had gone fine, and Rafe had probably taken Jaimie back to the motel. A hospital lobby wasn't exactly the best place in the world to care for an infant.

Picturing Jaimie, Maggie's arms ached to hold him. To feel his warm little body pressed against her. To breathe in that sweet baby smell. To touch his downy little head. *Jaimie*. She loved him so very much. No matter what price she had to pay to keep him safe, he was her consolation. Her only consolation.

"Hi there, angel face. They said you were finally awake."

Maggie turned to see Rafe crossing the room, the door swinging closed behind him. His stride was loose and slow. With each shift of his body, his hair caught the light, glistening like polished onyx. He had his coat draped over one shoulder, the tails concealing his right arm. His gaze swept the length of her, making her feel exposed even with the sheet and blanket over her. She tugged at the neck of her gown to be sure it was up.

"Where's Jaimie? You didn't let Lonnie take him?"

"Of course not. That's all taken care of. No more worries, just as I promised." As he reached the bed, he leaned down to flash her a conspiratorial grin. "I've got a stowaway." Brushing his coat aside, he revealed her sleeping son nestled in his arm. "He's not supposed to be in here. But I thought maybe a cuddle session with your favorite fella might be good medicine for what ails you."

Tears sprang to Maggie's eyes. Battling the IV, she eagerly took Jaimie into her arms. "Oh, Rafe, thank you. I've been missing him so much!"

"Now how did I know that?" he said with a silky chuckle. "If ever I've seen a good mama, you qualify."

"Not nearly good enough." Maggie's throat ached as she forced out the words. "My life is in such a mess."

"Not anymore," he assured her, a note of smugness lacing his tone. "Mr. Boyle won't cause any more problems, at least not for a while, I guarantee it."

Not for a while? Yes, Maggie thought, that just about summed it up. Lonnie Boyle was like radioactive waste buried deep in the ground; as long as he was on the same planet, there would always be a chance of contamination.

Maggie was about to insist that Rafe fill her in on all the details when an even more pressing concern occurred to her. "Jaimie won't get sick from being in here, will he? Maybe that's why babies aren't allowed."

Tossing his coat on the visitor's chair, Rafe sat on the edge of her bed and rested an arm on his bent knee. "I asked Dr. Hammish if it was safe. She's my partner in crime. She says there's no danger in a private room like this."

"Will we get in trouble?" Maggie whispered.

"Nah. Most of the nurses know he's here. They've just been pretending not to see him. I only covered him with my coat to surprise you."

"A nice surprise." She cupped a hand over her baby's head. "He's cool."

"You've still got a fever, honey." He touched her forehead. "You're like a little heater, turned up on high. How are you feeling?"

"Better now that Jaimie's here. This is even worse than when I left him with Mama while I worked. I was always a little afraid she'd forget she had him."

"You've been working since you gave birth? How soon did you go back to your job after having him?"

"I stayed in the hospital one day, then I took off three more."

"You've worked for years, haven't you? Ever since your dad died."

"I was afraid we'd go through his life insurance money if I didn't."

"And you were back on the job right after childbirth." He shook his head. "Never again."

She drew back the receiving blanket to admire the new blue sleeper. "I didn't have much choice. Having a baby is expensive."

"Yeah, I understand that," he said dryly. "So is postnatal care. You must have felt pretty awful when that kidney infection started."

Maggie shook her head. "My back ached a lot. But nothing so bad I thought it was a kidney infection and rushed to see a doctor. I have no health insurance, and it's thirty-eight dollars a visit.''

She heard him sigh. When she glanced up, he was fiddling with things on her bedside table. His hand grew still when he spied the apparatus resting there. Maggie's cheeks grew hot.

''Christ. It must feel like you're being attacked by a toilet plunger.''

Maggie gave a startled giggle. He chuckled, too. The tender warmth in his gaze made her uncomfortable. Uncertain what to say, she bent her head and toyed with Jaimie's blanket again.

''How long will they let you be in here?'' she finally asked.

''We were here while you slept. So far, they haven't hassled me. I'll call a cab soon and take Jaimie back to the motel. He seems to sleep all right with me holding him. But it has to be more restful being in his own bed.''

As much as Maggie hated the thought of parting with her son, she had to agree. ''Thank you for taking such good care of him.''

''I hope to make it a lifelong commitment,'' he said softly.

Maggie glanced up and then found she couldn't look away.

''I took care of Lonnie. You don't have to worry about Heidi. He'll leave her alone for the time being, and in the interim, we'll pull strings to get her out of there as fast as we can. I'll get my lawyer on it as soon as we get home.''

She'd never known anyone who had a lawyer on retainer all the time. ''How can you be sure Lonnie won't do anything? What did you do, murder him?''

He smiled. ''I was tempted, believe me. But we all have our price. I simply made him an offer he couldn't refuse.''

Maggie gnawed her lip, thinking of all the times her stepfather had threatened Heidi's safety to keep her in line. "Lonnie will promise one thing and do another. You can't trust him to keep his word."

"I thought of that. When we get to Oregon, I'll call frequently to check on Heidi. And in the morning, I'll place some phone calls and hire a private investigator to keep her under surveillance until I can get her out of there. Lonnie understands if I get a bad report, his ass is gonna be grass and I'll be a lawnmower. He also understands that if anything bad happens, even if it appears to be an accident, that his life won't be worth a sugar lump in a rainstorm." He winked at her. "I told him I'd find him, no matter where he went, and that when I did, I'd kill him."

"And he believed you?"

"Hell, I was so convincing, I damned near believed it myself." He shrugged. "I'm not so sure I don't mean it, actually. But fortunately, it isn't a worry. He jumped at the offer I made him."

Though she dreaded knowing the answer, morbid curiosity prompted Maggie to ask, "You bribed him, didn't you? How much did you offer to pay him?"

"I'm entering it in my little black book. You can worry about the exact amount later. Lonnie went for the bait. That's all that counts. And, typical of most bullies, he's too big a coward to cross me. Men like that don't take on anyone their own size or bigger. They prey on those who are weaker. They're bullies, Maggie. Fear is the turn-on. Having absolute power is their ultimate high. They pick on people who can't or won't stand up to them."

She fell into one of those categories—those who were weaker. She imagined her life, stretching endlessly before her, each day centered around the whims of her keeper. She should be glad Rafe had elected to fill that role. He didn't seem to be cruel like Lonnie, at least. But then, she couldn't be sure of that. Until you got backed into a corner, a man seldom showed his true colors.

Oh, God, what if she married him, and he started venting his temper on Jaimie? Jaimie wasn't his child. A lot of men resented their stepchildren.

Maggie cut the thought short. It wasn't as if she had a choice here. After all, there was no guarantee that the man who wanted to adopt Jaimie would be a good father, either. At least if she married Rafe, she'd be around to intervene for Jaimie if it was necessary, and she'd soon have Heidi with her as well.

"Having second thoughts?" he asked softly.

"I don't have that luxury. How about you?"

"I never second-guess myself, and even if I did, I'd circle back to where I am right now." He smoothed a palm over the fitted sheet. Then he glanced up and flashed a crooked grin. "I'm more into second chances, and that's what you and Jaimie are for me, a second chance. I've come to care about you, Maggie. I'm hoping that feeling will eventually be reciprocated. But even if it isn't, I'm still sure I'm doing the right thing."

"No matter how we circle it, this is an impulsive move."

"True. But sometimes if you stand around, thinking things to death for too long, by the time you reach a decision, it's too late." He searched her gaze. "Are you a religious person?"

"I believe there's a God, yes."

He winked at her. "You see? Already we have common ground. I'm a believer as well. But even if I weren't, I think I'd still believe in something. For some people, it's the universe. For others, it's a higher power. Regardless, I'm convinced there's something—call it fate or God or a guardian or the pull of the moon—that's at work in all our lives. Things happen for a reason."

"Your point?"

His vivid steel-blue gaze held hers. "That there were probably a number of empty boxcars in the train yard that night,'' he said softly. ''There usually are. What led you to the one I was in?''

''Poor judgment?''

He barked with laughter. When his mirth subsided, he shook his head. ''That, too, I guess. But I like to think it was also fate—or maybe your guardian angel. I was minding my own business, happy as a clam with my whiskey for company, and the next thing I knew, I was looking into a pair of big brown eyes I couldn't resist.''

Maggie had never seen him laugh like that, and for a moment, she felt she was glimpsing the man he'd once been. It gave her a good feeling to think that in some way, maybe she and Jaimie were responsible for the transformation.

''I think God looked down and decided I had better things to do than pickle my brain with whiskey.'' His smile faded, and the expression in his eyes grew solemn. ''I couldn't help Susan and my kids, Maggie. For whatever reason, it was time for them to go, and there was nothing I could do to stop it. I've lived with the memories, feeling angry and helpless and worthless—and wondering at least a thousand times why in the hell I didn't die, too. Now, I think I know. I can make a difference for you and Jaimie and Heidi, a little girl I've never even met. That's a very good feeling, and even if this marriage turns out badly, nothing can take that away from me.''

Tears filled Maggie's eyes. Embarrassed, she looked away.

''Jesus. Don't cry. It's nothing to feel sad about.''

''I'm not sad.'' She swiped at her cheeks. ''I'm just— well, if you want the truth, I'm praying you're really as nice as you seem to be.''

His mouth tipped into another of those lazy grins. ''Stick around and find out.''

''As I see it, I don't have much choice. No offense, but I can only hope I'm not making a terrible mistake.''

 *Chapter Nine*

Head resting against the back of the chair, Rafe sat with his legs bent. His scuffed boots bracketed the dresser drawer that served as Jaimie's bed. Taking care of a baby was no small responsibility, and he snored so loud, he wanted to be sure he woke up if Jaimie cried.

Just as Rafe started to snooze, a sharp rap on the door jerked him awake. His first thought was that Boyle had reneged on their deal and sent the police. Pushing to his feet, he finger-combed his hair and stepped over to the door.

"Who is it?" he growled, fully prepared to make a fast exit out the bathroom window if a cop answered.

"It's Ryan," a rough-edged voice replied.

Rafe curled his hand over the knob and flipped the lock with his thumb. He hesitated a moment. *Ryan.* His grip tightened on the brass.

For an instant when he saw the man on the porch, Rafe felt as if he were staring at his reflection. His brother wore a blue chambray shirt and well-fitting, faded jeans, the only difference between their garments the quality of the cloth.

Neither of them spoke. Rafe wasn't sure who moved first. The next thing he knew, they stood on the threshold, locked in a rib-cracking hug. As Ryan finally drew away, Rafe felt his brother's body shaking. He flipped the wall switch to turn on the bedside lamp.

Stepping farther into the room, Ryan cuffed Rafe lightly on the arm. His voice gruff and thick, he said, "You look like hell. If this is what booze does to a man, it doesn't come highly recommended."

Now that he was seeing his brother in better light, Rafe could detect vast differences between them, the most notable that Ryan outweighed him by a good twenty pounds, every ounce honed by grueling physical labor into rock-hard muscle. Broad shoulders, thighs roped with muscle, and a depth to his chest that Rafe had long since lost. It came as a bit of a shock to realize that his baby brother had matured into a man he would hesitate to take on in a fight.

"Damn, son." He pushed the door closed to prevent the cold night air from chilling the baby. "Last time I saw you, I still had to wipe your nose."

Ryan gave a derisive snort. "You never wiped my nose."

It was true; Rafe hadn't. They were only two years apart. Ryan was twenty-eight now, and it showed on his face. At the corners of his steel-blue eyes, he was beginning to get crow's-feet, and the dimple in his cheek so like Rafe's own had deepened into a long, sun-weathered crease. "You're right. Most of the time, I just wanted to thump you for being such a smart-ass."

Ryan sent his hat sailing onto the bed and then planted his hands on his hips. "You couldn't find anything better than this? It smells of mildew." He strode to the bathroom, gave the broken door a nudge, and shook his head at the dated fixtures. Turning back, he said, "At least that rattletrap heater works."

His gaze flicked to the drawer on the floor. He froze and stared at the sleeping infant. When he looked at Rafe again, his mouth hardened. "Where's the broad? Still in the hospital?"

Hearing his brother call Maggie a "broad" sent Rafe's temper rising. He tamped it down. Ryan hadn't seen Maggie for himself. Once he did, Rafe believed his brother's attitude toward her would undergo a fast change. He hoped so, anyway. If not, there would be some rough road to grade when Ryan found out Rafe planned to marry her. "Yeah, she's a pretty sick girl right now. A nasty kidney infection that went septic."

Ryan rubbed the corner of his eye. Then he sniffed and stepped soundlessly over to gaze at the baby. "You're right. He's a cute little fellow." He angled Rafe a look. "Is it the woman you're crazy about, or her kid?"

Rafe chuckled and pushed a hand through his hair. "I reckon I'd have to say it's a toss-up." He gestured at the bed. "Take a load off."

Ryan hadn't completed his snooping tour. After peeking in the empty closet, he said, "You weren't kidding about bumming the rails. No luggage."

"My Gucci was stolen."

"Who's the smart-ass?"

Rafe folded his length onto the broken-down cushion of the chair, propping his arms on his bent knees, his hands dangling. He watched as Ryan sat on the bed, assuming much the same posture. Until now, he'd never realized how very alike he and his brother were. "How'd you find me, anyway?"

"I sweet-talked a little gal at the hospital."

"I didn't expect you until morning."

"I got the Cessna ready faster than I hoped." He shrugged and rubbed his palms together. "Figured I might as well come, keep you out of trouble."

Rafe grinned. "If you're hoping to protect me from a conniving woman, you'll laugh at yourself when you meet Maggie."

Ryan frowned. "I just don't want you making any stupid mistakes, that's all. You've been through a bad time, Rafe. The folks and I are worried some little tramp's gotten her hooks into you."

"Maggie isn't a tramp."

"It's not like you to tie up with some gal you hardly

know, especially not the kind you'd meet on a boxcar. What type of people bum the rails?''

''You're looking at one.''

Ryan's mouth tightened. ''Not every bum has a reason like you did.''

''You're an expert?'' Rafe settled his gaze on Jaimie. ''Don't be so quick to judge people, Ryan. I could still be out there, you know. And if not for bumping into Maggie, I might never have sobered up enough to care.''

Ryan sighed. ''You should have called home. I would have come.''

''You were part of the memories. Can you understand that?''

''I'm trying.''

Rafe bent his head again. ''Yeah, well, that's all I can ask, I guess. I know you love me. But love isn't always enough. You've never lost anyone except our grandparents. I know you tried to understand how I felt, that you *wanted* to help me. But I had lost my whole life, my reason for breathing. There was nothing left in me. Nothing. That was impossible for you to relate to. It still is.''

''And this Maggie person can?'' He threw up his hands. ''Right.''

Rafe pushed to his feet and took a slow turn at the foot of the bed. ''It wasn't that Maggie talked sense into me. She was just—there, a battered young woman, down on her luck. I was passed out when she got on the boxcar. When I came around, there she was.'' He shrugged, the words to explain eluding him. ''She needed *me*, not the other way around. Do you understand what I'm saying? *She* needed *me*.''

Ryan propped his elbow on his knee and rubbed the bridge of his nose. Watching him, Rafe felt an ache of tension in the nape of his neck. ''I didn't mean to hurt you, Ryan, or Mom and Dad, either. I can see that I have.''

''You'll never know.''

"I was so wrapped up in my own pain, I couldn't see beyond it. That was selfish and inexcusable. And I'm very sorry. I had only one feeling left, pain. For a while, I was hurting too much to love any of you back. I know that sounds bad, but it's the truth. My feelings for you were there in me somewhere, but I couldn't tap into them or care about anything, and I just had to get out."

Ryan pushed to his feet. For an instant, they stared at each other. Then Ryan grabbed him in another bear hug. They held each other like that, their bodies tensed and quivering, emotions neither of them could express churning inside of them.

When they finally drew apart, Rafe knew everything would be all right.

The following morning, Maggie had just filled her mouth with oatmeal when Rafe Kendrick appeared in her hospital room—in duplicate. For an awful moment, she thought perhaps the nurse had misread the thermometer and she still had a high fever. Two tall cowboys in blue chambray shirts and jeans, with black Stetsons cocked at a jaunty angle on their heads?

But then she noticed that only one cowboy was carrying her baby, a half-filled bottle clutched in his hand. The other man looked slightly younger and less worn, his Stetson newer, his Western riding boots not as run-down.

"Maggie, honey, this is my brother, Ryan," the slightly older version said.

The younger man with the empty arms swept off his hat to reveal jet-black, slightly wavy hair exactly like Rafe's. Tall with a long-legged, well-muscled build, he stood with one lean hip cocked, his right leg slightly bent. The strong features of his face were sharpened by his stony expression, his gray-blue eyes intense and almost startling in contrast to his sun-bronzed skin.

"Ma'am," he said coolly, inclining his head. "Good to meet you."

"Mmmm," was the only response Maggie could utter.

She struggled to swallow and pushed at her hair, feeling horribly self-conscious. Though nearly a dead ringer for Rafe, Ryan Kendrick could have stepped straight off the set of the television series *Dallas*, one of her mom's favorite reruns. Despite the faded cowboy garb, he carried himself with the self-assurance of a wealthy rancher accustomed to barking orders. The gold watch on his wrist screamed, *Money*. Maggie doubted he was used to seeing women in hospital gowns, with no makeup and matted, tangled hair.

"I'm pleased to meet you as well," she finally managed to say around the stubborn bits of mush that felt glued to the walls of her throat.

Trying to gather her composure, Maggie glanced at Rafe. He had a predatory look that his brother lacked, as if suffering and deprivation had trimmed away all the excess, leaving only a core of hard-edged masculinity. Ryan Kendrick was bulkier, but Rafe was slightly taller and had the more dangerous air. His steely gaze was blade-sharp, the bunched tendons along his lean jaw more defined. There was also an alertness and tension radiating from him, as if he'd grown used to watching his back and fighting to survive.

Maggie's spoon rattled as it slipped into the bowl. She could feel Ryan's gaze taking measure of her. He was prepared to dislike everything he saw.

Rafe stepped around to the far side of her bed and held Jaimie up in the bend of his arm so she might admire the new snowsuit, a bit of blue pile lined with white. Despite her nervousness, she laughed.

Rafe drew the baby beyond her reach. "Breakfast first. You're thin as a fence rail."

Her oatmeal had lost appeal. "Please? Let me hold him for a minute."

Rafe narrowed an eye at her but relented, pushing the caster table aside to place the infant in her arms. Maggie immediately unzipped the snowsuit, anxious to feel her baby's sweet little body. This morning he felt delightfully warm when she curled her hands over him, a sign her temperature had dropped.

Dressed in another new sleeper, this one white with blue trim, Jaimie blinked and churned his feet, clearly not pleased to be disturbed from his nap. Then, feeling the softness of his mother's breast, he turned and nuzzled the front of her gown. Maggie gave a startled jerk when the baby found his mark.

Her cheeks went fiery hot. Even through the washworn hospital linen, Jaimie latched onto her like a little leech and sucked air when she broke the contact. Angry at having his attempt to breakfast interrupted, her son went crimson and screwed up his small face to scream. Rafe leaned over and plugged the infant's mouth with the nipple of the half-full baby bottle. He let loose with a deep, rumbling laugh at the way Jaimie's expression instantly changed from hungry outrage to complacent satisfaction.

"I think he's ready for brunch."

Maggie couldn't bring herself to look up. It was embarrassing to have two men watching while her baby went after her like that.

Seeing the crimson that flagged Maggie's cheeks, Rafe glanced over to gauge Ryan's reaction. Just as Rafe had predicted, his brother was staring down at her with a bemused expression, the stern set of his jaw and mouth softening. He glanced up and caught Rafe studying him. A hint of a grin tugged at his mouth, and Rafe knew Maggie had made another conquest. She radiated such sweetness, only a blind man could fail to see that it was genuine.

"He sure is a fine-looking boy," Ryan said smoothly, for all the world as if he hadn't entered the room loaded for bear. "I'll bet you're so proud of that baby you're about to bust."

Rafe suppressed a chuckle. Maggie's inherent wariness of men had made her one of the most difficult individuals to befriend that he had ever met, but when it came to Jaimie, the stiffness always went out of her. She cast his brother a shy smile, clearly disarmed. Damn Ryan's hide. He always had been slick with the ladies, and he hadn't lost the knack.

"Yes," she said softly. "I *am* proud of him. He's going to be handsome. I'm thankful he takes after my father and won't look like me. Perish the thought."

Ryan's forehead pleated in a frown, his raven-black brows drawing together over twinkling eyes that were focused with blatant male appreciation on Maggie's delicately sculpted features. Rafe knew exactly what his brother was thinking—that a cameo could be no more perfect. Maggie's cloud of tousled sable curls set off an ivory complexion touched with a strawberry-and-cream blush at the cheeks. And those huge, incredibly liquid brown eyes were the kind a man could drown in, their size accentuated by a dusky sweep of long, abundant lashes that clustered into silky spikes.

"Well, now, I don't know about that," Ryan replied. "Of course, if he looks too much like you when he matures out, he may be too pretty for a boy."

Maggie's cheeks bloomed again, and she glanced toward the ceiling, wrinkling her small nose to convey she'd never heard such blarney. Rafe and Ryan exchanged a long look, both of them grinning.

Ryan folded his considerable length to sit down on the visitor's chair by the bed. Propping one boot on his denim-clad thigh, he hooked his Stetson on his bent knee. A wave of homesickness washed over Rafe, for he could recall seeing his brother strike just that pose at least a thousand times in the kitchen of the main ranch house at home. Rafe could almost smell the coffee brewing.

He sniffed, and his gaze came to rest on the caster table angled across Maggie's bed. A cup of hot coffee sat on her pink plastic breakfast tray.

"So are you anxious to see the ranch, Maggie?" Ryan asked, all hint of animosity gone from his voice.

"I haven't told her much about the ranch yet," Rafe interjected.

Ryan tapped the toe of his boot on the tile. "You *haven't?*" He grinned at Maggie. "You're going to love it. Forty thousand acres of ranch and timberland that backs up to thousands more of BLM lease land. Pristine mountain wilderness. It's the perfect place for a boy. Rafe and I grew up there and never had a dull moment. In spring and summer, you can take off on horseback for days. Camp and fish at the mountain lakes. Hike until you drop. Winter sports are limitless. Do you enjoy downhill or cross-country skiing?"

"Horseback?" Maggie echoed, evidently hearing little else of what Ryan had said. "Oh, I don't think I want Jaimie around horses. He might get hurt."

Ryan's gaze sharpened. "Well, of course he'll be around horses." He glanced at Rafe. "We'll have him riding like a pro by the time he turns three."

Maggie cuddled her baby closer to her breast, looking dismayed.

Ryan quickly backtracked. "Only with your permission, of course. Once you're there and meet the horses, you'll relax about it. We've got some mares and geldings so gentle you can lay a baby at their feet. Right, Rafe?"

Maggie's face blanched.

"Of course, we wouldn't actually lay a baby—" Ryan broke off and threw Rafe a look that said, *Help me out here, brother.*

Forgetting her bruises, Rafe settled a comforting hand on Maggie's shoulder. He was about to assure her that she would always have the final word regarding her baby, but she winced under the light pressure of his grip, and he forgot what he meant to say. Jerking his hand away, he said, "I'm sorry, honey. I didn't mean to hurt you."

"I'm fine."

"Is something wrong with her shoulder?" Ryan asked.

"She's pretty bruised up."

"From what?" As he posed the question, Ryan focused a sharp gaze on Maggie, obviously looking her over closely from the neck down for the first time. She self-consciously tugged at the rounded neckline of the overlarge hospital gown, but not in time to keep Ryan from spotting the discolored skin. "Jesus. What happened?" His gaze darted to her exposed arms, which still sported the unmistakable marks of a man's brutal grip. A muscle along Ryan's jaw bunched, and his eyes took on a dangerous glint. He shot Rafe a querying glance.

"It's nothing," Maggie said faintly.

Ryan's neck turned a ruddy red, and the tattoo of his boot on the floor picked up speed. Rafe decided it was time to get Ryan out of there before he began riddling Maggie with questions he had no right to ask.

Checking the wall clock, he said, "I've got some business to take care of in town. While you're finishing breakfast, I'll go do that. Then we'll come back."

Maggie cuddled the baby closer. "Could I keep Jaimie with me?"

"It's probably not a good idea. You're supposed to be resting."

"I'm rested."

Rafe was beginning to realize he had the spine of a jellyfish where she was concerned. Maybe that was just as well. He had a feeling Maggie had heard the word "no" far too often. On this issue, though, he had to stand firm. According to Dr. Hammish, she was making great headway against the infection that still coursed through her, but she was a long way from well. As dearly as she loved that baby, keeping him in the room would tire her.

"I don't think so, honey." Taking the coward's way

out, Rafe quickly added, "The nurses have been really good about ignoring him. But if we take too much advantage, they may start enforcing the rules. Then I couldn't bring Jaimie to see you at all."

Her face fell, but even as her lips drew into a pout that made him yearn to kiss that sweet, vulnerable mouth, she set the bottle on the table, burped Jaimie, and then began putting the snowsuit back on him. "You're right, of course. I forgot about that. Rules are rules."

Rules. They were something she understood all too well, evidently. Rafe's throat tightened as he watched her dress the baby. He wished with all his heart that he could snatch her up from that bed and take her to the ranch where the only rules in force were ones that had been made to be broken. God, how he wanted to see her smile and make her eyes shine with happiness. He could blow every penny he had on her and never regret the loss.

As Rafe took the baby, Ryan pushed to his feet and settled his Stetson on his dark head. "It's been great meeting you, Maggie. Now I know why Rafe's so crazy about you."

Another painful blush flagged her cheeks. She started to extend her hand to Ryan, but the IV hampered her. He quickly leaned forward to lessen the distance and enfolded her slender fingers in a hard palm.

"I know you mentioned last night that she'd been battered. But I thought it was a figure of speech! Who the hell did that to her?"

Ryan's voice fairly vibrated with rage as he and Rafe walked along the east-wing hallway toward the hospital lobby.

"Her stepfather, Lonnie Boyle, a slimy little creep. I met him yesterday."

"Did you stomp the holy hell out of him?"

"No."

"Where is he?"

Rafe started to reply but bit back the answer. "Why?"

Ryan shot him a disgusted look. "He needs his ass kicked, that's why."

"And you've elected yourself to do the honors? Forget it. There's more to the situation than you understand."

"Like what?"

Rafe kept the query on hold as they crossed the crowded lobby. When they gained the front exit and stepped out the automatic doors into the freezing morning air, he tucked the blanket over Jaimie's face. "It's a long story, Rye."

"I've got nothing better to do than listen."

"I won't have you going off half-cocked. Maggie's my problem. Understand? In case that isn't clear enough for you, that translates into 'Butt out.' Don't embarrass her by asking a bunch of questions, and don't get it into your head that she needs you to be her champion. She's already got one."

"You? The brother I knew would have beaten a man to within an inch of his life for doing that to a woman. You've either lost your guts, Rafe, or you've pickled your brains with so much booze that your sense of justice went down the john. Where I come from, no man gets away with shit like that."

Rafe sighed. "We come from the same place. Remember? And how dare you judge me without knowing all the facts? An hour ago, you wanted me to dump Jaimie on the hospital steps and go home, leaving Maggie to fend for herself. Now you're all hot to go pick a fight on her behalf?"

"So? I changed my mind."

As they wove their way through the cars in the parking lot, Rafe began filling Ryan in on Maggie's past. When they reached the rented Toyota, Ryan rested his folded arms on the roof to gaze across the expanse of shiny red paint. "He arranged to adopt out her kid behind her back?"

"And then beat the hell out of her to make her sign the papers. The adoption attorney notarized them, which tells me he's a slimeball, too. He probably wouldn't hesitate to lie about her on the stand." Rafe inclined his head at the baby in his arms. "Would you unlock the damned doors? It's cold."

Ryan swore under his breath and shoved the key in the lock. An instant later, Rafe heard the latch mechanism pop inside the passenger door. He wrenched on the handle, jerked the door open, and slid onto the low-slung seat, cracking his knee on the dash.

"Son of a bitch!" He shifted Jaimie into one arm to rub the spot. "Did you have to rent a rollerskate? The leg room in here is for midgets." He sniffed and jerked open the ashtray to see cigarette butts. "It figures."

"This isn't Los Angeles. I took what I could get. And don't go lipping off at me. I don't appreciate it." Ryan pulled out the ashtray and rolled down the window to dump the butts on the asphalt. "There. Is that better? I don't remember you being such a priss butt."

"Lip off at you? You say I've lost my guts, and I'm the one lipping off."

Ryan hit the steering wheel with base of his palm. "I'm sorry. All right? How was I to know the son of a bitch had you by the balls?"

"Well, at least you acknowledge I've got some. Do you think it was easy, holding onto my temper? I wanted to kill the little asshole. You should see her shins. He kicked her with his boots. And he wears this big, honking diamond. Probably fake. I know damned well it was the prongs that cut her up. He's a vicious, cocky bastard who needs his teeth knocked down his throat."

Ryan tapped his fingers on the wheel. "We have to stop cussing."

Where that had come from, Rafe didn't know. He cast his brother a befuddled glance. "We can't talk like this around Maggie,'' Ryan elaborated. ''And what about the baby? You want him to be expelled from kindergarten for swearing? I don't want a pissed-off sister-in-law. Females don't fight fair.''

''Can I take that to mean you're no longer campaigning to make me come to my senses?''

Ryan rubbed beside his nose. ''She's not what I expected. So, yeah, you can take it to mean that.''

Rafe studied Jaimie. ''They say babies start learning their language skills in the womb.''

''You're shittin' me.'' Ryan made a choking sound. ''Kidding me, I mean.'' Silence. ''It's going to be a real bitch to stop cussing again. You know it? Saying 'dang' and 'gosh' just doesn't come naturally.''

''Maybe if we start now, we'll have it mastered before he starts talking.''

Ryan glanced in the rearview mirror to watch a slender brunette cross the lot. He gave a low whistle. When he glanced back at Rafe, his eyes were twinkling. In a low-pitched voice, he said, ''Maggie's a sweetheart, Rafe. I'm sorry I acted like such a jerk.''

Rafe smiled. ''I wish I'd had a camcorder in there.''

''For what?''

''To catch the expression on your face. You went from tiger to pussycat in three seconds, flat. My brother, the hard-ass.''

''It took more than three seconds—four, at least.'' Ryan laughed and shook his head. ''She doesn't have a poker face, that's for sure. I haven't seen anyone blush like that in a coon's age. Like we've never seen a baby go after its mama before? Give her a couple of years on the ranch, and she'll toughen up.''

''I hope not,'' Rafe replied. ''I like her just the way she is.''

''Yeah, I can tell.'' Ryan slanted his brother a measuring look. ''How much did it take to buy the pus pocket off? His last name fits, doesn't it? *Boil*.''

Rafe laughed. ''Yeah, and right now, I feel like lancing him. Offering him money didn't set well, I can tell you, and if it's all the same to you, I'd rather not discuss how much. It went against my grain. But the end justifies the means. I think she's had enough heartache.''

"How's she feel about marrying you?''

"About as enthusiastic as she'd be over a root canal.''

Ryan mulled that over. "Have you thought about giving her a little play in the rope? It's a bad way to start a marriage. You can probably keep Boyle off her back without tying the knot.''

Rafe knew his brother had a point. "I hear what you're saying. But all my instincts tell me I'm doing the right thing.''

"For who?'' Ryan asked softly. "Maggie, or you?''

"Not fair. She needs someone to watch out for her. You can't deny that.''

"No. And I'm not saying that. I'm just trying to point out that it can backfire when you deliberately toss a rope to foreleg a filly. It's a damned harsh way to take her down.''

"Maggie isn't a filly, and I'm not forelegging her. I'm doing what's best for her. The bastard will never dare mess with her again once she's a Kendrick.''

"That's true. Your name alone will protect her. Just make sure you don't fall into the trap of becoming a bastard yourself.'' He held up a staying hand when Rafe cut him a glittering glance. "I'm not saying you shouldn't marry her. No quarrels. Honestly. I'm just playing devil's advocate and trying to remind you she has feelings. If you make the mistake of ignoring them, you may regret it.''

Frustrated by the low ceiling of the car, Rafe swept his hat off. "You going to drive this rattletrap or sit here until we freeze to death?''

Ryan keyed the ignition. "Where to?''

"The main drag. I've got some unfinished business downtown.''

*　　*　　*

Rafe cranked up the heater of the rental car, his gaze scanning the street ahead. "There it is," he told Ryan. "Pull over. I'll only be a few minutes."

Ryan parked the red Toyota at one of the many unoccupied meters. After shoving the gearshift into park and cutting the engine, he looked surprised when Rafe handed him the baby. "If he cries, stick your knuckle in his mouth. It keeps him happy for a few minutes."

"Oh, thanks," Ryan said. "Now I get to play human pacifier."

"Just take care of him. All right? This won't take long. If the car starts to get cold, start the engine and run the heater."

Rafe climbed out and slammed the door. As he turned to face the pawnshop, his gaze came to rest on the diamond-studded gold band that lay on red velvet in the window. The overhead bell clanged to herald his arrival as he entered the shop. The place smelled of dust and hocked promises. Rafe breathed in the scent as he paced off the distance to the counter. The proprietor, a thin, balding man with strands of gray hair carefully arranged over his shiny scalp, glanced up from a notepad on which he was scribbling figures.

"May I help you?"

Rafe fished in his pants pocket for his receipt. "Yeah, I hocked a ring in here a couple of days ago. I want to pick it up."

The shopkeeper had the good grace to blush. "I didn't recognize you." He gestured vaguely at his jaw. "Quite a change without the hair and whiskers." He glanced toward the display window. "I never expected you back."

"As I understood it, you weren't supposed to sell the ring for thirty days. You're a little ahead of yourself, putting it in the window already."

The man rubbed his hands on the front of his green shirt. "Yes, well." He laughed nervously. "Like I said, I really didn't think you'd be back."

Rafe stabbed him with a hard look. "Surprise, surprise."

The owner scurried over to the window display to collect the ring. "This is a fine piece of jewelry." He held the diamonds up to the sunlight coming through the glass. "I'm sorry to see it redeemed. It's not often I get something this nice."

Rafe pulled out the wad of money Ryan had given him. "Twenty percent on top." He peeled off seven one-hundred dollar bills, then a like number of twenties, laying them to one side. "Good doing business with you."

With reluctance, the shopkeeper set the ring on the counter. Rafe picked it up reverently. He nearly slipped it onto the ring finger of his left hand, but at the last second, he clasped it in his fist instead. Tossing the crumpled pink receipt on the counter, he turned and left the shop without saying another word.

Once outside in the crisp morning air, Rafe stood on the sidewalk, absorbing the clean brightness of the sunlight. Its golden color reminded him of Susan's hair. Such sweet, precious memories. A wealth of them were buried in the dark folds of his mind. But they were only memories, a part of his past.

Rafe opened his clenched fist to stare at the ring that lay on his palm. *Susan.* He smiled again, for only in leaving him had she ever brought him sadness. What a beautiful, rare individual she had been. But God had called her home, and the time to turn loose and let her go was long since past.

Rafe stepped to the curb. Glancing up and down the gutter, he spied a grate. He moved toward it, feeling curiously free for the first time in over two years. When he stood over the hole, he took one last look at the ring that had been his only remaining link with her for so long. *Promise me, Rafe. Promise me you'll find someone else to love.*

Tears gathered in his eyes as he extended his hand

over the grate and opened his palm. "I think I've found her, Susan," he whispered softly. "I guess you probably know that. You'd approve of her. It makes me glad to know that."

With a flick of his wrist, Rafe dropped the wedding band. It hit the metal grate with a musical tinkling sound, and for a fanciful moment, he could almost believe it was the light, lilting sound of Susan's laughter. As the wedding ring tumbled between the grimy slats of the grate, the diamonds winked up at him, as if in final goodbye. And then the brightness was gone.

Rafe stood there for a long moment, gazing down into that endless darkness. He'd been trapped in it for so long. It was time to put it forever behind him. "Wish me luck, sweetheart," he whispered. "I'm going to need it."

When Rafe climbed back into the car, Ryan gave him a long, searching look. "Was that what I think it was?"

The tightness left Rafe's throat and he smiled. "*From the river to the sea,*" he said softly. "She used to throw flower petals into a stream and say that. It seemed like a nice way to say goodbye."

For a long moment, Ryan stared intently out the windshield. When he glanced at Rafe again, there was a new understanding in his eyes. "Last night you apologized for hurting me. Now it's my turn. I'm sorry I wasn't there for you the way I should have been." He took off his hat, lay it on the console, and rubbed a hand over his hair. "You said something else last night. It's been eating at me ever since. That I've never lost anyone I love. You're dead wrong about that. I have lost someone, and now I know how you felt."

Rafe's heart caught, his first thought being that one of his parents had died and Ryan had waited until now to tell him. "Dear God, who?"

"My brother."

Seeing the look in Ryan's eyes, Rafe finally understood just how much pain he had inflicted on his family. "Ryan, I'm—"

"Don't say it. You've apologized enough. I'm just glad to have you back." He carefully shifted Jaimie in his arms and handed the baby to his brother. Then he retrieved his hat and settled it on his head. "The extra baggage you're bringing along is kind of nice, too."

He started the car and pulled back out onto the street. At the stoplight, he glanced over. "Where to now? Anyplace special?"

Rafe released a cleansing sigh. "Yeah, as a matter of fact. How long's it been since you did something totally crazy?"

Waiting for the traffic light to change, Ryan kept his gaze fixed straight ahead. "I don't know. A while, I guess. Why?"

"I need you to help me do something."

"My calendar's clear. What is it?"

Rafe swallowed. "Something illegal. If anything goes wrong, we could both go to prison."

Ryan winced and jerked his gaze to Rafe's face. "Oh, Jesus. You're going to kill Boyle, aren't you?" He shook his head. "No way. I'll help you beat the hell out of him, but murder isn't my bag."

"I'm not going to murder anyone. Get real."

"What, then?"

"I want to snatch Maggie's sister."

A horn honked behind them. Ryan swore, stepping on the gas as he let out the clutch. The car leapfrogged through the intersection. "Have you lost your mind? That's kidnapping. It's a felony. If we get caught, we'll both be gray and impotent by the time we get out of the joint."

"Yeah, I know." Rafe passed a hand over his face. "But the way I plan to do it, it's really not that chancy. I called Mark yesterday to discuss the legalities of it. He—"

"Oh, God. You're actually serious. You've been on the phone with a lawyer?"

"Of course I'm serious. If I cover all the bases, Mark thinks I can do it without getting my tit in a wringer. It won't be precisely legal, but—"

"Which means it's technically kidnapping?"

"Technically, yes. But I've got to do it, Rye. I'm on pretty solid ground with the adoption thing if Boyle keeps his word and reimburses the adoptive parents. And I'm ninety-five percent sure Heidi will be fine for a while, left where she is. If I get a team of lawyers to work on it right away, chances are, she'll be out of the situation before Boyle does anything. But what if things go sour? I've got this bad feeling about that bastard. There's this look in his eyes. You know? Heidi's only ten years old. Just a baby. How can I take the chance that something might happen to her?"

"Easy. You pray for the wisdom to accept what you can't change."

"I gave Maggie my word I'd keep her safe, and by God, I will."

Ryan shoved the brim of his hat back. "Holy hell and high water! You can't do this. The kid'll be okay until you can get her out of there legally."

"This will be legal—sort of." Rafe turned in the seat to look at his brother. "Maggie's mom isn't real bright, and—"

"Wonderful. Now you're telling me you're about to dilute our gene pool? Not that you're displaying a genius I.Q yourself at the moment."

"Would you shut up and listen? Her mom's brain-damaged from a heart attack. She wasn't born that way. Maggie says she's childlike, but as far as Mark could find out, she hasn't been claimed legally incompetent. Mark drew me up a paper and faxed it to the hospital. It basically says Maggie's mom is authorizing me to transport the kid over the state line. If I can get Boyle out of the house long enough to pay her a visit, I think

I can con her into signing it before a notary public.''
Rafe shrugged. ''Afterward, I take the mother home,
snatch the kid when she comes in from school, and
we're out of there.'' Rafe waited a beat. ''Well, what
do you think?''

''I think you're out of your frigging mind. What reason will you give the mother for taking her kid out of
the state?''

Rafe smiled. ''Disneyland.''

''What?''

''I'll say Maggie and I are going to Disneyland for
our honeymoon, and that we want to take her sister.
Brilliant, right? That way, Helen won't be upset about
her kid disappearing, and it's technically legal for me to
take her out of Idaho. It's also something a not-very-
bright lady will go for. Disneyland, Mickey Mouse, and
all that? She'll be tickled for her kid to get a chance to
go.''

''Rafe, this is nuts. There are too many variables.
Boyle's no idiot. He'll come home, find out what you've
done, and go bananas. He'll call the cops.''

''Yeah, maybe. But possession is nine-tenths of the
law. We'll have the kid, and the paper signed by her
mother. Mark says Heidi is probably old enough to
speak for herself in front of a judge. Dr. Hammish is
willing to testify that Maggie's been savagely beaten.
Mark thinks we can plead a strong enough case to cast
suspicion on the home environment and get temporary
custody.''

''And if you can't?''

Rafe puffed air into his cheeks. ''Well, in that case,
we could both go to jail. I'd testify that you just flew
the plane, though, and didn't know what I was doing.''

''Ignorance of the law is a lousy defense,'' Ryan
pointed out.

''Maggie can't leave the hospital for two more days,''
Rafe retorted. ''We'll just be twiddling our thumbs. Why
not put the time to better use? Come on, Ryan. Where's

your sense of adventure? We've always made a good team. Remember all the shenanigans we used to pull? How often did we get caught?''

''Jesus Christ.'' Ryan pulled the car over to the curb, shoved the shift into neutral, and fixed Rafe with an incredulous look. ''This isn't exactly on a par with stealing a road sign. We're not kids anymore. Do you realize what you're asking?''

''Yeah. I'm asking you to put your neck on the chopping block. I think we can pull it off, Ryan. It'll be risky, but I think we can do it. My pilot's license is expired. I need you to fly the Cessna and watch Jaimie while I do the dirty work. Once we get Heidi, you can drop me off here, then fly her to the ranch. Becca's great with kids. She can watch Heidi while you fly back here to pick me and Maggie up. What do you say?''

''You're discussing kidnapping, and in the same breath, you're worried about flying without your license?'' Ryan stared out the windshield, his jaw muscle ticking as he thought it over. Then he released a weary sigh and met his brother's gaze. ''Some things never change. Every time I'm around you, I wind up doing something nuts.''

Chapter Ten

By the time Ryan Kendrick landed the Cessna 340 on the Rocking K airstrip two days later, Maggie was feeling like a pampered poodle with an overanxious owner. Since her release from the hospital that morning, Rafe had allowed her to do nothing for herself, not even walk. Dr. Hammish had said that for the next week, Maggie was not to be on her feet except to go to the bathroom. Determined to follow those orders, Rafe had carried her from the wheelchair to the car, and then from the car to the airplane, where he had deposited her on the rear passenger seats, which he'd already folded down to make a bed. Her first time to fly, and what did she see? The cabin ceiling.

Over the course of the three-hour flight, he'd drawn the doctor's instructions from his pocket several times. Time for fluid intake? He'd tapped an insulated water jug and filled a plastic sixteen-ounce glass to the brim, insisting she drink it. He'd even held the glass, as if she were incapable. Time for medication? Pills were shoved under her nose and she was made to drink more water. Only a few minutes later, it had been time for her to have fluid again. Maggie had had the feeling he might pinch her nose if she refused to swallow.

The Cessna had no toilet.

By the time the plane's wheels went *sprrt-sprrt* on the tarmac in Oregon, every jolt of the small craft was an agony for her. After Ryan exited the plane by the side door, she pushed up on her elbow to gaze out the oval passenger window near her head, hoping to see a house. Instead, the bright afternoon sunlight glanced off snow-swept fields and mountains for as far as she could see. She pushed up a bit higher to peek out the adjacent window, looking for buildings. *Nothing*. Just wilderness.

Signing off the radio, Rafe turned and saw her sitting halfway erect. He unfastened his seat belt and swung from the copilot's seat into the center aisle.

"Just rest easy, honey. Ryan has to start the four-runner and get it warm, so it'll be a few minutes before we get out." He bent over a first-row seat to check on the sleeping baby and then moved aft to hunker in front of her. Maggie half-expected him to whip a glass of water from behind his back. Instead he pressed a hand to her forehead. "How you feeling? Tired, I'll bet."

Maggie was too tense to be tired. She'd never been across the Idaho state line, and she'd never stepped foot on an airplane either. Now she was about to marry a man whose family owned two, this Cessna, which had a pressurized cabin for comfortable long-distance travel, and a small single-engine called an Eagle, which Rafe had explained was used for ranch work.

"What?" he asked softly.

Maggie shook her head. How could she explain her feelings when they were in such a tangle? This man, who'd poured sixty-four ounces of water into her in the last three hours and hadn't stopped to think she might need to use the rest room, had taken control of her life.

A part of Maggie knew Rafe meant her no harm. He treated her as if she were made of fragile glass, his so-licitousness almost suffocating. How could she fear someone who seemed so frantically concerned about her well-being?

Yet on a level where reason held no sway, Maggie did fear him. She'd been in a situation where a man had complete control of her world, and she'd learned from experience just how vulnerable that made her.

"Can you sit up, honey?"

Maggie did as he asked, relieved to find that she felt much stronger now than she had in days. He reached for her parka.

"I can do it," she protested as he began fishing her arm down a sleeve. When that didn't slow him down, she added, "I hate being so much trouble."

He tugged the jacket up onto her shoulder, then reached behind her to pull it around. "You're no trouble," he said huskily. He hesitated in his task to cup her chin in his big hand and make her look at him. "You'll never know how sincerely I mean that."

It seemed to Maggie that his dark face came closer, and for a moment, she felt sure he was about to kiss her. Her heart flip-flopped, sending a flutter into her throat. Her gaze went to his mouth. In the dimness of the plane, his firm lips had a satiny sheen. For a fleeting instant, she wondered what it might be like to kiss a man whose breath didn't reek of stale cigarettes and beer.

Shocked at herself, Maggie shoved the thought away. A mischievous glint danced in Rafe's eyes, as if he knew exactly what she was thinking. Letting the coat puddle behind her, he tightened his hold on her chin and curled his other hand over her nape, his hard fingers sifting through the strands of her hair to rest with intimate possessiveness on her skin. Shivers ribboned down her spine as he traced circles with his fingertips.

His features blurred as he pressed closer. Maggie planted a hand on his chest, intending to hold him away. The instant her palm connected with the front of his shirt, that hope fled. He felt as heavy and immovable as a wall of granite. Her breath snagged in her throat as his lips settled over hers. *Velvet heat.*

He tipped his head to gain better control of the kiss, parting his lips and touching the tip of his tongue lightly to hers. Maggie jerked. His arm tensed, the wide palm on her nape becoming a relentless but gentle restraint that held her fast. He tasted her as he might a sweet he meant to savor, with light brushes of his tongue that teased her sensitive flesh like the flutter of a butterfly wing. His breath mingled with hers, hot and laced with the rich taste of coffee and mint.

Maggie felt as if her bones were dissolving. The stutter of her pulse at the base of her throat became a pounding that seemed to echo in her temples. He wouldn't allow her to pull away, and she couldn't help but be frightened by the sheer power she felt radiating from his big body. She'd found herself on the receiving end of a man's greater strength too many times to easily discount the dangers. But at the same time, she was fascinated. Every other kiss she'd ever experienced had been a slobbery grinding of teeth that had hurt her lips and made her feel as if she were going to strangle on her own bile. By contrast, Rafe's mouth coaxed hers for a response she didn't know how to give.

When he drew back, there was a question in his eyes.

"I—" Maggie gulped and groped for the coat sleeve behind her. "I'm not a very good kisser, I'm afraid."

As she fumbled with the jacket, he continued to caress her neck, his touch seeming to become more electrical with every pass of his fingertips. Her stomach felt as if she had swallowed a giant-sized carton of live goldfish.

"Maggie?" he whispered.

She froze, her gaze drawn to his by the silky demand in his tone. He smiled slightly and rubbed his thumb over her mouth. "What?" she squeaked.

He leaned forward to graze his lips along her temple, his breath stirring the curls there as he whispered, "You kiss like an angel."

He drew back and released her. As he reached around her to finish helping her into the jacket, he smiled. "Is there anything I can do to make you feel a little less nervous? Correct me if I'm wrong, but I get the feeling you're a little afraid of me. There's no reason to be."

No reason? He'd made clear his intention to make this

a real marriage. She found the prospect of physical intimacy terrifying. Not that she would ever admit it. Fear was yet another weakness that a man could use against you.

Trying to keep her expression carefully blank, she bent her head to fumble with the zipper. "I'm not afraid of you. That's silly." *It truly is silly*, a small voice inside her mind chided. *Any fool can see he doesn't mean to hurt you.* Maggie guessed she was like those people who were afraid of heights. Even standing behind a sturdy guardrail, they couldn't breathe when they looked down. Sometimes a person's fears defied all reason. "Why would I be afraid?"

He brushed her fingers aside. "Is that why your hands are shaking? Because you trust me so much?"

Maggie looked down and saw that he was right; she was shaking. "I'm just—cold."

He zipped the jacket and rocked back on his heels, his well-muscled arms resting loosely on his knees. His expression was bemused as he regarded her. "I'll never hurt you. I want you to know that. And when the time comes that we make love, you'll *want* to do it. I promise you that."

Maggie barely managed to suppress a shudder. "Th-that would be nice."

"Better than nice," he assured her. "*Much* better than nice."

Maggie had her doubts. She would be greatly relieved if sexual intimacy with him turned out to be tolerable. *Nice* was a bit much to hope for.

He stood and drew her to her feet. Just then, Ryan opened the door of the plane. "The four-runner's heated up."

Rafe gathered Jaimie from the seat and handed him down to his brother, who promptly ran toward the waiting Ford to get the baby in out of the cold. Grabbing a hand strap suspended from the ceiling, Rafe swung from the plane, bypassing the drop-down steps. He caught his balance and turned, motioning her to the doorway. When she came within reach, he swept her into his arms.

As he carried her toward the expensive sport-utility vehicle parked a few feet away, she spied a small hangar in front of the plane that she'd been unable to see from the rear windows. "Does that building have a rest room?" she asked, hating herself for blushing.

"It sure does."

He broke stride and veered toward the hangar. It lay quite a distance away, and the snow at the edge of the plowed runway was over a foot deep.

"I can walk," she suggested. "I'm feeling much stronger today."

"It's farther than it looks," was his only reply.

Maggie stifled a sigh.

At the end of the tarmac, he jostled her in his arms to get a better hold and then struck off through the drifts. Maggie clutched his shirt, her body tense. She was only a few feet off the ground, but it seemed like much more. "It looks icy and slick in spots," she observed, thinking how easily he might slip.

"It is."

Maggie kept expecting him to get breathless. It was hard going, and he was lugging a lot of extra weight. But he trudged on without getting winded. Once at the hangar, he bent slightly to open a door, then carried her inside a small office furnished with only a desk, a chair, and a metal file cabinet. He set her on her feet in front of another door.

"Thank you."

He leaned around her to twist the knob and flip on the bathroom light. "You're very welcome. If you need any help, just holler."

Not in this lifetime.

Her legs felt weak, undoubtedly from lying in bed so long. She stepped inside, closed the door, and was about to turn the latch when he said, "Don't lock it, all right?

Just in case, I don't want to have to break down the door again.''

She quickly finished her business. When she emerged from the bathroom, she found him gazing at a picture on the wall.

"My son, Keefer," he said. "It was taken the summer before."

Before. Maggie moved closer, wondering what it must be like to have your life divided into two parts, before and after. The child perched on Rafe's bare shoulders in the snapshot looked about two, with chubby cherub cheeks and wavy dark brown hair. He bore a striking resemblance to his father.

The camera had caught Rafe laughing. He had been much younger then, if not in years, at least at heart, his eyes dancing with merriment. He'd also been huskier of build, his bronze upper body a sculpture of male strength, with bulging biceps, a powerfully padded chest, and an abdomen striated with rock-hard muscle. He'd been wearing jeans that skimmed his lean hips and long legs.

Her gaze returned to the child, whose dimpled fingers were clenched in his father's wind-tossed black hair. She almost said she knew how seeing the picture must hurt, but if she were to lose Jaimie, she wouldn't want people to pretend they understood how she felt. She didn't understand, she could only imagine, and she prayed to God it remained that way.

"Ready?"

Maggie glanced up. Rafe was smiling, but the shadows in his eyes were difficult to miss. "I'm so sorry." She hesitated and then heard herself saying exactly what she'd decided not to. "I know how it must hurt."

"That's the first picture I've seen since I left," he said softly. "It kind of blindsided me is all."

He swept her up into his arms. Maggie hugged his sturdy neck, once again feeling as if she were dangling from a skyscraper ledge. The sadness had left his eyes. "Worried I'll turn loose of you?"

"I'm hoping not," she replied.

A slow grin spread over his firm mouth. "Count on it, Maggie girl."

As he carried her to the waiting four-runner, Maggie wondered if he'd meant that as a reassurance or a threat.

En route to the house, Maggie hugged her sleeping baby close and peered out the windows of the four-runner for some sign of buildings. All she saw were distant mountains, pine and fir trees, open fields, and Herefords, all of which seemed to be running loose. It was beautiful landscape—like some of the winter scenes she'd seen on postcards. But admiring pictures and being smack-dab in the middle of the reality were two different things. After living in town all her life, she felt displaced here. And cut off from the world.

Even the luxurious interior of the Expedition smelled alien to her, the familiar scents of new-car leather and molded plastic blended with foreign odors. Grass of some kind, maybe? And horses? Glancing over her shoulder, Maggie saw that the back storage area of the Ford was strewn with pieces of rope, strange-looking leather straps, chunky metal gadgets, and bits of hay.

Rafe, who sat beside her in the back, finally noticed her craning her neck to see out his window and flashed her a questioning look.

Maggie glanced up at him. "Where's the house?"

"It's still quite a ways," Ryan said as he veered left to miss a muddy pothole in the gravel road. "Forty thousand acres is a mighty big spread. The main house is about seven more miles from here."

The main house? Ryan made it sound as if they had dozens. "Are all seven miles part of your ranch?"

Just as Maggie asked that, the Expedition hit a bump that snapped her teeth together and bounced her sideways on the plush leather seat. She tightened her hold on Jaimie. Rafe glanced down and curled a strong arm around her shoulders. "I think you need a little extra ballast." He dipped his head to look out his window. "In answer to your question, yes, we'll be on Rocking K land clear in to the main house. You see out through there?"

Maggie followed his gaze. All she saw was brutal wilderness. "Yes."

"Look as far into the distance as you can," he instructed. When she fixed her gaze on the most distant point of the horizon she could find, he said, "That's all either part of the Rocking K or land on a renewable ninety-nine-year lease. Our dad started the operation thirty-five years ago."

Incredulous, Maggie continued to stare at the horizon. "Wow. Why do I have the feeling you can't walk to the grocery store from here?"

"You're right. The closest store would be quite a trek."

Maggie peered out her window. "Is that all the Rocking K as well?"

"Yes. How's it going to feel to know you own that much dirt?"

The question was a reminder of their forthcoming marriage, and Maggie tightened her arms around Jaimie, her reason for being there. She wanted *her* world back—the one with sidewalks and corner markets and neighbors she'd known all her life. Minus Lonnie, of course. From the very beginning, he had messed up her life. Now he had obliterated it.

Ryan chuckled. "Now that's a unique way of putting it. Owning a lot of dirt!" He glanced in the mirror. "All she can see right now is snow. But in the summer, we've got dirt, Maggie. Lots of it."

Her joy knew no bounds.

Rafe drew her more snugly against him. "Honey, you're going to love the ranch. Don't look so worried."

"It's just that I'm a town person, I guess. Maybe I'll get used to it."

"We've got a large town only twenty minutes away."

"Once you get to the highway," Ryan pointed out, as if that were another highlight. "It's the ultimate in privacy out here. No prying eyes. No pesky neighbors. You can parade naked in the yard if you want."

"Don't even think about it," Rafe warned with a possessive growl in his voice. "With all the hired hands on the place, it isn't quite that private."

Maggie had no intention of parting with her clothing, period. Even as the thought rooted in her mind, she quickly qualified it. She'd part with her clothes quickly enough when Rafe decided she should.

"You keep saying the 'main' house. Is there more than one?"

"You could say that." Ryan braked to ease the vehicle over a rut. "There's my place, about a mile from Rafe's. And after the folks signed the ranch over to us, they built a cottage on the opposite side of the lake. Then there's the housing for our hired hands and families. Plus all the line shacks."

A few minutes later, the Expedition rounded a curve, and the wilderness gave way to white fencing that seemed to stretch forever. She spotted white outbuildings.

"There's the house," Rafe whispered.

She focused on the sprawling brick home that sat on a gentle, snow-covered knoll in the distance. As Ryan drove closer, she saw that the huge structure was a two-story with white trim and ivy trailing up the five exterior chimneys. The expansive, multi-pitched roof was covered with burnt red tiles.

That wasn't a house; it was a *mansion*.

"So, what do you think?"

She threw Rafe an incredulous look. What did she think? She remembered her cowboy bum in the ragged, filthy clothing, with his shoulder-length hair going every which way under the droopy brim of his dusty Stetson. Even later when he'd told her he was rich, she hadn't imagined *this*. How would she ever fit in here?

"I, um . . . it's beautiful," Maggie said hollowly.

"Honey, what's wrong?" He peered through the windshield at the house, as if he expected to see that the massive roof had caved in or something. When he looked back at her, he said, "If you hate it, I'll build you another one. We don't have to live there. This spring we'll go riding and look for a building site."

On a *horse*? "No, it isn't that. It's a—beautiful house. It's just—" Maggie broke off and stared at it some more. She'd get lost in there. "I'm not used to houses that are so—*big!*"

"It *is* big," Ryan agreed. "But you guys won't live in all of it. The basement floor is a huge industrial-scale kitchen to feed the crews during roundups, with a big dining area and another big room for dances and parties. The main floor is only—what, Rafe?—seven thousand square feet?"

"Thereabout," Rafe replied. "Eight, tops. And much of that is guest rooms."

Out the right back window, Maggie saw a gorgeous red horse on the opposite side of the fence. It pranced along with the car, its tail uplifted and its mane flying. Rafe spotted it at the same instant. "What's that son of a bitch still doing here? I told you to sell him or shoot him."

"He's a world-class stud. After you left, what was the point?"

Maggie had never heard Rafe's voice so cold. She glanced at the horse again and remembered the story he'd told her about the car wreck. She knew then that this was the stallion that had been kicking up a fuss in the trailer that night during the hailstorm. Maggie couldn't really blame Rafe for not being able to stand the sight of it.

His expression was still set in grim lines when he

carried Maggie to the house. Ryan followed, carrying Jaimie. They entered into what Ryan called the mudroom but was actually a huge atrium laced with stone walkways and beds of greenery. At the center was a bench-encircled fish pond with a waterfall.

For a long moment, Rafe stood just inside the door. Maggie suspected he had mixed emotions about this homecoming and was remembering his family.

After a moment, he smiled down at her. "You're right. It's big."

Maggie relaxed slightly, glad that the moment had passed. When she sensed his sadness, she wanted to comfort him. Not smart, under the circumstances. She would be inviting trouble. She'd seen the possessive gleam in Rafe Kendrick's eyes and knew it wouldn't take much to make him amorous.

He struck off for a set of sliders at the opposite end of the vaulted enclosure. She tightened her hold on his neck as he bent at the knees to open the glass door. He stepped into a huge country kitchen with copper-bottomed pots hanging from hooks over a butcher-block work island. One entire wall was dominated by a stone fireplace. A cheerful fire crackled in the grate, and two well-worn wooden rockers sat before the hearth, inviting tired souls to sit back and kick up their feet. Across the room from the hearth was a long plank table with cross-buck legs. Individual stools were positioned haphazardly around it.

At the sound of the door opening, a hefty woman with a wavy cap of gray hair turned from the sink. When she saw Rafe, her green eyes filled with tears. She wiped her wet hands on the starched white apron covering her brown dress.

"Rafael!" She lumbered across the room and launched her sizable self at him, sandwiching Maggie between his hard chest and her soft, ample one. A plump arm hooked Maggie around the neck, forcing her face against Rafe's jaw as it squeezed. "Oh, my boy! Praise the Lord. It's a miracle. I prayed and prayed you weren't dead, and now here you are, real as life!''

"Careful of Maggie, Becca," Rafe cautioned with a laugh. "She's still a little sore." He dipped his head to kiss her wrinkled cheek. When he straightened, he grinned. "What's to eat? I'm starving."

Becca stepped back and cupped her pudgy hands to her cheeks, her gaze fixed on his dark countenance. Then her face dissolved and she started to cry in earnest. "I didn't think I'd ever hear you ask me that again."

Rafe flashed Maggie an apologetic look and deposited her on one of the rockers. He went to take the older woman in his arms. Hunching his shoulders, he bent his head to kiss her temple.

"I never meant to put all of you through such a bad time," he said gruffly.

She ran her hands over his broad back as if she couldn't believe he was real even as she launched into a scolding. "Taking off without a word, and then never calling home. I've a good mind to warm your seat with my spatula!''

"Later," he said with a choked laugh. "I'm not grabbing my ankles in front of Maggie. It's not dignified."

Becca sobbed and then chuckled. "Well, then, you'd better straighten yourself up! Any more nonsense out of you, and I'll tan your hide right in front of her, mark my words. What you've put your mama through! For shame, Rafael! And your daddy, bless his heart. I've never seen that man shed a tear, mind you, and he cried like a baby the other night when he called to tell me!''

"I'm sorry. So sorry."

When Ryan stepped into the kitchen, Maggie held up her arms for the baby. He shook his head. "I think you're heading straight for bed."

Overhearing his brother's comment, Rafe pulled away from the housekeeper. Becca patted her cheeks dry and tugged at her dress and apron. "My, yes! What am I thinking, letting you sit there, Maggie? Forgive me."

"I'm perfectly fine," Maggie assured her.

"Fiddle. Rafael told me on the phone how sick you've been. Well, never you worry. The master suite is all ready for you. Rafael had the room completely redone before he left. You'll be the first to sleep in there since—well, in a good long while. And I've prepared the nursery as best I can. All the furniture in there was—" She broke off and glanced at Rafe. "Well, never mind. Rafael will have to buy more, is all. I've borrowed a few things from the wives of the hired hands that will do us for now."

"I'd prefer to have Jaimie in the same room with me," Maggie said.

"Only if I have your promise that you won't try to take care of him yourself," Rafe inserted. "Doctor's orders, remember? Complete bed rest."

The determined glint in his eyes told Maggie that arguing would get her nowhere. She decided a half a loaf was better than nothing. "I remember."

He came to lift her from the rocker. To Becca, he said, "She isn't supposed to be on her feet for a week."

"And she won't be," Becca said firmly.

"It's probably all right for me to get up for a little while if I'm—"

"No arguments!" Becca said, cutting Maggie short. "I'd like to give you a bit of time to settle in before I take after you with my spatula. But I won't hesitate if I catch you disobeying your doctor." She waddled from the kitchen into a long hallway, speaking to Rafe who followed behind her. "I already called Dr. Kirsch, so he's standing by. Did you bring all the medication she needs?"

"Got it."

"I'll want a list of instructions in her care. Don't be forgetting and taking off to the stables before you give it to me."

"I'm not taking off anywhere, Becca. You'll have your hands full with Jaimie and the household."

"Oh, pooh. I can accomplish more with a baby in one arm than three women and a girl." She threw open a door and stepped inside a huge room with mauve carpeting and creamy walls, her broad hips almost touching the door frame at both sides. "The bed is turned down," she said, scurrying over to a long bank of windows to draw the drapes against the late afternoon sunlight. "Just set her there on the edge."

"Did you get the nightgowns?"

"I sent Delores to town after you called me. You forgot to give me a shoe size, so she bought stretchy-type slippers. The robe is a nice heavy velour." She paused with one hand on a draw cord. "It's all there at the foot of the bed."

Maggie wanted to remind them she was an adult, not a sick child. They were talking back and forth as if she weren't there. Rafe set her on the mattress, which was covered with taut sheets that looked as if they had been ironed. He crouched to untie her shoes just as Maggie bent forward to do it herself, and they bumped heads. She blinked away stars and grabbed her temple.

"Sweetheart, are you all right?"

Much more help, and they were going to kill her. She stared at him, rubbing the throbbing place. It usually took a lot to make Maggie angry, but she was quickly getting there.

"I'll do it!" she said as he reached for her foot again.

"Don't be silly. It hurts your back to bend over." He unlaced one of her shoes and jerked it off. As he attacked her other sneaker, he glanced at the floral-print gown and burgundy velour robe at the foot of the bed. "Ankle-length flannel?" he said with a curl of his lip.

Finished with drawing the drapes, Becca ambled to the bedside table to flip on the light. "If you want negligees, go buy them yourself."

Rafe winked at Maggie as he brushed her hands aside to unzip her coat. "Maybe I'll just do that."

Maggie started to peel off the jacket. He drew it down

before she could move, trapping her arms at the elbows. As he tugged the sleeves off over her hands, Maggie got a bad feeling about this. Sure enough, after tossing the jacket aside, he reached for the buttons of her blouse.

Maggie grabbed his wrists. "I'll do it," she said.

"Honey, don't—"

Maggie's temper snapped. She slapped at his hands. "Out! Both of you. I appreciate your concern, but I'm not an invalid."

Rafe rocked back on his heels, looking mildly startled. Becca planted her hands on her ample hips. The two of them stared at her.

Maggie felt light-headed when she pushed to her feet. She grasped the ornately carved bedpost. "Out," she said firmly. "When I'm done, I'll holler."

Becca and Rafe exchanged worried looks. "She's just tired," he said.

"Poor dear," Becca said.

Maggie felt like pulling her hair. To her relief, though, they both left the room to afford her some privacy. She had just started to unbutton her blouse when Rafe opened the door and poked his head back in. She jerked her blouse closed. "If you need me, I'll be right here in the hall. Don't hesitate to call me."

Maggie felt guilty after he shut the door. He was only concerned about her, and here she was, biting his head off. Little wonder he was treating her like a child. She was behaving like one.

She finished undressing and slipped into the flannel nightgown before sitting on the edge of the bed. Taken separately, the things she was upset about seemed trivial. Not being allowed to hold her own glass. Having pills shoved in her mouth. Being packed around. Starting to do things, and having him stop her. It was a hundred little things. It was only when they were heaped together that they became something big. *He was suffocating her.*

Feeling drained, she slipped between the crisp sheets and fell back against the pillows. Scanning the large room, she took in the ecru walls and slightly darker drapes. There was no fire in the grate of the rock fireplace, a smaller version of the one in the kitchen, but Maggie could imagine the amber warmth, even so. In one corner, two easy chairs were cozied up around a small reading table. On a cold winter night, reading near a crackling fire would be nice, she guessed. It was just a little difficult to feature herself in here with a husband who might want to have sex with her after he closed his book.

She turned her face into the pillow, wanting to cry, which made no sense at all. She'd never been the weepy sort and had no patience with people who were. *Postnatal blues?* She'd read about the hormone imbalances women could get after having a baby. Was that what was wrong with her? She didn't feel as if her system was out of whack. It was the world around her that seemed to be careening.

She heard the bedroom door open. Thinking it was Rafe returning to check on her, she didn't look up.

"Maggie?"

At the sound of that sweet, familiar voice, Maggie's heart leaped. She sat bolt upright and stared at the child standing just inside the room, her small hand still clasping the doorknob. "Heidi?" Maggie couldn't believe her eyes. "Oh, Heidi! What—how did you get here?"

Her little sister gave a glad cry and came racing across the room. When she reached the bed, she bounded onto the mattress and flung both arms around Maggie's neck. "Oh, Maggie, I'm so glad you're here! It's been lots and lots of fun, but I've been so awful lonesome for you!"

Maggie barely noticed the pain of being hugged as she caught her sister in her arms. *Heidi.* She ran her hands over the child's back and pressed her face into her hair, breathing in the familiar, sweet scent of her. "Oh, Heidi. I've been lonesome for you, too. I had no idea you were here!"

''It was a surprise.'' Heidi reared back, her big brown eyes dancing with excitement. ''Guess what! Rafe and Ryan have horses. *Tons* of 'em, and Sly says he'll teach me to ride.''

''Who's Sly?''

''The ranch foreman. He's really nice. You'll like him lots. Just wait till you see him spit.''

''Spit?''

''Yeah. He chews.'' Heidi wrinkled her nose. Then she brightened. ''He says he can nail a fly at four paces.''

Maggie gave a startled laugh. ''What an amazing accomplishment.''

''He says he'll have me ready to barrel race at the rodeo next summer. Won't that be awesome?''

''Barrel race? Heidi, you're only ten.''

''That's old enough. Sly says the younger I start, the better chance I'll have to become a champion.'' She giggled at the worried expression on Maggie's face. ''I won't get hurt, Maggie. It's so fun. There are fourteen horses, just in the stable. I helped muck stalls this morning. As soon as you say it's okay, Sly says I can have my first riding lesson.''

Heidi had always wanted a horse. It was a wish that Maggie had never been able to grant.

''Say yes, Maggie. *Please?* I'll be real careful, I promise.''

''Give me some time to discuss it with Rafe,'' Maggie settled for saying. ''If he says it's safe, then I'll give the go-ahead. But in case he doesn't, don't go getting your hopes up. He may recommend that you wait until you're older.''

''Oh, he won't!'' Heidi assured her. Then with a giggle, she kissed Maggie's cheek. ''Thank you! Thank you! I'm so excited. Just wait and see, Maggie. I'll be an awesome rider. Rafe says I've got a great build for racing because I'll never weigh very much.''

Fantastic. "You mean he's already said you can learn to ride?"

"Not until you say I can. But when I asked him on the airplane, he said he'd talk to you. He started learning when he was a lot younger than me."

Rafe stepped into the open doorway just then. Loosely folding his arms, he leaned against the door frame, his gaze meeting Maggie's over the top of Heidi's dark head. He smiled slightly, then appeared to listen intently to the child's excited chatter.

Maggie was dying to question him. For the life of her, she couldn't imagine how he had managed to get Heidi away from Lonnie. Absently, she attended Heidi's enthusiastic accounts of her experiences at the stable. When the child wound down, Rafe finally spoke.

"Heidi, I know you've got all kinds of catching up to do with Maggie, but Sly's waiting for you. He says you asked to ride over to Ryan's with him this afternoon."

Heidi bounced off the bed. "To see the colt! Sly says he's beautiful." She whirled to glance back at Maggie. "Is it all right if I go? He's a brand-new baby. His name is Lightning Dancer, and I want to see him *so-o-o-o* much!"

Maggie no sooner gave her permission than Heidi raced from the room. Rafe gazed after her for a moment, still smiling. Then he returned his attention to Maggie. "She thinks of you more as her mother than a sister, doesn't she?"

Maggie nodded. "Mama's so childlike that Heidi naturally looked to me. The feeling's mutual. I've taken care of her since she was tiny."

"I suppose you're anxious to hear how I got her here."

"Day before yesterday, when you came by the hospital to tell me you'd be gone all day 'taking care of some business,' that's where you went, isn't it, to get Heidi?"

"I did it in a way that didn't upset your mom," he hastily assured her, "just in case you're concerned about that."

Naturally that worry had occurred to her. She loved her mother, and due to Helen's heart condition, the very thought of distressing her was terrifying to Maggie. "How did you manage not to upset her?"

He rubbed beside his nose, looking sheepish. "Well, actually, I lied through my teeth." He explained about the fictitious honeymoon plans to Disneyland. "Amazingly enough, she fell for it," he marveled. "There I was, a total stranger who popped up on her doorstep, and it never occurred to her to be suspicious." He gave her a slow wink. "She kept patting my arm, saying, 'It's about time my Maggie found herself a nice young man.'"

"I told you, she's not very—well, it doesn't occur to Mama that anyone might lie to her." Maggie searched his gaze. "How did you know how much she's always wanted to take Heidi to Disneyland?"

"It seemed like a sure bet." He sighed, bending his head and lightly scuffing the sole of his boot on the rug. "I would have told you what I was up to, Maggie, but I didn't want to worry you. A lot could have gone wrong, and I figured the less you knew, the better, until you could see for yourself that Heidi was here, safe and happy."

He launched into a detailed account of how he and Ryan had pulled it off. "Apparently she's enjoyed staying here the last two days," he concluded. "I've never seen a kid quite so wound up. She really loves horses, doesn't she?"

"Yes. She always has. I could never afford to get her one." Maggie smoothed a hand over the blanket that covered her knees. Her throat went tight when she met his gaze again, for she suspected that he'd glossed over the very real risk that he had taken in getting Heidi there. "If Lonnie gets Mama to file charges, isn't there a good chance you could go to jail for doing this?''

His mouth quirked at the corners. "Hoping to get rid of me?"

A pang of guilt stabbed into her chest. "No, of course not."

He pushed away from the door frame and stepped to the foot of her bed. "I've got my lawyer working on it. If I get my hand slapped, I get my hand slapped. The important thing is that Heidi's safe." His gaze held hers. "You may have to give a deposition, but my attorney feels we can present a strong case and that once we're married, we can get temporary custody of her. When that's accomplished, he'll start to work on a more permanent solution."

Maggie seriously doubted it was as cut and dry as that. Nothing that involved Lonnie Boyle ever was. "Thank you, Rafe." Her voice came out sounding tight and a little shrill. "Having Heidi here—knowing she's safe and happy—that means more to me than I can say. I don't know how I'll ever be able to repay you."

His firm mouth tipped into a grin, and a mischievous twinkle entered his eyes. "I'm sure I'll think of something."

 Chapter Eleven

Rafe tapped his pen on the desk and then tossed it on the blotter. Kicking back in the leather office chair, he propped his boots on the edge of an open drawer and stared at the check he'd just written to Lonnie Boyle. To someone like Boyle it would seem like a fortune. It was no small chunk of change, even to Rafe, and it rankled to give the bastard so much. Everything within him rebelled.

He sighed and ran his gaze over the richly appointed study. After being away for so long, he was acutely conscious of the smell of orange oil and furniture wax each time he drew breath, scents that had been nonexistent for him these last two years. Floor-to-ceiling bookshelves filled with leather-bound classics and agricultural and animal husbandry tomes lined most of the cedar-paneled walls. The few bare spots played host to paintings, all of them nature scenes by a local artist named Dobbs.

The last time he had sat in this chair, he'd felt as if his life was over. Now he had Maggie, Jaimie, and Heidi. He no longer mourned what he had lost. The future beckoned to him, as shiny-bright as a brand-new penny.

There was so very much that he could give them. *A second chance.* He remembered how Lonnie had thrown it up to Maggie about the advantaged childhood Jaimie could have with his adoptive parents, making it sound as if anything she had to offer was little better than chopped liver. Well, the boy would have even more advantages now, and so would Heidi. Maggie could pore over decorating books to her heart's content and bring in professionals to fix up their rooms. Those kids would never want for anything. As for college, Rafe would definitely encourage both children to further their educations, be they related to ranching or another field entirely. Rafe had two degrees himself, and no doors would be closed to his kids.

When it was all said and done, Maggie would never regret keeping her child or feel that by doing so, she had shortchanged Jaimie in any way. He would make damned sure of that. He already loved the boy, and he'd be a good father, not only seeing to it that Jaimie wanted for nothing, but that he was raised with a sterling set of values and work ethics.

Right now, Rafe suspected that Maggie found the vastness of the ranch intimidating, but she'd slowly acclimate and grow to love it here as much as he did. He just wished she were well enough to begin enjoying it now. But she wasn't.

Rafe sighed. It felt so strange, being back at his desk. True to his word, Ryan had closed none of Rafe's bank accounts. An authorized cosigner, Ryan had written occasional drafts to reimburse himself for Rafe's half of the ranch expenses and left the banking setup alone. Rafe needed to get his driver's and pilot's license reinstated, but otherwise, it was as if he'd never left. Yet so much had changed, all for the better. *Maggie.* God, he was so lucky to have found her.

A smile touched his mouth as he pictured her sweet face and recalled her telling him that she wasn't Susan. As if he had the two of them confused? That was another concern of hers that he needed to address, but everything in good time. She was nothing like Susan in looks or personality, and Rafe wouldn't have wanted it any other way. Maggie was a beautiful person, inside and out.

He drew his gaze back to the check. He was stalling. No matter how he circled it, paying Boyle off was a necessity. He could fantasize about beating the hell out of the son of a bitch, but for Maggie's sake, he had to set aside his feelings and get this settled, cleanly and as painlessly as possible.

He dropped his feet to the floor and pulled a business envelope from the drawer. After writing Boyle's address on the envelope, he sealed the flap, the muscles across his shoulders bunching with tension. *For Maggie.* Under any other circumstances, he'd never buy Boyle off. He had to think of this as an investment, the price he had to pay to have her in his life. Once he mailed this check, she'd be safe.

And his.

The thought jolted Rafe, and for a moment, he gave serious thought to the warning Ryan had voiced the other day. This was a hell of a foundation on which to build a relationship. Was he being selfish? What if he was wrong, and he couldn't make Maggie happy? If he put his mind to it, he could come up with alternative ways to help her without binding her to him in marriage. Legally, they wouldn't be as surefire, of course, especially when it came to Heidi. But he could give it a shot and only marry her as a last resort.

I could also climb out on a high limb and saw it off, he thought dryly. He needed her. That was all he could think about, how very much he needed her and how much she needed him. Despite her determination to control her own destiny and do everything on her own, underneath all of that, she was vulnerable and scared. When she looked at him, he felt like a man again, someone worthwhile with a purpose for existing.

He *would* make her happy. They were meant to be together. He sensed it every time he looked at her—a bone-deep feeling of rightness that defied explanation, but was no less compelling, for all that. Meeting her had given him a second chance, and this time, he wouldn't repeat the same mistakes. Nothing would ever be more important to him than his family. Nothing.

He couldn't let her go. He simply couldn't. If he was being selfish right now, he'd spend the rest of his life making it up to her.

Maggie surfaced from sleep slowly the next morning. The first thing she focused on was an ornately carved mahogany bedpost, and her stomach immediately knotted. At home she didn't even have a headboard, only a mattress and box springs on a cheap metal frame.

Last night, she'd fallen asleep staring at that bedpost, for in her mind, it was representative of everything in Rafe Kendrick's world—amounts of money beyond her comprehension and all the power that accompanied wealth. Maggie was used to choosing the cheapest brands of tuna. She felt as if she'd wandered into a maze and might never find a way out.

She heard a sound behind her and realized someone besides just Jaimie was in her room. No big surprise. Yesterday evening, she'd barely been able to yawn without getting pills shoved down her throat by Rafe or Becca. And water. They'd continually pushed tall glasses of the stuff at her. If it was possible for a person's pipes to rust, hers were corroded.

Rolling over, she sought the source of the sound that had awakened her and saw Rafe. This morning he wore a chocolate-brown shirt, the sleeves rolled back over strong, tanned forearms dusted with dark hair. Bent over the borrowed bassinet to change Jaimie's diaper, he held a cordless phone wedged between his jaw and shoulder to free his hands.

Maggie watched him care for her son with mixed emotions. When it came to Jaimie, he was the epitome of patience, every touch of his big hands gentle, his voice—which could boom when he barked orders into the phone—always pitched low and laced with affection.

Jaimie was *her* baby. Rafe didn't even know who the child's father was. Yet to watch him, a person would think Jaimie was his.

No big surprise. Almost from the beginning, his feelings about Jaimie had been glaringly apparent to her. He'd lost his own little boy, and in a twinkling, he'd had a substitute child dropped in his lap.

As grateful as Maggie was for all that he'd done for her, and all that he planned to do yet, a part of her grew frightened every time she considered the possible ramifications. A grief-stricken man who'd been running away from life. Now, he had put that grief on hold by submersing himself in a fantasy. Jaimie wasn't the little boy Rafe had lost. And, God help her, she wasn't Susan, the paragon, whose praises were continually sung by the plump housekeeper, Becca.

What was going to happen when Rafe Kendrick woke up one day and realized that his surrogate family could never replace the one that had been taken from him? That Maggie herself was a pathetic substitute for the woman he had adored? When he finally came to his senses, would he begin to resent her? And if that happened, wasn't it possible that he might vent his frustration on Jaimie?

As he tended to the baby, he listened to whoever was on the line, interjecting an occasional "Hmmm" or a low-pitched "I see."

Evidently unaware she was awake, he tossed the soiled disposable diaper in a nearby receptacle, then scooped Jaimie from the small bed, laid him over his shoulder, and stepped into the hall, drawing the door partly closed behind him. Through the crack, Maggie saw him pacing back and forth, patting the baby's back as he talked, his voice modulated so as not to disturb her. She found it amazing that a man who seemed so absorbed with other matters could, at the same time, give a child the attention it needed. Women did that sort of thing all the time, but in Maggie's experience, men rarely did.

Maggie wanted to believe his feelings toward Jaimie would never change. But if they did, he'd get the surprise of his life if he ever tried to mistreat her son. He'd have to go through her first.

"I called Harry yesterday right before he left the courthouse, and he's arranging for a waiver on the waiting period." Rafe turned to retrace his steps, jiggling Jaimie, who was starting to fuss. "How's the situation with Heidi looking?"

He listened for a moment.

"Yes, Becca got her enrolled in school this morning. I spoke with the principal on the phone and told him heads would roll if he allowed anyone but Becca or a family member to pick her up."

He gave a decisive nod.

"Got it covered. I understand we need to move fast. Dr. Kirsch is coming out this morning, and a courthouse clerk is coming by with the paperwork. So get on it, will you, Mark? Before we get married, I want my name on that birth certificate. This Boyle character is a fruitcake. I sent him the check, but according to Maggie, he can't be trusted. I tend to think she's right."

Silence. Then Rafe released a weary sigh.

"No problem there. She's willing to sign whatever's necessary. Just fill out the forms, draw up the papers, and bring them out."

Maggie drew the covers closer and gazed forlornly at the empty fireplace across the room. When Rafe Kendrick decided to do something, he was like a bowling ball rolling down a steep incline. She was glad, on the one hand. She didn't want there to be any chance she might lose Jaimie, and it was critical that they get temporary custody of Heidi as soon as possible, which probably couldn't be as easily accomplished if they weren't married. But having everything happen so fast was a little unnerving as well. She hadn't yet been in this house twenty-four hours, and Rafe had been making arrangements ever since they arrived. It sounded to her as if he was pushing for their marriage to take place immediately.

"I don't give a frigging damn about how you accomplish it," she heard him say.

Startled by the vehemence in Rafe's voice, Maggie jerked her gaze back to the partly open door. She saw him make another turn and then pause.

"Yeah? Jameson, huh. Never heard of him. How good is he?" Another silence. "Get him on retainer then."

Maggie glimpsed the housekeeper's stout form in the hallway. The next instant Rafe had a baby bottle in his hand. "Thanks, Becca," he murmured. He shifted Jaimie from his shoulder to the bend of his arm and began feeding him. "Hell, yes. I won't hesitate," he said. Then he laughed. "It's the least of many evils. I won't lose any sleep over it, I can tell you that."

He stopped pacing to gaze warmly at the baby in his arm. "The way I see it, in all the ways that count, he *is* mine." Another long silence. "I appreciate it, Mark."

She heard the phone bleep as the connection was broken. The next instant, Rafe poked his head in the doorway. When he saw that she was awake, he smiled and reentered the room. He clipped the phone to his belt as if it had become a necessary body part.

"Good morning, sleepyhead." He came to the bed. "Would you like to finish feeding your son his breakfast?"

Maggie held out her arms for the baby. Keeping his hand tilted so Jaimie wouldn't suck air, Rafe settled the child beside her. As she grasped the bottle, her fingers brushed against his, and a tingling sensation trailed up her arm. As though he sensed her reaction, he rested a twinkling gaze on hers. Maggie was so unnerved that she forgot to keep the bottle angled, and the nipple emitted a whistling sound.

"Oops." Rafe caught the end of the bottle to tilt it back up. A knowing grin tugged at one corner of his mouth. "Colic, here we come."

He stepped over to a cream-colored box mounted on the wall by the door. Pressing a button, he said, "Becca, Maggie's awake." An instant later, the housekeeper's voice came back, saying, "I almost have her tray ready now."

He pressed the button again. "Don't forget her medication, please. Oh, and Becca? Bring in a fresh pitcher of water, would you?"

Though Maggie kept her gaze on the baby as Rafe returned to the bed, she was aware of his every movement. She could feel him watching her and guessed that he was smiling. At least one of them was enjoying this situation. Personally, she felt as if she'd climbed onto a high-speed roller coaster with Rafe Kendrick manning the controls.

"Penny for them," he said as he sat on the edge of the mattress, the rich, faintly spicy smell of his shaving cologne surrounding her. "You're looking mighty solemn about something this morning."

Her thoughts *were* solemn. If left to her own devices, she would never get married. A little voice at the edge of her mind kept saying, *Don't do this, Maggie. It's not just a temporary arrangement.*

"Honey, can you talk about it? Whatever's upsetting you, just tell me. If you're still worrying about losing Jaimie or that we'll have to send Heidi home, don't," he told her in a husky voice. "The legal arrangements are being taken care of. I was just on the phone with Mark Danson, an old friend and attorney. He told me to tell you there's nothing for you to fret about, that he's on top of everything. He can handle the changes on Jaimie's birth certificate by fax and have it done this afternoon. He's also phoning an adoption attorney named Jameson. The guy is a guru. He'll handle any legal difficulties resulting from those papers you signed, and he'll be handling the situation with Heidi as well. Once we're married, we'll be one step closer to getting temporary custody of her, and in regards to Jaimie, Lonnie's hands will be completely tied.''

Oh, how Maggie wished she could be absolutely sure of that, but experience made her almost afraid to hope.

''And when will the marriage take place?'' she asked. ''It sounds as if you're pushing for soon.''

''In a situation like this, the sooner it's all a done deal, the safer we are.''

She couldn't bring herself to meet his gaze.

''Honey, what is it?''

''It just seems—'' Maggie bit her lip. ''It's all happening so fast, is all.'' She gathered her courage and looked up at him. ''Here I am, about to get married, and I can't even get out of bed yet.''

He touched a fingertip to the end of her nose. His voice was laced with amusement when he replied, ''If you were completely well, you'd probably spend the first week of our marriage in bed.''

Maggie's stomach felt as if it dropped through the mattress beneath her and plopped onto the floor. Fiery heat flooded into her face.

He sighed and braced a hand on each side of her, his broad chest forming a canopy of muscle over her and the baby. ''I'm sorry. I shouldn't tease you like that.'' When she averted her face, he leaned around to look her in the eye again. ''Maggie . . .'' he said in a gently scolding tone, ''I told you not to worry about it. Right? It'll be fine, I promise you. Whatever it is you're afraid of, just put it straight out of your head.''

He made it sound so easy, only it wasn't. At least not for her.

Shifting his weight to one arm, he trailed the back of his knuckles over her cheek. ''You're not going to back out on me at the last minute, are you?''

Jaimie's warm little body lay pressed against her, a reminder of all that she might lose if she did. ''No,'' she managed to say. "I don't want to back out."

She felt some of the tension ease from him. "You're sure? If you're having second thoughts, speak up now, sweetheart, before it's too late."

He acted as if she had a choice. "I'm sure," she said hollowly.

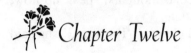 Chapter Twelve

Late the following afternoon, Maggie became Rafe Kendrick's wife, with only Heidi in attendance as one of her family members, and Ryan and Becca acting as witnesses. For Maggie, the quick bedside ceremony was an ordeal.

"Do you, Margaret Lynn Stanley, take this man, Rafael Paul Kendrick, as your lawfully wedded husband, promising to love and honor him, for better or worse, in sickness and in health, until death do you part?" the judge asked.

Maggie directed a panicked glance at Heidi and then at the bassinet. Through the flannel gown, Rafe's hand felt as big as a baseball mitt curled over her ribs. "I, um . . . I do."

His fingers tightened when the judge finished his recitation and it came his turn. Then, in a strong, steady voice, he said, "I do."

"Do you have the rings?"

When cued by the judge, Ryan stepped forward with the rings. When he flipped open the lid of a red velvet box and held it toward her, Maggie plucked the man's plain gold wedding band from the folds of white satin.

Rafe drew his arm from around her to extend his hand. She stared at his long fingers, the knuckles calloused and scarred from a lifetime of grueling work. She was aware of Becca sniffing and saying, "Oh" in a qua-very voice.

"As you slip on the ring, Maggie, please repeat after me . . ." Judge Barker instructed.

The sound of the judge's voice and her own tangled in her mind. As she aimed the ring at Rafe's finger, it slipped from her grasp and fell to the carpet, bouncing before it landed between her bare feet.

As Rafe crouched to retrieve it, he curled a warm hand over her ankle, which was hidden by the hem of her nightgown. Maggie leaped like a startled gazelle. He tipped her a look, his expression changing swiftly from concern to bewilderment. As he pushed erect, his gaze held hers. This time he helped guide the ring onto his finger.

After that, everything seemed to happen with dizzying haste, and the next thing she knew, Rafe was saying in a strong voice, "With this ring, I do thee wed."

Maggie gaped at the wedding set he slipped on her finger. The intertwined diamonds looked as big as a nickel in her blurred vision. When he released her hand, her arm fell to her side as though an anchor were attached.

He slipped his arm back around her waist. Was it only her imagination, or did he touch her differently now? Maggie felt certain the tips of his fingers nestled more intimately beneath her breast.

The judge smiled and snapped the book closed. The sound reminded Maggie of a lock tumbling. "Rafe, you may now kiss your bride."

Rafe framed her face with his hands and staked gentle claim to her mouth. Her mind went blank. She couldn't feel her lips and swayed when he let go.

"I wish you both all the best," the judge said.

"Thanks, Harry." Keeping his left arm locked around her, Rafe leaned forward to shake hands with the judge. "And you can stop worrying. I'll make her happy or die trying."

Maggie blinked. Rafe sounded almost defensive. She focused on the judge, who was eyeing her with concern. Ryan wore the same worried expression. Was her reluctance to marry Rafe so obvious?

Ryan tossed the ring boxes onto the foot of the bed. "Move aside, brother. It's my turn now to kiss the bride. Maybe I'll get a more enthusiastic response."

Rafe gave a halfhearted laugh and drew his arm from around her, whereupon Ryan grasped her by the shoulders. She found herself looking up into gray-blue eyes very like her husband's. Uncertain what to expect, she tensed as Ryan bent his head, his lips barely grazing hers. Then he whispered in her ear. "He's a big old teddy bear. Don't look so worried."

As Ryan released her and stepped away, she glanced up at her groom's dark face. His jaw muscle twitched, and she saw an unmistakable glitter in his eyes that reminded her of light glancing off ice chips. A teddy bear?

"Congratulations, Maggie! Wow, you're married. I can't believe it!" Heidi gave Maggie a quick hug. Then she turned to Rafe. He grinned and drew her close. "Does this mean you're my brother?" Heidi asked.

Ryan reached out to tousle the ten-year-old's hair. "It means you've got two brothers, pillbox. I've finally got a kid sister to torment." He tweaked the end of Heidi's nose. "What do you think about that?"

Heidi's eyes sparkled with gleeful anticipation as she glanced from Ryan to Rafe. Dressed in a brand-new pink top and a pair of pricey designer jeans, she looked glowingly happy, and the undiluted adoration in her gaze hinted that she had already developed a crush on Maggie's new husband and her brother-in-law. "Are you gonna torment me, too, Rafe?"

Rafe chuckled. "Probably. It's an irresistible pastime for older brothers. Only until you turn sixteen, though. Then we'll switch gears and make life miserable for all your boyfriends."

"Boyfriends? Yuck!"

The child's undisguised disgust at the thought made everyone in the room laugh. As the sound trailed away, Maggie felt the attention center on her.

She pasted on a smile and said, "Well, thank goodness that's done."

She winced even as she spoke, for she sounded like someone who'd just undergone surgery without anesthetic.

"Yeah," Rafe said dryly. "Thank goodness."

"Not quite," the judge said. "There are the papers yet to sign." He motioned at the dresser.

Rafe led Maggie to the opposite side of the room. Her hand shook as she signed her name to the documents, and she was acutely aware that her new husband kept his arm around her as he took the pen and bent to scrawl his own signature. As he straightened, he said, "Feel as if you just signed your life away, Mrs. Kendrick?"

How she felt—about anything—didn't really matter. In that moment, it seemed to her that it never had. "Don't we all when we get married? People don't usually think of it as a temporary thing, after all."

"My sentiments exactly." He grasped her lightly by the shoulders and steered her toward the bed. "You've been up long enough. Back to prison."

That was how she felt as she slipped between the crisp sheets, that he was returning her to a cage. He plumped the pillows. His knuckles grazed the flannel over her breasts as he smoothed the top fold of the sheet. Her nipples puckered into hard points. He felt the tips thrusting against his hands and glanced up. For several heartbeats, they stared at each other. Then he drew away, the backs of his fingers brushing against her even in retreat. She knew the touch was unintentional, but it was no less disturbing, for all of that.

"Well!" Becca said, wiping beneath her eyes and snuffling. "This wedding was as beautiful as any I've ever seen, absolutely beautiful."

Maggie glanced down at her flannel nightgown. *Beau-*

tiful? Her groom was dressed in jeans and a chambray work shirt. As a little girl, she'd imagined getting married someday in a lacy white wedding gown with a long train and veil. She'd abandoned that dream years ago, but she still felt sad. Real life never turned out to be anything like you imagined it might be when you were a child, not even if you married the modern-day equivalent of a handsome prince.

The rings winked on her finger as she toyed with the sheet and absently listened to Heidi's chortling. She wondered if Rafe had selected the rings or simply barked another order into the phone, leaving the jeweler to choose for him. As big as the diamonds were, the intertwining design was delicate and feminine.

"I hope you like them," he told her in a voice as scratchy as sandpaper.

Maggie jerked her head up to find him still standing over her. Angling her thumb across her palm, she touched the underside of the bands that felt so strange on her finger. "They're beautiful. How did you know my size?"

"I guessed. If you don't like my taste, we can exchange them." His mouth quirked at one corner, and he shrugged. "The design reminds me of you, somehow. Delicate but radiant."

So he had chosen the setting himself. Maggie was glad. Somehow it made the rings mean more to her, knowing that. "I like them just fine." They were lovelier than anything she might have chosen herself and had probably cost the earth. Unfortunately, her pleasure in them was ruined. This didn't feel like a real marriage to her. It was more a convenient arrangement. And if it happened that they split up later, she'd have to pay for the diamonds. She felt as if she were getting in deeper with every breath she drew. "Thank you."

Becca lifted Jaimie from the bassinet and motioned to Ryan. He began piling baby paraphernalia inside the basket under Becca's direction.

"What are they doing?" Maggie asked Rafe.

"Becca's taking Jaimie and Heidi to Ryan's place for the night so we can be alone. What with you being sick, we'll postpone the cake, champagne, and gift opening until next week. I was afraid too much hoopla today might tire you."

Her attention riveted to Jaimie, Maggie stifled her objections. This *was* their wedding night. Rafe had been patient about having Jaimie around, never once complaining or growing cross, not even when the baby cried. As her husband, he did have a right to expect at least one night alone with her.

With a worried gaze, she watched Becca exit the room with Jaimie in her arms and Heidi on her heels.

Ryan trailed behind them, the bassinet clutched waist-high. "Don't worry about any of the chores," he called over his shoulder. "I've got the men taking care of the cattle, and I'll drive back over to feed the horses."

The judge snapped his briefcase closed, flashed Maggie a farewell smile, and joined in the sudden exodus. "I'll be back in a while," Rafe told her. "I need to show Harry out and take care of a few things."

She was in no great hurry. When the door closed behind him, she relaxed against the pillows and closed her eyes, unable to forget how he had accidentally grazed the front of her gown with his knuckles. Her nerve endings felt raw, every brush of the flannel against her breasts making her skin burn.

A sick feeling settled in her stomach as she turned the rings on her finger. She'd done it. They were married. She had to remind herself that her sister and son were safe and try not to think of anything else.

She listened to the loud ticking of the case clock across the room, its pendulum marking off the seconds. Their wedding night. *Oh, God.* But she could think of no way around it. She supposed she could tell Rafe she still felt tender from giving birth, but she'd always been a lousy liar. Better to just take her medicine than to risk making him angry. Getting through tonight would be enough of an ordeal without that.

Nearly twenty minutes passed before he pushed open the door. He held a silver tray balanced in his hands. Tucked under one arm, he carried two silver candle-holders bearing long tapers. "Hi," he said, flashing a grin as he came toward her. "I decided we should celebrate by sipping fine wine from my grandmother's Waterford."

Maggie gazed at the delicate, long-stemmed goblets. "They're lovely."

"She collected it for years. My grandmother gave it to my mother on her wedding day, and she, in turn, gave it to Susan on hers. The entire set will be yours now."

A lump of resentment rose in Maggie's throat. She was living in Susan's house, had possibly been sleeping in her bed, and now she had married the woman's husband and was inheriting her wedding gifts. Secondhand Maggie. She felt like an interloper.

He shoved the lamp and telephone aside with his forearm to make room on the beside table. Becca had gone to a lot of trouble, laying out finger foods on lacy paper doilies: cheeses, slivers of dill pickle, green and black olives, sliced ham and beef, and dainty crackers. He'd also brought along the bottle of wine.

"For refills," he explained when he saw her looking at it. "I thought—" He straightened and pushed at his hair, which had fallen over his forehead in loose, glistening black waves. He looked nervous and sort of harried, as if he'd been rushing around and was only just now getting a chance to catch his breath. As he uncorked the bottle and poured them each some wine with an economy of motion, he said, "I know you're a little nervous. I thought this might help."

"Can I have the whole bottle?"

The words no sooner popped out than Maggie wanted to kick herself. But instead of seeming perturbed, Rafe only laughed. Still smiling, he sat down and settled a thoughtful gaze on her. Two seconds in, and Maggie started to feel as if those gray-blue eyes were turning her skin inside out. She plucked tensely at the dusty-rose fuzz of the blanket.

"You really *are* nervous," he finally said, his voice low and silky. "I apologize for that. I've been so busy making arrangements, I put you on hold and ignored you."

"You've taken care of the two people who matter most to me. I don't mind being put on hold. Really."

"I'll just bet you don't," he said, his tone laced with gentle amusement. "And that's my fault. I should have been trying to make you feel more at ease about this."

"You've tried." Maggie lifted her shoulders in a shrug. "I'm sorry I'm—it's just—kind of sudden. I mean, in ways I feel as if I've known you forever. I hate being in bed, so every minute I've been sick has seemed years long. But then I think—did I even know you a week ago? I'm—"

"You don't have to explain." He slipped his hand to her neck, his fingertips making those heart-stopping circles on her skin again, as he'd done when he kissed her in the Cessna. "I understand. We'll take it nice and slow."

Slow? She preferred the quick and painless approach. She was relieved beyond measure when he drew his hand away to reach for the wineglasses. Her fingers quivered as she grasped the cool stem of the goblet he handed to her. He extended his toward her. "To us and many happy years together."

When Maggie went to clink her glass against his, her goblet beat a tinkling tattoo, a telltale sign of how badly she was shaking. Dismayed, she jerked away to stop the noise and slopped wine over the front of her gown. "Oh, dear!"

Rafe grabbed a napkin and began dabbing at the flannel, each rub of the linen over her breast making her nerves leap. She instinctively grabbed for his wrist, spilling still more wine in the process. Scalding tears gathered behind her eyes. "I'm sorry. I'm making a complete mess of this. I'm sorry."

She had to stop this. *Now*. What if she blew this so badly that Rafe became disgusted and decided all deals were off? Until they consummated this marriage, he could get it annulled. He'd made it clear from the start that he expected them both to make this a real marriage in every way. She *needed* him. Without his protection, she'd have no way to keep her son and Heidi safe.

He grabbed another napkin to help her mop up. She decided to set aside her wine before she spilled the entire glass. She groped to find a clear spot on the tray. The instant she turned it loose, the goblet toppled and struck the wine bottle. Horrified, Maggie stared at the shattered remains.

"Oh, no! Susan's *crystal*!"

"Don't worry about it."

"Don't worry about it?" The very way he had said the name "Waterford" told her how special the crystal was. "I'm so sorry. I know how Susan must have treasured it. I didn't mean to break it."

He spared a long glance at the shattered glass, then went back to wiping at her gown. "It's not that big a deal, honestly."

"And I've ruined the food!"

"There's more where that came from."

He suddenly froze, his gaze locked on the outline of her erect nipple thrusting so pointedly against the crimson-soaked cloth. For an awful moment, Maggie stared down at it as well. Then she clamped her hand over her breast to hide the evidence.

When she glanced back up, Rafe was gazing out the window, a muscle ticking along his jaw. There was no laughter or tender understanding in his eyes now. He looked furious enough to chew through nails.

He pushed to his feet so suddenly that it startled her.

"I didn't mean to ruin the celebration," she hurried

to explain. "It was all an accident. Honestly, it was. I'm sorry about the glass."

He cursed under his breath and set his wine goblet back on the tray with a loud click. With his smoldering gaze riveted to her, Maggie's heart was already doing tumbles. Memories of Lonnie in a temper flashed through her mind. When Rafe made a sudden move with his hand, she instinctively flinched and threw up her arm.

He froze with his splayed fingers near his temple. When she realized he'd only meant to run his fingers through his hair, as he often did, she felt like a fool.

A pained expression crossed his dark face, and his lips drew back in a grimace. "I, um . . . I just remembered something I need to go do."

With that, he turned and strode from the room. The door closed behind him with a loud bang. Maggie just sat there, staring at the panel of wood, feeling sick. She should write a book, she thought a little hysterically. *How to Get Rid of Your Bridegroom in Five Easy Steps.*

Oh, God . . . oh, God. This wasn't funny. He was furious with her, and she couldn't blame him. He'd been so kind and patient with her. She had humiliated him during the ceremony. Now, to top it off, she'd broken his dead wife's Waterford and spoiled the little party he planned. Even the candles were splashed with wine.

They'd made a deal, and she had welshed on it. If he came back and told her to take her sister and baby and get out of his house, it would be no more than she deserved.

Rafe sank his boot into the hay, putting so much force behind the thrust that the bale slid across the feed-room floor. Pain shot to his knee. He swore and hobbled in a circle. "Son of a *bitch!*" Had he broken his toe? "God *damn!*"

This would teach him not pitch temper tantrums, he thought as he gimped toward the bale where it had come to rest against the unfinished wall. He sank gratefully onto the hay, braced one elbow on his knee, and reached to massage the throbbing digit through the leather. When the ache finally abated, he swore again and covered his face with his hands.

I just remembered something I need to go do. Every time he recalled saying that to Maggie, he got a sick urge to laugh. Big problem. It was a little difficult to go outside and kick himself in the ass. But, oh, God, how he wanted to. *Stupid.* He'd pulled some good ones in his time, but this took the prize. Where in the hell had his head been the last few days?

She was scared to death, and he'd bulldozed her into marrying him, paying her barely a second's notice since bringing her here, except to force pills or water down her. A person could suffer far more ills than just the physical, and he'd completely ignored that fact, so bent on getting what *he* wanted that he hadn't given a good God damn about her feelings.

Well, it was done. All legal and binding. He felt as though he'd been running a race for days, with a man-eating monster nipping at his heels, only to be caught just as he staggered into the safety zone. That look in her eyes. *Jesus.* He had prepared the food tray and taken it to the bedroom, intent on pulling off the smoothest seduction in history. Getting her a little looped on the wine, then gently kissing her until she forgot to keep a death grip on that damned nightgown that covered every sweet inch of her. Oh, yeah. Rafe Kendrick, the great lover, his chosen victim so terrified she couldn't hang onto a glass. But, oh, hey. No problem. She had all the usual body parts. He could just tease and kiss his way past her reservations, until she quivered in the throes of orgasm. Home free.

He had been ashamed of himself a few times in his life, but never like this. *Just be careful that you don't become a bastard yourself,* Ryan had warned him. If only he'd listened. Now, here he sat, hating himself. And

Maggie still lay in that bed, undoubtedly trembling, waiting for him to come back and ravish her. If it hadn't been so awful, he might have laughed. He'd never forced himself on a woman in his life, and he sure as hell didn't plan to start now.

"Aren't you the picture of wedded bliss. Trouble in paradise already?"

Rafe jerked his head up to see his brother standing in the feed-room doorway, a well-padded shoulder propped against the frame.

"Why in the hell didn't you knock some sense into me, Ryan?" He groaned again and passed a hand over his eyes. "Jesus. Since when have I started thinking of women as pieces of meat?"

Ryan pursed his lips and scratched just below the edge of his hat, which he wore cocked low over his eyes. "Aren't you being a little hard on yourself? You've been a little self-focused, sure, but you haven't mistreated her."

"Hell, yes, I have, and you damned well know it. Why didn't you say something?"

"Well, now. There's a question. I guess because I don't like getting my ass kicked."

Rafe took another long look at his brother's shoulder. "Yeah, right. I need a month to pack on weight before I take you on."

Ryan ran a finger under the loose collar of his shirt. "You aren't exactly puny." He studied Rafe for a moment. "You've changed since you left. There's a hard edge to you." His lips twitched. "I'd just as soon keep my face the way it is, thanks. And I try to stay out of other people's business when I can, my brother's included. I warned you, and I figured, enough said."

"I wish I'd listened."

"That bad, huh? Damn. I was only gone a few minutes. She seemed all right enough when I left."

" 'All right enough?' " Rafe considered that. "I

guess that describes it, not exactly leaping for joy, but not hysterical.'' He laughed bitterly.

''Maggie'll be okay. She's had a rough time, but she'll come through this.''

''I don't know what to say to her when I go back in there.''

''What in hell did you do, leap on her?''

''Of course not. I was just gearing up.''

''I knew you'd come to your senses before you went through with it.'' Ryan closed the distance between them, his boot heels thudding on the plank floor. ''Move over. If I've got to play counselor, I'm gonna sit.''

Rafe slid over to make room. ''On second thought, why am I even talking to you? You've never been married. You'll probably screw up your wedding night worse than I have.''

''I won't have the same set of problems. I'll sample the merchandise before I buy the goods. Trembling brides are passé. These days the girls give us boys instructions, and I like it that way. Born to please the ladies, that's me.''

Right then, an experienced woman with decided preferences in lovemaking techniques sounded damned good to Rafe. ''Maggie isn't like that.''

''Go to the head of the class. You're just now noticing?''

''Lay off. I feel bad enough, all right?''

Ryan leaned forward, resting his bent arms on his knees. He joined Rafe in staring down at the hay scattered over the floor. ''So . . . now that you realize what a jerk you've been, what are you going to do?''

''I *have* been a jerk, haven't I?''

''Class A.''

Rafe scuffed his heel through the hay. ''If I don't consummate the marriage, it isn't binding. She can still get an annulment.''

''You're incurable.'' Ryan shoved his hat back to fix

an incredulous gaze on his brother. "Would you listen to yourself?"

Rafe shook his head. "I *am* incurable, aren't I? Now that I've found her, I'm so afraid of losing her I'm paranoid. And not just about her deciding to leave me. This kidney thing, knowing it can go sour if the antibiotics stop working. I had Dr. Kirsch check her over. He says she's doing well. But it worries me, and I can't seem to stop hovering."

"We tend to worry about the people we love, Rafe. It's normal. You've just carried it a little too far." He shrugged. "Hell, a doctor knows his orders won't be followed to the letter once a patient goes home. If it were a life-and-death situation, don't you think patients would be kept in the hospital?"

"Probably," Rafe admitted.

"I'm sure it won't kill her if she goes to the kitchen and makes a sandwich. You've kept her chained to that bed since she got here, and there have been times I was afraid you might drown the poor girl." Ryan laughed. "All the clocks in the house being set to go off at pill time is another nice touch. I was having lunch with Becca today, and at precisely twelve-thirty, alarm clocks and radios started going off everywhere. It reminded me of living in the dorms. Like her kidneys will go bad if you're thirty minutes off schedule with her medication?"

Rafe winced. "Have I been *that* bad?"

"Not bad, exactly. I think everyone knows you mean well, even Maggie. It's just so—" He frowned and tipped his hat back. "You can relax a little, you know? She's going to be fine—if your idea of in-home care doesn't kill her."

Rafe laughed. It was true, he realized. He'd been behaving as if Maggie were terminally ill, and that was only the half of it. He considered his actions over the last few days and tried to see himself as others must. The picture that formed wasn't a pleasant one to face.

"I've really messed up, Rye. I shouldn't have pushed her into this marriage."

"Well, you have pushed her into it. Now you have to make the best of it. It isn't just Jaimie's welfare you have to think about now, but Heidi's, too. If you call it off at this late date and let Boyle take that girl back to Idaho, you'll have more problems than you can handle, and they'll have my initials on them."

"She's a cute kid, isn't she?"

Ryan smiled and nodded. "She asked me today if I've got a girlfriend. I think I'm the target of a serious case of puppy love." He rubbed beside his nose again. "She sure looks a lot like Maggie. It's good to know she'll be able to grow up here and not have all the same heartaches."

"Yeah, it is. And that tells me exactly what? That the road to hell is paved with good intentions?"

"You can work this out, brother. You just need to sit down and hash it out with Maggie, that's all. The results of the arrangement are great. Now instead of bulldozing, move forward slowly, taking one thing at a time."

Rafe heaved a weary sigh laced with self-disgust. "I thought I could make it all up to her later, you know? Work past her reluctance, make her—well, you know—enjoy the intimacies. And once that was done, I wouldn't lose either of them because she'd be married to me."

Ryan nodded. "I know that, and I understand—sort of." He gestured with his hand. "Don't get mad, all right? But I'm gonna be flat-out honest here for a minute. You're an emotional mess, and your feelings for Maggie have you so mixed up, you don't seem to be thinking straight."

"What are you saying? That I don't really love her?"

"No, I'm not saying that at all. I think you do love her, and, knowing you, probably deeply. You never have done anything slowly or gone into it half-ass. It was love at first sight for you with Susan, too, if you'll remember back. You're one of those lucky people who somehow just knows when things feel right. It's just—oh, hell, I don't know. You aren't yourself. You seem almost—well, sort of frantic. Maybe even a little grasping.''

Rafe's guts balled into a cold knot in the pit of his belly. ''Grasping?'' It was an ugly word, one that he'd never dreamed might be used to describe him.

''You lost the three people you loved most in the world, Rafe. When we've been hurt like that, I think we all have a fear of it happening again. It's like you saw Maggie, fell for her hard and fast, and saw a way to grab hold. Do you know what I'm saying? That's no way to treat a woman.'' He shrugged again. ''Deep down, you know that. Especially not someone like Maggie. She has her own past history and her own set of fears. She needs a slow hand.''

Rafe knew that. It had just escaped him for a while. Thinking back to those long-ago days when he'd first met Susan, he could remember all the hours they'd spent simply talking and laughing together, falling more and more in love with each passing second. Long before they'd ever become lovers, they had been best friends, double-dating, studying together, and talking endlessly on the telephone, sharing their innermost thoughts and secrets.

Rafe closed his eyes, thinking about what he knew of Maggie's teen years. School, work, and then home at night to do even more work. Had she ever steamed up the windows of a car parked on Lovers' Loop? Or fended off the advances of a horny boy at the movies? Probably not. Hell, no. When would there have been time for her to date? Unlike Susan, who'd been pampered, indulged by her daddy, and sheltered from the harsh realities, Maggie had jumped into adulthood and responsibility when she was little more than a child herself. There had been no one to watch out for her, no one to protect her, and absolutely no one to indulge her.

Instead, she'd fallen into that bastard Lonnie's clutches, and, unless Rafe missed his guess, he'd put a halt to any semblance of normalcy in her life after that.

Rafe sighed again and rubbed his forehead. His brother was right. Instead of courting Maggie and winning her heart, he had laid siege, fashioning a velvet-lined trap, leading her into it, and snapping the teeth closed.

"Thank you, Ryan."

"For what? All I've done is try to point out the problem."

Rafe pushed wearily to his feet. "Sometimes just recognizing the problem is half the solution."

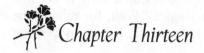 *Chapter Thirteen*

Maggie's heart leaped when she heard the doorknob turn. An instant later, Rafe stood in the doorway. She wasn't sure what she expected to see in his expression. Anger, perhaps? Instead the set of his chiseled features was impossible to read, shadows darkening his smoke-blue eyes to a somber slate that reminded her of the summer sky right before a storm.

"Hi," he said huskily, his gaze moving slowly over her as he stepped into the room. After closing the door, he leaned against it, the breadth of his shoulders spanning a large share of its width. His black hair lay in wind-tousled waves across his high forehead. His blue chambray shirt was open at the collar to reveal a patch of burnished chest that Maggie knew would feel as hard as a granite slab.

"Hi," she said weakly. "I was beginning to think you weren't coming back."

He folded his arms. "An exercise in wishful thinking?"

She felt heat flood into her face. Since it was obvious she was less than enthusiastic about their wedding night, she saw no point in making denials. "I'm sorry I ruined the little celebration you planned. Especially about breaking Susan's crystal. I accidentally set the goblet on an olive. Stupid of me. I should have looked before I turned it loose."

"I really don't give a hang about the crystal, and it's yours now, not Susan's."

"Oh." She wished he would stop staring at her like that. It made her nerves jangle. "Well, for ruining the party then. If you'd like to try again, I'll do my best not to spoil it."

"I don't care much about that, either. It was bad timing." He rubbed the bridge of his nose. "I've heard of being saved by the bell. But by an olive?"

He straightened and moved toward her, his stride slow and unhurried. As he drew nearer, her heart skittered madly.

He came to a stop near the nightstand and rested his hands on his lean hips, the very picture of a rugged male, his long, denim-clad legs braced apart, his firm mouth tipping into a crooked grin. Maggie tried to meet his gaze and return his smile. A twinkle came into his eyes.

"Maggie, you look as nervous as a long-tailed cat in a roomful of rockers. I'm not going to attack you. I just want to talk to you. I think we'll both feel a whole lot better once I do."

She lowered her gaze to her hands, realized she was toying with her wedding ring, and began picking fuzz from the blanket instead. He resumed his seat on the edge of the bed and rested his arms on his knees.

"There won't be much blanket left if you keep that up," he observed dryly. "I'll have to go hunt up a quilt so we don't freeze to death during the night."

She didn't miss the fact that he had made clear his intention to sleep with her.

"Maggie," he said softly, "can you look at me, please?"

She forced herself to meet his gaze again.

"This has all been pretty hard for you, hasn't it?"

"All what?"

He sighed and looked away. "Everything, from start to finish. Here you are, apologizing to me about making a mess of things? I'm the one who needs to apologize."

He gave a low laugh. "The hell of it is, I don't know where to start."

He dug the heel of his boot into the rug. Maggie watched him, her heart pounding for an entirely different reason now. She had an awful feeling he was about to tell her this had all been a disastrous mistake.

"You're going to send us away, aren't you?"

He looked startled. "Away? Hell, no. What gave you that idea?"

Maggie tried to moisten her lips. Her tongue felt as rough and parched as a line-dried washcloth. "I, um . . ." She gestured limply with one hand. "I'm not unwilling to hold up my end of the bargain. Honestly, I'm not. I was just nervous earlier, that's all. I'll—" She couldn't bear to look at him as she said it, so she went back to picking at the blanket. "I'll be fine now—and do whatever you want—if you'll just give me another chance to hold up my end of the bargain."

"I'm the one who wants to ask for another chance."

That brought her head up. "You?"

"Yes, me." He laced his fingers and bent them backward, making his knuckles pop. "I went through everything I wanted to say to you while I was walking back to the house. Do you think I can remember one damned thing? Hell, no." He shook his head. "Why is it, do you think, that when it's really important to say all the right things, a person usually says all the wrong ones?"

He looked so genuinely distressed that Maggie momentarily forgot her own concerns. "What is it you want to say?"

He closed his eyes, the muscle along his jaw rippling under coppery skin as he clenched his teeth. "That I'm sorry for being such a jerk, for starters."

A jerk? A picture flashed in her mind of him pacing the floor during the night with her baby. This man had been controlling. She secretly felt like a commodity he'd purchased to replace something he'd lost. But in spite of that, she couldn't recall a single instance when he'd been what she would term a jerk. "You've actually been very kind to us."

The smile that crept over his firm mouth was pained. "Kind? On the surface, maybe." He pushed suddenly to his feet and started stepping off the distance to the fireplace with long strides, the tendons in his legs bunching under the denim of his jeans with every movement. As he pivoted back toward her, he hooked his thumbs over his belt. "I'm no good at this kind of thing, so I'm just going to jump into it with both feet. Bear with me, okay?"

Maggie nodded.

"First off, you're afraid I'm going to hit you. We have to talk about that." His eyes went dark with shadows again. "Call it a quirk, but I don't want a wife who feels afraid every time I scratch my head."

Maggie's lungs hitched, and an airless pounding reverberated in her temples. She *had* flinched away from him. She couldn't deny it. *Oh, God.* It was her turn to close her eyes. Despite his denial, she felt certain he was about to tell her this wasn't going to work, and she didn't know what she was going to do.

He cleared his throat and muttered under his breath. "I have a bad habit of talking with my hands. Rubbing my jaw, shoving my fingers through my hair. My dad does it. I think it's something Rye and I picked up from him. I seriously doubt it's a trait I can overcome because I do it unconsciously."

"I'm sorry for throwing my arm up like that," she said in a wobbly voice. "I didn't think you were going to hit me. Really I didn't."

"Yes, you did."

His words cut sharply through the air and seemed to echo. "No," she assured him hoarsely. "Maybe it looked that way. But it was only a reflex reaction. You've never struck me, and I've no reason to think you might."

"Maggie, I'm not scolding you. All right? You *do*

have reason to believe I might hit you. More reason than I probably know about. And like I just said, reflexes or unconscious gestures are something none of us can control. I'm not asking that of you. I just need for us to come to an understanding about it. I want you to know that I'll never hurt you.

"I wish I could tell you that I've never in my life struck a female, but the honest-to-God truth is that I did once." He rubbed the back of his neck. "I doubled up my fist and let her have it, square in the face. Bloodied her nose, busted her lip, and knocked her flat on her ass."

Nausea rolled through Maggie's stomach. She was fairly certain that she'd have no nose left if Rafe Kendrick punched her. "Wh-what did she do to make you so mad?"

"You plan to take notes so you never make the same mistake? Probably not a bad plan." His eyes took on a distant expression. "What did she do?" He seemed to mull that over. "Well, she scratched me, to start with. And then she hit me. I might've let both those things slide, but then she smashed my Twinkie. *That* pissed me off."

Maggie blinked and refocused on his face. "Pardon?"

He narrowed an eye at her. "You heard me." That narrowed eye closed in a slow, teasing wink. "Don't screw with my Twinkies. I tend to react violently."

"Twinkies. The kind you eat?"

"Is there another kind?" He got a contented look on his face. "You know, the ones with the creamy centers? I used to be crazy about them. Still am."

Maggie was still thinking of that poor woman's smashed nose.

"Anyway, when my Twinkie got smashed, I lost my temper and let her have it. My first-grade teacher called my dad and told on me."

"You were a *first*-grader?"

His lips twitched. "That afternoon when I got home,

my father escorted me to the tack room where he wore out the seat of my jeans with his belt, giving me one of the few spankings I ever got.'' He held up a finger. ''Rule number one in the Kendrick family: men never, under any circumstances, hit women. My dad is absolute death on that. I always kind of thought he overreacted, since I was only six and the girl was bigger than I was. But I think it was a lesson he wanted to drive home to me early on.'' He shrugged. ''He did, and with a vengeance. The lesson took.'' He frowned, but his eyes still twinkled with mischief. ''I think it's branded on my ass. I don't have it in me to strike a woman, Maggie, and I have no respect for any man who does. It goes against everything I was raised to believe in. When I get pissed at you, I may fantasize about wringing your neck, but when push comes to shove, I'll never retaliate physically. It's not in my nature.''

''Oh.''

''You can smash all my Twinkies, honey. By the case, if you want. I'll never lift a hand to you.'' He folded his arms across his chest. ''No matter how mad I get, when the smoke clears, there won't be a hair on your head harmed. I promise you that.'' He glanced over his shoulder. ''There's a Bible around here someplace. I'll give my solemn oath on it, if you'd like.''

''That won't be necessary,'' she said softly.

''I know it's probably not the best idea for me to talk a lot about Susan, and I apologize for doing it now. But would it help you to know that Susan and I had knockdown, drag-out fights sometimes, and I never once so much as slapped her?''

''You loved her, though.''

He nodded. ''Yeah, I loved her. More than anything. I won't lie to you about that. I adored her, worshiped her. But sometimes she still made me so mad I wanted to strangle her.'' He smiled slightly. ''Married people get angry with each other sometimes. Really angry. Any man worth the powder it'd take to blow him to hell doesn't use his fists to settle the dispute. I'll walk out and go cool off before I'll ever hit you. I promise you that.''

Maggie nodded, wanting with all her heart to believe him. Her father had never hit her mom. She knew on some level that men like Rafe described truly existed. She'd just spent so many years dodging Lonnie's fists that it no longer seemed like a reality to her.

Rafe dug his heel against the rug again, then traced the sculpture pattern with the toe of his boot. ''On the subject of Susan and how much I loved her,'' he went on. ''That's something else we need to talk about. A part of my heart will always belong to her and my kids.'' His voice went husky. ''I wouldn't be much of a man, and my love wouldn't be worth a damn if I could simply bury people I care about and forget them. But please, understand that my memories of them have nothing to do with how I feel about you and Jaimie. Susan's gone, my kids are gone. Life goes on. A man can love and love deeply more than once.'' Tenderness clouded his eyes as he studied her. ''I love you like that now.''

''You're starting to love me?''

''Starting?'' He gave a self-deprecating laugh and ran a hand over his face. ''I guess this seems sudden to you.''

''A little. Actually, a lot.''

''Do you think love has to conform to a mean and follow a time chart?''

''No, of course not.''

''Or make sense?'' He shrugged. ''Nine times out of ten, it makes no apparent sense at all, except to the person who feels it. I can't explain how it happened. Or exactly when. I didn't want to care about you. It made me feel like I was betraying Susan. But the feeling blindsided me anyway.'' He broke off and swallowed, avoiding her gaze for a moment. ''You're a very special person, Maggie. I don't think you realize how special.'' He looked deeply into her eyes again. ''Remember telling me that you could never replace Susan? When you said that, I got the feeling you felt inferior somehow, that no matter how you tried, you'd never be able to measure up.''

''You said yourself that she was really wonderful, and Becca talks about her like she was a saint.''

''When people die, we tend to canonize them, I guess. Not to say she wasn't wonderful. She was. But as much as I loved her, when it comes to measuring up, she's the one who comes up short, Maggie, not you. And if she were here, she'd be the first person who'd tell you that.''

''She would?''

''Susan was a sweetheart, no question, but never once was she put to the test like you have been. At fourteen, she was a cheerleader. A little rich girl. For her sixteenth birthday, her daddy bought her a brand-new car.

''When we got out of college and decided to get married, she worked at a hamburger joint to buy my wedding ring, which set her back about four grand. Every cent she earned went for that ring. Not for clothes. Her dad gave her a charge card for that, and anything she wanted or needed, she just went and bought. Her earnings never went to pay bills. She had none. She lived with her folks, and they paid for everything. She had no real responsibilities until we got married, and even then, I tried my best to provide well for her. I'm not knocking her for that or saying it isn't the way it should be. I'm just pointing out that you've never had it that easy.''

''No, but that doesn't mean I wouldn't have jumped at the chance. In high school, I envied girls like that.''

''I'll be damned. You mean to tell me you have an ignoble trait?'' He arched an eyebrow. ''I'll bet you never once had the luxury of spending your wages on something as frivolous as a four-thousand-dollar ring. Or on anything else frivolous, for that matter. You just did what you had to, taking care of your mom and Heidi.''

''I love my mom and Heidi, but even so, it wasn't quite that simple. Sometimes I—well, to be honest, I resented both of them because I couldn't be like other kids my age. I wished—'' Maggie's throat went dry. "Sometimes I wished I were someone else.''

"Another ignoble streak?'' He gave a low laugh. "My God, you're riddled with them, aren't you? Don't tell me you feel guilty for that? Feeling resentful— honey, that was *normal*. You must have hated them sometimes. If you sit there and say you didn't, it's time to make you an appointment with a good shrink.''

A scalding heat seared Maggie's cheeks.

"The point is that, despite those feelings, you didn't shirk the responsibility.'' He smiled and shook his head. "Measure up, Maggie? Think again. Compared to your life, Susan's was a cakewalk. In high school, she never had to worry about supporting her family. And later, she never once had to worry about getting food for her babies. She sure as hell was never in a situation where she had to bargain with her body in order to get her hands on a bottle and formula. I'm not saying she wouldn't have, if faced with the same circumstances. She was a wonderful mom. She just never had to prove her mettle. You have.''

She couldn't think what to say.

"Do I need to list a few more reasons?'' he asked softly.

"Reasons for what?''

"For loving you. Or maybe, to be more precise, to convince you that you deserve to be. I can go on, if you like. But in the end, Maggie, we'll be right back where we started, with me saying I love you, and you not sure you believe it. I wish I could lay it all out for you in black and white and somehow justify my feelings. But that's not how love works. It just happens.''

"I never meant to make you think you had to justify anything.''

"Good, because I probably can't. The feeling hit me, fast and hard. Now it's just there, and I'd rather die than lose you, which brings me to the rest of my apology.''

He walked back to the bed and hunkered to look up at her. "There's no excuse for the way I've handled all this. I've tried like hell to think of a good one, believe me. But the truth is, I screwed up. Screwed up royally." His throat muscles convulsed, and his larynx bobbed. "Have you ever wanted something so bad—needed it so bad—that you went a little crazy?"

"I almost stole a necklace once," she admitted shakily.

"A necklace?"

"A gold locket. All the girls at school wore them." She touched her throat. "You know—to carry pictures of their boyfriends. I, um . . . didn't have a boyfriend and I felt—" She shrugged. "I don't know. Left out, I guess. I thought if I wore a locket, I'd be more like everybody else, and people would think someone liked me. But the lockets cost fifteen dollars, and I couldn't afford that. So I almost stole one."

She half-expected him to laugh. Instead he just looked sad, as if he knew exactly how she must have felt. After a moment, he said, "It's not exactly on the same plane, but I guess that's sort of how I feel about you. Only my character isn't quite as sterling. I went ahead and took what I wanted."

While Maggie was trying to digest that, he went on to say, "Loving Susan and my kids like I did and then losing them . . . it nearly destroyed me. One day, I had the world by the tail, and the next, my wife and kids were dead. Worse, I blamed myself. When I met you, I was a drunk. I won't color it pretty. I went from one bottle to the next, and that was all I cared about, staying drunk. I didn't have a life. I didn't want a life. Before I left the ranch, I considered shooting myself. For several nights, I sat in here in the dark with the nose of a revolver shoved against my temple, but I was too big a coward to pull the trigger."

Maggie had seen him take on four armed men with

nothing but a whiskey bottle to protect himself. ''You're no coward.''

''Yeah,'' he said huskily. ''Yeah, I am, Maggie. I ran from the pain, tried to drown it in a bottle. There are all kinds of cowardice. For me, terror wasn't in facing death, though I did draw the line at blowing my brains out. It was facing life without the people I loved.'' He swiped his hand over his mouth. ''I couldn't handle it, so instead, I drank. Meeting you changed all that. You needed me. Knowing that gave me a reason to sober up. In a very real sense, you were a lifeline tossed to me as I went under for the last time. You know?''

She recalled the wild-haired, scruffy bum she'd met on the boxcar. Was this even the same man? ''I think I do, yes,'' she said tightly.

He rested his arms on his thighs and turned up his palms to examine the deeply etched lines there. ''I think I started falling for you the first time I looked at you. I tried not to. I was so mixed up in the head at the time that I felt guilty, like I said. But that passed. Right before she died, Susan made me promise I'd find someone else to love if anything ever happened to her. I kept remembering that when I looked at you, and I couldn't fight the feelings. I knew she wouldn't have wanted me to. And once I accepted how I was coming to feel about you, I started to—'' A shine came into his eyes, and he blinked. ''I, um, felt scared.'' He interlaced his spread fingers and popped his knuckles again. ''That's a hell of a thing for a man to admit, but there it is. I was afraid I might lose you, and I still am. Only now I'm getting my head on straight, and then I was just reacting. All I could think about was how to make sure you wouldn't leave.''

''I'm not going to leave. Where would I go? Lonnie would eventually find me, and when he did, I'd be back to square one. And now there's Heidi to think of, too. It'd be a lot harder for me to get custody of her if I was working two jobs and living in a crummy apartment in a bad neighborhood, which is probably what I'd have to do to make ends meet. Where would that leave her?''

''I know all that,'' he said in a gravelly voice. ''And to my shame, I used it to my advantage. I knew you were in a hell of a fix. To my credit, I did offer you a way out, but only one way out. There were alternatives. Hiring a team of lawyers for you. Giving you enough money that working two jobs and living in a crummy apartment never would have been in the game plan. There were lots of things I could have offered to do for you, Maggie, and I didn't.''

Once again, she couldn't think what to say, so she said nothing.

''Instead I offered to do those things for you only if you married me, and I knew when I made you the offer that you'd take me up on it, that you essentially had no choice.'' The shine in his eyes became unmistakable wetness. ''When a man robs a woman of her right to choose, something is way out of whack.

''Now you're mine. I got what I wanted. I wouldn't undo any of it, not for the world, because I know what a hell of a mess you'd be in if I did. Not to mention what would happen to Heidi now that I've snatched her from Idaho and brought her here. For her sake, we have to push ahead and try to get temporary custody.''

''I don't *want* you to undo any of it.''

''Because of Jaimie and Heidi. That's a hell of a way to start a marriage. If not for that olive, I would have pressed you to make love. I feel like a heel, but there it is. Saved by an olive.'' He passed a hand over his face again. ''I know it's asking a lot. But I'd like a second chance to do things right this time. Will you give it to me? Another chance, I mean?''

Maggie's throat tightened. She'd almost started to believe he meant to give her a reprieve. *Stupid, Maggie.* ''I already told you, I'm perfectly willing,'' she said thinly, pushing aside the blankets to make room on the bed beside her. "Just don't hand me any wine this time."

He laughed and reached out to grasp her wrist. "No, no. That's not what I mean. A second chance, from start to finish, honey. That's what I'm asking for." He drew the blankets back to where they had been and gave them a solid pat as if to stick them to the sheet. "Normally a man wins a woman's heart before he tries to make love to her. Walks in the moonlight, kissing her until her knees go weak. Taking her out to dinner. You know, dating and—" He shrugged. "I need to run all the bases. Even if you can never love me, at least I can make the intimacies of this relationship a little easier for you."

Maggie smoothed her hand over the blanket as well. "We're, um . . . married now. You don't have to finagle your way into my bed. I'm supposed to fix dinner for you, not expect to be taken out on dates. And even if we went somewhere, we'd come home together. I don't see how we can make dating work or why you'd even bother."

"Well, it won't be the normal kind of dating. That's true." He ran his knuckles along the edge of the mattress cording that showed through the fitted sheet. "But allowing you some time to get used to me isn't impossible." He gave her a slow smile. "Before I make love to you, it'd be nice if my touch didn't make you so nervous that you douse us both with cabernet. Don't you think? The least we can do is work on being good friends before we become lovers."

"Friends?" she echoed.

"You think a husband can't be your friend? I'd like to be your *best* friend, honey. I can't promise you fireworks and bells ringing when I make love to you. You'll have to love me—a *lot*—for that to be possible, or anything even close. But friendship is attainable. I can be the person in your life you know will always be there for you. Someone who cares about your feelings. Who'll listen and try to help. And I think we can have

fun together if I can coax you into relaxing around me.''
He held her gaze for a long, searching moment. "Well?
What do you say? Do you want to give it a try?''

Maggie circled the offer. Why did he want to do this?
They were married. He had every right to demand that
she surrender her body to him. "Are you saying we
aren't going to—well, you know, have a wedding
night?''

"Sure we'll have a wedding night. Only a very different kind.''

"What kind, exactly?''

He laughed. "You don't trust easily, do you?'' He
shrugged and glanced around. "A walk in the moonlight
is out for another three days. How about making eyes
at each other over a game of chess? I'll fix a new tray.
We can drink a little wine. Have some fun. And then
when we're tired, we'll crash. We'll save the lovemaking for when you're ready.''

Maggie stared at him, half-expecting him to suddenly
throw back his head, guffaw, and say, *Gotcha!* Only he
didn't. He just kept searching her gaze, as if waiting for
her response. Finally, she said, "Are you serious?''

"Of course I'm serious. Tell me you're willing to start
over with a clean slate, and you've got a deal.''

"Until I'm ready?'' she repeated incredulously.

He nodded. "That's the whole point, waiting until
you're ready.'' That mischievous glint returned to his
eyes. "It's not like we need to wait until I am.''

"And what's the catch?''

"There isn't one. Unless it's that I'm counting mighty
heavily on my ability to win you over. But that's my
problem, right? And my gamble.''

"And what if—''

"What?'' he asked gently. "Don't be afraid to speak
your mind. What's worrying you?''

"What if I'm never ready?'' she blurted. "I, um . . .
think it's only fair to tell you that I don't like it very
well.''

"Lovemaking, you mean?"

"Yes," she admitted faintly.

"When did you try it?"

"When?"

He caught her chin on the crook of his finger. "Maggie, don't write it off as something you don't like until you've tried it with the right guy. It'll be nice for you when it happens. And if I can manage it, it'll be far, far better than just nice. Fantastic, maybe."

Looking down at him, Maggie could almost believe that anything was possible, even that. He wanted to spend their wedding night playing chess? When she thought of all the things she'd envisioned that he might demand of her tonight, she got tears in her eyes.

"What?" he asked.

Maggie shook her head, unable to speak for the sudden thickness in her throat. The moment she'd been dreading had arrived. She was his wife. He had staked a paternal claim to Jaimie that he could easily use as leverage against her, and Heidi's well-being depended totally upon his benevolence as well. She was completely alone in this huge house with him, miles from the closest town, and she wasn't even certain where that town might be. He had absolute control over her and the situation. Anything he wanted from her, he could simply take. But instead he was offering to spend the evening playing board games?

"Honey, *what?* Talk to me."

Maggie shook her head again, trying frantically to blink back the tears. But a sob was locked in her chest. She thought of all the countless times when she'd been at Lonnie's mercy and wished he knew the meaning of the word.

Why that made her want to cry, she didn't know. But it did. An awful, horrible ache crawled up her throat as she attempted to hold back the tears.

"Sweetheart, don't," he said, smoothing her hair. "Whatever it was I said, I take it back. I didn't mean it. Was it the making-love business? You're afraid? Or you think you'll never be ready? Whatever it is, we can work it out.''

Maggie couldn't have answered to save her soul. His heavy hand on her hair felt wonderfully warm, his touch gentle, as always. She reached up to close her fingers over his wrist. At the contact, he swore under his breath. The next thing Maggie knew he was sitting on the edge of the bed again, and she was locked in his strong arms, his chest a sturdy wall of strength to cradle her. Even more amazing than finding herself there was that she had absolutely no desire to leave. It felt good to be held close by this man—good and perfectly right.

''Son of a bitch,'' he muttered.

The sob in her chest broke free with a surge of wet laughter, the combination nearly strangling her as it came up her throat. He pressed a hand over the back of her head, the span of his thumb and fingers nearly stretching from ear to ear. Normally the reminder of how tall and powerfully built he was would have made her heart catch. But, for reasons beyond her, now it seemed comforting. He meant her no harm. Not this man. *Chess.* Maggie clung to his neck and pressed closer to his heat, feeling utterly safe. It was the most wonderful feeling, one that made her muscles feel limp and sent a radiant sense of peace clear through her.

He tightened his embrace. ''It's going to be all right. I promise. It's going to be all right.''

For the first time in so very long that Maggie had lost track, she truly believed it might be.

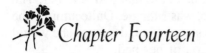

Chapter Fourteen

Rafe usually enjoyed chess, but after three games, he found it difficult to concentrate on strategy, especially with Maggie lying on the bed across from him, her cheeks turning pink from the wine and her lashes fluttering as she struggled to stifle her yawns.

Glancing up from making his last move, he said, "I think it's about time for lights out. You're really tired."

She batted her lashes and made an obvious effort to look wide awake. As he watched her, tenderness welled within Rafe. "Oh, no! I'm not tired at all," she assured him. "Are you?"

Not wishing to rush her, he returned his attention to the game. Five minutes later, he heard her stifle another yawn. He glanced up and saw that she was drooping with weariness, her long, dark lashes veiling her lovely eyes. A smile tugged at his mouth. He was quickly coming to suspect that his wife's reluctance to call it a night stemmed from her dread of sharing a bed with him.

For a brief moment, he entertained the thought of returning to his own room. The notion had scarcely occurred to him than he firmly set it from his mind. The entire purpose of waiting to make love to her was to ease her into this relationship, giving her an opportunity to grow accustomed to him a little at a time. If he kept his distance and never touched her, accomplishing that goal would take forever.

It wasn't an entirely selfish decision, though Rafe freely admitted, if only to himself, that he eagerly anticipated the moment when he could make love to her. The deciding factor, however, was Maggie. Quite simply, the longer he allowed her to sleep alone, the more she would come to dread his invasion of her bed.

Fear was a funny thing, with common characteristics shared by humans and animals alike. If left alone, instead of healing, it festered, increasing in proportion until it became gargantuan.

He sat up and faked a yawn, stretching his spine and shrugging his shoulders. "I forfeit the game. Call me a party pooper, but I'm beat."

She sat up as well, her gaze fixed on the marble chess pieces as if they were long-lost friends. Rafe began gathering them up and returning them to the hand-carved oak box. Then he folded the board, fitted it inside, and snapped the lid closed.

After setting the game on the floor next to the bed, he pushed to his feet and corked the wine bottle, which was still a quarter full. Maggie had consumed two glasses, and he'd nursed only one over the course of the evening, half-afraid the taste of alcohol might make him start craving whiskey again. Luckily it hadn't, which told him his dependency had been more emotional than physical.

Finished tidying up, he turned to regard his bride. She gazed back at him with unmistakable wariness. In that moment, she looked about twelve years old, the biggest thing about her those huge brown eyes. Rafe found himself struggling not to smile again. A pixie perched on a rosy blanket.

Skimming his gaze over her, he noted the feminine and inarguably mature curves of her body caressed by the flannel. It was the first time in Rafe's life that he could recall envying a nightgown. His attention snagged on the crimson splash of cabernet over one softly peaked breast.

"I guess the first order of business is to give you your pills and then find you a fresh gown," he said.

She released a long-suffering sigh as she took the capsules he shook out onto his palm. Rafe poured her some water from the pitcher he kept filled on the nightstand. After handing her the glass, he glanced at his watch and silently congratulated himself on making progress. He was twenty minutes behind schedule, and he hadn't pressed her to drink any fluids all evening.

While she swallowed the pills, he stepped over to the dresser and began rummaging through the items of clothing Becca had gotten for her. When he turned back with a neatly folded length of flannel clutched in his fist, he found Maggie standing at the foot of the bed.

"I . . ." She gestured toward the bathroom. "I'll be a few minutes."

He gave her the clean gown as she swept quickly past him. When the bathroom door closed and he heard the lock click, he sighed and shook his head. His wife was painfully shy, which was becoming more apparent by the moment.

While waiting for her, Rafe kicked off his boots and sat on the edge of the bed. He considered stripping off his clothes and lying down, but given Maggie's nervousness, that might not be a wise idea. Better to get her settled first and then join her. He also decided he'd be well advised to keep his pants on. His boxer shorts, at least.

It seemed to him that an interminable amount of time passed before she finally emerged from the bathroom, and when she did, she blushed as if she'd been doing something shameful. She wore the clean nightgown and she'd brushed her hair. Sable curtains lay like rich silk over her shoulders.

She came to a stop several feet away, her nervous fingers plucking at her nightgown, her gaze avoiding his. Observing her, he searched his mind for something he might say to help her relax. Not even a banal comment came to mind. Zeroing in on her sleepy eyes, which he considered quite a feat given the fact that her face had turned such a startling shade of pink, he said, "Sweetheart, you look completely exhausted."

"Mmmm."

She rubbed her palms on the flannel, looking as jumpy as a flea at a pesticide convention. Her gaze kept darting from him to the bed he sat on, as if she couldn't decide which posed the greatest threat.

He'd never been adept at small talk, especially not when his companion was tense and seemed to have no inclination to hold up her end of the conversation. Instead she just stood there as if her feet had put down roots.

"Well . . ." he said, then immediately wondered why. Well, *what*, exactly? A few possibilities ran through his brain. *Well . . . ain't this a hell of a mess?* Somehow he doubted she'd appreciate the attempt at humor. He settled for clearing his throat, which made him sound like sick diesel engine trying to ascend a steep grade.

Since he'd foregone his conjugal rights, Rafe couldn't imagine what she thought might happen when they went to bed. As the seconds of deafening silence ticked past, it occurred to him that maybe she didn't trust him to keep his promise. For just an instant, he felt offended. If there was one thing he prided himself on, it was keeping his word. But then he recalled what Ryan had said about people being afraid history might repeat itself.

Lonnie Boyle, the pus pocket. The bastard had undoubtedly made Maggie countless promises over the years, never honoring a single one, unless it was to carry out a threat. Coming from that kind of environment, was it really any wonder that she found it difficult to trust? In her experience, a man's code of honor wasn't worth much.

What really broke Rafe's heart was knowing how very badly she wanted to trust him. The yearning was there in her beautiful eyes. There was also a pleading look in her expression, as if she were silently imploring him to do something, the problem being that he didn't know what she needed from him. More promises? He could talk himself blue in the face and never take the edge off the anxiety she felt.

Rafe stood and crossed the room toward her, his movements slow and deliberate so as not to frighten her. Judging by the way her eyes widened as he approached, he might as well not have bothered. He heaved a weary inward sigh.

"Maggie," he said softly, grasping her lightly by the shoulders. "Don't be nervous. I'm not going hurt you."

"Oh, I know that," she assured him in a quavery voice.

Like hell. The truth was, she hoped and prayed he wouldn't, but Lonnie had robbed her of the ability to feel certain of it. "Come on, sweetheart," he said, steering her toward the bed. "Let's get you tucked in."

She moved before him like a condemned person being guided to the execution chamber. When her knees connected with the mattress, she jerked. Beneath his hands, Rafe could feel her slender body trembling. He felt like the world's worst bastard for ignoring that and sweeping back the covers.

"In you go," he urged.

Her movements stiff and awkward, she slipped between the sheets, then scooted so close to the opposite edge she was in danger of falling off. Lying rigidly on her side with her back to him, she drew the blankets to her ears.

"Good night," she said faintly. Then: "Should I turn out the light?"

"Please," Rafe told her as he began removing his shirt.

Studiously keeping her gaze averted from him, she reached for the lamp switch. The next instant, the room was plunged into darkness. Blessed with good night vision, Rafe's eyes adjusted quickly. Moonlight spilled in through the windows, painting the mauve carpet silvery gray and casting the furniture that lined the room's perimeters into shadow.

After tossing his shirt aside, he stripped off his jeans. His belt buckle and the change in his pockets sounded off in the taut silence like a tambourine as the denim fell to the floor. He sat on the edge of the bed to pull off his socks and drape them over his boot tops. When he finally slipped between the sheets to join Maggie, he wore nothing but his boxers, which, considering the fact that he usually slept naked, was a concession.

When he settled a hand on her flannel-draped hip, she flinched as though he had touched her with a hot coal. Rafe pressed close, his chest against her back. Clinging to the edge of the bed as she was, she'd left herself no room to escape. That suited his purposes perfectly. He slipped his hand from her hip to her abdomen, splaying his fingers over her softness. Her stomach muscles convulsed the instant his hand settled. Even through the flannel, he could feel the looseness of her skin there, a sign of her recent pregnancy.

Her silky hair lay over the pillow. Letting his eyes drift closed, Rafe rested his cheek on a spray of curls, his lips and nose buried in the strands. She smelled wonderful, the faint scents of shampoo and bathing soap mingling with a sweet fragrance that was exclusively her own.

He could have sworn he felt her pulse quicken. How that could be, he didn't know. His hand was on her belly, not her chest. He increased the pressure of his fingertips. Sure enough, he felt a rapid thrumming. The poor girl was so scared, she was one big heartbeat.

He cracked open one eye. "Maggie, honey, can you try to relax?"

"I'm relaxed," she said, clutching his wrist even as she spoke.

Rafe lay there for a long moment, wondering if she realized she was digging her nails into his skin. He decided probably not. Judging by the force of her grip, it was a panic reaction. Every line and curve of her body felt knotted with tension. He waited for several minutes, hoping she might turn loose or at least relax her hold. No such luck. His fingers started going numb.

"Maggie?" he whispered.

"What?" she asked in a thin voice.

"Do you think by holding my hand that you can stop me from touching you someplace else?"

Her breathing stuttered and stopped. When at last she replied, her voice sounded choked. "No, of course not."

"Then why bother?"

She relaxed her grip but kept her hand on his wrist. Rafe flexed his fingers to get the blood flowing through them, which instantly earned him another lacerating assault from her fingernails.

He considered trying to reassure her again, but since that hadn't worked thus far, he opted to fake slumber instead, his hope being that she might feel safe if she believed he'd fallen asleep. He forced his body to relax and his breathing to change. Still, she lay there, body taut, hand vised on his wrist.

Rafe had a feeling it was going to be a very long night and far more torturous for her than for him. He counted the ticks of the clock pendulum. He tried to think about something else. When his thoughts returned to the woman in his arms, she was still taut as a well-tuned piano wire.

How much time had passed? Twenty minutes, possibly thirty? He only knew she couldn't possibly get any rest this way. *Christ.* In that moment, Rafe detested Lonnie Boyle with a virulence that nearly choked him.

Even worse, it wasn't a problem Rafe could openly discuss with her. She had yet to admit Boyle was even the father of her child, let alone give specifics about what the son of a bitch had done to her. How could Rafe swear to her he'd never do the same if they couldn't discuss it openly?

I can't let him do to Heidi what he did to me, she'd cried that afternoon in the hospital. The instant she'd said that, Rafe had guessed exactly what Boyle had done to her. When he thought about it, he still felt just as sick. Sooner or later, he would have to get her to talk to him about it. She needed to do that, to purge herself of the ugliness, if for no other reason. As it stood, she believed no one else knew the entire truth—that her stepfather had not only physically abused her, but raped her as well.

Rafe closed his eyes, hurting for her in a way that went bone deep. God. He wanted so badly to say, *What are you so afraid of, Maggie? That I might do what Lonnie did?*

The ability to trust in others was such a fragile thing and shattered so easily. Maggie had been betrayed by a man who should have been the one male in her life she could trust implicitly. Boyle had made a mockery of that familial bond by doing what he had, and in doing so, he'd left Maggie believing that men held nothing sacred.

Rafe wanted to tell her differently. But as deeply as he yearned to soothe her fears, he knew words alone would never be enough. The only way he could prove to Maggie that she could trust him was with his actions, holding her close like this and doing nothing more, teaching her by experience that the touch of his hands would never bring her pain. Slowly—moment by moment, day by day.

There was no quick cure. She needed time, and probably lots of it. Rafe's only consolation was that she would be well worth the wait. Cradling her against him, he continued to feign slumber, hoping with every breath he drew that she would grow so exhausted soon that she could relax and drift off to sleep.

It seemed to him that an eternity passed before her grip on his wrist finally went lax and the tension left her body. She sighed then, her breath catching in a whispery huff like that of a child who had cried itself to sleep.

She leaned more heavily into him, twisting slightly at the waist, her soft hip nudging his manhood. His shaft twitched and sprang to attention. Rafe stopped breathing, afraid the unaccustomed hardness might wake her.

He needn't have worried. She was asleep. Cramped from maintaining one position for so long, he eased onto his back, gently drawing her with him. She murmured and turned. Seeking the hollow of his shoulder with her satiny cheek, she snuggled close, angling her bent leg across his thighs, her pelvis against his hip, her breasts molding to the hard planes of his chest.

He let his eyes fall closed. *Maggie.* God, she felt so soft and incredibly sweet. Being able to hold her like this was like receiving a miracle. It didn't matter that he couldn't make love to her. In time, that would change.

For now, he would take her just as she was and count himself blessed. As he drifted toward sleep, Rafe vowed to himself that no matter what it took, he would protect her and the people she loved from any more pain and ugliness. But as he slipped from semiconsciousness into troubled dreams, his confidence in his ability to do that left him.

He was once again in the back of the horse trailer, peering through the fury of a terrible hailstorm at the station wagon as it hovered at the edge of the embankment, about to carry the people he loved to their deaths. Only this time, instead of it being Susan and his children in the car, he somehow knew it was Maggie and Jaimie.

In that split second that somehow became an eternity in his dreams, just before the car plunged over the cliff, the face of the driver turned toward him. To his horror, it wasn't Susan's face he saw anymore. And, God help him, it wasn't Maggie's, either.

The face was that of Lonnie Boyle, and he was laughing maniacally.

 *Chapter Fifteen*

Everything will be all right.

Over the next three days while Maggie was still confined mostly to the bedroom, Rafe reaffirmed that promise in dozens of different ways. Each morning, without fail, he and Heidi joined her in the bedroom for breakfast, then before Heidi left for school, he placed a long-distance call to Prior, running interference with Lonnie and handing Maggie or Heidi the receiver only after their mom got on the line. Maggie was relieved beyond words to talk with her mother and know firsthand that she was all right, and she knew it meant a lot to Heidi as well. Given Helen's mental and emotional immaturity, Heidi had always looked to Maggie for parenting and wasn't as attached to or dependent upon her mother as most children her age might be. But she did love Helen and worry about her.

For the remainder of each day, Rafe staved off boredom, entertaining Maggie with a host of restful activities. He watched romantic movies with her one afternoon, taught her to play poker the next, and then, on the last day, piled her bed high with decorating catalogs so she might choose a theme for Heidi's bedroom and Jaimie's nursery.

As much as Maggie appreciated his thoughtfulness, though, what really touched her were all the silly, incredibly sweet things he did. He frequently telephoned her on a separate line from another room in the house to engage her in ridiculous conversations. Talking on the phone, he explained, was an essential part of dating. Sometimes they simply teased each other about silly things. At other times, they exchanged information about themselves, sharing stories from their childhood or relating their most embarrassing moments. Maggie learned that his favorite color had once been blue, but that his tastes had changed recently and now he loved brown—the exact color of her eyes. His favorite meal was a steak and a baked potato, slathered with butter, sour cream, and fresh chives. His favorite song was "The Way We Were," his favorite movie *The Yearling*, his favorite book *Where the Red Fern Grows*, and his pet peeves warm beer and wet toilet paper.

Because she knew his time might be better spent tending to ranch business, Maggie felt guilty about all the hours he wasted on the phone with her. When she suggested that he might use the time to begin familiarizing her with the bookkeeping system, he insisted that silly phone conversations were a courtship ritual every woman should experience. He also maintained it was far easier to speak openly on the phone than in person, and since he wanted to learn all he could about her, it seemed a small price to pay. Maggie thought he was a little crazy, but it was the very nicest kind of crazy.

One morning during her confinement, he invited her "out" to breakfast and escorted her and Heidi to the kitchen where he whipped up one of his "famous Kendrick omelets." The following evening, he invited her "out" for a candlelight dinner and movie. It didn't matter that going out with him was actually only a short trek from her bedroom to another part of the house. It didn't matter that his omelet fell or that the steaks were a little charred. No, what counted to Maggie was that he cared enough to make the gestures.

On her first day of freedom from the bedroom, Rafe took her to town to see Dr. Kirsch for a follow-up exam, after which she was given another ten-day round of antibiotics and told she was recovering nicely.

"You can resume your usual activities," the physician told her with a kindly smile, "the only exception being that you shouldn't breast-feed your son until you finish your course of medication. I'd suggest you wait at least two days after taking the last dose, just to make sure it's entirely out of your system."

Maggie felt as if she'd just been released from prison. She wanted to throw back her head and shout that she was well. As though Rafe sensed exactly how she felt, he flashed her a huge grin as they left the clinic and headed down the busy sidewalk. His breath formed puffs of vapor in the chill air. "Becca's watching Jaimie. No reason to rush home. Let's celebrate."

Sidestepping with him to avoid a collision with an oncoming pedestrian, Maggie laughed and shrugged. "How can we celebrate?"

He curled an arm loosely around her shoulders, the spicy scent of his aftershave teasing her senses. "How about an early lunch downtown and then shopping till we drop?"

"Shopping? For what?"

He cast her a mock frown. "For *what?* Mrs. Kendrick, need I remind you that your wardrobe is sorely lacking?"

"I can't pay this much!" she whispered later when they entered a women's apparel shop and she saw the price tag on a blouse he liked.

"Sweetheart, money isn't at a premium anymore, remember?"

With numb fingers, Maggie checked some other garment tags, and the least expensive blouse she found was eighty-nine dollars. One was two hundred forty-nine dollars, and it was plain *cotton*. Oh, God. Rafe wanted to buy her several tops, and at these costs, he would blow a thousand dollars before she could blink.

A tight, airless feeling filled her chest. If he broke it

off with her, she still wanted to reimburse him for all the money he'd spent. On a waitress's income, it would take her forever to settle the debt unless she put a cap on expenditures.

"I admit I need clothes, but this is highway robbery," she insisted. "Isn't there a K Mart or Wal-Mart in Crystal?"

Instead of answering, he bunched the blouse he held in his fists and just stood there, clenching his teeth and staring down at one of the buttons, which she felt fairly certain was made of 14-karat gold. For an awful moment, she feared he was about to lace her up one side and down the other. Instead, he took a deep breath, relaxed his grip on the cloth, and seemed to shrug it off.

When he turned toward her, he was smiling. He nudged his hat back, held the blouse up to see how it would look on her, and told the clerk, "She'll try this one on."

The clerk took the blouse to the dressing room.

"Rafe, didn't you hear me?" Maggie whispered as he turned away to resume browsing.

"I heard you." He regarded yet another expensive top that he had selected from the rack, then draped it over his arm. "I'm ignoring you."

"I've always worked and paid my own way. I feel uncomfortable about letting someone else buy me things."

He cut her a sharp glance. "Why don't you say what you mean, Maggie? That you feel uncomfortable letting a *man* buy you things. More specifically me."

"That isn't it."

"Isn't it? You talk about paying your own way. 'No free rides.' But it's so much bullshit, and we both know it. The truth is, you're afraid I'll insist on another kind of payback."

With growing alarm, Maggie watched him pluck another blouse from the rack. It was the one that cost two hundred forty-nine dollars. "It's a matter of pride. It's *your* money, not mine. I've done nothing to earn it. I haven't so much as washed a dirty dish or dusted a piece of furniture in your house. Can't you understand how I feel?''

He sighed and finally stopped rummaging to give her his full attention. His gray-blue eyes delved deeply into hers. After a moment, he softly said, ''Is this going to be an issue with you forever? From day one, it's always been something. The motel room, the food, the hot plate. It's all right to let your husband buy you things. You're not on the payroll. You're my *wife*.''

''There's no crime in being thrifty, is there? Why throw money away? Give the extra to charity.''

''Before I left the ranch, I donated plenty. I'll continue to do that now, and probably on a much larger scale. I'll never waste money that could be put to better use, just for the joy of blowing it. But, by the same token, since I have the means, I refuse to count pennies when it comes to providing for my wife and child. Or for Heidi, either, for that matter. It makes me feel good, being able to buy nice things for the three of you. Is there a crime in *that?*''

Maggie's gaze fell to the price tag. Her heart stuttered. ''Can we compromise and find a *medium*-priced store?''

''Jesus Christ,'' he said under his breath.

''Don't get mad, please?''

He gave a humorless huff of laughter. ''Mad? You're hurting my feelings, damn it. I do have some, you know.'' He leaned closer to avoid being overheard. ''We have *millions* in the bank. *Millions*, Maggie. And you're haggling about the prices of necessities? Why? I can think of only one reason. If there's another I'm overlooking, please enlighten me because, otherwise, this little dialogue is a slap in the face. I've *never* demanded a thing from you. *Nothing, zilch!* Do you think I'm keeping a tally, saving up for an all-*weeker?*''

Maggie inched back to put some distance between

their noses. "I told you, it isn't that. I'm just frugal by nature and prefer to bargain-shop."

"What's your solution? To own one pair of jeans and one blouse? To go around looking like a beggar? People will think I'm a cheap-ass jerk, making my wife go without while I wear a Rolex and five-hundred-dollar boots."

"It isn't my aim to look like a beggar. I'd just prefer to shop at a discount department store. I don't have to spend a fortune to look nice."

He laid the second blouse over his arm. Maggie suspected he was counting to ten. Slowly. He shifted his weight from one foot to the other, looking out of place among the racks of feminine apparel. Tall, dark, rugged. In the leather jacket, with the black Stetson tipped back to reveal his burnished features, he was so handsome he made her pulse race.

Evidently, counting to ten didn't work very well. His eyes glinted as he ran his gaze the length of her. "True. You'd look great in a burlap sack. But that doesn't mean I intend to let you wear one."

"I wasn't planning to go with any burlap this season." She glanced over her shoulder to be sure no one was standing nearby. "Honestly, Rafe, I'll be perfectly happy with cheaper clothes. If I want something special later, I'll go to work part-time and buy it myself. I'd feel better, doing it that way."

"Maybe you'd be happy with cheaper clothes," he conceded, "but I wouldn't. I can afford to buy you nice things. I want to buy you nice things. As for you earning the money yourself, if you're talking about waiting tables, even mention doing that again, and I'm going to make Hiroshima look like a cap gun going off."

Maggie refrained from pointing out that he seemed pretty close to detonation already.

"You wanna go to college? Fine by me. Wanna pursue a career? Fine by me. I'll never try to hold you back. But as God is my witness, it'll be over my dead body that you *ever* wait tables again, letting some trucker pinch your butt so he'll give you a better tip. Got it?''

"I *never* let anyone pinch my butt to get a better tip!" she cried, her voice carrying the length of the store. She no sooner spoke than she winced and felt fiery heat rush to her cheeks. She saw the clerk poke her head out of the dressing room to gape at them.

Rafe rubbed his jaw, looking sheepish. "Low blow. I'm sorry. I know you didn't." When he focused on her again, his eyes had begun to twinkle, all trace of anger gone. "*This* is one for the record books. I'm fighting with my wife in one of the classiest joints in town." He cocked a dark eyebrow. "Please tell me you don't throw stuff or break things when you get pissed. The clerks in here give women lessons on how to put their bras on right."

A startled giggle erupted from Maggie. This man. Sometimes she felt as if he had attached invisible strings to her emotions and that he could play her like a well-tuned harp. There was nothing funny about this. Why in the world was she laughing? Relief, she guessed. He seemed willing to declare a truce, and she couldn't help but leap at the offer.

"There's more than one way to put on a bra?"

A mischievous grin slanted across his mouth. "Let's go home and I'll show you."

"Like you know? As I recall, you flunked Bra Clasps 101."

"That doesn't mean I don't know my logistics. Susan came in here sometimes, and she gave me a blow-by-blow account."

"Really."

He leaned close. "No push-and-stuff allowed in a place like this. You bend forward and gently *ease* into the cups. It's the only way to get a proper fit."

She couldn't quite credit that they were having this conversation, let alone in a public place. "That cinches it," she said, keeping her tone light. "We have to find a discount store. I'm a 'push-and-stuff' gal.''

"Married to a guy who's doing his damnedest to *ease* you into some decent clothes. Get used to it.''

"I'm trying.''

"Good.'' His voice went low and husky. "Seriously, Maggie. Oregon's a community property state. What's mine is yours, what's yours is mine. That means my money is your money. You insist on paying me back for every cent I ever spent if we end up splitting the sheets? Fine by me. You can pay me back out of your half of our assets.''

"That isn't what we stipulated in the agreement we signed. The little black book, remember? Keeping a tally, and me paying you back with my own money.''

"That may have been your take on it, but it wasn't necessarily mine. Where in that agreement did it say *'your own money'*? No waiting tables again, period, end of discussion.'' He chucked her under the chin. "Just relax and enjoy shopping. Please?''

Maggie knew when she was beaten. She either had to let him buy her clothes, or they would get in a huge fight. Since he was more than a little frightening when he got really angry, she opted to take the easy way out. "All right. But in my opinion, these clothes in here cost the earth. I could happily *ease* into cheaper ones.''

"But you'll look so beautiful.'' He leaned down and kissed the tip of her nose. "Think of it as your gift to me. I'm the fellow who has to look at you.''

Put to her like that, Maggie applied herself to the task of choosing a wardrobe.

By the end of the afternoon, he had bought her everything from ranch clothing, purchased at a spendy Western-wear store, to day clothes and evening wear from elite women's apparel shops all over town.

When Maggie attempted to avoid the lingerie department in the last store they visited, he chuckled and steered her directly toward it. Her face went scalding hot when he began holding up lacy, scantily cut panties and bras, glancing at her as if he were trying to picture her wearing them. He also selected several sexy nightgowns and draped them over the sales counter. When he noted her worried expression, he waggled his eyebrows, winked, and then whispered, "I firmly believe in the power of positive thinking."

Maggie laughed in spite of herself. "Positive thinking?"

"Trust me," he whispered. "I have no intention of making you wear any of this. Not anytime soon, anyway. You can stop looking so worried."

"I'm not worried," she popped back, a little amazed to realize she meant it. Rafe might contemplate making love to her, but she was coming to trust that he would never force her into anything until she was ready. It was such a wonderful feeling, knowing that.

During the following ten days while she finished the last round of medication, they slipped into a pattern, Rafe spending the giant's share of each day outdoors with Ryan, Maggie staying inside, caring for her son. On most afternoons when twilight descended, Rafe came in from the stables, grabbed a quick shower and shaved, then spent the remainder of the night with her and Jaimie and Heidi.

On those evenings, Ryan often joined them for a casual dinner in the kitchen, which afforded Maggie an opportunity to become better acquainted with her brother-in-law, who proved to be a tease and as nice as her husband.

Afterward when Heidi and the baby were down for the night, Rafe always took Maggie for a long walk along the lakeshore, weather allowing. She had never seen anything so beautiful or fairy-tale perfect as the frozen lake and the snow-swept woodlands when all was bathed in moonlight. The windows of the house glowed lantern yellow through the stands of snow-laden fir and pine, the smell of wood smoke from the chimneys seasoned the mountain air, and when the wind blew in over the towering snowcapped peaks that hugged the basin, she likened the sound to angels whispering. The serenity of the setting soothed her, and she gradually came to see why Rafe loved the ranch so much.

During those walks along the lake, they sometimes talked or cavorted playfully in the snow, but at other times, they said little, merely sharing the night sounds of the wilderness. Either way, Maggie learned something new about her husband during each stroll. He was fiercely protective of her, often grasping her elbow or looping an arm around her shoulders to prevent her from slipping on the ice. He was also innately gentle, never forgetting his strength even when they horsed around.

On the three evenings during that time when they dined out alone, he treated her to candlelight dinners at what she called ''dress-up restaurants'' where the men were required to wear suits and the women wore cocktail dresses. On those occasions, Maggie was glad he had bought her beautiful clothing, for it was becoming more important to her with each passing day that her appearance should please him. She never wanted him to compare her to one of the other women they encountered and find her lacking.

The food served in these establishments was so fancy Maggie couldn't pronounce the names of half the dishes. Ashamed to admit ignorance, she bluffed her way through and frequently had no idea what she might be ordering. On one such occasion, Rafe's eyes filled with twinkling laughter when he saw the expression that crossed her face when she learned the appetizer she had ordered was snails. He came to her rescue by telling the waiter that he had ordered the escargot, not his wife. Maggie suspected that his trading dishes with her was a monumental sacrifice. He didn't appear to be overly fond of snails himself. But to save her embarrassment, he ate them.

After that when they visited a restaurant, he gave her obscure guidance by mulling over the menu selections aloud. Pinot Noir? A bit too dry. Tonight his palate called for a wine with just a touch more sweetness. What cabernets did the house have on hand? he would ask the waiter.

Maggie realized exactly what Rafe was doing, but he carried it off so unobtrusively that she didn't feel humiliated. She became adept at surreptitiously watching every move he made. She draped her napkin over her lap when he did and soon learned by observation that the bowl containing water and a lemon wedge wasn't to drink and that the itty-bitty fork wasn't used for salad. The one time he glanced up and caught her emulating him, he winked and mouthed, "*I love you*," making her feel incredibly special when he might have belittled her instead.

It had been so long since a man had shown any concern at all about her feelings. Her father had, certainly, but many years had passed since his death and Maggie's memories of him had long since faded. For seven endless years, Lonnie had polluted her life, day in and day out.

By comparison, Rafe was wonderful. From the beginning, he'd been unfailingly generous, giving her so very much. Yet he'd never demanded anything of her in return, except that she marry him, and on that count, Maggie absolved him, believing with all her heart that he'd done it to protect her. Now he was her lawful husband, with every right to possess her, and he held off.

Maggie couldn't explain it, but somehow, as one day passed into the next, being around him bolstered her confidence. Before meeting him, she'd felt inadequate. Maggie the nobody, an inconsequential little creature, squirming and ducking to avoid being squashed.

By contrast, Rafe made her feel smart, talented, and important. When she insisted that he familiarize her with the bookkeeping system and turn over the accounts to her, he marveled at how quickly she mastered the computer and became adept with the different software.

When she compiled data from the last three fiscal years and developed flowcharts depicting profits and losses, he didn't simply pat her on the head and say, *Good job.* He spent an entire afternoon and evening in the office with Ryan, poring over the information and frequently calling upon her to explain some of the variances, concluding in the end that operational changes were indicated that might substantially increase their annual profits. Maggie could scarcely believe her ears. These intelligent, highly successful men were about to change the way they'd been doing things for years, simply because she had suggested they should?

"You're amazing, Maggie," both men said more than once, and the respect she saw in their eyes told her that they meant it. "You've literally saved us thousands of dollars, just in crop rotation alone."

Having come from a male-dominated household where she was slapped for speaking her mind and told she was stupid more times than not, Maggie loved all the praise, but more importantly, she felt her efforts were a worthwhile contribution which, by extension, made her feel worthwhile herself. One evening Rafe asked her if they should consider making cash outlays to begin replacing some of the ranch equipment. After looking into the matter and charting the cost of seasonal equipment repairs versus the possible purchase costs, Maggie recommended that they buy a new tractor and Cat, whereupon Rafe immediately got on the phone to do some price comparisons. As she became more familiar with the ranch's accounts, she also determined there might be some large tax breaks if they incorporated, and Rafe called a tax lawyer to discuss the possibility.

For the first time in her adult life, Maggie felt important, and the timidity that had been beaten into her began to fall away, to be replaced by self-assurance. She *wasn't* stupid. Rafe believed in her and because he did, she began to believe in herself. He called her "our computer guru," and while on the phone with the tax attorney, she heard him say, "The ranch manager says we could save substantial amounts by incorporating." *The ranch manager*. She suddenly had a title, and by bestowing it upon her, Rafe was giving her credit she'd never expected to receive. One evening he laughingly said, "Rye and I are the muscle in this operation, and Maggie's the brains." *The brains*. She walked a little taller after hearing him say that.

He went out of his way to make her feel incredibly special in other ways as well. If she yearned aloud for chocolate, the next thing she knew, a box of chocolates appeared on the nightstand. When she mentioned how much she loved lemonade, a pitcherful magically appeared in the refrigerator. He spoiled her shamelessly, and though unaccustomed to the attention, she enjoyed every single thoughtful gesture.

Each night when he joined her in bed and took her into his arms, Maggie could feel the throbbing hardness of his manhood pressed against her and she'd think, *This is it. My reprieve is over. He'll force the issue this time.* Only he never did, and because he didn't, she slowly came to realize that he placed more importance on her feelings and needs than he did on his own.

As Maggie came to that realization, what she had previously believed was impossible began to happen. She found herself falling in love with him. No longer did she lie awake in his arms, sick with dread. Instead she found herself wondering what it might be like to make love with him. She enjoyed the way his hands felt when he touched her, so big and hard and warm, yet always so gentle. And she longed to touch him in return—to trail her fingertips over the play of muscle in his back, to mold her palms to the firm contours of his chest, to test the resilient bulges of strength in his shoulders.

Sometimes, after she felt certain he was asleep, she satisfied her curiosity, tracing his features with her fingertips and running her hands lightly over his arms. Touching him made her pulse quicken and filled her with a yearning to move closer. As a young girl, she'd dreamed of one day meeting Mr. Right, someone tall, dark, and handsome who was gentle, sweet, and wonderfully romantic. Rafe Kendrick met or exceeded all her requirements. He was definitely tall, and except for his smoke-blue eyes, he was about as dark as a man could get with his bronze skin and jet-black hair. As for being handsome? He was no pretty boy, certainly, but there was something about the chiseled planes of his dusky face that made her insides flutter. He was also, hands down, the kindest and most thoughtful man she'd ever known.

Love. She would catch herself watching him, terrified by the feelings she was developing for him but unable to stop herself. Those feelings gave rise to a paralyzing new fear, that of losing him.

And there were things about her that Rafe didn't know—things so shameful she had never admitted them to anyone. She felt certain that when he learned of them, he'd turn away from her.

It was awful of her, she knew, but she entertained the idea of simply never telling him the truth. She could invent a fictitious father for Jaimie easily enough.

Such was her desperation that she might have chosen that route had it not been for her fear that Rafe might discover her duplicity later. Someday he might glance at Jaimie and note some small resemblance he bore to his real father. Or Lonnie might barge back into her life and spill the beans. Either way, Rafe could discover her secret and hate her for deceiving him.

Honesty. All Maggie's life she'd been told it was always best never to lie. But how could the truth be best in this instance? As things stood, Rafe held her in high regard. *Dear God, you are so sweet*, he often whispered to her at night. Well, he would no longer suffer from that illusion if she blurted out the truth.

Around and around Maggie went, ceaselessly circling the dilemma, her instinct for self-preservation tempting her to keep her secret, her sense of fairness filling her with guilt for even considering it.

Having reached that decision, Maggie found herself haggling over *when* she would tell him. That night after dinner, she would promise herself. Only when the time came, Ryan was there or Jaimie cried and needed attention, or Heidi needed help with her math, providing Maggie with a convenient excuse to put off the inevitable.

On the Tuesday right before Thanksgiving, she was finished taking the last of the antibiotics, and Rafe once again took her to see Dr. Kirsch, who gave her a clean bill of health. After leaving the clinic, Rafe insisted they mark the occasion this time by shopping for Jaimie.

They visited several infant stores where Maggie agonized over the prices of cribs, hesitating to make a choice because they were all so expensive. As they wandered through the last shop, she leaned closer to Rafe so as not to be overheard and whispered, "Don't they have any less expensive baby shops in town? All of these prices are absurd."

His gaze sharpened on hers. "Less expensive? Don't tell me that's why you've dragged me to five different stores, because you're looking for a bargain."

"All right. I won't tell you that."

He glanced around them. "That cuts it." He checked his watch. "You have five minutes to make a choice between natural or dark oak, two-toned or single-tone. When the five minutes are up, I'm buying a shitload of baby furniture. I strongly advise you tell me what your preferences are before then because you're going to be stuck with what I choose if you don't."

Maggie already knew which of the cribs she loved. But it cost over a *thousand* dollars. If she wound up having to pay him back for everything, she had to keep an eye on the total debt, and a thousand bucks seemed an outlandish price to pay for a baby bed. There were surely nice ones for far less.

Rafe followed her gaze to the crib she preferred and asked, "Is that the one you like?"

"It's beautiful," she admitted. "The dark oak looks so rich."

"Dark oak it is, then."

With that proclamation, he began selecting things for the baby as if he were killing snakes, his raven-black eyebrows drawn into an angry scowl and his voice so clipped and harsh that the clerk was all over herself, trying to pacify him. In the space of five minutes, he chose a cradle, a stroller, a crib, a bureau, and a bathing table, never once looking at Maggie to see if she approved of his choices. Then, as if he hadn't spent enough money, he proceeded to buy a glider rocker with matching ottoman, a Noah's Arc bumper pad and bedding set, several matching contour sheets and blankets, and oodles of toys. He arranged for all the purchases to be delivered to the ranch the next day, except for the cradle, which, he insisted, would fit in the back of the Expedition.

When he left the store, carrying said cradle, Maggie tagged along behind him, so upset she was about to wring her hands. She'd never seen him this angry. When they reached the back of the Expedition, she stood to one side, watching as he shoved the bed in the back storage compartment, gouging one of the side slats in the process. She stared at the scar on the dark oak. It was deep and permanent, representative to her of the wound she had just inflicted on him.

"It's a beautiful cradle, Rafe." She ran a hand over the gleaming oak. "Something this nice used to be so far beyond my reach, I never even let myself *wish!*"

"I'm glad you like it," he bit out.

He slammed the rear cargo door closed and turned the full blast of his gaze on her, his square chin jutting, a muscle ticking in his lean cheek. His blue-gray eyes glinted so brightly with anger, they reminded her of sparking flint.

Never more than in that moment had Maggie been

aware of the dangerous edge to this man. He'd put weight back on. He stood with his booted feet apart, his long, powerful legs braced against the buffeting wind that molded his Western-cut leather jacket to his well-muscled torso. The fading afternoon sunlight slanted across him, its soft, muted gold striking a sharp contrast to his darkness. Beneath the brim of his Stetson, his ebony hair lay in breeze-tousled strands over his forehead. He looked elemental, like the brutal peaks that rose in the distance behind him, tall, forceful, and honed to a lethal sharpness.

A month before, Maggie would have quaked in terror. He looked furious, and in her past experience, a furious man was an unpredictable one. Not Rafe, though. He might get so mad he could chew through nails, but he'd never lay a hand on her. She believed that with all her heart.

The knowledge filled Maggie with gladness. It was an inappropriate moment for her to yearn to hug him. But, oh, how she wanted to. He was such a sweetheart, this man—even when he was glaring at her as if he were inches away from strangling her.

The depth of her trust in him rocked Maggie and made her emotions teeter on a perilous edge between regret and happiness. Oh, God. She didn't just love him. She *adored* him. Over the last few weeks, he had slowly and systematically sneaked past her guard, laying claim to her heart as surely as if he'd grabbed hold of it with one of those brutal fists. And right now, she felt as if he were squeezing it. The pain in her chest knifed like a blade.

"You're very angry at me," she ventured.

"Yes." He said the word with such sibilance, he fairly hissed it at her.

"Would you mind telling me why?"

Even as she asked that question, Maggie felt ashamed. Recalling their quarrel at Monique's Boutique, she knew exactly why he was upset with her. Knew and regretted having hurt his feelings again with all her heart.

He was dead wrong about her reasons for not wanting him to buy the expensive crib. But to set him straight, she would have to tell him the truth about Lonnie. A public parking lot didn't strike her as an ideal place to have that conversation, especially not when Rafe was already furious with her. Waiting to broach that subject until the timing was right was the only hope she had.

"It's a little hard to say I'm sorry if I don't know what I did," she settled for saying. "I'm not able to read your mind."

If it was possible for his already sparking eyes to glint even more dangerously, his did. In a tone completely at odds with the distended, pulsating veins along each side of his throat, he calmly said, "As if you don't damned well know? Let's not play games, Maggie."

She shoved her freezing hands into the pockets of the warm down parka he'd bought for her. She owed him for so very much. Knowing that she had hurt him made her feel awful. "Good plan. No games. That includes guessing games. Can't you just tell me what I did?"

From the edge of her vision, she saw his right hand close into a knotted fist that could have easily flattened a full-grown steer. When he swung that fist toward her face, Maggie stood her ground and kept her hands in her pockets. Her faith in him wasn't misplaced. Instead of hitting her, as she might have expected weeks ago, he thrust a rigid finger at her nose.

"If you don't know, damn it, what good will it do to spell it out for you? I do my best talking with my actions. That doesn't count for shit with you, does it? Nobody does something for someone else without expecting a payback. Right, Maggie? Remember telling me that?"

She remembered, and with a clarity that made her feel sick. A denial welled at the back of her throat, but before she could voice it, he continued railing at her.

"Right now is *not* a good time to discuss this," he

informed her in a throbbing voice. "Trust me on that. If I once get started, I'll let you have it with both barrels and say things I shouldn't. So just leave it alone until I calm down."

With that, he stormed around to the driver's door, jabbing the button on the remote key device with such force that Maggie feared it would never work again. Icy wind gusted around her where she stood at the rear of the vehicle.

After climbing into the Ford, he glanced back at her through the rear window. "Why are you standing there?" he yelled. "Get in the rig!"

Feeling oddly separated from her feet, Maggie moved to obey him, half-afraid he might leave her in the parking lot. The door opened just before she reached it, compliments of her enraged husband. As she started to crawl inside, his deeply tanned hand snaked out to grasp her left arm and lend her unneeded assistance. Even in a snit, he unconsciously made caring gestures.

He turned the key in the ignition and gunned the engine. For seven years, her instinctive response to masculine rage had been to cover her head and duck. Now, here she was with a man who not only didn't start swinging when he got mad, but refused to discuss the problem with her until he calmed down. As if his saying cruel and mean things to her would be the worst thing on earth? Not even close.

As Maggie adjusted her seat and fastened her safety belt, her eyes stung with tears. She blinked them away, not entirely sure why she felt like crying. She only knew there was a lump at the base of her throat that felt the size of a baseball and that her face tingled with scalding heat.

He jerked the gearshift into first and peeled rubber leaving the parking lot, making Maggie worry that he might be one of those men who drove like a maniac when he got angry. But no. Once on the street, he stayed within the speed limit and handled the vehicle with calm precision, coming slowly to a stop and then accelerating with exaggerated smoothness.

The tension inside the vehicle was so thick it was almost palpable. He didn't speak, didn't look at her. Maggie's stomach clenched. It seemed to her that it took hours to maneuver through the busy city streets to reach the highway. After they merged with the eastbound traffic, she could bear the silence no longer.

''Are you going to give me the silent treatment all the way home?''

He ignored the question, sweeping off his hat to lay it on the console between them. Ducking his head slightly to see the rearview mirror, he flashed the turning signal to change lanes.

''Rafe?''

''God *damn* it, Maggie, leave it alone!'' he said, baring his teeth in a snarl. ''I can't talk to you right now. All right? Be smart and back off.''

She huddled against her door, staring fixedly at the white line ahead of them that divided the two traffic lanes. *Coward*, a small voice at the back of her mind chastised. She *knew* why he was so hurt. Why couldn't she just explain that he had misinterpreted her motives?

She clenched her hand over the shoulder harness that angled across her body, hating herself for remaining silent. But, oh, God, if she opened that can of worms, then what? She would have to tell him the whole ugly truth. Sooner or later, she planned to do that, anyway. But not *now*. Not when he was so mad he wouldn't even look at her.

Engaging in a stint of self-recrimination, she went back over everything that had been said at the infant store. He'd been so sweet all afternoon, escorting her from shop to shop, never once complaining or insisting she make up her mind about a crib. His mood had been mellow. There had been an indulgent smile on his mouth and a twinkle in his eyes every time he looked at her. Then, whammo. She had asked him if there were any less expensive baby shops in town, and he had detonated.

Outwardly, it might appear that he'd gotten angry over nothing, but Maggie knew better. From the very start, he had been touchy about the money issue. And he'd been completely up front with her about it, admitting that he took it as an insult and that it hurt his feelings. How many men were willing to swallow their pride and admit to a woman when their feelings got hurt?

He did his best talking with his actions? Not entirely. He'd reassured her with words as well, countless times. *No paybacks, Maggie.* And bless his heart, he'd meant it. Night after night, he'd lain in bed beside her, his arms a gentle circle around her, his big frame pressed against her. She wasn't so naïve as to believe his restraint hadn't cost him dearly.

Remembering all those nights made her feel so small. It was just so scary to think about telling him the truth about herself. *You are so sweet.* He'd never look at her in the same way once she talked to him. Never.

Rafe. He was every hope and dream she'd ever had. He was the answer to every prayer she'd uttered over the last seven years. *Please, God, help me.* How many times had she wept into her pillow, whispering those words to a God she'd long since decided didn't hear her? Her life had been a trap. Toward the end, she had nearly stopped praying. Nearly stopped dreaming. Wishes were for fools, she'd told herself, and she'd been far too busy trying to survive.

Then she'd hit bottom. No way out. No way to fight back. No strength to continue the struggle. So she'd run. Straight into the arms of a boxcar bum. Her frog who had turned out to be a handsome cowboy prince.

She gulped to stifle a sob, the highway a swimming blur before her. Sometimes he called her his little angel face. Well, she had news for him. *He* was the one who was heaven-sent. And if he learned the truth about her, she might lose him. Was it so wrong to hold off and let the days pass in silence? He was the only miracle she was ever likely to get. If she lost him, that'd be it. And, God help her, now that she'd gotten a taste of a life with him, she didn't think she could go on without him, figuratively or literally. Lonnie had nearly killed her the last time he beat her up. Without Rafe to protect her, what was to stop him from having another go? Next time, he might finish the job.

Maggie took a ragged breath, knowing she couldn't allow this to continue. If Rafe had said or done something to hurt her feelings, he wouldn't remain silent and let her go on bleeding. He'd fix things, no matter what the risks to himself. How could she do less? Let the chips fall where they may, she had to tell him. Not later this evening. Not tomorrow morning. She had to do it now.

Minutes passed. Long, agonizing, excruciating minutes. Then, up ahead, she saw the turnoff to the Rocking K. When he turned off the highway, the Expedition bounced over some ruts, jarring her teeth.

"Rafe?" she managed to squeeze out. "Would you mind pulling over? I need to talk to you, and it's a little hard to have a conversation on rough road."

He kept driving, his jaw muscle bunched, his lips pressed together in grim silence. Maggie waited. It seemed to her they drove ten miles. In reality, it was probably only two, but every second of quiet seemed years long. If she was going to tell him, she couldn't let it go until they reached the house. She'd die of shame if Becca or Ryan happened to hear snatches of the conversation, and she absolutely couldn't take the chance that Heidi might overhear them. At all costs, Heidi was never to know. Maggie never wanted her to feel guilty or indebted to her for what she had gone through to protect her. *Never.*

"Rafe?" she tried again.

He slammed the heel of his hand against the steering wheel, shot her a glare, and without slowing down, pulled off to the side of the road. When he finally slammed on the brakes, the Ford jounced and rocked to a jarring stop on the snow-packed shoulder edging the bar ditch.

"You just won't let it be, will you?" he raged. "Okay, fine. You wanna talk, Maggie? By God, let's talk. Who starts? You?" He waited a beat. "Oh, that's right. Little Miss Innocent has no idea what the hell I'm pissed about!"

"I—"

"Shut up!" he snapped, cutting her short. "You wanna play games with me, honey? Well, keep your head down. You're way out of your league."

"I'm sorry," she managed to insert, her voice quaking.

"You're sorry. That's supposed to fix everything, right? My heart bleeds. Well, you know what? I'm sick-to-death tired of playing Mr. Nice Guy. So we'll play this crappy little game your way. 'Paybacks are hell.' Isn't that what it's called? I give, you pay back. Sounds good to me. I'm so horny, I could screw a knothole right now."

Maggie saw the pain that lurked behind the anger in his eyes. She wanted to avert her face, to get angry right back for all the awful things he was saying, but she wouldn't let herself off that easy. This was her fault.

"Would you listen, just for a minute?"

He gave a bitter laugh. "I'm fed up with your bullshit. New game, new rules. A little addition and division is called for at this point. How much do you owe me? Let's see. There's the five hundred grand I paid Lonnie."

Maggie's breath snagged. "Five hundred *what?*"

"You heard me," he rasped out. "Do you think the bastard backed off out of the goodness of his heart? And then there was the money I spent on clothes for you. What did that come to? Dumbass that I am, I never totaled up the tab. Four thousand, five, maybe? Oh, hey, I'll be fair and cut you some slack. We'll call it three thousand, five hundred. Then there's the thirty-seven hundred I blew today. And what do you figure a roof over your head and food in your belly is worth? And the mountain of medical bills, of course." He fell silent, his glittering gaze fixed on her expectantly. "Quick. You're a smart girl. Put that calculator brain of yours to work. You're a lot better with figures than I am. How much do you owe me?"

Maggie couldn't speak. She just sat there, staring at him, his words barely registering. All she could really concentrate on was that awful, wounded look in his eyes.

"I'll leave off the food for you and the baby. What the hell. I'll toss in free board as well and forget the hospital and doctor bills. Off the top of my head, I calculate you're into my wallet for approximately five hundred and seven thousand. Honey, where I come from, there's not a piece of ass on God's green earth worth that much!"

The door handle jabbed Maggie in the back. She realized she had turned in the seat and was shrinking away from him. She straightened, keeping her gaze fixed on his.

"Are you finished now?" she asked. "There's something I need to say."

"Am I finished?" He raked a hand through his hair. "Hell, no. Would you be? What's your going rate these days, Maggie? I hope to God you place a higher value on yourself than when I first met you. A baby bottle and a can of formula?" He gave another humorless huff of laughter. "Five or six bucks, maybe? I'd be dipping for honey until the cows came home and *still* not get my money's worth. A hundred bucks a pop. How's that sound? You'll only have to spread your legs five thousand and seventy times that way. Divide three hundred and sixty-five days into that, sweet cheeks. Getting laid once a day, you'll be working off the debt on your back for thirteen years, give or take a few months."

Maggie felt as if he had slapped her. *Both barrels*. He

was being mean and dirty, no question about it. He made her feel like a piece of trash.

She guessed that was fitting.

"Of course, playing the game your way, you'll be getting into my wallet every day for those thirteen years, adding to the debt even as you work it off. Living costs being what they are, I think it's fair to charge fifty bucks a day for your and Jaimie's and Heidi's keep. And clothes, of course. Hell, the bottom line, not counting clothes, is that you'll be hanging around here for twenty-six years or so, and still owe me. Sweet for me, a real bitch for you, but life's hell. Even worse, I'm older than you are by six years. When my sex drive dwindles, I may only take a crack at you once a week and drag it the hell out until you're tits up and six feet under!"

Inside the pockets of her parka, Maggie clenched her fists so tightly that her nails lacerated her palms. She knew she had no right to feel angry. But it was there inside her, roiling like acid. Before she could stop herself, she cried, "Is that my cue to run screaming up the road, Rafe?" She drew her hands from her pockets and jerked open her parka, the snaps popping loudly in the silence. "Well, guess again! I've been whoring to keep Heidi safe for three years! You really should have stuck to playing Mr. Nice Guy. Trying to play the bastard, you're the one way out of your league! Compared to Lonnie, you're a pussycat."

He jerked as if she had punched him. His burnished face went pasty, and the mask of anger fell from his features, revealing only the hurt. He stared at her for a long, seemingly endless second. Then, as if a fist drove all the breath from him, he released a ragged sigh and rested his forearms on the steering wheel to pillow his head. "Oh, Jesus, Maggie . . ." The tendons in his throat became swollen and starkly defined as his face contorted in a tortured grimace. "I didn't mean it. Please believe that. I didn't mean it."

"I know you didn't," she said in a voice that sounded

distant and off-key. "But I mean this. I'd count myself the luckiest woman alive to work off the debt I owe you for the next twenty-six years. On my back. Standing on my head. Once a day, twice a day. I don't care. I'd thank God for every minute I was with you. You want me on those terms? Please, say yes. I'll strip and start paying you back right now!"

His head came up. He turned a bewildered gaze on her. "Say what?"

"You heard me. I stopped feeling terrified of having sex with you days ago. A week or two, maybe. At this point, I've moved up to just feeling a whole lot nervous about it, which is something I can handle. There's only one problem. I can't in good conscience charge you a hundred dollars a time. Let's keep it at five dollars. That way, you don't get ripped off and I have a guarantee you'll let me stay!"

He blinked and rubbed a hand over his face. As he dropped his arm, he blinked at her again, as if he thought the picture might change if he brought it into better focus.

"I wasn't edgy about you spending so much on a crib for the reasons you think," she forced herself to say. "I admit, I was worried about possibly having to pay you back if things went wrong between us. But I never for a moment thought I might be so lucky as to pay you off by making love with you. I was thinking in terms of getting a job after you sent me away and paying you back by the month, a little at a time." She laughed a little hysterically. "Of course, I didn't know how much you paid Lonnie. Even working two jobs, I'll never be able to pay that off."

He sat erect, his expression still conveying befuddlement. "After I what? Maggie, for God's sake. Send you away? We've covered that ground. All of this because you've got some maggot in your brain about me telling you to leave? I'd never do that. *Never*. How many times do I have to tell you I love you to make you believe me?''

''You love an illusion,'' she threw back shrilly, tears rushing to her eyes and nearly blinding her. ''Sweet little Maggie, your innocent angel. Well, wake up! I'm not innocent, and I'm sure as hell no angel. Do you remember when I told you Jaimie had no father?''

''Yes,'' he said hoarsely.

''I lied.''

''Well, of course you lied. Unless you experienced the second Immaculate Conception, that is.''

''Lonnie is Jaimie's father.'' Maggie felt as if she might vomit. She swung her hand, unable to go on until she gulped. ''My stepfather. I slept with him for three years. Whenever he wanted, however he wanted. You name it, I did it. You can't speak to me like I'm a whore and insult me. That's what I am!''

He raked his fingers through his hair again, this time pausing to make a tight fist in the strands before releasing them. ''How can you say that? A whore? The bastard raped you.''

It seemed to Maggie that the interior of the Expedition had been stripped of oxygen. Black spots danced. Her throat felt frozen. ''No, Rafe. Lonnie Boyle never raped me. You've believed that because it's what you wanted to believe, and I was too ashamed to tell you differently.'' She watched the incredulous look that slowly came over his face. ''He never forced me. Never once. He's an animal, and his sins are many, but rape is one thing I can't pin on him.''

A muscle under his eye began to jerk as he gaped at her. The silence between them crackled. Maggie held her breath, mindless prayers bouncing around in her mind, all of them disjointed, none making sense. It didn't matter. She'd begged God dozens of times to make Rafe not care when she told him, to somehow work a miracle and make him still love her.

Now was the telling moment.

He just kept staring at her as if he'd never seen her before, his dark face frozen with shock. With a jerky laugh, he said, "You were willing, you mean?"

Maggie couldn't force out a reply, so she merely nodded, watching his face for some sign of his reaction. What she saw was fleeting but soul-shattering. *Disgust.* He regained control quickly. She'd give him that. But she had seen, nevertheless.

Reaching behind her, she grabbed the handle and threw open the passenger door. Toppling backward off the seat, she grappled to land on her feet on the packed snow. She didn't pause to close the door. She just ran. Blindly, not really caring where she went, just as long as she didn't have to see that look on his face again.

Honesty wasn't always the best policy, she thought wildly, as she struggled through the deep drifts between the trees. She'd told him the truth. She had played fair. And she'd lost. It was as simple and as heartbreaking as that.

 Chapter Sixteen

For a frozen instant, Rafe was so taken aback that he couldn't move. *Willing?* The images that word called to mind were so contradictory to everything he knew about his wife that he couldn't credit them.

As the first shock wave subsided, he regained his senses, saw that Maggie was running away from him into the woods, and leaped out of the Ford. "Maggie, get back here!" he roared.

Approximately forty feet away from him already, she whirled to look back, staggering to keep her footing in the deep snow. Even at a distance, Rafe could see the pain that contorted her features. Her stance and the expression on her face brought him reeling to a halt at the front bumper. She looked poised to flee, and he had a feeling one wrong move on his part would be all the impetus she needed. It would be dark soon. The sun was already behind the mountains, and at this elevation, once dusk fell, darkness came with treacherous speed.

"Come back, honey. Please? We'll talk. We can—"

"No!" she shrieked, bending forward at the waist and pressing a fist to her chest. "I *knew* you'd hate me if I told you. I *knew* it."

"I don't hate you, Maggie. That's crazy. I love you. Let's talk this out."

If she heard him, she gave no indication. She shook her head wildly. Rafe measured the distance between them, confident that his longer legs would give him the advantage if it came to a footrace. He hoped it didn't.

"I don't *want* to talk. Just leave me alone!" She'd reversed their situation—she had wanted to talk and he'd refused. Now she was the one who wouldn't communicate. She sobbed again. "Just leave me *alone!*"

With that, she turned to run, lost her footing, and fell full-length in a drift. As she scrambled back to her feet, Rafe sprang after her. "Maggie, for God's sake, don't run off. You'll get lost!"

She darted away, each step taking her deeper into the woods. Rafe could remember at least a half dozen times over the years when visitors to the ranch had gotten lost out here, the most memorable occurring one summer when a cattle buyer had parked along the road to take a leak. He'd walked only a few feet into woods, just far enough so no one could happen along and see him. When he'd tried to return to his truck, he'd gone the wrong way. A search party had finally found him alive three days later, eight miles from his vehicle.

Rafe crossed the shoulder of the road in two loping strides, tensing to leap over the ditch. As his boot touched ground with his third step, he hit ice where the snowmelt on the road had drained off and refrozen like polished glass. The smooth sole of his riding boot shot out from under him.

He scrambled to keep from falling. The ice was slicker than snot. One of his legs shot forward, the other went backward. He landed *hard* in a graceless rendition of a ballerina doing the splits. Pain exploded through his groin and lower abdomen. A rock. He had landed on a rock buried in the snow.

He grabbed for his crotch and rolled onto his side in a fetal position. He couldn't see around the red haze that swam before his eyes. Couldn't breathe. Couldn't even move except to roll back and forth. *Jesus*. He was going to die.

The agony held him in a paralyzing grip. For seconds?

Minutes? When the pain subsided and his senses started to clear, he realized he had slid down the bank into the ditch and lay in the rushing current of snowmelt. He pushed up on his elbows, dug for purchase, and managed to pull himself out. Once he reached more level ground, a convulsive tide of nausea purged his stomach.

Trembling with weakness, he lifted his head to search the trees. "Maggie?" he called, a little amazed that his voice hadn't changed to a high-pitched soprano. "Maggie!"

Silence. He rose to his feet and, staggering like a drunk, started after her. Even though it was getting dark, he really wasn't too worried. He doubted she could be very far ahead of him. Besides, even if it took until after dark to find her, the moon would rise soon. Reflecting off the snow, its brightness would provide fair visibility. Her tracks should be easy to follow. If the trees filtered out the light, he could always go to the house and get a nine-volt torch.

"Maggie! Honey, if you can hear me, holler out and I'll find you."

Nothing.

"Sweetheart, I don't hate you. I love you!" In the dusky light, Rafe missed seeing a low-hanging branch. It caught him across the forehead and almost knocked him off his feet. He swore and executed a drunken side-step to keep his balance. Now both ends of him were throbbing.

"I don't give a shit about Lonnie!" he yelled, not exactly in a loving tone of voice. "Maggie, goddamn it, answer me! It's childish to run off and hide like this. We need to talk this out like two mature adults!"

No answer.

"We need to discuss this!" he cried, his volume inching up another decibel. The words seemed to bounce back at him, diminished and muted. *The snow.* In places the wind had layered it in gently rounded banks of white nearly as high as his waist. A deep snowpack absorbed sound, and it was entirely possible his voice didn't carry very far. Could Maggie even hear him? She couldn't be too far ahead of him, but his calls might not be reaching her.

As he zigzagged through the trees, he plunged through the crust of a drift and dropped to mid-thigh. "Son of a bitch! Damn it, Maggie, I know you can hear me!" He just prayed she really could. Straining with his unencumbered leg to escape the hole, his other foot broke through. He fell sideways, only managing to stay standing by grabbing hold of a tree limb. He was going to kill himself trying to catch up with her. He crawled from the icy wallow.

"I outweigh you by over a hundred pounds! I'm falling through the ice. You want me to break a goddamned leg?"

Only silence. Rafe knelt there, grabbing for breath. Peering through the darkening twilight, he searched the stands of pine for movement. She couldn't have gone *that* far. Even someone as slightly built as Maggie would fall through occasionally, which made for slow going.

He stared ahead at her tracks. Her sneakers had left a quarter-inch depression on the icy white surface. A glance over his shoulder at his own footprints revealed that his boots sank in at least an inch with every step.

Wonderful. She was racing ahead of him with the speed of a gazelle while he floundered back here like an overweight buffalo.

"*Maaaagheee!*" he yelled as loudly as he could. "*Maaaa—ghee!*"

When he caught up with her, he'd be tempted to wring her neck. Of all the damned fool stunts to pull. There were cougars in these woods, and recently there had allegedly been sightings of wolves that had migrated down from the Washington Cascades. Odds were against her encountering a dangerous animal, but what if she did?

Regaining his feet, Rafe began following her tracks again. He moved cautiously. No worries. Every step she took left an imprint on the snow. It wasn't as if he might lose her trail. Right?

Rafe no sooner assured himself of that than he broke into a small clearing where cows had bedded down. The snow had been so badly churned that he couldn't detect Maggie's footprints in the maze. Not in such dim light.

He paused to listen. All he heard were the lodgepole pines creaking in the wind. *Cold.* His wet clothes were freezing to his body. The sopping side of his leather jacket lay over his shoulder like a chunk of ice. *God.* Shortly after dark, the temperature would plummet twenty degrees, taking the mercury well below ten. With the wind-chill factor, it could dive below zero. If he failed to find Maggie and she spent the night out here—

He cut the thought short. No point in borrowing trouble. He would catch up with her. Why scare himself spitless by thinking of the awful fates that might befall her? It just tied his gut in knots and kept him from thinking straight.

But he couldn't stop the pictures from forming in his mind. What if she had fallen through the drifts? Her clothing might be as wet as his. She was wearing the new down parka, but the damned thing was designed more for fashion than practicality.

"Maggie!" he yelled, growing frightened in spite of himself. He cupped his hands around his mouth and turned, yelling her name in all directions. Only the whisper of pine boughs offered a response.

Bent low over the ground in an attempt to pick up her tracks, he moved in an ever-widening circle. She had to have left some sign of her passing. Deep snow lay in all directions. He would come across her trail. He had to.

Minutes later, his patience was rewarded. He found a faint imprint of her sneaker. Heading in that direction, he soon picked up a plain trail. Holding himself under rigid control, he stepped slowly and lightly. He couldn't afford to hurry and fall through. Maggie really would be in a pickle if he broke a leg.

When they didn't show up back at the ranch, Ryan would get worried. His first move would be to try contacting Rafe on the Expedition's built-in cellular phone. He might piss away as much as two hours before he decided to look for them. When he found the Expedition parked on the side of the road, he'd realize something was wrong. But how long would it take him to organize a search party?

By that time, where would Maggie be? If she were woods-smart, Rafe wouldn't have been so worried. But she was a town girl, and due to her illness, he hadn't had time yet to teach her how to take care of herself out here. Did she even know how to tell her directions? Had anyone ever explained to her how she could wander in circles, getting more and more lost with every step she took? Or that the smartest thing to do if she did get lost was to stay put? Was she aware that digging deep into a snowbank might keep her from freezing?

He kept seeing her face. That sweet, vulnerable mouth. Those big, expressive eyes. The pain that had twisted her features. *You were willing, you mean?* Why in God's name had he asked her something so stupid? Of course she hadn't been willing. No matter what she said or how she had come to believe such a thing of herself, he knew better. Not his Maggie.

I whored to protect Heidi for three years. Whenever he wanted, however he wanted. You name it. I did it. When she'd told him that, why hadn't he grabbed her into his arms? Told her he loved her. But, oh, no. He'd sat there like a mindless imbecile. Just gaped at her with his mouth hanging open.

"Maggie! I'm sorry!" he shouted. "It's not like you think! I love you!"

Nothing.

"I *love* you! Do you hear me? I love you. I'll always love you! I don't care if you slept with Lonnie!"

Silence.

"I don't *care!*" he yelled, his vocal chords aching

with the strain. ''If you slept with every trucker on the interstate from Idaho to California, I don't care!'' When she didn't answer, he screamed, *''Maaa—ghee!''*

He was getting panicky. He couldn't let himself do this. He had to keep a level head. Think. Systematically follow her tracks.

Her life might depend on it.

Oh, God. She was lost. There was no question. She'd walked every which way, finding the same exact thing each time, nothing but more trees. She'd only gone a short distance from the road. How on earth had she gotten turned around?

Maggie swung about in the small clearing. Above her, all she could see were treetops and tiny patches of velvet-black, star-specked sky. She couldn't get her bearings without being able to study the constellations.

She'd first tried to return to the road at least two hours ago. Instead of following her own tracks like any sane person would have done, she had wanted to avoid facing Rafe again, so she'd walked north/northeast, hoping to hit the road at a different place from where he had parked. After walking for what she'd guessed then to be about thirty minutes, she knew she'd gone the wrong way. Definitely not north/northeast. She had then tried to correct her course, walked at least another thirty minutes, and eventually concluded that wasn't the right way, either.

At that point, she had done what she should have in the first place and tried to follow her own tracks. Simple, right? She'd thought so. But she'd left three sets of prints by then, and the ones she chose to follow weren't the ones that led to the road. Worse, the next set didn't either, and by then, her tracks were so confusingly criss-crossed, she had no idea which were which.

She had spent the last hour going first one way, then another, her terror mounting. Her clothes were soaked, the down parka soggy and heavy, making it hard to swing her arms for balance. Her legs had long since moved past being merely cold to an awful, frozen numbness.

"Rafe!" she screamed. "Rafe! Can you hear me?"

He was out here searching for her. She knew he was. She just had to keep moving until he found her, that was all. And he would. She knew he would. No matter how angry he might be. No matter how disgusted. He would set aside his personal feelings and search for her.

Stupid, Maggie. So stupid. Why on earth had she run off like that? At the time, she'd intended to go only so far into the woods—just deeply enough that he wouldn't be able to see her—and then walk parallel with the road until she reached the house. It had seemed like a good plan then, her only way of getting home without suffering his company and seeing that awful, sick look on his face the entire way. By her estimation, it had been only about five miles to the house. She had walked that far to work in a little over an hour more times than she could count. *Nothing to it*, she'd told herself. Only the first thing she knew, she hadn't been able to *find* the road, let alone walk parallel to it.

Her chest burned. The air was so cold, it seared her lungs. A gust of wind came whistling through the trees, slicing at her wet coat like a razor. Tall pines snapped and creaked all around her, the sound eerie and frightening. She thanked God for the moonlight, which at least helped her see.

Keep moving. If she gave in to the exhaustion, she would freeze to death. Heidi and Jaimie needed her. For them, she had to stay on her feet and keep walking. If she stopped to rest, even for a minute, she might not get back up.

Was this how it felt to freeze to death, your lungs on fire, your heart slogging as if your blood had thickened to molasses? Her thoughts were jumbled and disjointed, the icy coldness making the top of her head feel as if it might blow off. Her cheekbones and eyebrows ached. Even her hair hurt.

Her leg buckled. The next instant, she lay facedown in the snow. She struggled to get up. Couldn't. The ice burned her palms and her grasping fingers quivered. Tears squeezed hotly from her eyes, only to freeze the instant they trailed onto her cheeks.

After a while, she didn't feel as cold. That was good. Vaguely, she wondered if perhaps a warm front was moving in. She could still feel the wind buffeting her, but it no longer seemed to slice through her clothing.

A faint sense of alarm slipped into her foggy thoughts. *Warm?* People started to feel warm when they were freezing to death. Next, she'd feel sleepy. Oh, God, she already felt sort of sleepy.

She blinked, her alarm increasing when her upper and lower eyelashes clung together. Heaven help her, her eyes were freezing shut. She had to get up. Only how? Just moving a leg took a Herculean effort.

An awful sound drifted to her through the woods. *Muh-rrhaww!* Maggie raised her head. *Muh-rrhaww!* An animal of some kind. A really *big* animal. A bear, maybe? No, they were in hibernation right now. The sound came again, and she listened, trying to determine what it was. After a moment, she nearly laughed. A cow. Only a cow. Even if there was a small herd of them, they weren't likely to hurt her. Rafe said most cows on the ranch were accustomed to humans.

Maggie was wandering aimlessly now. Rafe could determine that much by the meandering trail he'd been following. Why didn't she stop so he could catch up with her? No such luck. Her irregular tracks told him she was exhausted. Common sense told him she was probably also freezing cold. He sure as hell was.

Rafe staggered to a stop. This was getting him nowhere. He had to head back to the road and call Ryan. Get a search party out here. Several men on snowmobiles could cover a lot more ground than a lone man on foot. *Damn.* With every step, he'd expected to come upon her, sitting forlornly under a tree, hugging her knees to stay warm. To turn around and leave with that picture of her in his mind had been damned near impossible.

"Maggie!" he yelled for what seemed like the thousandth time. "Maggie?"

Rafe's heart skipped a beat when he heard an answering sound. He cocked his head. There it was again. He turned to listen, pinpointing the direction. *A cow.* Defeated, Rafe stared down at her footprints on the snow, noting the zigzagging pattern of her steps. She was about to go down, judging by the lurching pattern of those tracks. His eyes burned from the cold blast of the wind. Should he go for help or follow her trail for a few more minutes? If she collapsed, a search party might not find her in time. It would take at least an hour to get men rounded up and all the snowmobiles filled with gas. Another thirty minutes would be wasted while they drove from the ranch to where the Ford was parked. Tack on the additional time that it could take to penetrate the woods and find her, and she could be dead before they reached her.

Rafe prayed he wasn't making the worst decision of his life as he started to follow her tracks again. But, mistake or not, he couldn't make himself give up. Just a few more minutes, he promised himself. If he hadn't found her by then, he'd head for the road.

Her trail became more and more erratic as it went along. His heart caught again when he came upon a place where it looked as if she'd fallen full-length in the snow. He knelt to examine the disturbed surface, touching his fingertips to depressions he felt certain had been made by hers. He imagined her lying there, digging her fingers into the ice, sobbing and terrified. *Jesus.* He'd never forgive himself for this. He'd known all along that Lonnie was the father of her baby. Why in the hell hadn't he forced her to talk to him about it?

Pushing back to his feet, Rafe began to bird-dog her tracks again, certain now that she couldn't press on much longer. *Please, God*. He remembered how resolutely she had endured whatever came her way when he first met her, suffering the cold without a coat, nursing Jaimie even when it brought tears to her eyes. Maggie was delicate-looking, but that fragile spine of hers was laced with steel. His luck, she'd keep walking until she froze to death standing up.

A few minutes later, Rafe came to a clearing where a half dozen cows and heifers had bedded down for the night. They lay bunched together to keep warm, their breath sending up ribbons of steam that looked like smoke in the moonlight. Maggie's tracks circled to the left. He followed her footprints. About halfway around the opening, she hung a sharp right. Straight toward the cows.

Rafe turned to peer at the dark bovine lumps that lay in a cluster. The cows' white faces shone eerily in the moonlight. Two of the creatures had their heads up, their eyes dark pits as they stared stupidly at him, chewing their cuds.

Almost afraid to hope, Rafe moved slowly toward them. "Easy, ladies," he said soothingly. "I just wanna check to see if you've got company."

Maggie lay huddled between two heifers. Tears of relief turning to ice trails on his cheeks, Rafe made his way carefully toward her. He placed a boot on each side of her torso, the sides of his legs pressing against the hot bovine bodies that he felt certain had kept her from freezing to death.

"Hee-yah!" he yelled, slapping the back of the cow to his right.

The huge beasts scrambled to their feet, bawling in protest at the disturbance. Rafe shoved away the two heifers that flanked his wife, protecting her from being stepped on with the brace of his legs. As the animals trotted away, he sank to one knee.

"Maggie?" He grasped her shoulder, fear lancing through him when he felt the frozen nylon of her parka. *Oh, God.* Just as he had feared, she was wet to the skin. "Maggie? Wake up," he ordered, shaking her.

She didn't respond. His fear became terror. "Maggie, damn it! Wake up!" He grabbed her hands and began chafing them. Then he lightly tapped her cheeks. Please, God . . . He couldn't bear it if he lost her. "Maggie?"

"Rafe?" Her lashes fluttered and she opened her eyes. His relief was so great, he felt boneless. She rolled onto her back . "I *knew* you'd come."

It terrified him to think how close he'd been to turning back. "Of course I came, sweetheart."

How in hell could she have so much faith in him on that score and so little in other ways? He yearned to ask, but now wasn't the time or place to hash out their problems. Maggie seemed to have put their troubles on a back burner as well. No big surprise. Their first order of business had to be getting out of here. All else took a second seat.

"I've been bird-dogging your tracks the whole time," he told her. "Why the hell didn't you stop and stay put so I could catch up?"

Stiffly she rose to her knees. Her voice still gruff with sleep, she replied, "It was so cold. Until I found the cows, I was afraid to stop for fear I'd freeze to death."

It was a miracle that the cows hadn't spooked, leaving her to lie there and die. Just the thought made his guts tighten like a fist. He loved her so much.

He laughed shakily and cupped his hands over her hair. The unruly curls had become wet, probably from snow falling from tree boughs. Now the strands were stiff with ice.

Rafe wanted to hug the very breath out of her and make long avowals of love. But that would have to wait.

He had to get her out of here. Strip those damned wet clothes off her. Get her warm.

"I owe those cows," he settled for saying. "Tomorrow I'll bring out a sack of grain to show my appreciation." He bent to press a quick kiss to her forehead, his heart squeezing when her skin felt warm against his cold lips. "Two sacks of grain," he amended. "Thank God you had the good sense to cuddle up."

"With me, necessity is the mother of courage. It was my only option." She wrinkled her nose. "I'm so sorry about this, Rafe. It was stupid of me to take off like that. I meant to follow the road, only then I couldn't find it."

"That happens out here. The trees are so thick, even experienced woodsmen have gotten lost. If you don't know some of the landmarks to give you your bearings, you're shit out of luck."

She laughed weakly. "That pretty much describes how it went. No matter which way I walked, it wasn't the right way. Take away sidewalks and I'm inept."

Rafe did hug her then. Weak though it was, that spunky little laugh melted his heart, and he couldn't resist. His arms trembled with the intensity of his feelings as he squeezed her close. "Inept? You used your head." He pressed his lips to her hair. "I'll make a great rancher's wife out of you yet. All you need is some mountain know-how, and you'll do fine."

She stiffened slightly. "A rancher's wife?"

"Damned straight, a rancher's wife. *My* wife. I'll chain you to the bedpost before I'll let you leave me, Maggie. Understand that and get used to it."

Tears filled her eyes, and her mouth trembled as she gazed up at him. "You mean it?" she asked faintly.

Rafe realized he was kneeling there in the snow like a damned fool, wasting precious minutes. Beginning tomorrow, he was going to make it his mission in life to teach her some survival skills. He'd also drive it into her brain with chisel and hammer that he loved her and nothing was going to change that. But, for now, he had far more pressing concerns.

"I mean it," he assured her gruffly. "You about ready to go home?"

"Oh, yes . . . I hope Becca kept dinner hot. I'm cold and I'm starving."

Starving? Rafe had an unreasoning urge to laugh again. *Starving.* He'd pictured her lying out here, half-dead. He'd bring those cows three sacks of grain. Scratch that. He'd bring a whole damned truckload.

He pushed himself erect, prepared to lend her assistance in standing, but to his surprise, she managed on her own. That figured. This girl had been doing just the opposite of what he expected ever since he first clapped eyes on her. She shivered at a gust of icy wind. He found reason to rejoice even in that. It was when a person stopped shivering that there was cause for true alarm.

"Can you walk?" he asked.

She lifted one sneaker and gave her foot a shake. "Yeah. I was on my last legs earlier, but the breather and getting warmer really helped."

He encircled her shoulders with an arm, pulling her snugly against him. It felt so good to have her with him, safe and sound. So damned good. Once he got her back to the truck, they'd be home free.

Rafe took only one step, then came to a stop, his gaze fixed in the direction of the road. He wasn't sure exactly how far away it was. By quick estimate, it would take them over an hour, and that was if nothing went wrong—like falling through the ice, which was a probability. By the time he got Maggie to the rig, she'd be chilled to the bone again, not to mention so worn out she probably wouldn't be able to put one foot in front of the other one.

Could he carry her through this snow? On the one hand, Rafe vowed that he would crawl out with her on his back if he had to, but on the other hand, he had to face facts. With her weight tacked onto his, he'd break through the ice far more often. Managing to scramble free from each wallow would take precious time and stores of energy, both of which would slow him down. What if it took two hours or even three to get her to the vehicle?

Concern tightened his throat. He cast his gaze westward. Just over that steep ridge was a line shack, which would be stocked with canned food and plenty of firewood. It would be equipped with other emergency necessities as well, including lanterns, warm bedding, and a radio or cellular phone to call out, powered by a thousand-volt generator with a DC outlet. The Rocking K was peppered with line shacks like that. They were a necessary feature on a huge spread, often meaning the difference between life and death for ranch hands who got stranded miles from anywhere. The rough dwellings also served as overnight accommodations for the men during roundups.

If he remembered correctly, it would take less than half an hour to reach the line shack, but it would be one hell of a rough climb to scale that ridge. On the plus side, though, the snow wouldn't be packed as deeply on a steep slope like that. He glanced at Maggie, who wobbled slightly. She probably didn't have the strength left to make it. He could throw her over his shoulder in a fireman's carry if she gave out. He would call Ryan from the line shack and make arrangements for men on snowmobiles to pick them up in the morning.

Drawing her along with him, Rafe veered west, heading for the ridge that loomed like a black specter against the moonlit sky. With every step they took, he sent up a silent prayer that they could make it.

Chapter Seventeen

Her feet braced on protrusions of granite, Maggie clung to the snowy branch of a pine whose roots had taken hold on the steep, icy slope. Her legs quivered with exhaustion, and she was so cold, her fingers barely felt the bite of frost that encased the tree's rough bark. Her lungs grabbed for breath, each inhalation making a soft, wheezing noise that knifed down her windpipe.

Halted in his ascent, Rafe stood about three feet above her, one long leg straightened behind him, his other bent to take another step. He looked over his shoulder, his face bathed in black shadows. She couldn't see his eyes, but Maggie had never been more intensely aware of his ability to strip away a person's veneer with that piercing gaze of his.

"You're done for, aren't you?" he called softly.

As far as Maggie could see, being "done for" wasn't exactly an option. It had turned out to be a lot farther to the base of the slope than Rafe had estimated. High-elevation air, he'd explained, often made things look closer than they actually were, especially at night. "A magnifying effect," he'd called it. In the time since, he had apologized to her several times and berated himself under his breath for misjudging the distance. It had been two years since he'd been up here, he explained, and he never should have trusted in his memory.

Maggie knew little about high elevations except that

the thin air made it hard to breathe. Now the crest of the ridge looked no closer to her than it had when they'd started the climb. She couldn't just lie down and say she was finished. To reach shelter, she had to make it to the top, and Rafe said it was still some distance after that to the line shack.

"I'm fine," she said between panting breaths. "I just need to rest a sec."

He nodded and braced his hands on his hips, throwing back his head to pull in a huge draught of icy air. "Hell of a climb, isn't it? I'm sorry. In summer, when there's no ice, it's not such rough going. I'm about done for myself."

Maggie could see he was tired, but he looked far from the point of collapse. He was breathing heavily. Anyone making a climb like this would. But he wasn't frantically struggling for breath, and those long, powerful legs of his looked rock-steady. Her own were trembling and jerking.

"Yeah," she agreed. "Steep."

She couldn't manage a lengthier response. Right now, what little oxygen she could filch from the air was needed to fuel her body.

Seconds passed. She could feel him staring at her, an unvoiced *You ready to go on yet?* hanging between them. She gulped and drew on the last reserves of her strength. "Let's go," she squeezed out.

Standing above her, Rafe watched Maggie push off, his heart catching when one of her feet slipped on the ice. She scrambled for footing, caught her balance, and then stood there, shaking. Whether she would admit it or not, she was finished. He admired her pluck. As exhausted as she obviously was, most people would have been whining and saying they couldn't make it.

Not Maggie. She would keep going until her legs gave out, and then she would try to claw her way up, bless her heart. *Jesus.* He couldn't believe he'd underestimated the distance here. Some rescuer he was turning out to be. If he couldn't get her to the line shack, they'd die of exposure, and it'd be his fault.

To make himself feel better, Rafe kept reminding himself that he'd been away from the ranch for a long while. Naturally he had forgotten some things. It was just a hell of a note when his memory failed him in a life-or-death situation. He was a frigging moron, and Maggie was paying the price.

He extended his left hand to her. "Grab hold."

She stared at his outstretched palm. "I can make it," she huffed. "You just worry about yourself. I'll be right behind you."

Rafe had ceased worrying only about himself the instant he'd clapped eyes on her in that boxcar a month ago. She was an irresistible combination of spunk and fragility, his Maggie, the kind of woman who made a man applaud her gutsiness even as he burned to protect her.

Tensing, he watched her struggle to gain more ground. When she got within reach of him, he grabbed her arm. The look she gave him was a mixture of stung pride and gratitude. Through the soggy sleeve of her parka, he could feel how badly her muscles were quivering. Before she could anticipate what he meant to do, he bent to catch her behind the right knee.

When he slung her across his shoulders in a fireman's carry, she wailed, "Oh, my God! Rafe, p-put me d-down!"

"I won't drop you, honey."

"I'm too heavy. You can't make a climb like this, carrying me."

"I've carried calves heavier than you are, and for a hell of a lot farther." He failed to mention it had been a while since he'd done so or that he'd been in much better shape at the time. "I won't even notice I'm packing you."

Ha-ha. Just in pushing erect, he felt the strain in his legs. He had no intention of wasting his breath to argue the point with Maggie, however, so he gave no further response to her many objections as he resumed the climb.

"I'm not helpless!"

No, not helpless, he thought. But she did have physical limitations that had been intensified recently by pregnancy and serious illness.

"I can make it on my own."

Yeah, even if she had to crawl.

"Oh, God, Rafe, please . . . don't do this to yourself. You'll never make it."

I'll make it, he vowed grimly to himself. He had to.

When you were being carried on a man's back, Maggie decided, the thoughts that went through your head were as rough and jarring as the ride. That he was wonderful . . . and infuriatingly stubborn. That if he had a brain, he'd put her down and make her walk. That she loved him . . . and wanted to slug him. Or maybe just hug him, instead.

He fought his way to the top of the ridge, killing her a little with every labored breath he drew and every straining step he took. The way was steep and treacherously slick. There was no path to follow. It was a brutal climb over boulders and loose rock that rolled out from under his feet. More than once she felt sure they would go down, but somehow he managed to keep his footing. He was exhausted. She knew he couldn't possibly go on like this. Yet he did. And the stress of worrying about what a burden she must be to him made the idea of walking on her own seem much easier.

She relaxed somewhat after he reached the top of the ridge where the ground evened out, but even then, she felt him stumble under her weight at times. Her heart twisted. She willed herself to be as light as a feather. Fat chance of that. She considered pulling his hair to shock some sense into him.

And, meanwhile, he just kept going, placing one foot

doggedly in front of the other in an excruciating endurance test of his tendon-roped body. She could hear his chest whistling as he drew each tortured breath. Sometimes when he shifted her weight, she could feel the violent pounding of his heart between his shoulder blades. At one point, he crashed through the ice and fell to his knees. Maggie pleaded with him to put her down as he struggled to stand back up.

He never spoke, not even to tell her to shut up. Maggie suspected he didn't have the breath, and knowing that broke her heart. Oh, God. She was afraid he'd keep pushing himself until he dropped, and then what would she do? As dearly as she loved him, she'd never be able to carry him as he was her.

Hot tears squeezed from her eyes. She could *feel* his exhaustion. Almost taste it. Never—not once in her entire life—had she felt so small and ashamed. He was killing himself for her. She could feel the quivering weariness in his body, every movement an effort that vibrated into her. Yet he kept going, taking just one more step, and then one more.

How much farther was it to the line shack, anyway? *Please, God, don't let it be far.* This was her doing. She'd gone haring off into the woods. Poor little Maggie, running away to hide. It had been such a stupid and childish thing for her to do. And why? Because she hadn't believed he could love her after hearing the ugly truth.

Well . . . if this wasn't love, what was it? A serious case of like?

He fell again. This time, he hit the snow chest-first. Maggie's right knee dug through the ice. Her frozen flesh felt as if it shattered, pain lancing from her toes to her hip. She blocked out the pain, her concern all for Rafe. He just lay there for a moment with her hipbone riding the back of his neck, his face shoved against the ice. She struggled to get off of him, but his hold on her was unbreakable.

"Oh, God, Rafe, let me go!" she cried with a sob. "You can't do this."

With strength she couldn't believe he had, he straightened his back with all her weight still riding his shoulders. Maggie realized he meant to keep her there, no matter what, so she stopped struggling.

"Rafe, please. I'm rested now." It was a lie. She wasn't sure she could walk. But, oh, God, she had to try. "I can make it on my own. Honest."

"Snow—too deep," he rasped out. "Not much farther."

He struggled back to his feet. She had a horrible suspicion he'd used the last reserves of his strength a half mile back, and that now he was operating on sheer force of will. What if his heart gave out? Her mom had seemed perfectly healthy before her illness began to manifest itself. Oh, God, she would never forgive herself for this.

Maggie nearly wept when she finally saw the dark outline of a structure ahead of them. She fixed her gaze on the bleary silhouette of the building, hoping Rafe wouldn't fall again before they reached it.

When he staggered to a stop a few feet from the line shack's door, he just stood there with his legs braced apart, staring at it. Maggie suspected that he was so exhausted, he could scarcely think, let alone determine what he needed to do next. She was about to suggest he put her down when his knees buckled. He dropped hard, somehow managing even then to keep her on his shoulders.

She heard his lungs whining and saw clouds of vapor rising in front of his face. Through tears, she stared at his sharply carved profile. Wet shocks of hair lay flat against his forehead. Droplets of sweat had frozen on his cheeks. His mouth hung open as he grabbed for oxygen.

"Rafe?"

He relaxed his hold on her, and she slid down his

back to plop on the frozen snow. As she rolled onto her hands and knees, he braced his palms on his thighs and hung his head. Even with the thick leather coat blanketing his torso, she could see that he was shaking violently.

"Made it." He heaved out the words.

Maggie shoved herself erect. Her legs felt rubbery and numb. She staggered to keep her feet, accepting as she did that he'd been right; she couldn't have walked all the way here.

Done for. Those two words had aptly described her condition back on the slope, and they described his now. Maggie swung toward the shack. As she covered the distance to the door, she careened like a drunk. The crudely fashioned portal was held closed with a piece of board nailed to the wood. Her half-frozen fingers screamed with pain as she fumbled to turn it.

She stepped back to draw the door open. It didn't budge. She glanced down and saw that a frozen drift held it closed. Sinking to her knees and blocking out the agony that exploded from her fingers to her shoulders, she clawed at the ice, her one thought to get the door open and Rafe inside.

He was still kneeling on the ice when she went back for him. She leaned over and grabbed his arm with both hands. "Rafe? Let's go in."

He shook his head as if to come awake and then stared at the doorway as if it were a thousand miles away. Then he began struggling to his feet. Maggie tried to help, but her arms were so leaden, she couldn't lend much assistance.

When he threw an arm over her shoulders and his weight came down, her legs nearly buckled. She staggered, regained her balance, and somehow aimed their lurching footsteps toward the shack. Three steps, four. She strained with all her might to support him.

Suddenly—like a huge tree knocked flat in a gale— he started to go down. Maggie screamed, twisting to shove her shoulder against his chest in an attempt to catch him. The next thing she knew, she was lying on her back like a kid making snow angels. She blinked and stared stupidly at the stars twinkling above her. As her senses cleared, she twisted onto her knees, got back up, and stared dizzily at her husband.

Husband. Not a fairy-tale prince on temporary loan. Not some dream come true that she could blink away and pretend wasn't real when the going got rough. He was a flesh-and-blood man who'd laid his heart at her feet, and God forgive her, she'd walked all over it, throwing his love for her back in his face, denying him the right to touch her, and doubting him at every turn. Then, as the proverbial icing on the cake, she'd run away from him into the woods like a spoiled, not-very-bright child.

On legs that wobbled, Maggie made her way back to him. He had carried her on his shoulders for miles, half of that distance straight uphill and on ice that had made every step treacherous. She could surely get him into the cabin.

She leaned down and grabbed his hands, not allowing herself to think the word "can't." She *would.* Straining with all she had, she dragged him an inch at a time to the doorway. Then, stripping off her parka and bundling it under his head to protect his face, she managed to pull him across the threshold into the black void of the shack. He muttered something unintelligible.

"It's all right," she panted out. "It'll be all right now, Rafe. We made it."

Her back connected with a sharp corner of wood as she struggled to get him far enough into the dark room to close the door. She ignored the pain, just as she did the quivering weariness in her limbs. *It'll be all right.* She remembered how he'd held her so gently in his arms on their so-called wedding night, whispering that promise to her, over and over.

Except for the labored whine of her breathing, silence

descended when she slammed and bolted the plank door. No wind. She'd been hearing it whistle for so long that the sudden cessation made her ears ring.

"It'll be all right now," she said again.

And she meant it. With all her heart. With all she was. She'd get him warm, get some hot food into him. He'd be okay. Oh, God, he had to be. He was breathing. Sure he was. Her own huffing was just so loud, she couldn't hear him. Rafe wasn't her mother. He was big and strong and healthy. His heart was fine. Just fine.

She stumbled through the pitch blackness, waving her arms in front of her. First order of necessity was some light. Oh, God, she needed a light. After cracking her knees on several unseen obstacles, she ran into what felt like a crudely fashioned table. Praying mindlessly, she groped and patted the rough planks. When her hands bumped into a lantern, a sob tore from her. A box of kitchen matches lay beside it. *Thank you, God. Thank you*. Fumbling with numb fingers, she struck a match. Flame flared. She stared dumbly at the lamp, having no clue how to light the damned thing.

Several wasted matches later, half of which sputtered out because she was shaking so violently, she deduced that the handle at the lantern's base was the pump mentioned in the nearly obliterated instructions just below the charred glass globe. She pumped, twisted the stem to lock the valve, and thrust a lighted match through an opening to light the little net sacks suspended inside.

Ka—whoosh! Excess fuel vapor ignited, the heat blasting her in the face. She fell back, throwing up her arm, fairly sure her hair would be afire if not for its being so wet. *God*. The idea wasn't to burn the place down. With a palsied hand, she adjusted the fuel valve. The explosive brightness dimmed, becoming a mellow spill of light.

She ran back to Rafe. As she fell to her knees beside him, she could see his chest rising and falling. Old habits died hard. She touched her fingertips to his throat, just to be sure her eyes weren't deceiving her. His pulse thrummed against her fingers, strong and steady. *Foolishness*. But after living with a person who had serious heart problems, she couldn't help but feel a sick fear for him. Just exhausted. That was all. He'd be all right soon. He would.

Struggling to stand, she took stock of their temporary shelter. Along one wall was a wood-framed cot, the bare striped ticking of the mattress and single pillow a blur. She blinked to bring the stripes into focus. The mattress was scarcely wide enough to sleep one person comfortably. Above it on two board shelves was an assortment of old but clean clothing—faded jeans, what looked like a stack of red, insulated long johns, some rolled boot socks, and a couple of old work shirts, the usual ranch-issue blue chambray. There was also a stack of wool blankets that would come in handy.

Rafe had said this place was kept stocked for emergencies. Maggie could see that it was. Definitely not fancy, but it seemed like a palace. She turned toward an old iron cookstove, so relieved to see the huge pile of wood stacked neatly beside it she nearly wept. She'd never used a wood cookstove, but she'd never used a lantern before, either, and now she had light.

In a frantic hurry, she went to work, her one thought to get Rafe warm.

Once she had a fire roaring in the stove, she went back to him. Just stripping the wet leather coat off him was exhausting work. He was heavy and limp, and so was the jacket. But she managed because she had to.

"I'll make it, Maggie," he muttered. "I'll make it."

Tears scalded her eyes as she tossed the jacket aside. She leaned over to cup his cold face between her hands, remembering all the many times he'd touched her in much the same way, gazing down at her as if to memorize every line of her features. Well . . . his face was carved on her heart. The stubborn thrust of his square chin. The muscular ridge along his jaw. The jutting bridge of his slightly crooked nose. The arch of his thick, black eyebrows. The light of laughter in his smoky blue eyes.

"You already made it. You got us here, Rafe. You got us here."

His dark lashes fluttered. "Love you, Maggie. I do."

The tears in her eyes became a swimming blur. "I know. I know, Rafe. Just rest now. You don't need to talk. There's nothing that needs saying."

"Don't care." He tried to touch her cheek. His arm fell before he spanned the distance. He blinked, his eyes unfocused. "About Lonnie. It doesn't matter."

"I know."

His eyelids drooped. "Love you, no matter what."

Maggie no longer doubted it. If what he'd done tonight wasn't proof enough, nothing ever would be. "I love you, too. No matter what."

As she said those words, Maggie knew she was taking that final step toward a commitment that would last a lifetime, and such a step didn't come quite as easily for her as she had insinuated to Rafe while they were arguing in the Ford. She loved him, yes. And she was no longer terrified to have sex with him. But that didn't mean she was exactly eager to do so, either. Old terrors weren't quite that easily overcome.

No matter. She would simply follow Rafe's example, setting aside her own wants and needs in favor of his. When he wanted to make love, she would do it, and if the experience was a trial, she would somehow get through it and pretend she liked it. For him.

His mouth twisted in a ghost of a smile and then his face went lax as Maggie applied herself to the task of tearing the wet clothes off of him. She had to stand up and pull to remove his boots. When he and the second boot parted company, it happened so suddenly that she fell against the door.

A few minutes later when she began fumbling with the zipper of his jeans, he jerked, clamped a hand over his crotch, and opened his eyes to focus blearily on her. "Maggie?" he slurred, shuddering with the cold.

"It's me."

His eyes fell closed again. She smiled tremulously. Evidently he trusted her, for he drew away his hand and plopped it on the floor. As she peeled off his wet jeans and boxers, she was peripherally aware that he was as ruggedly gorgeous naked as he was fully clothed. His skin was the color of aged oak. Thick overlays of muscle padded his long frame. At the juncture of his thighs, his sex rested in limp glory against a shiny thatch of coarse ebony. As she unbuttoned his shirt, she discovered that a narrowing swath of equally dark hair led from there up to his flat, striated belly.

She couldn't waste precious seconds to admire him properly, but, oh, how she wanted to. He was beautiful, like a wood sculpture, rubbed to a high sheen.

She jerked her gaze away and went to fetch a set of the long johns. Once she had tugged a pair of the bottoms on him, she sat back on her heels, so drained it was all she could do not to collapse beside him. He could survive without a shirt. She'd pile all the blankets on him once she got him in bed.

"Rafe?"

He moaned.

"Rafe, I can't get you to bed. You have to wake up." She patted his cheeks, coaxing a groan from him. "I know you're exhausted, but you have to help me." She slipped an arm under his shoulders and strained to lift him. "Come on. It's only a few feet."

"Oh, God." He struggled to sit up, then waved her off. "I can do it."

He twisted onto his knees and crawled. She hovered anxiously over him. Once beside the cot, he grabbed the frame and flung a leg onto the mattress like a drunk trying to mount a horse. She got behind him and pushed. After a few false starts, he finally made it, sprawling facedown on the pillow.

"Sorry," he mumbled into the bare ticking. "So sorry, honey."

Maggie dragged the entire stack of blankets off the shelf and covered him with multiple layers of wool. "I'm the one who's sorry, Rafe. Running off like that. It was such a *stupid* thing to do. I'm so sorry."

He just lay there for a moment. Maggie thought he'd passed back out. Then he mumbled, "Maggie?"

"What?" she asked, yearning to hear him say he forgave her.

"Shut up."

That said, he went back to sleep. Maggie stood over him, grinning like a fool. It wasn't exactly an absolution, but it would pass. *Shut up*. He didn't want to hear her apologies. And he was right. She had more important things to do than stand here, pleading for forgiveness when she knew very well that he'd never held her foolishness against her in the first place.

She figured out how to prime the old water pump at the rusty sink. After that, she mastered the cookstove burner plates and made coffee in a tin pot that looked as if it had been trampled by a horse. On overhead shelves above the sink, there were odds-and-ends dishes, some old flatware and cookware, plus an assortment of canned food. Maggie grabbed a pot, a can opener, a spoon, and two cans of chili beans, the labels of which read, *Hot*.

She was so cold that any kind of hot sounded divine.

When she took a mug of steaming coffee to Rafe, he was shuddering so violently she didn't trust him to manage alone without scalding himself. Not that her own hands were much steadier. Remembering how he'd once fed her when she was sick, she returned the favor now. "It's straight off the stove."

He slurped eagerly at the coffee and swore when it burned his tongue. Then he curled a shaking hand over hers to guide the cup back to his mouth. This time he sipped more cautiously. When he fell back, too exhausted to take more, she managed to spoon a little chili into his mouth before he fell asleep.

Now that she could tend to her own needs, all she wanted was to lie down and sleep. The lantern could burn itself out. She was too tired to walk back to the table and turn it off. Standing beside the cot, she kicked off her sneakers and peeled off her wet clothes, dropping them in a puddle at her feet. Then, grabbing a set of oversize long johns, she dressed and slipped under the blankets with her husband. The cot was just barely wide enough to accommodate both of them, which suited her fine. She was freezing.

He jumped when her icy body touched his side. She pulled his arm around her and snuggled up as close as she could get, throwing a leg across his and half-lying on his chest. Under the blankets, he groped clumsily with his free hand, feeling of her shoulder, her arm, and then her butt.

The warmth that rolled off him was wonderful, and she rested her chilled cheek in the hollow of his shoulder. An instant later, she was asleep.

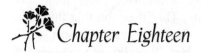 Chapter Eighteen

A beeping noise woke Maggie. As she rolled onto her side, she saw Rafe standing across the room, looking incredibly handsome in a red, long-sleeved undershirt and faded Wrangler jeans that fit him like a second skin, the legs riding high on the still wet tops of his boots.

He stood near the sink, facing the counter, his broad back rippling under the snug undershirt. He appeared to be speaking softly on a phone. Maggie frowned. They were still at the line shack. The glow of the lantern told her it must still be nighttime. Where had he found a phone?

"Like I said, Rye, we'll be fine." A pause. "First thing in the morning would be great. Hell, around noon will be better. That way we can sleep in. We've got plenty of wood and food. It's nice and cozy, actually. We'll make the most of it and rest. It was one hell of a night. If it weren't for Maggie, I'd be history. I collapsed just outside. I don't know how, but she got me indoors."

He braced the heel of his hand on the sink edge, the jut of his hip and the backward thrust of one leg forming a ruggedly masculine stance. Maggie half-expected him to inform his brother that the reason he'd collapsed was because he'd carried her so far through deep snow. But, typically, he said nothing, letting Ryan draw his own conclusion. No one could accuse Rafe of being a braggart.

He chuckled suddenly. "Don't you dare. If you aren't here by noon, I'll have your head. If I want to take her on a honeymoon, it'll be someplace nicer than this. How's Jaimie, by the way? That'll be the first thing she asks." Silence. "He did? Is Becca sure it wasn't gas?" He laughed. "I'll tell her. Hey, Rye, be sure to tell Heidi not to worry, all right? Yeah. Same here."

As he broke the connection and returned the phone to the black leather case on the counter, Maggie drew the blankets to her chin, horribly conscious as she did that the wool felt wet where it had lain against her undershirt. It had been a long time since she'd last used her breast pump. If they wouldn't be going home until after noon tomorrow, what on earth was she going to do?

"You're awake," Rafe said softly when he turned. The tap of his boots resounded on the floor as he moved toward her. "That was Ryan. I got in touch with him just in time to stop him from launching a search. Luckily he figured we'd stayed in town for dinner and a movie and had forgotten to tell Becca. He didn't get worried until about an hour ago."

"What time is it?"

He glanced at his watch. "Twelve-thirty. I only snoozed for a while." He winked at her. "Becca says we missed a first this afternoon. Jaimie smiled, and she swears up and down it wasn't just gas, but an honest-to-goodness grin. She told Ryan he's got the Kendrick dimple."

Hearing that, Maggie smiled herself. "It's sweet of them, pretending he's really yours."

"He *is* mine. If he ends up looking like me, don't be surprised. That happens, you know. Mannerisms, I guess—and personality traits. I used to know a couple of boys who were adopted. They weren't biological brothers, but they acted so much alike, they resembled each other."

"I hope he grows up to be just like you."

He rubbed his jaw. "Thank you, Maggie. That's about the nicest thing anyone ever said to me."

"Well, it's sincerely meant." She hugged the blanket closer. "I already miss the little stinker."

"It won't be long before we're home." He ran a hand over his hair, his gaze searching hers for a long moment. Then he bent his head and scuffed the heel of his boot over a floorboard, his brow pleating in a thoughtful frown. When he looked back up, his expression was solemn. "We need to have a long talk. The sooner, the better."

Maggie agreed, but that didn't mean she was looking forward to it.

He hauled in a deep breath, then slowly released it. "I realize right now isn't an ideal time, so we can put it off for a few minutes while you use the rest room and"—he gestured vaguely with his hand—"do other things. I'm sure you'd like to eat and have some coffee. But I do want to get a couple of things said straightaway to put your mind at ease. The first is that I love you." His voice went raspy and deep. "If you tell me you hog-tied Lonnie and had your way with his body three times a day, I'll still love you."

She threw him a horrified look.

He shrugged. "It's the truth. Aside from how it has hurt you, I don't care what happened in your past. It'll have no effect on how I feel about you. Is that understood? No matter what you tell me—or how bad you think it is, sweetheart—it's not going to change my feelings for you."

Maggie felt tears burning at the backs of her eyes.

"The second thing I want to say is that I'm instituting a new rule in this relationship, starting now."

"What's that?"

"I learned an important lesson today. No problem ever gets solved by pretending it doesn't exist. All it does is complicate matters, making huge problems out of what should have been small ones."

She couldn't very well argue the point, so she nodded.

"Almost from the first, I figured that Lonnie was Jaimie's father. I didn't push you to talk about it, believing at the time that I was sparing you humiliation. That was the worst mistake of my life, and today it damned near cost you yours."

Maggie drew up her knees and stared at the gray blanket covering them.

"All this time," he went on, "I was under the assumption that you found it hard to tell me the truth about Jaimie because Lonnie is your stepfather. That maybe you were afraid I'd press you for details you're reluctant to talk about. Now I realize that's only part of it, that it isn't just what the creep did to you, but that he's got you so messed up in your thinking you blame yourself for it."

Maggie squeezed her eyes closed.

"Well, no more," he said, his tone ringing with finality. "No more secrets. No more tiptoeing around. No more assuming on my part. Little issues, big issues. From here on out, we're going to be open with each other about everything. There may be times when I'll embarrass you. Scratch that. I undoubtedly will, and I apologize to you for that in advance. I tend to be straightforward and blunt, and there's not a whole hell of a lot I feel shy about discussing. You're a hundred and eighty degrees out from that. But I'd rather embarrass you than hurt you, honey, and hurt you is exactly what I've done. Starting right now, nothing is sacred. Understand that."

She lifted her lashes. Trying to inject a note of levity into her voice, she said, "That sounds almost like a threat."

"A warning," he corrected. "When we have that talk in a few minutes, I'll make it as easy for you as I can. But there'll be no more secrets between us, period. So prepare yourself for that."

"You're angry."

"Yes, but not with you. I'm mad at myself for letting this go for so long and for allowing it to get so out of hand." He paused and then said, "This is a talk we should have had weeks ago, and it's entirely my fault that we didn't."

"It's as much my fault as yours."

He gave a low laugh. "Let's save that debate for our discussion, shall we? Right now, I'm sure you've got more pressing concerns." He gestured toward a three-pound coffee can beside the bed. "I hunted up a chamber pot. It's not very convenient, but it beats wading through the snow to the outhouse."

Maggie seconded that. She'd had quite enough of snow for one night.

"I, um . . ." He hooked a thumb over his shoulder to indicate yet another can sitting on the table, his gaze flicking to her chest. "I found that one for your other needs." He shifted his weight from one foot to the other. "I've got some stuff I need to do out in the shed. You'll have some privacy while I'm out there, messing around. I'll knock before I come back in."

Maggie nodded. As he turned to fetch his coat from where he'd draped it and the other wet clothing over crossbuck stools in front of the stove, she threw an appalled glance at the can he'd left on the table. There was no question in her mind as to what he'd meant by her "other needs." Major problem. She had only a vague notion of how to address those needs without her pump, and it was back at the house.

A blast of frigid air washed into the room as he opened the door to step outside. The moment the planked portal swung shut, Maggie slipped from the cot and grabbed a blanket to drape around her shoulders.

Rafe cursed under his breath, calling himself a hundred kinds of fool. She didn't have a clue! He'd seen befuddlement written all over her face. And what had he done? He'd run like hell.

It wasn't that he felt uncomfortable discussing the functions of the female body. Raised from infancy on an operating cattle and horse ranch, there wasn't much that embarrassed him. She was just so painfully shy.

As that thought settled, Rafe hesitated where he was bent over the generator making choke and carburetor adjustments. Damned if he wasn't doing it again, tiptoeing around her and holding back for fear of embarrassing her. Even worse, he'd just sworn to her that he'd never do it again. If this was any indication, he wasn't getting off to a great start.

He grabbed a rag to wipe the smudges of grease from his hands. Enough of this. Starting right now, he wasn't going to hold back about anything. She was his wife, and in all the ways that mattered, that baby was his. It was time he began acting like a husband instead of some over-polite stranger.

It wasn't as if a woman's body came with an instruction manual. He distinctly remembered how often Susan had sought advice as a new mother—calling her doctor every few days to ask questions or going to Rafe's mom, who'd once been a registered nurse. Was this normal? Was that normal?

Maggie had no one to turn to—except him.

He tossed down the rag, turned off the flashlight, exited the lean-to, and strode around to the front of the line shack to pound on the door. He winced at the way the planks vibrated under his fist. His aim wasn't to scare her to death.

"Come in," she called faintly.

He turned the bar and opened the door. She sat on a stool at the table with a blanket draped around her shoulders, the lengthy legs of a pair of overlarge red long johns bunched at her ankles over the tops of some equally overlarge boot socks. Eyeing the can on the table in front of her, Rafe closed and bolted the door.

Now that he was in here, he wasn't exactly sure what

to say. He settled for jumping right in. "You don't know how to do that, do you?"

She flashed an appalled glance at the can. Her cheeks turned a startling shade of red. He told himself the color went well with her long johns.

"Well . . . I'm getting there—I think."

As he peeled off his jacket, he stepped over to peer into the can. There wasn't much inside.

He tossed down his jacket, grabbed the container, and stepped to the foot of the table. "Come here, honey," he urged as he centered the can at the edge.

She shot him a look filled with suspicion. "Why?"

Rafe felt his reasons were patently obvious. "Don't be shy. I won't even touch you. I'm just going to give you some pointers."

She made tight fists over the edges of the wool. "Oh, no, that isn't necessary. I can manage fine. Really."

He crooked a finger at her. "Maggie, it's no big deal. Trust me. I won't lay a hand on you, I promise, and you can keep the blanket on."

"How do you know so much about it?"

"I was married before, remember? Susan misplaced her pump once."

"You *watched?*" she asked, her tone scandalized.

Rafe bit back a smile and scratched beside his nose. He'd walked right into that one. "Well, no, it's not exactly a spectator sport. I just, um—my mom used to be a nurse. Susan was all upset because we were planning to be gone overnight. It was too late to drive clear into town to buy another pump, so Mom told her how to express her milk without one."

"They discussed it in front of you?"

"Would you look so horrified if they had been talking about elbows?"

"No, of course not."

"Well, then?"

"Elbows are slightly different."

"Different from . . ." He inclined his head, urging her to say the word.

"Other body parts."

He laughed in spite of himself. "You can't even bring yourself to say it."

"Don't be silly. I've said it lots of times."

"When?"

She shrugged, doing her damnedest to avoid looking him in the eye. "I don't know. Lots of times, is all."

"Good. Then it's no big deal, and you can say it now." He leaned sideways to meet her gaze, which immediately skittered away in the opposite direction. He followed, giving her no choice but to look at him. "Come on. Real quick. Just blurt it out. I promise not to clap my hand to my forehead and drop over in a dead faint."

She rolled her eyes. "This is the silliest thing I've ever heard."

"Isn't it, though? I'm sorry, but I don't think it's a workable plan for us to go the next fifty years pretending you don't have any—" He broke off and sighed. "Sweetheart, I'm gonna be the guy who holds your head when you get sick, and vice versa. What if you get a female infection and need to see the doctor? You need to be able to tell me things like that. What're you gonna say, that you've got a problem down yonder? Unless you can talk openly with me, I'm liable to think you've got an ingrown toenail and put off taking you to town."

"I can drive and make my own doctor appointments. I'm not a child."

He conceded the point with a nod. "I don't mean to imply you need a keeper. It's just—" God, he hated this. If they were already being intimate, it wouldn't be so difficult. But they weren't, and he felt like a slug. He braced the heels of his hands on the edge of the table and stared thoughtfully at the can. The nearly *empty* can. Shit. "A vaginal infection can make having sexual intercourse excruciatingly painful," he forged on. "That's not to mention that some infections are contracted by the man without his having symptoms, and he has to take antibiotics so he won't infect his wife again every time he touches her. What are you going to do? Hand me pills and not tell me why?''

"I can't see how that pertains to—"

"Trust me, it pertains. Your body and anything that goes wrong with it is my business from now on. You're my wife. I love you. Your health and well-being are extremely important to me. Can you understand that?"

"Of course," she agreed, her tone defeated.

"We're stuck up here. It'll be another twelve hours, at least, before we get home. You should express your milk every four. You haven't done that since yesterday before noon when we went to town."

"No," she admitted forlornly.

"If you don't do it now, it could create some big-time problems. Chances are, probably not. But why push your luck? Engorgement, inflammation. You name it. You've drawn your milk all this time, hoping to nurse Jaimie again. You've finished taking your medication. You wanna risk blowing it now, just because you're embarrassed?''

"No."

She pushed to her feet and moved reluctantly to stand beside him. Rafe knew he'd won only the battle, not the war. Strategy was called for, his aim being to make this as easy for her as possible while he conveyed to her the necessary information. He decided a little kidding around tossed into the mix wouldn't hurt. A laugh here and there, some teasing. If he kept the tone casual, she'd be better able to relax.

"Mom said this is actually easier than using a pump," he told her. "And once Susan tried it, she never messed with a device again. This is quicker."

"Trust you to know."

Rafe let that one pass. He positioned her facing the table, and then he stood beside her, leaned slightly forward at the waist, and cupped his hands in front of his chest. "You hold your"—she flashed him a warning look—"*thingamajig* like this." He saw her roll her eyes again. "Well? What shall I call it, then? A doohickey?"

Her mouth twitched at the corners. "You're incorrigible."

"But you love me anyway." He glanced at her hands. "Are you going to do this? Or are you just going to stand there, turning interesting shades of red?"

She leaned forward and positioned her hands well away from her chest. "Now what?"

"You entering a taffy pull?"

She made an odd sound at the back of her throat that he hoped was a stifled giggle. He watched as she positioned her hands closer to her body.

He nodded. "That's it. Now you massage at the base with a forward motion. Mom said about ten times. *Gently*, Maggie. We're not kneading bread dough, for God's sake."

A startled laugh escaped her. He grinned and winked at her. "Good. Now you move forward, closer to the—" He hesitated. "What are we gonna call the tip?"

"The tip," she replied, her voice taut with suppressed laughter. "Are you like this with everyone, or did I just get lucky?"

"You just got lucky. Do you think I'd make a fool of myself like this for just anybody?"

"I sincerely hope not."

"It's a damned good thing. Tell Ryan I did this, and I'll wring your neck. A guy's got an image to uphold, and he'd never let me live this down."

"I assure you that I'll never have occasion to discuss this with Ryan."

She had relaxed, at least. He gave himself a pat on the back for sheer genius. "Now you squeeze about ten more times."

"Will nine times do?"

He narrowed an eye at her. "You gonna be serious

about this, or do I have to do it for you?''

"Touch me, and you're dead."

He laughed under his breath. "For a woman who hasn't got any, you're damned territorial."

"I never said I didn't have any. I simply prefer not to advertise it."

He glanced at her blanketed front. "If that's what you call low profile, darlin', you're in trouble."

She ignored the observation. "What next?"

He gave her explicit instructions, ending with: "And make sure you aim at the can. I'm checking it when I come back inside."

"For what?"

"Yield." He bent to kiss her cheek, which was so hot with embarrassment, he was half-afraid she'd go up in flames. "Any questions?"

She kept her face slightly averted. "No. I think I can handle it easily enough. Thank you." She graced him with eye-to-eye contact for a brief moment. "When will your mom come back?"

He laughed again, appropriate reaction or not. "Trust me. I'm the better confidant. Ask her for advice, and she'll bring it up at the dinner table, with Dad and Rye throwing in their two cents' worth. You can count on me to keep my mouth shut."

"Your dad and Ryan?" she repeated, her expression appalled again.

"In my family, nothing's sacred. Guard your secrets well, or they'll be the best-kept secrets this side of Texas. It's kind of nice, actually." She averted her gaze again. "Maggie, it's silly to be embarrassed about this. Like I've never noticed you've got breasts? You're definitely packing. That was one of the first things I noticed about you."

She gave him another of those appalled looks. "It was?"

"Absolutely."

"What else?"

"What else what?"

"What else did you notice about me?"

He winked at her. "Those beautiful eyes. They were the first thing. One look, and I was a goner. I just didn't have the good sense to stop kicking."

"And? What else about me did you—like?"

"You really don't want to know."

"Yes, I do."

"That world-class ass of yours," he whispered. "And those gorgeous legs." He grabbed his jacket from the bench. He paused at the door, gave her a slow, sweeping glance, and grinned. "If you have problems, call me. I'll be right outside."

"I won't need you," she assured him again.

Rafe could hope. If she did, he wasn't sure who'd suffer the most, him or her.

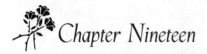 Chapter Nineteen

Thirty minutes later when Rafe reentered the cabin, Maggie was sitting on the cot with a blanket still around her shoulders. Now, however, he glimpsed the red sleeve of an undershirt and guessed she was covered again, top to bottom. *Hallelujah.* "Everything go all right?"

She nodded, and when he glanced at the can, she said, "Don't bother looking. I dumped it down the sink." She waited a beat, and then, in an obvious attempt to change the subject, said, "What'd you do outside?"

He'd spent the last fifteen minutes of exile sitting on the generator freezing his buns off. "Just this and that. Mostly, I worked on the generator." He stepped to the sink, pumped some water into the washbasin, and scrubbed his hands. "It needed oil and some minor adjustments. I figured I'd better tend to it in case we need to use the phone again. The DC outlet is the only way to power it up."

He grabbed a towel off the shelf above the sink, turning as he dried his hands. Studying his wife, he decided she looked miserably nervous, either in anticipation of their talk or because she feared he'd want to take advantage of the isolation here to make love. He drew off his jacket and hung it in front of the stove beside hers to let it finish drying. Then he added some wood to the firebox.

"Maggie, I'm not going to jump you just because you

mentioned you no longer dread the thought of having sex with me.''

She blinked. ''Did I say that?''

He dusted his hands on his jeans and moved slowly toward her. ''Yes, you did say that. When we were in the Expedition talking. Remember?''

She fiddled with the folds of the blanket. ''I guess I did, didn't I?''

''You regretting the statement?''

''No. I am, mostly.''

''You are mostly what? Regretting it?''

''No, mostly ready.''

Rafe sat on the edge of the cot and braced his forearms on his knees. *Mostly?* What the hell did that mean?

''Before we worry about making love and when we're going to, I think we need to have that talk,'' he told her.

She nodded.

''Main topic, Lonnie, as unpleasant as that may be. I want you to tell me everything, Maggie. No more secrets, please? I'd specifically like to know why on earth you feel he didn't rape you. I know damned well he did.''

Her eyes darkened and the color drained from her face. ''Is that why you don't care about what I told you, because you don't believe it's true?''

Rafe released a weary breath. ''No, I meant exactly what I said earlier. Insofar as our marriage goes, your past sexual relationships really don't matter to me. If you screwed the entire Seattle Seahawks football team, including the coach and water boy, I honestly don't care. That has no bearing on my feelings for you, or on yours for me. The reason I'm asking about Lonnie, specifically, isn't because it makes a difference to me if you slept with him—willingly or not. But because it's bothering you.''

Silver-tongued, he definitely wasn't. Being up front about everything was proving to be a real bitch. He pinched the bridge of his nose.

"Did that make any sense?"

She pressed her lips together, saying nothing for a long moment. Then her eyes filled and her chin started to quiver. "You really, really don't care? I mean—he wasn't just anybody. He was my stepfather. Just like you're Jaimie's. It's so ugly—almost incestuous, even if we aren't actually related."

"I don't think there's any comparison between my feelings for Jaimie and Lonnie's for you. I love Jaimie, and I can't believe Lonnie Boyle has feelings for anyone but himself. Incestuous, yes. In my books, it was. He broke every code of decency when he touched you. But that was his sin, never yours." He cupped her chin in his hand. "Sweetheart, you're the best thing that's ever happened to me, barring none. I love *you*, not your past history. I'm not exactly uncharted territory. You gonna throw me back because I've been with other women?"

A tear rolled onto her cheek and shimmered in the lantern light like a diamond on ivory satin. "Of course not." She gulped. "Have you been with lots?"

He chuckled. "Promise not to hold it against me?" At her nod, he said, "Then the truth is, I don't have many notches on my belt. I met Susan when I was pretty young, and even before we got married, I was never unfaithful to her. After she died, I never looked at another woman until I met you." He winked at her. "I'm damned near a virgin, so be gentle."

She gave a startled laugh that ended with a wet sob, and then, before he guessed what she meant to do, she launched herself at him. Rafe caught her to his chest, his heart breaking a little at the desperate way she clung to his neck.

"Tell me again," she whispered. "That it doesn't matter about Lonnie."

He tightened his arms around her. "It doesn't matter. Never has, never will. I love you, Maggie. There's nothing, *nothing*, you can tell me that will ever make me stop loving you. I mean that."

She shuddered and pressed closer. "I was never with the Seahawks."

He laughed and curled a hand over the back of her head. Dear God, how he loved her. His feelings for her ran so deep, even his bones seemed to ache when he held her. "Seriously? I never would have guessed."

"Only Lonnie," she whispered, "and I *hated* it."

That came as no surprise, either.

"He always hurt me, and I—" She broke off and turned her face against his neck. "I never wanted to. Never."

"But you let him?" Rafe asked cautiously.

Her body went rigid, and for a moment, she stopped breathing. "Yes," she finally admitted brokenly. "I was afraid. I was so afraid. He went crazy when I refused him. He said I was his. *His.*" Her breath snagged and she shrank closer to him. "He was so obsessively jealous he wouldn't even let me take the Pill so I wouldn't get pregnant. He thought if I was safe, I might mess around with men I met at work, and the thought made him crazy. I went behind his back once and got a prescription. When he found out, I thought he'd kill me. He took me down by the river—to this isolated place he knew—and—" She made a strangled sound. "He was so furious, he choked me. I couldn't get away. Finally I blacked out. When I came to, he was leaning against the car, smoking a cigarette. He said it was a good thing I woke up because he was about to chunk me in the water. He didn't act as if it even bothered him, thinking I might die. He would've preferred that, I think, to letting anyone else touch me. After that, I never dared take anything to protect myself again."

Rafe stroked her hair. "And that's how Jaimie came to be."

She nodded. "I'm lucky it didn't happen a lot sooner than it did. It's been three years since he added on to the back of the house so I had my own room."

"Your own room?" Rafe circled that, not entirely sure how it related.

"Before then, I shared with Heidi. He looked at me funny up until then, but he never did anything. It was only when I was sleeping at the back of the house, where he knew Mama couldn't hear, that he started—waking me up at night."

Rafe's stomach lurched. He tightened his arms around her. "And after you had your own room—did he wake you a lot?"

She shivered. "Yes." She fell quiet for several seconds. "I suppose you find it disgusting that I didn't leave. You probably think I'm one of those weak people who allow themselves to be victims."

He closed his eyes. "No, Maggie. You're one of the strongest people I know. If you stayed, I know you had a reason, and I think I know what it was."

"He said if I left, Heidi would be next. That she was almost old enough." Her voice went shrill. "I went to legal aid then. Tried to get custody of her. But the lawyer said I didn't stand a chance until I could prove Lonnie had actually done something to her. Proof. They needed proof. It was my word against his. He even kept me home from work when I had bruises. How could I get proof?"

"So you stayed—subjecting yourself to the abuse, rather than let him victimize Heidi." Rafe felt physically sick.

"After seeing the lawyer, I took Heidi and tried to leave. That time I used the car. It was in Mama and Lonnie's name, but I made the payments, so it wasn't like I really stole it or anything."

"What happened?"

"Lonnie reported it missing, and the cops pulled me over. Lonnie came and took us back to Prior. He was so mad, I thought he'd kill me that time. A part of me almost wished he would."

Rafe had experienced that feeling himself a time or

two. "And you were right back where you started, with Lonnie visiting your room."

"Yes. He started coming again, and just like before, when I told him no, he'd become so enraged, he'd beat me up. I couldn't scream. I was terrified if I did that Mama or Heidi might hear, and I was afraid he'd kill one of them if they burst in."

He squeezed his eyes closed again, his heart breaking for her. Recalling the bruises he'd seen on her body, he knew Lonnie had pulled none of his punches. "Ah, Maggie. How could you help but scream?"

"I pulled my pillow over my face."

"*What?*"

"My pillow—to muffle the noises I made."

His stomach lurched, and nausea slithered up the back of his throat.

"And after he beat you up," he managed to say. "Then he would rape you?"

She went unnaturally still. "No," she whispered. "Then he'd leave."

Rafe felt sure he hadn't heard her correctly. "Leave?"

"He always came back. Sometimes the same night, sometimes the next. He told me he'd never had to rape a woman, and he wasn't going to start with me. That when he came back, my attitude better be improved or he'd give it another adjustment."

Rafe could feel her tears slipping down his neck. He began to rock her and massage her back. "And when he came back, rather than take another beating, you did what he wanted."

It wasn't a question. Rafe could see it so clearly, and the pictures that took shape in his mind made him want to do murder. *Whenever he wanted, however he wanted. You name it, I did it*, she'd told him that afternoon. At the time, he couldn't conceive how that might have been possible, not with Maggie. But he understood now. Imagining her, pressing the pillow over her mouth to stifle her screams . . . Oh, God. He wanted to hold her tight and never let her go. Until this moment, Rafe had known Lonnie was sick, but he hadn't realized just how sick.

"I had to do what he wanted or he would hurt me again. He'd never stop until I gave in. The worst part was, if hurting me didn't work, he'd threaten to go to Heidi's room. She was so little. I was so afraid he'd do it."

The whole ugly story came pouring from her then, the details so sordid that Rafe cringed.

To rape a woman was horrible enough. Rafe could think of few things that were worse. But for the bastard to beat her into submission and then return later so he could pretend she wanted it?

A sob erupted from her, wet and tearing, the sound coming from so deep within her that it frightened him.

"Oh, sweetheart. Don't. Please, don't. It wasn't your fault."

If she heard him, she gave no sign of it. Rafe cradled her against him, rocking more violently, yearning to make her hurting stop, but not knowing how. So he let her cry. Until she lay limp against him. Until she ran out of tears. Until an awful silence settled over them— demanding that he say something. Only, heaven help him, he couldn't think what.

When he finally did speak, he was so focused on her and her pain that the words came instinctively. "I love you, Maggie girl. I didn't think anything could make me love you more than I already did, but this has. Do you have any idea how extraordinary you are?"

"Extraordinary?" she echoed faintly.

"Extraordinary. Wonderful. Amazing. That you stayed there—for Heidi. And that you never let the bastard break you. I'm so proud of you, knowing that. Most people wouldn't have taken the beatings, over and over. He tried his damnedest to break your spirit, to strip you of your dignity and take you to your knees—and you never allowed him to win."

He felt her grow unnaturally still. After a moment, she made tight fists on his shirt. "Oh, Rafe. He won every time. That was the nightmare."

He pressed his nose against her hair, which smelled of wood smoke, evergreen boughs, and the scent that was exclusively Maggie's. "No, sweetheart, *no*. He never really won, not in any way that counts."

The clench of her arms became almost frantic. "I feel so sick inside. When I think about the things I did, I feel like worms are crawling around inside of me. An awful, dirty feeling I can't wash off."

"Ah, Maggie." Rafe felt as if a sock had been shoved down his windpipe. His larynx refused to budge when he attempted to swallow. He damned near choked trying to clear his throat. "You can't wash away those kinds of feelings with soap and water."

"I know," she said hollowly. "I've tried. Scrubbed until my skin was raw. It never worked."

Tears filled his eyes. He twisted to lie on his back, drawing her down with him. He pulled the blankets over them, his hand threaded through her hair to cradle her head on his shoulder. "When you're ready, we'll wash that feeling away together."

"With what?" she asked warily.

He smiled, aware even as he did that tears were trailing down his cheeks and into her hair. "Trust me, I've got just the cure. There's only one way to get rid of bad memories, Maggie girl, and that's to make beautiful new ones."

"Oh, Rafe, I wish I could believe that."

His heart caught at the desperation he heard in her voice. "Well, believe it then. Have I ever lied to you?"

"No."

"Well, then? What seems dirty or ugly or frightening with someone else seems magical and perfectly right with the person you love, Maggie. You do love me. Don't you?"

"Oh, yes."

"Then it'll be like that for us—sheer magic. So beautiful and good and sweet that there won't be room in your head for any bad memories. They'll be crowded out by fantastic new ones, and all that will be left is that wonderful, magical feeling."

She hooked a heel over his leg to pull her body closer to his. Rafe accommodated her by tightening his embrace. He felt her hand make a fist on his shirt again. "Then let's *do* it," she whispered fiercely. "Do it *now*."

It was the last thing he expected her to say. He lay there a moment, his body taut, his pulse pounding. "Maggie," he finally said gruffly, "I don't think now is the best time."

Where her hand had closed over his shirt, he felt a tug on his chest hair.

"Sometimes," she whispered shakily, "after you go to sleep, I touch you when you don't know it and I— wonder about it."

He knew the times she referred to, and he hadn't been asleep. She had traced his features, etched the shape of his mouth with a fingertip, and lightly run her hands over his arms.

"You wonder about making love, you mean?"

"Yes," she said thinly. "What it'll be like."

He curled a hand over her shoulder. "What do you think it'll be like?"

For the longest time, she didn't answer. "I'm hoping it'll be nice. I like it when you touch me. Like right now. It feels good."

He realized he was gently caressing her shoulder through the cotton weave of the baggy shirt and stopped. Then, reminding himself that she'd just admitted to liking it, he began again, deliberately this time. "Like that?"

"Mmmm." She dragged in a shaky breath. "It makes my skin tingle."

Knowing she liked it made his borrowed jeans feel another size too small. This was dangerous. She was encouraging him to do something he wasn't sure she was ready for yet. And he was a little *too* ready.

"Only as nice as I hope it'll be, I'm afraid, too," she admitted. "Not really of you anymore. Just afraid. That maybe it won't be nice. That maybe it'll even be—terrible. And I never woke you up because I was scared to find out."

"I swear to you, Maggie, it won't be terrible."

"What you said about the magic?" She suddenly pushed up on an elbow to gaze into his eyes. He felt as if he were drowning in wet silk. "If you—" She broke off and swallowed. "If you can make magic and chase this awful feeling in me away, I want you to."

Rafe studied her small face, which had been ravaged by weeping. Tear streaks lined her pale cheeks. Her eyelids were puffy and red. The end of her nose was pink. And her mouth. Oh, God. It was swollen and shiny and soft-looking—and begged to be kissed. He reached up to smooth a dark tendril of hair from her cheek, and somehow his hand ended up cupped over the back of her head.

"Sweetheart, you're upset. We've just talked about Lonnie. It's all fresh in your mind. I think we should wait until another time."

"Don't you want me?"

Oh, God. He'd never wanted anyone or anything more. But he also wanted the timing to be right. What if he failed to make it magical for her? Let her down? "Oh, sweetheart, I want you. Of course I want you. More than I can say."

"I don't mean to push. It's just—it's like having a monster in the closet. You know?"

Where that had come from, he had no idea. "A what?"

"A monster in the closet. When you were little, didn't you ever believe there was a monster in your closet?"

He'd never seen eyes as beautiful as hers. Her every thought and feeling was reflected in those liquid brown depths, and the mixture of emotions terrified him. She obviously wanted to face her demons, and somehow, in her mind, he was one of them.

"I never believed a monster was in my closet. But I used to think there were ghosts in the stable after dark."

"How'd you come to realize there weren't?"

"When I was about twelve, I took a sleeping bag out and slept in the tack room. It was a hell of a cure, but by the time daylight rolled around, I wasn't afraid anymore."

"Well, when I was young, I thought there was a monster in my closet. Night after night, I lay in bed, staring at the closet door, afraid to go to sleep. Finally one night I couldn't stand it anymore, and I jumped up and opened the door. Guess what? No monsters. I was never afraid again."

"Maggie, are you saying I'm a monster in your closet?"

Her gaze clung to his as she shook her head. "No. Lonnie's my monster now, and you're the door I'm afraid to open." She nibbled her lip, her eyes pleading with him to understand. "I know it's stupid. Please don't be hurt. It's just—"

Rafe angled a fingertip across her lips. "You don't have to explain. I understand, and I'm not hurt. There's nothing inside me you haven't seen, Maggie. No monsters lurking. Nothing of Lonnie in me."

"I know that. I've known for quite a while," she admitted shakily. "But I need to prove it to myself. You know? Unfortunately, it's not quite as simple as grabbing hold of a doorknob this time." She smiled tremulously. "You don't come equipped with one."

He could think of other things she might grab that would get the job done in damned short order. He drew her face closer to his. He'd never contemplated making love to anyone who looked more frightened, and conversely, that scared the ever-loving hell out of him as well.

"If you really want to make love, Maggie, all you have to do is kiss me," he told her. "I'll take it from there."

To his shame, he was hoping she'd back off. Give herself some time. Wait until her mood was better. Instead, her gaze dropped to his mouth. She licked her lips, then flicked the corners with the pink tip of her tongue. His guts knotted and fire sluiced through him, liquid and racing.

"I've never," she murmured. "Been the one to start, I mean."

She dipped her head, then drew back and angled her face in the opposite direction. Several false starts later, her silken lips finally grazed his—so lightly, so shyly and tentatively, that he made a fist in her hair, yearning to draw her closer. But no. As she'd so aptly put it, this was her door to open, her monster that needed to be vanquished. And he had to let her do it in her own way and at her own pace.

 Chapter Twenty

Maggie had barely begun kissing Rafe when she realized he meant to just lie there and let her run the show.
For an instant, she found the idea appealing. It was a
novel experience to feel in control—to be the aggressor
and know nothing would happen unless she wanted it to
happen.

But that feeling quickly waned. She remembered how
it had felt that day in the airplane when he kissed her—
the breathless, exciting, heady sensation that had come
over her. She wasn't experiencing the same feeling now.
She was new at this and wasn't sure how to proceed.
She'd always found Lonnie's lips revolting, and she had
tried to twist her face away, swallowing her gorge.

Her heart squeezing with nervousness, she touched the
tip of her tongue to Rafe's lips, hoping that might inspire
him to take over. But he still just lay there, kissing her
back—sort of—but not touching her and making her
nerve endings sing like he had the other time. She
wanted that, needed that. As it was, she felt awkward,
not to mention nervous. After kissing him, what was she
supposed to do next? Touch him? Undress him? If he
intended to follow her lead, they might lie here all night
with their lips glued together.

Wholly unsatisfied with their progress thus far, she
drew back to search his gaze. His eyes glittered
strangely, the twinkling warmth she was accustomed to

gone. He was aroused, she decided. He wanted her. So why didn't he do anything about it?

"You said you'd take it from here," she reminded him shakily.

His satiny lips twitched, and his long, black lashes dipped low, momentarily veiling his eyes. "I changed my mind. It's better if you set the pace. I'm afraid I'll rush you."

"Maybe I'd rather be rushed."

His eyes filled with questions.

She shrugged, her gaze drawn to his mouth. "The last time you kissed me, I could scarcely think."

"You couldn't?" He looked surprised to hear that. "I thought you were scared to death."

She gave a nervous laugh. "I was." She caught the inside of her cheek in her teeth, working the sensitive tissue until the sting made her quit. "I need you to start this," she blurted. "I, um—feel self-conscious doing it."

Issuing no warning, he shoved her elbow out from under her. The next instant, she found herself flat on her back with him looming over her. "Self-conscious, huh? Well, Maggie girl, we can't have that." The warmth had returned to his eyes. He bent his head to kiss the tip of her nose. "I feel like I've been waiting a lifetime for this," he whispered huskily. "It's hard to decide which part of you I want to taste first."

"My mouth?" she suggested hopefully.

He slowly shook his head and grinned. "Can I choose?"

Maggie's heart thumped wildly at the base of her throat. She'd been counting on him to kiss her and make her feel mindless before he started exploring elsewhere. "I guess," she agreed reluctantly.

"Your ears," he whispered.

"My what?"

He arched a raven brow. "I have this thing about your ears. I can't explain it. They've been driving me crazy for weeks. I've dreamed about kissing them. Fantasized about it. Those ears of yours have been responsible for my taking at least a dozen ice-cold showers.'' His gaze burned a slow path to her hair. ''I like to drool for a while before I actually taste the entrée. Is there any chance I can convince you to push your hair back?''

''You want to look at my ear? You're kidding, right?''

''I'm dead serious. You're not territorial about those, too, are you?'' When she didn't immediately push her hair back, he gave her a mock scowl. ''Maggie,'' he said in a low, scolding tone. ''I'm only asking to kiss your *ear*. I promise not to ravish your canal.''

She giggled in spite of herself. His putting it like that made her feel silly.

''Please?'' he cajoled. ''I'm at the end of my rope. If I don't get to kiss one of those ears soon, I'm going to get pneumonia from cold showers, I swear to God.''

She smiled and reached up to push her hair back. It was insane, but she felt shy. *Stupid, so stupid.* He wasn't asking her to strip. It was only her ear he wanted to see, for pity's sake. When she lowered her hand, she glanced up and saw that he was staring at the side of her head like a starving man who had just spied a heavily laden banquet table.

''That is, without a doubt, the cutest little ear I've ever clapped eyes on.'' With a twist of his waist, he rolled off of her and sat up, resting his broad shoulders against the wall. ''Come here, Mrs. Kendrick,'' he said softly.

Maggie gave him a wary look. He chuckled and grasped her arm. ''Come on. I'm only going to nibble on that ear, not chew it off.''

As she rose to her knees, he released her arm, straightened his legs, and patted his thigh.

''This seems like a lot of preparation just so you can kiss my ear,'' she grumped, trying to inject a blasé tone into her voice, even though her insides were quivering.

''Just?'' His chest rumbled with a low, vibrant

chuckle. "Maggie, Maggie. Ear kissing is an art, and I am a master."

She believed it.

After a good deal of twisting, grunting, and elbowing each other, they finally got comfortably settled with her astride his hard thighs. *Silence*. They regarded each other.

"Can I ask you something?" she ventured.

"Shoot."

"What is it about my ear that you find so appealing?"

"The way I know you'll feel when I kiss it," he said with a mischievous grin.

Maggie couldn't fault him for lack of honesty. "How will I feel?"

"Let me kiss it and find out for yourself." He reached up to push a stray curl out of the way. "You ever done this?"

He'd barely touched her yet, and already she was having trouble thinking. "No, I've never done this."

"Well, I feel duty-bound to tell you you're in for an experience." His velvety warm mouth was at her temple. "Dear God, you smell so wonderful."

"I do?" she asked, her heart lurching as his lips tantalized the sensitive places along her hairline.

"Absolutely," he replied in a whisper that jangled all her nerve endings. "Bathing soap and shampoo and another scent that's uniquely yours."

She probably needed a shower.

"Oh, Maggie, have you any idea what you do to me?"

His lips found her ear. Maggie curled her hands over his shoulders, whether to hang on or shove him away, she wasn't sure. A tingling warmth settled low in her abdomen as his breath wafted softly into her ear canal. The tingling became electrical shocks of melting heat when he drew her lobe into his mouth and teased it lightly with his tongue.

She couldn't move. The sensations were mesmerizing. A restrained breath shuddered from her.

"Oh, Maggie . . . Maggie . . . I love you so."

His voice seemed to radiate clear through her. She clutched his shirt in tight fists, tipping her head to accommodate his mouth, so focused on the feelings he elicited within her that she no longer even felt nervous. *Heaven*. No one had ever kissed one of her ears. Over the years, she had regarded those twin body parts mainly as things that needed to be scrubbed on a regular basis.

Now, suddenly, that ear seemed central to her being, the multitude of nerve endings making her whole body tingle.

She forgot everything. Lonnie. Her dread of sex. Even her name. His mouth moved to the hollow beneath her ear, his teeth nibbling and teasing the spot, his lips grazing her skin like warm, wet satin. Oh, dear heaven. He made her *want*. Way low in her belly, she started to ache—a throbbing ache that transmitted itself to her skin and breasts, making her toes curl inside the floppy socks she wore.

All this, just by kissing her ear?

She blinked when she felt him lightly run his hands down her arms, then back up to grip her shoulders. She let her head fall back as he began to kiss her throat. "Oh, Rafe . . ."

A sudden dizzy sensation made her head swim. She moved back a bit, needing a moment to collect her wits. He made no attempt to restrain her, just allowed her to push away and then gazed up at her, the hue of his eyes smoky and warm.

"Afraid, Maggie?"

It came as a surprise to realize she wasn't. Still bracing her hands on his chest, she said, "No, not really."

"Going somewhere?"

"No," she replied shakily and knew she meant it.

She gazed down at his mouth, yearning for him to kiss her. When he made no move to do so, she leaned hesitantly closer until her lips hovered a scant inch from his. Her heart went *wham-wham* inside her chest. Her stomach tightened, making it difficult to breathe.

This time she scarcely thought about how to kiss him. She just pressed her mouth to his.

Unwilling to let this kiss end as the last one had, Rafe curled a hand over the back of her head, aware as he tightened his hold that even her skull felt small to him. He slanted his mouth over hers, taking control. When he first touched the tip of his tongue to her lips, she stiffened. But after a moment, she opened her mouth ever so slightly.

It was all the encouragement Rafe needed. *Sweetness.* It seemed to him he had waited forever to taste her again, and he wasn't disappointed. Remembering an old song, he thought, *Kisses sweeter than wine.* It was no exaggeration. She was intoxicating.

Yearning hit him, fast and hard. He wanted to lay his hands on her satiny skin, to slowly trace every curve and plane of her body, to suckle her breasts. *Maggie.* This went beyond desire. He burned with such a fierce need to have her that he felt afire.

She pressed against him, her slender body soft, deliciously warm, and trembling with what he hoped was desire. *Maggie.* He slid his hands beneath the hem of her top and found bare skin. To actually touch her felt so wonderful his guts knotted.

At the edge of his mind, warning bells clamored. He had to go slowly. It was just so damned difficult when he'd wanted her so badly for so long. Never for a minute had he dreamed she might respond to him like this, or with such abandon. *Slow down. Don't rush her.* He wanted their first time together to be perfect. She had experienced less than perfect too many times as it was.

He tamped down his rising passion, afraid he'd lose control and frighten her. As if she sensed his tension, she suddenly drew back, her beautiful eyes slightly unfocused, her lashes fluttering. "What is it?" she whispered throatily.

His hands anchored at her waist, he feathered his fingertips over her silken skin, the yearning within him to skim his palms upward so intense that he clenched his teeth. He let out a shaky breath, forcing himself to relax. *Honesty*. His rule. No more secrets between them, he'd told her.

"I'm scared to death," he confessed.

An incredulous bewilderment entered her eyes. "Scared? Of me, you mean?"

"For you," he whispered. "Scared for you. And for me. I'm afraid of screwing this up. Of doing the wrong thing." He drew his hands from her waist to frame her face with his palms. He trailed the pads of his thumbs over her cheeks, reveling in the silky smoothness, knowing full well she'd be just that soft everywhere—if not softer. "I love you so much, Maggie. I want to make this perfect for you, and I'm afraid I won't. That I'll blow it, and you'll never want me again. That—" He released another shaky breath and gave a self-deprecating laugh. "I'm so nervous, I couldn't spit if you yelled fire. Can you believe it?"

She sat back, her soft bottom settling on his thighs just above his knees. Even in that, he found sweet torture. The heat of her. The alluring way her lush roundness molded to his firmness. Curling her slender hands over his wrists, she gazed at him for a long moment, saying nothing. Then her eyes filled with tears, and a tremulous smile touched her swollen lips.

"I thought for a moment you'd decided you didn't want me."

"Oh, I want you," he assured her. "That's the problem. I want you so much, it's scary, and I'm—" He didn't want to alarm her, even with words. "I'm afraid I'll lose control and—" He swallowed. "I just don't want to do anything that reminds you of Lonnie, you know?" He tried to inject a note of humor into his shaking voice. ''The old monster in the closet, jumping out at you.''

Maggie had never loved him more than she did then. She searched his eyes and knew he actually was afraid. Bone-deep afraid. He was shaking slightly, whether with nerves or the strain of holding back, she wasn't sure. And it didn't really matter, for either way, it told her how very much he did love her. She thought of all the nights that he'd held her, the hardness of his need pressed rigidly against her. Night after night, needing and never taking. Now, when he could finally have her, he still held back? That meant more to Maggie than she could say. In fact, out of all the things he might have said or done to make this easier for her, his doing nothing at all was the most disarming. It nearly broke her heart.

The old monster in the closet. Her words, and she realized now that she'd been inadvertently cruel, telling him she had a deep-rooted fear that there was a little of Lonnie in him. Now he was afraid to be himself for fear she would draw comparisons. Not this man. Never. He was so sweet and dear, the very antithesis of Lonnie Boyle in every way. Granted, Rafe was big—and he was definitely strong, his body roped and padded with steely tendon and muscle. He embodied all that was masculine and all that Lonnie had taught her to fear. But Rafe Kendrick was more than just that, so very much more. Hard as he might be on the outside, he was a softie at the center, the most gentle and caring man she'd ever known.

And he loved her. *For keeps*. Not just a physical attraction, though that was undeniably interlaced with his feelings for her. But he loved her beyond that, more deeply than that, in a way that transcended the physical and would persevere even if she denied him the physical. She could bring this to a halt right now, tell him she wasn't ready and might never be ready, and he would accept it. She could see it in his eyes. More than that—she felt it in her heart.

Knowing that gave her the most incredible feeling. It was madness, she knew, but she felt like a prisoner being miraculously released from manacles and chains. A heavy weight, slipping off her shoulders. A wondrous, almost giddy sensation of lightness. Nothing to fear. Nothing to hold her. Knowing Rafe, loving him—he had somehow set her free, yet in doing so, he had also bound her to him.

Maggie didn't allow herself to think it through. She just drew her hands from his broad wrists and grasped the hem of her undershirt. When he saw what she was about to do, he tensed, his forearms turning rock-hard and his palms pressing more firmly against the sides of her face.

"Maggie," he said in a gravelly whisper, "don't bite off what you can't chew. Please, be sure you're ready first."

She could only pull the undershirt up so far with his arms in the way. "Let me, Rafe. Please?"

He darted a glance downward, glimpsed her bared breasts, and said, "*Jesus*. Didn't you hear me? I'm inches away from—" He closed his eyes, his larynx bobbing, the tendons along his throat distended. "Holy hell."

Maggie twisted to escape his hold and jerked the shirt off over her head. As she tossed it aside and felt cool air washing over her skin, a wave of embarrassment hit her, and right behind it came a rush of insecurities. That maybe he'd find fault with her. That she wouldn't be what he had expected. That once he saw her, he might not want her.

She caught her breath, waiting for his reaction, and all he did was continue to sit there with his eyes closed, his shoulders pressed hard against the wall behind him. An airless pounding began in her temples. She waited. Waited. Finally she had to draw in oxygen.

"Rafe?" she said shakily, fearing that he'd not liked what he saw when he glanced down. "Aren't y-you going to l-look at me?"

A muscle rippled along his jaw. In a taut, gruff whisper, he asked, "Do you *want* me to lose it? Damn, Maggie. I'm not made of stone. One look, and you'll be flat on your back in two seconds, tops."

"Just as long as you're there with me."

He didn't say anything for a beat. Then he narrowly cracked open one eye. "What?"

Maggie laughed tremulously. "You're torturing me. Would you please just look and get it over with? I'm scared to death you won't like me."

The crack of his eye widened a hair. He looked down. "Jesus, Mary, and Joseph."

Maggie crossed her arms over herself. "I'm sort of saggy."

He opened both eyes. "You're sort of *what?*"

"Um . . . saggy. And there's stretch marks. Do you hate stretch marks?"

He searched her gaze as if he couldn't quite believe she was seriously asking. Suddenly his expression softened. "You're worried I might not—" He chuckled, albeit a bit shakily. "Sweetheart, don't hate me, all right? But I've already checked out the terrain."

"You have? When?"

He smiled slightly. "In the motel when you were so sick."

"Oh." Maggie hugged herself more tightly. "And?"

"And what?"

"Did you—well, you know—like what you saw?"

He did laugh then—a full-blown rumble of laughter that rocked his broad shoulders. "Like? Did I *like* what I saw? I'm here, aren't I? Maggie, you're beautiful. Gorgeous. *Perfect*. I didn't see any stretch marks."

"Then you didn't check very close. It must have been a sneak peek, and you missed the bad stuff."

He sighed. "The bad stuff?" He dropped his gaze to

her arms. "The moment of reckoning. Let me see."

Maggie forced herself to lower her arms. It was the most awful moment of her life, just sitting there while he looked her over. Every place his gaze touched, her skin burned. And why didn't he say something? She imagined he was thinking all kinds of awful things— that they were shaped like balloons that had lost some of their air, maybe. And that the stretch marks, silvery white, were ugly. Oh, God. If he didn't like her, she'd die.

"Well?" she demanded, hearing the quiver in her own voice.

He drew his gaze back to hers, his face so solemn she just knew he was going to say something terrible. "Those," he said slowly, "are, without question, the most beautiful, perfect, *gorgeous* thingamajigs I've ever seen in my life."

The next instant, he hooked an arm around her waist, and before Maggie knew quite how it happened, she was flat on her back with him braced on his arms over her. "I warned you," he said huskily. "You can't say I didn't." He bent his dark head to nibble below her ear. "Oh, God, Maggie, forgive me. I know you need me to go slow."

At this point, Maggie was just pleased to have him go forward at any speed. "I guess I should warn you. I've got some stretch marks on my tummy, too. And a couple on each hip." When he just kept kissing her neck, she added, "Not real bad ones. Just little white lines like I've got up top."

"Does that mean you probably won't ever wear a string bikini in public?"

Maggie wouldn't wear a string bikini anywhere. Just the thought made her cringe. "Oh, no. I couldn't."

"Good," he growled, the deep timber of his voice seeming to rumble through her. "I'd kill the first man who looked twice at you. You're mine, Maggie girl." He trailed feverish kisses along her throat, suckling her skin as if to savor her taste. "Mine," he repeated fiercely.

You're mine. The words echoed through her mind, calling up memories. For an instant, everything within her recoiled. But then she turned her gaze to the man who'd said them. The blurry darkness of his profile, the glint of lantern light playing over his jet-black hair. *Rafe.* Not Lonnie. *Rafe.* She wanted to belong to him. Needed to belong to him. And just hearing him say the words filled her with joy. She was his now, not Lonnie's. *His.* And that made her feel absolutely safe.

"Yes, yours," she murmured.

He groaned deep in his throat. "Say it again."

"Yours," she said more loudly. "Yours, Rafe."

His mouth burned a searing path over her collarbone, his teeth nipping lightly at her skin. His tone throbbing with need, he said, "If I do anything you don't want me to, just tell me. I give you my word, I'll try my damnedest to stop."

Try? That should have alarmed her, but oddly, it didn't. He would try. No guarantees. No promises. He wanted her so badly, she could feel him shaking. But if she asked him to stop, he would try.

She smoothed her hands over his shoulders, wishing she could feel his skin and the play of steely muscle beneath. "Rafe, could you take off your shirt?"

He reared up, grabbed the hem of the undershirt, and peeled it off over his head. He knelt astride her hips, and as he tossed the shirt aside, Maggie took in the bronze splendor of his upper torso—the broad, well-padded shoulders, the striated belly, the mounded pectorals and biceps. The skin of his upper body, more frequently exposed to the sun, was the color of rich caramel, one of her favorites, and looking at him made her want to taste him just as he had her.

He raked at his hair to settle the tousled waves, his gunmetal-blue eyes glinting as he gazed back at her. "Anything else you want off?" He gave her a mischievous wink. "Be careful what you ask for. I believe in equal opportunity."

Maggie giggled. He was mercurial, this man, hotly passionate one second and teasing her the next. "Does that mean you'll demand I remove any articles of clothing I ask you to take off?"

"Damn straight."

She pretended to consider. "That isn't equitable. You've got no thingamajigs."

He chuckled and ran a hand over his chest, ruffling the light dusting of black hair that she yearned to run her fingers through. "Thank God."

He fell forward, catching his weight with his hands, his chest a scant inch from hers. Maggie gave a startled squeak. He smiled and dipped his head. His silken mouth settled over hers. Maggie moaned, her breath spilling into him in a rush when his chest lightly grazed hers. Sensation ribboned from the tips of her breasts like jolts of lightning, streaking fire into her belly.

His lips molded gently to hers. *Wet heat.* He traced the shape of her lower lip with his tongue, then drew the sensitive flesh between his teeth to lave it and suckle. The fire in her middle turned white-hot. She clung to his shoulders, overcome by the feelings.

He suddenly drew his mouth from hers, plucked one of her hands from his shoulder, and began kissing her fingertips, his gaze locked with hers. When he drew the tip of her forefinger into his mouth, she was sure she'd never felt anything like that warm, wet, incredibly soft pulling on her flesh. He worked his way down the underside of her finger to her palm, tracing the lines there with his tongue. Then he moved on to her wrist. Then up to the bend of her elbow. Every touch of his mouth struck a chord within her, enlivening and torturing nerve endings she hadn't realized existed. She felt like a delicate string instrument being played by a maestro.

Oh, yes. Her whole body tingled and she wanted to experience the sensation of his mouth on her skin in other places. Everywhere. He drew her arm out from her side and began nibbling his way up the ladder of her ribs. She sucked in her breath, her stomach so concave it felt glued to her backbone. Airless pressure hummed inside her head. Like the caress of feathers, tendrils of his black hair teased over her breast. Oh, God. She wanted his mouth there, ached to feel his lips on her there.

He nibbled a path to the sensitive hollow beneath her armpit instead. It tickled, and she tried to jerk her arm back to her side to protect the spot. He seized her wrist and pinned her hand to the bed. "Oh, no, you don't. I've been dreaming about doing this. Every sweet inch of you, Maggie girl. Finally all mine. There isn't a spot on you I'm gonna miss out on."

Not a single spot? She tried to laugh, but just breathing seemed to be beyond her. This was—oh, God. He pushed her arm straight out to give him better access. Her underarm? In all her wildest imaginings—not that she'd traveled down that path very often—she'd never for a moment considered her armpit as an erogenous zone.

"It—tickles," she gasped out, squirming to escape the delicious torture.

He trailed the tip of his tongue up the side of her breast, licking the swell as if she were a melting cone of his favorite ice cream. Her nipple hardened and thrust upward shamelessly, aching for him to reach it. *Almost there.* Maggie was lost to the need building inside her. She turned slightly to bring the throbbing peak closer to his seeking mouth.

He circled to kiss the underside of her breast instead, the brush of his hair on her screaming flesh an exquisite torment. Up. Wet heat. His teeth nibbling and teasing. At the edge of her pebbled aureole, he backed off and resumed kissing the under-swell of her breast again. Maggie sobbed. At the back of her mind, she heard the echo of Lonnie's voice. *Ask me for it. Say please. Beg me for it*. She'd sworn each time that she never would again. But now the pleas were there at the back of her throat, aching to burst forth.

She started to swallow them back. Only she *wanted*. And this was Rafe. There was no shame. No wrong. No degradation.

"Rafe, kiss me," she whispered raggedly. "Please, kiss me there."

In a distant part of his mind, Rafe was aware that she had run the slender fingers of her free hand into his hair and was hanging onto him for dear life. She arched her spine and let her head fall back, offering herself to him in a way no sane man could refuse.

As he bathed her thrusting nipple with his tongue, she jerked and cried out. He could feel every beat of her heart in that swollen, erect tip. He drew her gently into his mouth, his mind spinning with multiple shades of red that blinded him. *Maggie*. She sobbed, a tremor coursing through her that was so violent it rocked his own body. *His*. She was his. The need to have her raged through him, blanking out all else.

He drew urgently on her. The sweet, dizzying taste of her inflamed him. He caught the turgid peak between his teeth and teased her captured flesh with flicks of his tongue until she quivered and moaned, begging him with inarticulate cries to ease away the ache. He more than happily obliged her, dragging hard with his tongue, then suckling.

She bucked and sobbed. When he released her hand, she promptly caught his hair in both fists. She was so sweet and infinitely precious. While keeping her mindless with the ministrations of his mouth, he pushed her bottoms to her knees, then jerked them off, removing socks and all in one tug.

He ran a hand up her slender leg, slipped his fingers between her thighs, and then turned his hand so the width of his palm pushed her knees apart. She flinched when his fingertips caressed the thatch of tight curls he sought. He separated the silken folds, slipping his fingers over slick heat to gently invade the velvety sheath of her femininity. Thrusting deep, then withdrawing, his rhythm slow.

She sobbed again and lifted her hips, bumping awkwardly against his hand. He abandoned the one breast to give some attention to the other one. Her nipple gave him sweet welcome, so swollen and eager, begging for the pull of his mouth. He granted the request, waited a beat, and then slipped his fingers over her wetness at the apex of her thighs. Lightly stroking her. The node of vulnerable flesh beneath his fingertips went instantly turgid. He increased pressure and speed of stroke. Faster, harder.

Her slender body suddenly went rigid. Her breathing stopped. Then she emitted a low cry, her muscles quivering and jerking with each pass of his fingers. He gloried in the hot, wet rush.

When she went limp, he smothered her soft sobs with his mouth, kissing her deeply while he fumbled with his belt buckle and jeans. His zipper caught. Frustrated, he gave it a hard jerk. As the denim parted, he rose over her, then knelt between her open legs.

Grasping her hips, he slowly entered her. Her eyes fluttered open. She moaned. With his first thrust, she sobbed again, her breath whining in her slender throat.

Heaven, hell. Explosive need roiled low in his abdomen, the ache for relief so sharp it was nearly unbearable. He held back, determined not to let go until he took her over the edge again. White-hot. Then a red, swirling haze formed before his eyes. *Maggie.* He couldn't see her face.

"Rafe!" she cried out.

He felt her tightness convulse around him. That was all it took to snap his self-control. He made one, final thrust and let go, his body jerking taut as he went over the edge with her.

Afterward they lay intertwined on the bed like two

wax figures that had melted and run together. Exhausted, replete, so drained that even coherent thought evaded them. Rafe held Maggie close, content in a way he'd never been. She lay snuggled against him like a well-fed kitten that had been petted to sleep, her cheek resting in the hollow of his shoulder.

Sleepily and disjointedly, he tried to recall all that had taken place, wanting to analyze and grade his performance. He couldn't hold onto his thoughts. He had wanted so badly to make it perfect for her this first time.

Unable to succumb to exhaustion until he had assured himself he'd accomplished his goal, he hovered between consciousness and blackness, blurry images of her spiraling through his head. A smile touched his mouth when he recalled how she had come apart in his arms when that first orgasm had rocked her.

Perfect? His smile deepened. Probably not. But he'd come damned close.

His last thought as he plunged into the blackness of slumber was *Practice makes perfect*. He was more than willing to repeat his performance until he got it right.

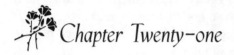 *Chapter Twenty-one*

Maggie awakened to the crackling of the fire in the woodstove, the muted sound of popping embers filling her with a feeling of cozy warmth. She blinked, saw the blur of striped pillow ticking under her cheek, and came wide awake, acutely aware of the man who held her in his arms, his wide chest a sturdy wall of vibrant muscle against her back.

Her heart skittered when she realized one of his big, callused palms was cupping her bare breast. She'd never awakened naked in a man's arms before. Unlike last night when only the dim glow of lantern light had illuminated the room, now the harsh brilliance of a snow-bright morning spilled over the bed.

She lay there and stared at the wall, uncertain what to do. If she moved, she'd wake him. And then what?

"Good morning."

The husky timber of his voice next to her ear startled her. His long fingers curled lightly over her breast, his thumb dragging on her nipple in such a way that her muscles jerked involuntarily. When he made another pass, her stomach did flip-flops.

"This is like waking up with my arms full of heaven," he whispered.

She sucked in a sharp breath, her senses reeling. Then she felt his mouth nibbling her bare shoulder. The sensation, coupled with his teasing strokes over her nipple, obliterated all rational thought from her mind.

Magic. He had promised her magic, and that was what he gave her. Pure, sweet magic that made her feel mindless . . .

Ryan and another man arrived at the line shack around one-thirty that afternoon, whereupon Rafe went out to help refuel the snowmobiles and check their oil. Watching from a window inside the shack, Maggie had eyes for only her husband as he carried a large gas can from the lean-to. She loved the way he walked, his long-legged stride loose, his broad shoulders shifting with every step. In the frosty winter sunlight, he looked so rugged and deliciously masculine, his badly soiled leather jacket hanging open to reveal the faded red undershirt, which skimmed the muscular bulges of his chest. Without his Stetson, which he had left in the Expedition yesterday, his hair glistened like polished jet in the bright sunlight that shafted down through the snow-laden evergreen boughs.

Ryan and the other man offered to ride double on one snowmobile, leaving the other machine for Rafe and Maggie. After dousing the fire in the stove and helping her to straighten the room, Rafe led her outside, his hand locked on her arm so she wouldn't slip on the ice. His protective behavior made her feel cherished.

"You ever ridden a snow horse?" Ryan called.

Maggie shook her head, eyeing the snowmobile with wariness. She'd seen how Ryan and the other man drove the things—their bodies angled low for balance as they zigzagged the machines through the thick growth of trees and went airborne over the deep drifts.

Never releasing her arm, Rafe swung a leg over the seat and then scooted forward to make room for her behind him. "Climb on, sweetheart," he urged, then helped her as she complied. "Now—lock your arms around my waist."

The man had no waist. He was built like a wedge.

Maggie put her arms around him, nonetheless, her fingertips barely meeting. He glanced over his shoulder, his eyes twinkling. In a low voice meant only for her, he said, "I know I'm not that big around. What's shortening your reach, sugar?"

Maggie blushed. "It's the parka."

"Bullshit. But I'll settle the argument later." He winked at her as he revved the motor to deafening decibels. "You ready?"

Maggie nodded, and the next second, she was clinging to him for dear life as they flew over the frozen snow. As they executed the first sharp turn, Rafe roared, "Lean with me!" Maggie leaned and lost her stomach in the apex of the curve, her heart in her mouth. His emphatic "Hold tight!" was an unnecessary warning. She even had her thighs clamped to his hips.

Ryan zoomed up on his snowmobile beside them, swung his Stetson above his head, and whooped, his dark face creased in a grin. "Eat my dust!" he yelled, and then shot ahead of them.

Maggie felt Rafe's back jerk with laughter. She half-expected him to take up the challenge, but he lagged behind, keeping their speed within reasonable limits. To her surprise, she began to enjoy the ride. It was exhilarating, and she was almost disappointed when she finally saw the road ahead. Ryan and the hired hand had already dismounted from their machine and were awaiting Rafe's arrival, their stances conveying intense boredom.

As Rafe parked on the shoulder of the road near the Expedition, Ryan yelled, "What is this? You turn into a wimp the last two years?"

Rafe steadied Maggie as she swung off the seat, then got off behind her. "I was carrying precious cargo. Challenge me to a race when I'm riding alone, and I'll whip your ass."

Ryan hooted. "That'll be the day. Marriage! It ruins all of a man's fun."

Rafe looped an arm around Maggie's shoulders. "Jealous, little brother?"

Ryan fixed a twinkling gaze on Maggie. "If I were, I'd never admit it. Well, sis, what do you think of snow horses?"

"It was fun," Maggie said breathlessly. "I'd like to do it again."

To Rafe, Ryan said, "You wanna ride on in? I can drive the Ford."

Rafe grinned. "I think Maggie's had enough excitement the last two days. We'll drive. You gonna meet us at the main house?"

Ryan glanced at his watch. "I've got work scheduled. Unlike some lazy cusses, I can't play around all day." He narrowed an eye at his older brother. "That vacation you promised me is sounding better all the time."

"Take off anytime. I can handle it."

"I just might do that. A warm tropical island sounds good right now."

Rafe led Maggie toward the Ford. "Catch you later," he called to his brother over his shoulder. "Don't work too hard. I'm taking the rest of the day off."

"Newlyweds," Ryan said with a teasing note of disgust in his voice. "The world comes to a screeching halt."

It was nearly four o'clock in the afternoon when they finally reached the driveway to the main house. As Rafe drove up the long, curving road, Maggie gazed at the sprawling brick home on the distant knoll. For the first time since marrying Rafe, she had reason to believe she might actually be able to spend the rest of her life there.

She recalled how intimidated she had been when she'd first seen the house. Now it seemed familiar and comforting—a safe haven she could call home. *Home.* If all went well, Heidi would call this home as well, and it would be where her son grew up. He would play someday on that knoll and run wild in the surrounding woods, a healthy, happy little boy with every advantage.

If all went well . . . That was the kicker. There were no guarantees in life. Oh, how she wished that there were.

"Penny for them."

Jerked from her reverie, Maggie looked over at her husband. His black hair, still damp and windblown from their ride on the snowmobile, lay in loose waves over his forehead. His smoky gaze glinted with a new possessiveness and bold familiarity as he gazed back at her, a result, she felt sure, of their recent intimacy.

Afraid he might think her silly, Maggie nearly fibbed about what was on her mind. But then she looked deeply into his eyes and couldn't, for the life of her, lie to him.

"I was just thinking that this really is my home now," she admitted. "Until last night, it was always in the back of my mind that I might have to leave soon."

She glimpsed an aching regret in his eyes just before he returned his attention to the road. "I never would have asked you to leave. I hope you realize that now."

Hugging her waist, Maggie smiled. "Yeah, I realize that now. It's just—I don't know quite how to explain it. But there's a part of me that's almost afraid to feel this happy. Oh, Rafe. It's magical, just like you promised. And you know what they say about magic. It can vanish in a puff of smoke."

"Is it Lonnie you're worried about?"

After all he'd done to protect her and her loved ones, Maggie hated to admit she still felt threatened by Lonnie, but the truth was she did. "It's just so hard to believe he's out of my life forever. You know?" She looked over at him, fairly certain her heart and all her fears were shining in her eyes. "Oh, Rafe, I love you so, and being here has made me so happy. Most of the time, I try not to even think of Lonnie, but sometimes, like now, I just get this awful, frightened feeling, and I can't shake it off. I'm so afraid something may happen to ruin everything. Do you think that's silly?"

"No, not silly. But sweetheart, I really do think the danger is mostly over now. And if something does crop up, I'll handle it. I promise you that. He's never going to hurt you again." Flashing her one of those grins that always made her heartbeat skitter, he backed off the gas and slowed the Expedition to a crawl. "The sky won't fall just because you're happy, Maggie. And this particular brand of magic isn't going to vanish in a puff of smoke. I'm real. My love for you is real. If you can't trust in anything else, trust in that."

"I'm trying."

Feeling almost giddy with happiness as they drew closer to the house, Maggie noticed an unfamiliar vehicle parked near the side door where the Expedition usually sat. "Somebody's here."

As the Ford rounded the final curve of the driveway, Rafe studied the dark blue, sporty Cadillac parked by the atrium door. Then he grinned. "I'll be damned. Ten bucks says it's my folks. Ryan told me they bought a new Cadillac right before they left. I wasn't expecting them until next week. They didn't think they could make it for Thanksgiving."

Maggie's stomach lurched. His folks? Ever since her marriage to Rafe, she'd been dreading their return to Oregon. Unless they were rare individuals indeed, they weren't likely to be very happy about their son's marrying so suddenly.

"Sweetheart, you look scared to death. Mom and Dad don't bite."

Maggie gulped and shot him a beseeching look. "Could I go in by another door? I'm a wreck. I'd really like to freshen up before I meet them."

"Don't be silly. You look beautiful. If you run off to the bedroom without even saying hello, it'll hurt their feelings. Just excuse yourself after the introductions and go change. I'm sure Becca's told them you got lost yesterday. They won't expect you to look like a fashion model. I sure as hell don't."

Maggie curled her hand over the door handle and made a tight fist. "What if they don't like me?"

"They're going to love you." He killed the engine, drew the keys from the ignition, and leaned across the console to kiss her. "Sweetheart, don't do this. Just relax and be yourself."

With a sinking sensation, she opened her door and climbed from the vehicle. Rafe fell in beside her as they walked to the house, one strong arm encircling her shoulders. Maggie tried to draw away from him as they entered the atrium, but he tightened his hold. "Always present a united front."

The kitchen was bustling with activity when they entered by way of the sliding glass door. Her heart squeezing with anxiety, Maggie breathed in a fishy smell. She was so nervous, it made her feel a little sick to her stomach. She pressed closer to Rafe, suddenly glad for the hard, warm strength of his arm.

Across the room, Becca and a diminutive blonde dressed in gray slacks and a burgundy sweater were preparing dinner. In front of the hearth, a dark-skinned man with steel-gray hair sat on one of the rockers. Dressed in the usual rancher garb, a blue chambray shirt and Wrangler jeans, he looked like an older version of Rafe. Holding Jaimie in the bend of one arm, he was trying to read the evening newspaper with only one hand, a task greatly complicated by the baby's wiggling and the rhythmic motion of the chair.

Maggie couldn't stop staring at him. The family resemblance was so strong, there was no mistaking him for anyone but Rafe's father. He had the Kendrick chiseled profile, and even with him sitting down, she could see where his sons had gotten their height and well-muscled builds.

As if he sensed her gaze on him, he glanced over his shoulder. Maggie found herself staring into twinkling, gray-blue eyes very like her husband's. "Well, now," he said as he pushed to his feet, "just look what the cat dragged in!'' He dropped the newspaper and jiggled Jaimie to get a better hold on him. Then in a booming voice that made Maggie's nerves leap, he hollered, ''Annie, the kids are finally home!''

Clutching green-leaf lettuce in her slender hands, Ann Kendrick whirled from the sink. She gave a glad cry when she saw her son, and her wide gray eyes went bright with tears. ''Rafael!'' She flung the lettuce back in the sink and came racing across the room. ''Oh, Rafael!''

Rafe drew away from Maggie in the nick of time to catch his mother in his arms. He chuckled and lifted her off her feet to swing her in a circle. Ann hugged his neck, laughing and crying at once.

''I've never been so glad to see anyone in my life!'' she told him.

''The feeling's mutual,'' Rafe assured her as he set her down. ''Damn, Mom, I've missed you! I didn't expect you today. I thought Dad had a stress test early next week.''

''They had a cancellation, and he got in early. We didn't phone because we wanted to surprise you for Thanksgiving.''

''And the test results?''

''There's not a thing wrong with him that some common sense wouldn't cure. The chest pain isn't from his heart. It's indigestion from eating too much fatty food. So what did your father do? He celebrated his clean bill of health by eating country-fried steak with biscuits and gravy at a greasy-spoon restaurant!''

''And topped it off with a cigarette, I'll bet.'' Rafe grinned at his dad. ''Ornery as the day is long. Why do you put up with him?''

''I don't know. I guess I'm fond of him.'' Ann ran her hands over her son's face. ''Oh, Rafael. It's so good to have you back.''

Rafe bent to kiss her cheek. ''I'm home to stay now. I promise.''

Ann gave him another hug. "You'd better be," she said as she stepped away to let him greet his father.

Rafe turned and locked gazes with his dad. The room went suddenly quiet, and for what seemed to Maggie an interminably long moment, the two men just stared at each other. Then, as if by mutual decision, they stepped off the distance between them.

Still holding Jaimie, Keefe returned Rafe's exuberant hug with only one arm. He sniffed, patted his son on the back, and said, "Careful of my grandson. We don't wanna squash the little guy."

Rafe drew back slightly to look down at the baby. "What do you think of him, Dad? Does he pass muster?"

Keefe smiled. "Your mama swears up and down he's damned near as good-lookin' as I am, so I reckon he's a keeper."

Ann, who stood slightly off to the side watching her husband and son, smiled and inserted, "Actually, I said he was better-looking than you are."

"Don't split hairs." Keefe handed the baby to Rafe and then turned to regard Maggie. Still hanging back by the door, she felt impaled by those slate-blue eyes. Like Rafe, Keefe Kendrick seemed to miss nothing as he swept his gaze slowly over her. His expression sober and unreadable, he strode toward her, coming to a halt half an arm's length away. Every bit as tall and broad across the chest as his son, he seemed to loom over her.

"And this must be Maggie." He grasped her elbow, drew her away from the wall, and then proceeded to step a circle around her. Maggie felt like a mare on the auction block. "She's a little on the scrawny side, son."

Maggie threw Rafe a horrified glance. His mouth twitched, and he gave her a reassuring wink. Then, to his father, he said, "I've been trying to fatten her up. No matter what I feed her, though, I can't seem to get any meat on her bones."

"Hmmm," was Keefe's reply to that. "I have the

same problem with your mother.'' Completing his circle around Maggie, Keefe came to a stop in front of her and cupped her chin in his big, hard hand. After turning her face this way and that, he nodded. ''On the plus side, she's a pretty little thing. Nice, clean lines. She'll wear good. Only problem with her that I can see is that you'll have to beat the fellows off with a club.''

''I can handle it.'' Rafe fixed a laughing gaze on Maggie. ''Any other man looks twice at her, and he's dead.''

''How are her teeth?''

''She bites, so I haven't been able to check. I haven't glimpsed any cavities when she snarls, though, so I'm hoping she won't bankrupt me with dental bills.''

Keefe nodded. ''She'll do, I reckon.''

Ann Kendrick clucked her tongue. ''Keefe, leave off. He's only teasing you, Maggie. Don't pay him a second's notice.''

Keefe chuckled, and before Maggie guessed what he meant to do, he gathered her into his arms for a gentle hug and bent his head to kiss her cheek. ''Welcome to our family, Maggie.''

Maggie frantically searched her mind for a suitable response, but she was so surprised by Keefe Kendrick's overture that she drew a total blank. He kept a strong arm around her shoulders as he led her toward his wife. ''Well, Annie? What do you think of our new daughter?''

Ann stepped closer and framed Maggie's face between her fine-boned hands. ''She's beautiful, Rafael,'' she said warmly. And the next thing Maggie knew, she was receiving another affectionate hug. As Ann drew away, she said, ''I'm so glad to have another woman in the family again! I need all the reinforcement I can get with these big galoots. And Jaimie! I spent the whole afternoon cuddling him. He's adorable! What a joy to have another grandchild to spoil.''

''You'll have to excuse my folks, Maggie,'' Rafe said, his voice laced with amusement. ''They forget that all families aren't quite so demonstrative. It may take a while, but you'll get used to them."

Maggie felt tears burning at the backs of her eyes. To be instantly accepted like this—to have them hug her and call her daughter . . . *Oh, God.* Maggie was horrified to realize she was about to cry.

The weight of her father-in-law's arm around her shoulders reminded Maggie of her dad. She glanced up at Keefe's dark face. He flashed her a grin that was so much like Rafe's, she couldn't help but smile back. He gave her shoulder an affectionate squeeze.

"You two got home just in time for dinner," Ann informed them. To Maggie, she said, "After the ordeal you've been through, I'm sure you want to clean up." She glanced at the kitchen clock. "You've got about thirty minutes. We can watch Jaimie while you shower."

Maggie did feel in dire need of a good scrubbing. She glanced at the baby in Rafe's arms. "I can just take him with me. I'm sure you'll want some one-on-one time with your parents."

"Don't be silly," Ann said with a smile. "We can visit while we watch the baby. Keefe and I are so taken with him, we'll enjoy every minute."

Maggie glanced uncertainly at Rafe. He gave her a slight, almost imperceptible nod. "Well, if you're sure. I really would like to freshen up."

"How about if I bring the cradle in, honey?" Rafe asked as she started to leave the kitchen. "That way, we can just keep Jaimie out here this evening while we're visiting."

Until that moment, Maggie had forgotten all about the cradle in the back of the Expedition. A thought occurred to her. "Oh, gosh. They're supposed to deliver all that stuff today before five, aren't they?"

Rafe checked his watch. "Damn. That's right."

"All what stuff?" Keefe asked.

"I came close to buying out an entire baby store yesterday," Rafe explained. He glanced at Maggie, his eyes dancing with mischief. "I got a little impatient with Maggie because she was agonizing over the prices, so I took over and bought one of just about everything in the place."

"You got a fever, son? When a woman agonizes over the prices, let her agonize." Keefe chuckled and directed his gaze toward Maggie. "Whatever it is ailing you, honey, I hope Annie contracts the disease." To Rafe, he added, "Your mama can spend money faster than any female I've ever seen. And you know the kicker? She tells me afterward how much she *saved* me. I've never quite been able to follow that line of reasoning."

"That's because you're a man and think mostly left-brain." Ann shrugged. "It makes perfect sense to me. If I buy on sale, I save."

Maggie was so entertained by their teasing banter that she nearly forgot why she'd been about to leave the room.

Half an hour later when Maggie reentered the kitchen after freshening up, the adjoining sitting and eating area was filled nearly wall-to-wall with newly delivered baby furniture. Heidi had gotten home from school, and she was examining everything like a kid in the center of a toy shop. Rafe and his dad were ripping open a cardboard crate to look at the unassembled crib.

"Why didn't you pay extra to have them put it together?" Keefe asked. "We'll be all evening figuring the damned thing out."

"Oh, come on, Dad. Where would be the fun in that?"

The two men wrestled the crib pieces from the box, laid them out on the floor, and then stood staring down at the parts as if it were a creation from another planet.

"Read the directions!" Ann called from the sink. "Just once, Keefe?"

Rafe snorted. "We don't need directions. It's a simple enough assembly, Mom. Do you think we're total imbeciles?"

"I've heard that before."

"No cracks from anyone who doesn't know a Phillips from a flat-blade screwdriver," Keefe warned.

"I know a Phillips, just as I know a blockhead when I see one."

Smiling at their teasing, Maggie gave Heidi a hard hug and then wandered through the maze of stuff to find her son. Recently fed, Jaimie was sleeping peacefully in his new cradle. Someone had spread a receiving blanket over the tiny, plastic-covered pad for him to lie on, and he was warmly bundled in another blanket. Maggie touched a hand to the baby's dark head, remembering a time in the not so distant past when she'd felt almost overwhelmed by the prospect of raising him alone. Now he had a nanny in the loving Becca, a doting father, and grandparents to help look after him.

"Dinner is ready," Ann called. "You fellas can string that stuff everywhere and lose all the screws later."

"We won't lose the screws," Rafe huffed.

Neither man looked up from the task at hand. Neither of them had reached for the instruction sheet yet, either. Keefe held up an end piece. "Oh, yeah," he said, his tone laced with confidence. "This is self-explanatory. Piece of cake."

Ten minutes later, the men still hadn't responded to the meal call, and Ann stood over them with her hands at her hips. "Can this wait, guys?" she asked, but got no answer as the two men bent their heads to their task.

Ann sat on the rocker, glaring at her son and husband. "Twenty seconds and counting. We've got a hungry ten-year-old to feed, and dinner's getting cold."

Her stern look finally convinced the Kendrick males to leave the crib assembling for later.

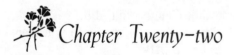 Chapter Twenty-two

It was ten-thirty that night when Rafe's parents left for their cottage on the other side of the lake, and even then, Ryan, who had also dropped by to visit, remained behind to help Rafe finish assembling the crib. While the men worked, Maggie got Jaimie comfortably settled for the night in the bedroom, checked in on Heidi, and then she decided to take a hot bath. She'd had time to grab only a quick shower earlier, and after her escapade in the woods, she felt in need of a thorough scrubbing.

She had just settled back in a deliciously hot tubful of water and closed her eyes when she heard the bathroom door open. Startled, she turned to see Rafe slowly crossing the tiled floor. He'd washed up earlier and thrown on a white dress shirt, the collar open to reveal a V of bronze chest, the sleeves rolled back over his corded forearms.

He smiled slightly at her look of surprise, and his smoky blue eyes took on a mischievous twinkle when she glanced over the edge of the tub in search of a towel or anything else she might use to cover herself. She had to settle for using her washcloth, which she draped over her chest. Unfortunately, it covered only the main points, leaving the rest of her exposed.

Thrusting a hand between her thighs to conceal her nether regions, she managed a squeaky, "Hello. I thought you were working on the crib."

"We decided to leave the rest for tomorrow after dinner."

"Oh. I expected you to be a while."

"I can see that you did. Caught you, didn't I?"

Maggie decided to ignore that. "Um . . . do you want something? I can be out in a jiffy."

He sat on the tile step that led up to the garden tub. Maggie didn't take it as a good sign when he rolled each of his sleeves higher. She gulped and gave him a wondering look which he greeted with a grin. "You don't act very happy to see me," he said in a gruff, low-pitched voice. "And yes, I do want something."

She swallowed convulsively again. "Oh? What?"

His firm mouth quirked at the corners. "You know very well what." He settled his gaze on the washcloth, which seemed to be shrinking under the heat of his regard. Maggie clamped her free hand over one edge. He reacted by leaning around slightly to regard the unveiled swell of her other breast.

His eyes gleaming, he lowered a hand to the water, trailing his fingertips over the surface. Maggie didn't know if he meant to conjure images in her mind, but he did, nonetheless. She couldn't help but recall how he'd caressed her skin in just that way, and remembering gave her goose bumps. Even worse, she had a bad feeling that her washcloth had suddenly developed peaks.

"I—um—" Her toes curled when his gaze came to rest on the hand she held clamped between her legs. "I can be out of here in a flash. Why don't you step out, and I'll be right there."

"And miss this opportunity?" He slowly shook his head. "My mama didn't raise no fool. You know, don't you, that there's nothing quite so delectable as a beautiful woman fresh from her bath—unless it's a beautiful woman still *in* the bath. Clean, rosy-pink skin . . . with droplets of water to sip away. Every part of her body sweet and just waiting to be kissed or nibbled. It'd take a team of draft horses to drag me out of here."

"Oh," she said weakly.

He chuckled, the sound deep and warm, curling around her like an embrace. "Sweetheart, don't be nervous."

Easily said. Maggie had never taken a bath in front of a man. Her skin tingled as if the water itself was electrified. "I'm not nervous, exactly." She momentarily forgot the washcloth and lifted her hand to gesture a little wildly. "Not at all. It's just—you're gaping at me." She clamped her hand back over the edge of the terry cloth.

His lean cheek creased in a slow grin. "I'm sorry. I can't help myself. You're as pretty as sunrise and sunset and everything in between."

He cupped water in his hand and spilled it in a tickling dribble over her chest. The unanchored edge of her washcloth floated away. Maggie grabbed for it with both hands, leaving her nether regions unguarded for only the briefest of moments. It was all the opportunity he needed. Before Maggie guessed what he meant to do, he cupped his hand over her thatch of curls.

She gasped and grabbed his wrist. "What're you doing?"

"Helping you keep everything hidden," he replied teasingly. "With three hands to do the job, that leaves both of yours free to wrestle with that washcloth." His long fingers flexed where they cupped her. Maggie jerked in reaction. "Aren't I thoughtful?"

She gripped his wrist more tightly, her stomach beset by swirling heat as he pressed firmly against that spot with the heel of his hand, then released the pressure. Her breath caught, and her throat convulsed to stifle a moan. He twisted at the waist, slipped his other hand behind her head, and lifted her slightly, settling his mouth over hers.

Maggie's head went into a spin. She clenched her wet hands on the front of his shirt, forgetting all about the washcloth. Forgetting all about everything. *Rafe.* In a distant corner of her mind, she was shocked at herself. But she could no more break the contact of their mouths than she could stop breathing.

She gave a startled squeak when he suddenly caught her behind the knees and scooped her from the water. She blinked, trying to orient her dizzied senses as he carried her from the brightly lit bathroom to the shadowy bedroom. Upon reaching the bed, he gently laid her on the mattress.

''I'll get the bed damp,'' she protested.

''Like I care?'' He jerked off his shirt and opened his jeans. The next instant, he covered her, his hard shaft thrusting fast and deep.

Maggie hadn't thought she could feel anything more intense than what she had experienced last night. But she was wrong. *Rafe*. His name was like a sweet refrain in her mind, and once again, his gift to her was sheer magic.

Much later, Maggie awakened to find Rafe leaning over her with Jaimie in his arms. He'd pulled his jeans back on, but his upper torso was bare, his wedge-like form gleaming like seasoned oak in the moonlight. She yawned and stretched, smiling up at him. ''Is he hungry again already?''

''You could say that.'' As though to punctuate the sentence, Jaimie whimpered and squirmed. Rafe smiled. ''Go to the bathroom and wash up, Mama. You've been off the meds for two full days. No more bottles and formula for this kid.''

Maggie started to sit up, remembered she had no clothes on, and reached over the side of the bed to grab his discarded shirt. She held the blankets to her chest as she straightened and shoved her arms down the sleeves.

Jostling the fussy baby, Rafe said, ''Worried that I'll see something I've seen before?''

She shrugged and slipped from the bed. ''Maybe all of this is old hat to you, but it isn't to me.''

"Trust me. Seeing you in that shirt isn't old hat." He laid the baby over his shoulder and started to pace as she went to the bathroom. When she returned a few moments later, he followed her to the bed. "Hurry, Mom. He's working his way up to a full roar. I can feel it coming."

Maggie fluffed up a pillow and sat with her back against the headboard. After taking the baby from him, she looked up at him expectantly. He gazed back at her, smiling. Instead of turning away as she hoped, he lowered himself onto the mattress beside her. Jaimie thrashed his legs and let loose with an angry cry.

"You'd better feed him. He's getting pissed. The Kendrick temper is getting the best of him."

Maggie unbuttoned the shirt, hoping to keep herself covered with the loose front plackets. Only when she tried to get Jaimie to nurse, he turned away, stiffened his body, and started to shriek. Her heart sank. Her son obviously wanted his baby bottle back.

Watching Maggie's face, Rafe could see how upset she was getting.

"He wants his bottle," she said forlornly, trying once more to interest the furious baby. Jaimie pulled an awful face and just screamed more loudly.

"He just doesn't remember, honey." Rafe cupped his hand over the side of Jaimie's small head, forcing his face back toward his mother. When the baby tasted the milk, he broke off in mid-cry and latched on, suckling eagerly. Maggie gave a startled jerk. "There, you see?" Rafe said with a laugh. "How's that for enthusiasm?"

Maggie smiled and touched the baby's cheek. When Rafe looped an arm over her shoulders, she settled against him. Gazing down at her and the baby, he felt his chest go tight, for he'd never seen anything as beautiful as Maggie with their child's dark head at her breast. He feathered his fingertips over the baby's silken hair, thinking to himself that this was what love was all about—the quiet times, the sharing. He was more grateful than he could say that Maggie had set aside her modesty to let him experience it with her.

"Thank you," he whispered.

She turned her luminous gaze up to him. In the moonlight, she looked like an angel, her sable hair falling in a dark cloud of tousled curls around her shoulders. "For what?"

He pressed a kiss to the tip of her nose. "For letting me stay."

She sighed and rested her cheek on his shoulder. "It seems perfectly right, doesn't it? The three of us together like this."

"That's because it *is* perfectly right."

When the baby had finished nursing and was sleeping peacefully in his new cradle again, Rafe made love to his wife once more, slowly this time, and with infinite care. It was the perfect ending to a perfect night.

Bright and early the next morning, Maggie entered the study with Jaimie in her arms to find Rafe on the telephone and pacing the floor. Leaning her hip against the desk, she rocked the baby while listening to her husband's side of the conversation, which she instantly deduced was about gaining custody of Heidi.

"If that's what it takes, that's what it takes," Rafe bit out. "I don't want there to be any chance that Boyle can take her away from us, which might happen if he decides to convince Helen to pursue it." He pivoted and came to a stop when he saw Maggie. A fleeting smile touched his mouth. Then he raked a hand through his hair. "Half up front?" He laughed humorlessly. "I don't think so. No more than a fourth of it. Give him too much now, and he's liable to get slippery. We can't trust the son of a bitch."

Maggie's heart caught. Rafe was offering Lonnie money again. She'd been nothing but a drain on his bank account since the day he met her.

"Tell him that's my offer, a quarter up front, another

quarter when he gets her to sign the papers, and the remainder when I've got the documents in my hands. Maggie may be her sister and better able to provide a stable environment, but even so, I'm essentially trying to buy a child, you know? It's not as if I can take him to court if he backs out.'' Rafe listened for a moment, then cast his gaze toward the ceiling, the very picture of frustration. ''Then we'll have to cough it up. Yeah, you're right. I won't be surprised if that's how it goes.'' He nodded. ''I know. But on the other hand, which is more important, the child or having to cough up more money? No contest, Jameson. If that's his game, I'll play.''

Rafe ended the conversation with an apology for telephoning on Thanksgiving, then muttered a curt farewell. He punched the button at the base of the portable and set it on his desk, his gaze shifting back to Maggie. His mouth instantly slanted into a grin. ''In the bag,'' he told her with a wink. ''Jameson spoke with Lonnie last night. For a price, he'll play ball. Our only hurdle is your mom. He has to get her to sign the papers.''

''You're giving Lonnie even more money, this time for custody of Heidi?'' she said incredulously. ''When did you decide to do that?''

''I got the ball rolling with Jameson right after we got home yesterday. I called him while you were in the shower.'' He winked at her. ''I figured I'd tell you after dinner—a special gift of sorts to mark our first Thanksgiving together.''

''You never mentioned doing this before. What made you suddenly decide—''

''You,'' he said huskily. ''Hearing about what he did to you. I used to think the son of a bitch had limits, Maggie. I don't anymore. I won't rest until I know he can't get Heidi away from us.'' He shrugged. ''The man's crazy, and in a very sick way.''

A lump rose in Maggie's throat. ''I just wish we could do it without it costing you even more money.''

He grinned. "I can afford it."

"Thank you so much, Rafe."

"Don't thank me. She's your sister. And I'll remind you that in the past two weeks, you've saved this ranch thousands of dollars with your accounting skills. By the time Heidi is in college, you'll have paid for her education twice over." He smiled. "I think she likes it here. Don't you?"

"Oh, yes," Maggie said tightly. She cuddled Jaimie closer. "Mama may refuse to sign the papers though. She's slow and easily manipulated, but she truly does love me and Heidi."

He stepped close to kiss her cheek. "I know she does, honey. But my money's on Lonnie. He knows how to work her, and I'm giving him plenty of motivation. He'll find a way to convince your mother and have her believing she's doing Heidi a favor in the process."

Oh, how Maggie prayed he was right.

"How much did you offer him?" she asked, almost dreading his answer.

"Does it matter?" He drew the baby blanket back to kiss his sleeping son. "We can't put a price on a child's happiness, possibly even her life. Where do we draw a line? When is the price too high?" He shook his head. "I want her safe from him, and I'll damned well do it if it takes every dime we've got and I'm forced to ask my family to help me."

Maggie knew he meant that, and it filled her with quiet joy to know that he loved her that much. Essentially that was what it boiled down to, his love for her. She just thanked God that his financial situation was such that the expenditures probably wouldn't hurt him too badly.

"You'll never know how happy it's made me to have Heidi here where I can watch after her myself and keep her safe. She's a very lucky little girl to have you in her life."

"I'm the lucky one." He looped an arm around her

shoulders. "In fact, I feel like the luckiest man alive. And before you know it, we'll have permanent custody of her, guaranteed."

"I have every confidence," she said in all honesty. "Has there ever been anything you decided to do that you failed to accomplish?"

He cast her a suspicious look. "What's that supposed to mean? That I'm overbearing?"

Maggie giggled. "You do tend to take matters in hand—people included. And you're extremely determined and relentless once you set your mind to something. Not that I'm complaining."

A mischievous twinkle crept into his eyes. "It's a damned good thing. Now that I've got you in hand, I'm not about to turn you loose. You're mine, sugar. Every sweet inch of you." He glanced at the sleeping baby, then fixed his gaze on Maggie again. "Let's have breakfast in bed this morning."

"What?" she said with a laugh. "We're already up and dressed."

"So? What goes on can come off."

"I've already eaten my breakfast."

"I haven't, and Becca's scrambled eggs aren't what I'm craving. Think of it as a special Thanksgiving Day gift to me."

He leaned down and whispered suggestively in Maggie's ear, describing what he wanted in such vivid detail that her face went bright red.

"Oh, I couldn't. People don't really—that's *indecent!*"

"*Glorious*," he countered.

"Scandalous, more like!"

"*Incredible*," he insisted. "You'll think you've died and gone to heaven."

Her knees went a little watery. "We made love three times last night."

"So?"

"Will you draw the drapes?"

He paused in nibbling on her ear, his voice a grumble. "No way."

"Please?"

"Do I have to?"

"Yes!"

"You drive a hard bargain, Maggie Kendrick, but I'll take you any way I can get you."

Loving Rafe. Being loved by him. She felt as if her life had been touched with magic, just as he'd promised, and if there were times when she felt a sense of impending doom, fearful that their happiness might go up in a puff of smoke, she kept her thoughts to herself. As long as Lonnie Boyle drew breath, he would always pose a possible threat, but did that mean she had to let thoughts of him ruin her happiness?

No, absolutely not. Determined not to let him taint her new life, Maggie thrust him firmly from her mind and concentrated on being a good wife. Over the next few days, she settled in at the ranch and truly began to feel it was her home. It wasn't only Rafe who filled her with a sense of belonging, but his family as well. Within a day of meeting his parents, Maggie received orders from Keefe that she was to call him Dad, and whenever she forgot, he corrected her. If the edict had come from anyone else, Maggie might have balked, but Keefe Kendrick was as impossible to resist as his elder son. When he entered the house, Maggie often felt as if her home had been invaded by a big, lovable grizzly bear, and she invariably found herself captured in his brawny arms for a gentle hug.

"How's my girl this morning?" he would ask. Maggie soon learned that a standard response of "Fine" wasn't what Keefe wanted to hear. How was Jaimie doing? Was that boy of his treating her good? What were her plans for the day? Had she gotten a good rest last night? Any word yet about when they might get custody of Heidi? He pelted her with questions, to which he demanded lengthy answers, and to Maggie's amazement, he listened with undivided attention, making her feel like one of the most important people in his world.

Though less overwhelming, Ann Kendrick was no less loving. She took to Jaimie as if the baby were truly her grandchild, swooping him from his cradle the instant she entered the house, cooing and kissing him as she headed for the rocker before the hearth. To Maggie's delight, Ann also took an active interest in decorating the nursery, spending hours leafing through the decorating catalogs and offering her opinion.

One morning, she glanced up from an earmarked page and said, "Why don't you run in to town and get the wallpaper and paint? I'll watch Jaimie. When you get back, we'll get started on the room."

"I think Rafe plans to hire it done."

Ann frowned. "What fun will that be?"

Maggie secretly agreed, but every time she approached Rafe about painting the room and hanging the wallpaper herself, he vetoed the idea, saying he could well afford the cost of hiring professionals. "Rafe doesn't want me to do it," Maggie tried to explain. "And I don't suppose I can blame him. I've painted, but I've never hung wallpaper. I'd probably make a mess of it."

"Oh, piddle." Seated in the rocker with Jaimie cuddled close, Ann smiled and tossed her head. "I'm an expert at painting and hanging wallpaper. Grab Rafe's checkbook and run get the stuff we need. I'll watch Jaimie while you're gone."

Maggie went and got the checkbook. Imbued with courage after listening to Ann, she filled out a check and took it to the stable to ask that Rafe sign it. When she finally found him and his father in the tack room, however, her bravado had already begun to wane. "Um, Rafe?"

Seated on a hay bale across from his dad, he glanced up from a stirrup he was mending. "Hi, sweetheart."

His gaze fell to the check in her hands. "What's that?"

"One of your checks. I, um, wrote it to cash for five hundred dollars. Would you sign it for me and lend me the car keys?"

He set aside the stirrup and pushed to his feet. "What do you need five hundred dollars for?"

"Paint and wallpaper for the nursery."

He winced. "I'm sorry, honey. It slipped my mind. I'll call this afternoon and hire a crew to get that done, I promise."

Maggie imagined the look she'd get from Ann if she failed to stand her ground. "Actually, Rafe, I want to do it myself. Your mom says she'll help me."

"Oh, shit," Keefe muttered under his breath.

"Mom? She can't paint. She gets it on her butt and in her hair and all over everything around her. Trust me, you don't want to turn her loose in the nursery with a paint roller."

Maggie's heart squeezed. Her instinct was to nod and give in rather than quarrel with him. But Ann was waiting. "She says she's an expert painter and paper hanger."

"Oh, hell," Keefe said.

Rafe scratched beside his nose and nudged his Stetson back to regard her with a scowl. "Can't you wait a couple of days? I'll get a crew in there, I promise, and it'll be done before you can blink."

"I want to do it myself."

"I'm busy, Maggie. I really don't have time right now to help you."

"I don't expect you to help."

"Oh, boy," Keefe grumped.

Rafe sighed, plucked a pen from his shirt pocket, and took the check. Smoothing the draft against a bare wall stud, he quickly scratched out his signature. "I need to get your name on the account. This is a pain in the ass, and I really don't like the idea of you carrying a bunch of cash around. It isn't safe." He handed back the check. "Is Mom going to town with you?"

"Um, no. She's going to baby-sit."

"So who's taking you?"

"I'm just going to drive myself."

"Say what?"

Maggie gulped. "I do have my driver's license."

"Yeah, but you don't know the area. Crystal's a big town."

"I've been there a few times. I think I can find my way around." Maggie held out her hand for the keys. "I'll be fine."

Rafe glanced at his dad. "I'll be back in a couple of hours, Dad."

"No!" she blurted.

He swung back to stare at her in surprise. "It's no big deal, Maggie. I'll just drive you in."

Maggie straightened her shoulders. "It *is* a big deal. You're treating me like a child, and a not-very-bright child, at that."

"It isn't like that at all," he argued. "It's just that you've never driven all the way to town by yourself. You could get lost."

"I'll call you on the cell phone if I do, but I honestly don't think I will."

"I need to get things straightened out at the bank, anyway, so you can write checks."

"You can do that another time. Today I want to go by myself. I have to do it sooner or later, right? Why not now?"

He fished in his jeans pocket for the keys and reluctantly handed them over. Then he trailed behind her to the Ford like a well-trained hound. "How much gas is there?"

Maggie turned the key in the ignition. "Three-quarters of a tank."

He leaned in to check the computerized dash readouts. "You know how to use the phone?"

Maggie picked it up and studied the buttons. "It looks simple enough."

"You ever used a cell phone?"

"You figured it out the first time you used it, didn't you?"

He huffed and scraped the sole of his boot over the snowy gravel. "You're being just slightly irritating. It's no crime for me to worry about you."

"No, it's actually very sweet. But I *am* twenty-four years old. Remember?"

"And you grew up in a town I can spit across."

"Prior's not *that* small."

"Close."

He was still standing in the drive, gazing after the Expedition, when Maggie executed the first curve and drove out of sight.

Shortly after Maggie and Ann opened the first paint can later that afternoon, Rafe and Keefe magically appeared in the nursery. Rafe leaned down to peer at the paint. "That the color you like?"

Ann smiled and put her hands on her hips. "It's perfect," she said, eyeing the chiffon yellow.

"You have them shake it?" Rafe asked Maggie as he tossed aside his hat and began rolling up his sleeves.

Shoving his own shirtsleeves up, Keefe said, "Better stir it, to be safe."

The next thing Maggie knew, the two men were painting the nursery. Ann strolled in from the kitchen a few minutes after they began, still tidily dressed and coifed, with a mug of fresh, steaming coffee cupped between her slender hands. After watching the men work for a moment, she smiled at Maggie.

"See? I told you I was an expert and could get a room painted in nothing flat."

Acutely conscious of the weight of Rafe's arm around her shoulders, Maggie gazed through the window glass, watching the taillights of his parents' Cadillac fade to pinpricks of red in the twilight. She sighed as the car disappeared around a curve. She smiled slightly as she recalled the excited anticipation in Heidi's eyes when she'd been invited to spend the night with her "grandparents." Maggie suspected that Keefe and Ann would see to it that their newly adopted granddaughter had the time of her life at their cottage.

"Tired?" he asked huskily, his fingertips toying idly with a curl at her temple.

"Painting's hard work."

He chuckled and bent to kiss her hair. "My mother's something else, isn't she? She knew the whole time we'd end up doing it all."

Maggie smiled. "I think she's wonderful. I wish—"

"What?"

She shrugged. "Being around her makes me miss my mom. Not the way she is now, but how she used to be. When I was younger, before she got sick, she was so bright and funny. She could always make Daddy laugh. When he got home at night, they always teased and cut up. And every chance they got, they'd kiss when they thought I wasn't looking. It's so sad to not have her with me anymore. You know?"

He grew still, his lips pressed against her hair. "I'm sorry," he whispered. "I guess it must be hard. It's a shame it happened to her, Maggie, but now all you can do is love her for who she is."

"Do you think she might come here someday?"

"It's hard for me to say. She loves you and Heidi. I guess it's a possibility."

"She'll probably drive you crazy. She's flighty and scatterbrained. And she gets all in a dither over the silliest things. Like if she forgets to write something on the grocery list when we run out of it. You'd think the world was about to end."

"It probably frustrates her because she can't remember things."

"I suppose."

"She won't drive me crazy," he assured her. "*You* drive me over the edge, though."

"Me?"

"I haven't been able to take my eyes off of you all afternoon. God, Maggie, I can't get enough of you. Jaimie's asleep. Come make love with me."

She threw him an incredulous look. "What will Becca think if we just disappear?" She glanced at the plump housekeeper, who was bustling around in the adjoining kitchen, preparing dinner. "She'll wonder what we're doing."

"She'll wonder, but she won't know. It's a big house. We'll be clear back in the bedroom." His breath sifted through her hair, warming her scalp and igniting her imagination. "Please, Maggie. I need to hold you."

She leaned against him, giving her answer without speaking. Just as he turned to lead her from the room, the phone rang. "Damn it. It's probably for me." He bent to nibble her ear and the hollow beneath, making chills run up her spine. "Hold the thought. I'll be right back."

He stepped over to the counter and grabbed the phone. "Kendrick residence."

Maggie resumed gazing out the window at the swiftly descending darkness, her thoughts no longer on her parents-in-law, but on making love. *Rafe*. She was so happy. Sometimes she wanted to pinch herself to make sure she wasn't dreaming.

"Helen? Is that you?"

Hearing her mother's name, Maggie whirled from the window. As she stepped toward Rafe, she could hear the muted sounds of a woman's voice.

"Helen, calm down. Start at the beginning. Lonnie did what?" He listened for a moment, then cupped a palm over the mouthpiece. "She says Lonnie's left her. She's horribly upset."

Maggie's stomach dropped, not because she would

regret seeing the last of Lonnie Boyle, but because with the heart condition, her mother wasn't supposed to get upset.

"Write down her street address and the name of her doctor for me," Rafe whispered urgently. Then, to Helen, he said, "I'm sure he'll come back, Helen. Just calm down. When did he leave?" A pause. "I see. And he didn't say why in the note?"

Maggie was searching frantically for a pen. She finally found one inside the phone book. Snatching up a piece of paper, she quickly scribbled out the address of her childhood home. When she thrust the slip of paper at Rafe, he once again cupped a hand over the mouthpiece. "She thought Lonnie was sleeping. He's been using your bed since you left, she says, and keeping odd hours, staying up all night, sleeping during the day. She just went in to tell him supper was done, and he wasn't there. She found a note on the pillow, saying he's leaving her."

Maggie pressed a hand to her throat. "Oh, God, Rafe, her heart! She could collapse. There's no one there to call an ambulance."

He pushed the phone at her. "Keep her talking. Try your best to calm her down. I'll get on another line, call her doctor, and arrange for an ambulance to get over there."

Maggie nodded. "Mama? Mama, this is Maggie. Oh, Mama, don't cry. Lonnie will come back. He probably just got upset about some little thing." Maggie forced out the next words. "You know he loves you."

"He says he doesn't!" her mother wailed. "Oh, Maggie, I can't bear it. What'll I do? Now I'll be all alone."

Her mother sounded like an abandoned, terrified child. Maggie squeezed her eyes closed, wishing with all her heart that she were closer. "You're not going to be alone, Mama. You know I won't leave you there all alone."

"You'll come? I need you, Maggie. I'm scared. It's

getting dark. You know I can't sleep if I'm here all alone after dark.''

Maggie had no idea how long it might take her to reach Prior. Becca's dinner preparations had come to a halt, and she came to slip a plump arm around Maggie's shoulders, offering silent comfort. "Mama, listen to me. Are you listening? Rafe's calling your doctor right now, and someone is coming to be with you. I won't let you stay there all alone. It's going to be all right. And I'll be with you as soon as I can.''

"Oh, Maggie. How come did he leave me?''

Maggie could almost see her mother's brown eyes, wide with fright and swimming with confusion. "I'm sure he'll be back very soon. I don't know why he left, but he'll come to his senses.'' Maggie's gorge rose as she mouthed the lies. Lonnie never did anything that wasn't calculated. He undoubtedly had left her mother because the pickings there had ceased to be appealing. An older, mentally incapacitated woman? Now that he was into the big money and no longer had a young plaything to keep him entertained, he wanted out.

Keeping odd hours and sleeping in your bed, Rafe had told her. Maggie's stomach rolled. Lonnie was obsessed with her, and she was glad he'd left. *Glad.* She just prayed the emotional upheaval didn't end up killing her mother. "Please, Mama, stop crying. Your doctor will be there soon, and until he gets there, I'll stay on the phone with you. Rafe and I are a long way from you, but we'll be there as soon as we can.''

With half an ear, Maggie listened to her mother babble and sob. The rest of her attention was fixed on the background noise that came over the telephone line. It seemed like forever before she finally heard the muted wail of a siren.

"There's an ambulance here!'' Helen cried.

"It's all right, Mama. Rafe called your doctor. Remember I told you that? I'm sure the doctor sent the ambulance.''

"But I'm not sick."

"I know. The doctor is just making sure you don't get sick. The paramedics will probably give you a shot to make you feel calmer. Won't that be nice? Get on the portable and keep talking to me while you go open the door to let them in."

Maggie listened. In a moment, she heard male voices. The phone clattered in her ear, telling her that Helen had dropped the receiver. Believing her mother might have collapsed, Maggie's legs turned to water. She was so relieved when she heard Helen talking in the background a second later that she nearly wept.

"Hello?" a male voice said. "Who am I speaking with?"

"Her daughter in Oregon. Are you one of the ambulance attendants?"

The man assured her he was and that her mother was very upset but doing fine.

Rafe returned to the kitchen. Maggie threw him an agonized look. He took the phone, spoke briefly with the medic, and then said, "They're giving her a shot, Maggie. Her vitals look good. So far, so good." He listened for a moment. Then he hung up the phone. "They're taking her to the hospital now. They can watch her there and keep her calm until we arrive."

Rafe stepped over to hug her. Feeling his hard strength and warmth calmed her and imbued her with strength. She leaned against him, letting him support her weight. "Oh, Rafe, how could he do something so cruel?"

"Think past it, sweetheart. By leaving, he's opened the door for us to bring her here. She'll be with you and Heidi and Jaimie. And she'll have me and Dad and Rye to make her feel secure. As rough as this is right now, she'll be much better off in the long run."

Maggie glanced up at him. "How long will it take for us to get there?"

"I'll have to call Ryan. He'll need to arrange for a

preflight to be done on the Cessna.'' He glanced at his watch. ''We'll probably get there sometime during the night and be there to see her at the hospital first thing in the morning.''

Maggie leaned against him and closed her eyes. He held her for a moment, and then he whispered, ''Don't get upset with me. All right? But I can't help but worry that there's something rotten in Denmark. It doesn't make sense that Lonnie took off like this. When the lawyer spoke to him the night before Thanksgiving, he seemed eager to work things out so we can get permanent custody of Heidi. He was quibbling over the money and trying to drive the price up. Why would he suddenly decide to take off without first getting his hands on the cash?''

''I don't know,'' Maggie said hollowly. ''Oh, Rafe, I'm so worried about my mother.''

''I know you are, and you're not going to like what I'm about to suggest.''

Maggie looked up at him. ''You don't think I should go, do you?''

He sighed. ''No, I really don't. You'd be going back across the Idaho state line. I have a bad feeling. You know? What if this is all a ploy on Lonnie's part to lure you back there? He may have the groundwork laid to have you arrested for kidnapping or some damned thing. Or to meet us at the plane with those damned adoption papers and take Jaimie.''

''I need to go be with my mom, though.''

He gave her a comforting squeeze. ''Let me call Mark and see what he thinks. If it isn't safe for you to go, Maggie, it isn't safe. I can handle your mom. We've met once and talked a lot on the phone. It's not as if I'm a complete stranger to her. If her health allows, we'll be back here sometime tomorrow. I guess it depends on whether or not the doctor thinks she should fly. If not, I'll have to rent a car to bring her back. Either way, it'll be all right. She's in good hands right now. They've sedated her. She'll come through this.''

Maggie prayed he was right as he dialed Mark's home. She listened intently to Rafe's side of the conversation as he discussed the situation with his friend and attorney. Before Rafe said goodbye, Maggie already knew the outcome of the phone call.

''He doesn't think it's wise for me to go. Does he?''

''No. Here in Oregon, you've got a measure of protection. Interstate red tape. They have to extradite you to prosecute. But if you return to Idaho . . .'' He shrugged. ''Lonnie supposedly reimbursed the adoptive parents and they've given up on getting Jaimie. But until we see documented verification of that, which Mark is working on getting, you could be wide open to criminal charges. Lonnie can't make them stick. I've been named on his birth certificate as the father, and we're married. But it could be a hell of a mess until we got it all straightened out.''

Maggie nodded and clasped her waist with her arms. ''It's only a day. I'll just have to wait for you to get back.'' She tried to smile. ''Mama already loves you. I'm sure she'll be fine once she's got a big, strong fellow to lean on. I think that's her main attraction to Lonnie, that she misses Daddy so much.''

''That's like cozying up to a rattlesnake.''

Maggie agreed.

''I've got to call Ryan,'' Rafe told her. ''I haven't renewed my pilot's license yet, so he'll have to fly me there.'' He gazed down at the phone, frowning thoughtfully. ''I think I'll call Mom and Dad and have them come stay with you.''

''I'm sure that's not necessary. It'll spoil Heidi's sleepover, and I'll be fine here with Becca.''

''I'll feel better if Dad's here, nonetheless. There's no point in taking any chances, and something about this just doesn't feel right.'' He smiled slightly. ''If Boyle comes around with Dad guarding the fort, he'll rue the day he was born. My father may be sixty, but he's in damned good shape. He'd chew Lonnie up and pick his teeth with the bastard's bones.''

"I'll feel better with him here, for sure,'' Becca inserted. "Better safe than sorry, I always say. Tell Miz Kendrick I'll fix extra and to plan on eating dinner here.''

Rafe made the two phone calls, the first to his folks, the second to Ryan. After hanging up, he said, "I'm going to go throw some clothes in a duffel bag.'' He glanced at his watch. "Ryan's coming right over to pick me up. He says the plane was checked out after the last trip. He'll file a flight plan, give the plane a quick going-over, gas it up, and we'll be ready to lift off. Mom and Dad are packing to stay for a few days, just in case it takes me longer than I hope to get back. They'll be here in about an hour.''

Maggie forced a smile. "I'm sure Becca and I will be fine here by ourselves for a little bit.''

Rafe bent to kiss her. "I'm sure you will be, too, or I wouldn't leave until they got here.''

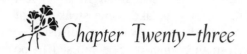

Chapter Twenty-three

Watching Rafe drive away was the hardest thing Maggie had ever done. She wanted so badly to go with him to Idaho. Her mother needed her. Staying behind was the wisest thing to do, but her heart urged her to throw caution to the wind.

Right before leaving, he had pressed a kiss on her palm and closed her fingers around it. Now Maggie made a tight fist over the place where his lips had touched, clinging to it as she watched taillights fade from sight for the second time in less than an hour.

"Your parents-in-law will be here shortly," Becca assured her. "And Rafael will be back tomorrow. Don't look so glum."

Maggie heard the concern in the housekeeper's voice and was able to laugh at herself. "I know. I'm being silly. I think my mother's childish? Now Rafe's leaving me overnight, and I'm acting the same way."

"Well, now, it's a bit more than just that. I know you're very worried about your mama, and well you should be. Rafael's got a good heart, though. He'll hug her up and have her set to rights in no time."

"Yes." Maggie remembered how he had hugged her up when she first met him. Her ragtag cowboy. In a twinkling, he had become her staunch defender, picking up the pieces of her shattered world and rearranging them into a magical dream. She sighed. "You're absolutely right, Becca. With Rafe there to handle it, everything will be all right.''

"I need to go change the bed linen in the guest room,'' Becca said. "Can you take some steak out of the freezer and toss it in the microwave on defrost?''

Maggie turned from the window. She refused to be like her mother, helpless and falling apart just because her man had left her. Rafe was taking care of her family. While she waited here for him to return, she would be the wife he deserved, keeping her perspective and taking care of business, which at the moment happened to be helping with dinner preparations.

As Maggie set the dial on the microwave a few minutes later, she smiled sadly, recalling that Rafe's favorite meal was steak and a baked potato. It was a shame he wasn't going to be there to enjoy it.

"Scream, and I'll blow your head off.''

Maggie froze with her finger on the start button. *Lonnie*. Something cold pressed against her ear. She realized it was a gun, and her legs nearly buckled. "Lonnie?''

"Lonnie?'' he mimicked in a singsong voice. "You faithless little bitch. You think you've got it made, here with your rich cowboy? That I'd just kiss off if he offered me more money?'' He bumped the barrel of the gun against her head, making her ear throb. "Think again. You're mine, sweetness, and your cowboy's one stupid son of a bitch. He already gave me money. Lots of it. And that's gonna be our ticket out of here. We'll go where he can never find us. Oh, I like the sound of that. Way off alone, just you and me and the little brat. You don't do what I tell you, and the kid's brains will decorate a wall.''

He shoved at her with the gun again, knocking Maggie slightly off balance. She bit down hard on the inside of her cheek as she struggled to keep her footing. *Becca*. She was just down the hall in the guest room. Maybe she would hear Lonnie's voice and telephone for help.

"Let's go get Junior. We have to get out of here before your daddy-in-law gets here.'' He laughed evilly. ''Didn't think I knew about that, did you?''

Maggie realized he'd been in the house, listening to everything they said. For how long? Before Rafe even left? Oh, God. *Think.* She couldn't leave here with him. She had to stall, hold him up. Once Rafe's dad got here, everything would be all right. Lonnie was a coward, according to Rafe. She could remember him telling her that so clearly. *He gets off on fear*, he'd said. *He won't pick on someone his own size or bigger. Only those who are weaker, or people who won't or can't fight back.* Maggie's head reeled. *He gets off on fear. Power is the ultimate turn-on.*

Maggie was plenty terrified now. As she walked ahead of Lonnie down the hall to the bedroom she shared with Rafe, her legs felt watery. *Jaimie.* Oh, God. His brains decorating a wall. The picture those words formed in her mind made Maggie shake. Her baby. Her sweet, precious baby. Would Lonnie go so far as to actually kill him? Jaimie was his own flesh and blood.

Maggie's arms felt numb when she entered the bedroom and went to the cradle to collect her son.

''Get everything you need. We ain't comin' back.''

Maggie quickly stuffed things into the diaper bag Rafe had gotten her.

''Get your driver's license. You're gonna be my chauffeur while I keep the gun trained on Junior. One wrong move, and he's history.''

She still had her driver's license in her jeans pocket. ''I have it right here,'' she said in a voice that trembled. ''Lonnie, why are you doing this? I love Rafe. Do you really want a woman who doesn't want you?''

He laughed, the sound ringing with insanity. ''Oh, you'll want me. You'll get on your knees and beg me for it, girl. We ain't gonna have your mama around no more so we gotta sneak. You know? I'll have you whenever I want you. And you'll want me back. Got it? If you don't, I'll kill your brat.''

He swung the gun toward the door. "*Move*. Don't think you can stall me until your daddy-in-law comes to the rescue. I'll shoot the son of a bitch and anyone else who gets in our way."

Maggie remembered reading once that even maniacs had limits. How she prayed that was true. Surely Lonnie wasn't so crazy that he'd kill someone in cold blood.

But, oh, God, she couldn't count on that. The diaper bag bumped against her leg, reminding her with every step of the night she had fled from this man. She exited the bedroom and started to retrace her path up the hallway to the kitchen. Halfway there, Becca emerged from the guest room, her stout form blocking Maggie from going farther.

"There," she said, straightening her apron. "That's all done."

Becca's eyes widened when she saw Lonnie behind Maggie. The next instant, Maggie saw the gun in her side vision. "Lonnie, no!"

The blast of the weapon deafened Maggie. Becca grabbed for her chest, her gaze bewildered and disbelieving as she reeled backward and hit the wall. She fell with a thud to the carpeted floor, crimson spreading across the upper right side of her chest. *Blood. Everywhere.*

"Oh, my God. Oh, my God. Lonnie! Oh, dear God."

Maggie started toward Becca. Her stepfather jerked her back by the hair. "He's next," he said, shoving the gun against the baby she cradled in her arms. "Walk or he's dead."

Maggie staggered over Becca's body, horror blanking out all rational thought. This wasn't happening. It was a terrible nightmare. Rafe wasn't gone. Becca wasn't dead. Lonnie wasn't really here. It was simply her worst fear come to life in a terrible dream. Any moment now, she'd wake up and be safe in Rafe's strong arms.

Everything seemed to happen in a blur. Hurrying through the kitchen. Spilling out into the atrium. Stepping outside without a coat, to feel the blast of the chill winter night slicing through her clothes.

Lonnie had hidden a rental car in the woods. He'd come onto the ranch on a back road—a logging road that had been excavated after the forest fire when Rafe and Ryan had tried to salvage what they could of the charred timber. It seemed to Maggie that they walked forever. No strong hand held her elbow now to keep her from slipping on the ice. She was all alone.

With a monster.

The luminescent glow of the instrument panel bathed the otherwise dark cockpit in ghostly green. Rafe stared straight ahead, unable to shake the feeling that he shouldn't have left Maggie. For some reason, Rafe kept remembering the nightmare he'd once had of Lonnie in the station wagon, laughing maniacally just before the vehicle plunged off the cliff. The image made his blood run cold, and he prayed to God it hadn't been some kind of premonition.

"Penny for them," Ryan said as he put the plane on autopilot.

"I'm just worried about Maggie and the kids. I've got this bad feeling I shouldn't have left them."

Ryan sighed. "That's why you called the folks. Right? Dad's there by now. He can handle anything that comes up, Rafe. And you know what else?"

"No. But I'm sure you're going to tell me."

"Yeah, I am. I think Maggie's got a hell of a lot more grit than you give her credit for. Not saying I think anything's going to go wrong while you're gone." Ryan leaned forward to adjust the controls. "But if it did, I think she'd surprise everyone in how well she handled it."

"Trust me, no one on earth gives Maggie more credit for gutsiness than I do. She's a strong-minded woman, and just because I'm worried about her doesn't mean I think she lacks courage. It's just that she's been through enough. You know? My natural inclination is to protect her from any more heartache, and I sure as hell don't want her having to face Boyle alone again. She felt so helpless, with no way out. The memories of that will affect her for the rest of her life as it is.''

"She wasn't helpless. She could've left and gone to a shelter.''

"And abandoned Heidi? Give me a break.''

"I'm not saying she was wrong to stay. But there's a difference between being helpless and deciding to sacrifice yourself to save someone else.''

"True.'' Rafe passed a hand over his face. "I guess I shouldn't worry so much. If anything happens, she can probably handle it just fine without me. I just have this bad feeling. You know? Boyle can't be trusted. My first thought when I decided to come get Helen was that he might have planned it this way. What if he did this, hoping to lure me away so he could get to Maggie and the kids?''

Ryan scowled. "Damn. Do you really think he's that crazy?''

"He's pretty damned crazy.''

Ryan fell quiet for a long moment. Then he said, "No matter how you circle it, Rafe, someone's got to go get Maggie's mom. I'd go do it for you, but the woman's never even met me.''

"I know. Thanks for offering, all the same.''

"Maggie'll be fine. If anything happens, Dad's there, and what he can't handle, Mom will.''

Rafe chuckled. "You're right about that.'' He peered through the gloom at his brother. "Talk about steel in the backbone. I think she gets a little ornerier with each passing day. I swear, she needles Dad for the fun of it.''

In the eerie green illumination of the cockpit, Ryan's teeth looked phosphorescent when he grinned. "She's a little lippy, but Dad seems to love it. You know what he told me right before they left for Florida? That the sex was so good, he was afraid he'd croak in bed. 'Hell of a way to go,' he said.''

Rafe barked with laughter. ''God, he's bad. He's not supposed to tell his sons stuff like that. He'll warp us emotionally. Somehow, you just don't picture your folks—well, you know.''

''Especially not Mom. It's sort of—hell, I don't know, sacrilegious or something—''

A static blast from the radio interrupted them. Ryan keyed his mike to signal a go-ahead. A second later, their father's voice came over the air. ''You boys need to get your asses back here,'' he said. ''We've got trouble.''

Rafe's stomach dropped and felt as if it bounced on the floor of the aircraft.

Maggie's hands felt as if they were frozen on the steering wheel. She had taken the on-ramp onto the interstate approximately five minutes ago. The rental car's headlights illuminated the white divider lines, making them seem to come at her in a dizzying rush. She tried frantically to think, but the fear that held her in its grip blanked out rational thought.

Lonnie sat sideways on the passenger seat, the gun aimed at Jaimie, who lay in back. *Damn* him. He knew her weak spot. By threatening the life of her child, he had absolute power over her.

He gets off on fear. It turns him on. Rafe's voice kept zigzagging through her head. Sweat beaded on her face. *Boyle's a bully. He picks on those who are weaker. To men like him, power is exciting. They thrive on it and on being in control.*

Well, he had to be turned on now, Maggie thought frantically. She was plenty scared. Pictures flashed through her mind of Becca, lying dead in the hall, her blood smeared over the wall. Call his bluff? Oh, God, how did she dare? The man was insane. Absolutely insane. If she bucked him, he'd kill Jaimie.

In that moment, Maggie would have given anything to have her son safely away from there. Then she'd have nothing to lose by calling Lonnie's bluff. The slimy worm. He grabbed for power in any way he could, even if it meant using a tiny baby as leverage. He wouldn't be so smug if it were only the two of them. The bottom line was, Maggie wasn't as afraid of dying as she was of staying alive and under his thumb. If it weren't for his having Jaimie to use as a bargaining chip, she'd give Lonnie more trouble than he could handle.

The thought stuck in Maggie's brain. *Without Jaimie as a bargaining chip.* A rush of adrenaline moved through her. Lonnie was maniacal, but he wasn't stupid. He kept threatening to kill Jaimie, but if he did that, he'd compromise his position of power.

Boyle's a bully.

He gets off on power.

Rafe's voice bounced around in Maggie's head. She struggled to calm down. *Think. Shove the fear away, clear your mind. Think.* There had to be a way out of this. She needed to get help before he took her someplace isolated. And, God help her, she needed to think of some way to get her son safely away from him.

She remembered reading somewhere about a woman who had been abducted and forced to drive the getaway car. She had kept her cool and unobtrusively tapped her brake pedal to flash her rear lights, sending out an SOS. Maggie didn't know the signal, which ruled out her doing that. But if she kept her head, maybe she could think of something else.

She saw a blue road sign: REST AREA, ½ MILE. Up ahead, she could see the lights off to her right. Several passenger cars were in the parking area as well as three semi trucks. A lump of raw terror rose into her throat. She backed off the gas.

"Why you slowin' down?"

Maggie gulped to steady her voice. "I have to go to the rest room."

"Bullshit. You can squat alongside the road. We ain't stoppin' around a bunch of people."

Maggie forced herself to laugh. "God, Lonnie, you're something else. You want me to stop alongside a busy highway? Forget it. Besides, I have to *go*. You get my drift? It's not going to be a quick process."

"Pick up speed!" he yelled. "We ain't stoppin', I said. Don't screw around with me, girl. That kid don't mean nothin' to me. I'd as soon shoot him as look at him."

Maggie continued to slow down. "That *kid* better rise in your estimation, Mr. Boyle. He's your only ace in the hole." She shot her stepfather a glare. "Go ahead, Lonnie. Shoot him! With him gone, I've got nothing to lose. *Nothing*. Are you reading me, loud and clear? You want me on my knees, asshole? Well, here's a news bulletin. Kill my child, and you can kiss that plan goodbye! I'll fight you with my last breath, and the minute you turn your back on me, you're a dead man. Got it?"

Rafe sat forward in his seat, his father's voice replaying inside his mind. *Maggie and the baby are gone. Becca's been shot. I think the son of a bitch was hiding in the house.*

Glancing at Ryan, Rafe snarled out, "Hurry, damn it! Is this as fast as you can fly this thing?"

Ryan sighed. "I'm circling to land, Rafe. You want them picking up our pieces after a crash? Calm down, for God's sake. You'll be no use to Maggie or anyone else in this state."

Rafe propped his elbows on his knees and rested his face in his hands. "Oh, sweet Jesus. Oh, sweet Jesus. I should never have left her. I smelled a rat. Why didn't I listen to my instinct and stay with her? The *bastard*. God, Ryan, he's a lunatic. He shot Becca! And he's got Maggie and the baby!"

Ryan's voice sounded thin when he said, "They'll be

okay, Rafe. They'll be okay.'' He reached out to squeeze Rafe's shoulder. "Hey, bro, get a grip.''

"I can't lose them," Rafe cried raggedly. "I'll put a gun to my head and pull the trigger this time, I swear to God. I can't go through that again. Oh, Jesus. *Maggie*. I promised her he'd never lay a hand on her again. I promised her.''

"They're probably traveling right now. He won't mess with her until they get where they're going. Dad's called the cops. The state boys will have an APB out in nothing flat. They'll find them, Rafe. Have a little faith, huh? You already lost one family. Lightning doesn't strike twice in the same place.''

Magic can vanish in a puff of smoke. Rafe could remember Maggie saying that to him. He'd pooh-poohed the notion. Christ! Why did he always do that? Looking back, he knew now that Susan had sensed she didn't have long to live when she'd pleaded with him that night down by the lake. *Promise me, Rafe. If something happens to me, promise that you'll find someone else to love. I don't want you to be all alone.* He'd laughed it off. Not taken her seriously. Only a short while later, she'd been dead. And now Maggie, his sweet angel face, the one touch of magic in his life, vanishing in a puff of smoke. She'd sensed that their happiness couldn't last, and instead of heeding the warning, he'd patted her on the head and ignored it.

"You know the worst part?'' Rafe said to his brother.

"No, what?''

"When we first got together, I told her men like Lonnie are turned on by fear. That he was a bully. What if she listened to me?''

"Well, it's true. He is a bully.''

"Yeah, but—'' Rafe broke off and swallowed. "Dear God, I hope she doesn't do anything stupid. When I told her that, I thought she was safe from him. I never dreamed she might be around him again without me there to shove his teeth down his throat. What if she does something crazy, Rye? It'll be my fault.''

"She won't. The lady's not dumb.''

Dumb, no. But with Jaimie's life on the line, she would be desperate.

Maggie drew the rental car to a stop in one of the rest area parking places, shoved the shift into park, and cut the engine. Staring at the steady trickle of women who were entering and exiting the ladies' rest room, she said a quick prayer. Then she shifted her gaze to Lonnie. Inside, she was shaking with terror, but somehow she managed to keep her hands steady and meet his incredulous gaze without flinching. He still had the gun trained on Jaimie.

"Start the car back up,'' he said in a dangerously silken voice. "Now. Or I swear to God, I'll splatter his brains all over the seat.''

"And lose your only leverage, all because I have to use the toilet? Brilliant thinking, Lonnie.'' She tossed the car keys in his lap. "There's only one way in. Those rest rooms never have back windows. Where am I going to go, down the sewer? You'll see me if I come back out. It's not like I can get away.''

"I'm warning you!''

Maggie opened her door. "Yeah, I hear you. And you know what, Lonnie? I think you're bluffing.''

"Get out of this car, and find out!''

"Yeah, yeah. The bottom line is, with Jaimie out of the picture, you'll lose your advantage.'' She smiled at him. God only knew how she managed to do it, but she actually smiled at him. From somewhere inside her, a reckless but calculating hard core sprang to life. A hard core that gave her just enough courage to put on a front of bravado. "No Heidi to threaten me with, no mother, and no baby. Just you and me. That thought frightens you, doesn't it? That's why you came to get me, because you knew you were about to lose custody of Heidi, that even if you fought him, tooth and nail, Rafe had more money, better lawyers, and the ability to hold out until he got what he wanted.''

The gun began to shake. Maggie's heart caught, for if he accidentally pulled the trigger in his agitation, Jaimie would pay for it with his life. She swallowed, determined to keep talking. She'd taken the other route for seven endless years, letting this man bully her into submission. That path led to hell, and this time, she'd be taking her son along with her. Maggie couldn't let that happen. She had little hope of escaping from Lonnie herself, but there was a chance for Jaimie.

''If you didn't regain custody of Heidi and get her back in your clutches, you knew you'd have no way to coerce *me* into going back to you, and that was your plan all along, wasn't it? To take Rafe's money and bide your time for a bit. Then threaten me with Heidi's life if I didn't get my tail back home.''

He said nothing.

''That's what it's all about. Isn't it, Lonnie? Your sick obsession with me. Your last hold on me would slip away if you permanently lost custody of Heidi. So you pretended to be interested in Rafe's offer and then you walked out on Mama, knowing she'd fall apart. Then you headed for Oregon to get me, knowing all the while that Rafe would have no choice but to go to Idaho.''

''Shut your mouth.''

''You knew Rafe wouldn't allow me to step foot over the Idaho state line, didn't you? That he'd feel duty-bound to go get my mother, but that he'd go without me. Very smart, Lonnie. I'm impressed. Don't ruin it by threatening to shoot Jaimie. We both know how dumb that would be.''

''Shut *up!*'' He pointed the gun at Maggie's forehead. ''You shut up, you little bitch! I'm the one with the gun.''

''Yeah, and with all the witnesses.'' She gestured at the cars around them. ''I'll gladly shut up if you stop threatening to kill my child.''

"I'll threaten whatever I want."

She heaved a weary sigh. "And that's all it is, a threat. Kill him, and you lose your power over me. I'll be a good girl to keep him safe. No question. We both know it. So stop aiming the gun at him and running the threat into the ground. After a while, it gets repetitive."

Maggie slipped from the car, sending up feverish, disjointed pleas to God. She slammed the driver's door closed and then opened the rear passenger door to scoop Jaimie off the seat. Thank God the door had been unlocked.

"What're you doing?" Lonnie cried.

Maggie grabbed the diaper bag. "What's it look like I'm doing? While I'm in there, I may as well kill two birds with one stone and change him. Or would you rather waste even more time by stopping again a few miles up the road?"

"You're not taking him in there with you. Do you think I'm stupid?" He threw open his door and jumped from the car. As he hurried around to Maggie's side, he shoved the gun in the pocket of his jacket but kept it aimed at her. "Put him back. Now."

"Don't be silly." Maggie started walking. "Do you think I can go through concrete walls? If you're so damned worried, come stand outside and guard the door. I'm going to use the bathroom and change my son's diaper."

With every step she took, Maggie cringed, half-expecting to get a bullet in the back. Nothing happened.

"I'll be watchin' that door," he called softly. "Don't think I won't. Try to pull a fast one, and I'll open fire. I swear to God. And I'll be right outside. No askin' for help. Do it, and I'll kill everyone in there." She heard a jangling sound. "Hear that? It's bullets. I've got plenty in my pockets."

Thank you, God. Thank you. Maggie nearly wept with relief. He was going to let her go in. "I'm not stupid, Lonnie," she called back. "And guess what, no lipstick to write a message on the mirror! You're safe. Stand outside. Keep an ear cocked and your eyes peeled. I'll only be a few minutes.''

Rafe didn't wait for Ryan's pickup to come to a stop before he jumped from the vehicle. His riding boots slipped on the packed snow at the edge of the driveway as he raced toward the house. Police cars everywhere. The bubble lights flashed, throwing a rotating blur of blue over the house and outbuildings.

He found his father and mother sitting on the bench by the atrium fountain, their arms locked around Heidi, who huddled between them. Ann Kendrick's shoulders were hunched around the child. Keefe had an arm around both his wife and the girl, his expression grim. There was a gray cast to his skin, and his eyes looked haunted when he met Rafe's gaze.

''They just took Becca away in the ambulance.''

Rafe struggled to collect his thoughts. To his shame, as deeply as he loved the housekeeper, he could focus only on his fear for Maggie and Jaimie. ''How is Becca, Dad? Will she live?''

''It's a shoulder wound, so there's hope. It's serious, though, son.''

Rafe closed his eyes for a moment, his heart catching at the sound of his mother's soft weeping and Heidi's ragged sobs. He crouched before the child and touched a hand to her head. ''Hey, sweetheart. How's my girl?''

Heidi flung her arms around Rafe's neck. ''He took Maggie and Jaimie!'' she cried.

''I know, honey.'' Oh, God. It was all Rafe could do not to break down and sob himself. ''They're going to be all right, Heidi. We just have to pray really hard and think good thoughts. God will watch over them and bring them safely home.'' Stroking the little girl's hair, Rafe met his father's gaze. ''Get her out of here, Dad. Take her to your place and—'' Completing the message with his eyes, Rafe drew Heidi's arms from around his neck, wiped away her tears, and returned her to his mother's embrace. "You go with Mom and Dad, Heidi. All right? I'll keep in touch with you by phone and let you know the minute Maggie gets back."

The little girl nodded and then turned to cling to Ann again. Rafe straightened, clasped his dad's shoulder in farewell, and then crossed the atrium to the sliding glass door. As he entered the kitchen, he scanned the room. Two police officers stood talking in the hallway that led to the rest of the house. Rafe walked toward them, his gaze drawn like a magnet to the smears of blood on the wall behind them.

"Oh, Jesus," Ryan whispered.

Until that moment, Rafe hadn't realized that his brother had caught up with him. They approached the policemen together. Rafe heard the younger officer say something about the Dallas Cowboys. Then he spotted Rafe and Ryan and broke off in mid-sentence.

"I'm Sergeant Hall," the older officer said. Hooking a thumb toward his companion, he added, "This is Officer Townsend. I take it you must be the younger Mr. Kendrick?"

"Yeah," Rafe bit out, "I'm Rafe Kendrick. This is my residence. It's my wife and baby who've been abducted. What's been done so far to find them? Any word at all of their whereabouts?"

Instead of answering his question, the two officers began expressing their condolences.

Rafe held up a hand. "I realize you sympathize. All right? But right now, all I want to know is what you're doing to find my wife and baby."

Sergeant Hall, a gray-haired, grandfatherly type with a paunch, nodded in understanding. "We immediately ran a trace to get the make and plate number of Boyle's automobile. Then we put out an APB, hoping another officer might spot the car."

Rafe could tell by the expression in the man's blue eyes that the news wasn't good. "And?"

The sergeant sighed. "We located the vehicle almost immediately. The Idaho police found it abandoned at the edge of Prior about ten minutes ago." He cleared his throat. "We, um, believe Boyle rented a car before he left town, and that he must have done so under an assumed name, using fake ID."

"Can't you have the clerk that was on duty do a photo identification?"

"Of course," the policeman assured Rafe, "but first we have to get our hands on a photo. The local police went to his residence. No one was there. Right now, the Idaho State Police are running a computer search for his driver's license photograph. As soon as they pull it up, they'll have something to show the rental-car clerk. These things take time."

"We don't have time," Rafe bit out. "Lonnie Boyle is a frigging lunatic. He's got my wife and baby! He could kill them."

"We're doing everything humanly possible, Mr. Kendrick. I know it's hard to be patient, but all of this takes time. We haven't been dragging our heels."

Rafe passed a hand over his eyes. He felt Ryan's hand gripping his arm. "I'm sorry. I, um . . . without a description of the rental car, how in the hell will you find them?"

"Rafe," Ryan said softly. "Hey, bro. How about some coffee? Hmmm? Let these fellows do their job."

"I don't want any goddamned coffee," Rafe snarled, jerking his arm from his brother's grasp. "I want them to find my wife! The assholes are standing here with their thumbs up their asses, talking about football scores!"

The younger officer blushed to the roots of his blond hair.

"All just part of the job, right?" Rafe cut him a scathing glance and whipped around to return to the kitchen. Upon entering the room, he braced the heels of his hands on the counter and hung his head. When he closed his eyes, all he could see was Maggie's sweet face. Aware of Ryan beside him, he whispered, "I don't even know which direction he went, Rye. She's out there somewhere, scared to death, praying I'll find them in time. And I don't know wh-where to l-look."

A sob tore up from Rafe, jerking his shoulders. His body started to shake, and no matter how he struggled to control it, he couldn't make the shaking stop. He felt Ryan's arm encircle his back.

"Rafe. Dear God, don't do this. You can't fall apart."

Rafe took several deep, shuddering breaths. "I know. I have to stay calm. But I'm coming apart inside. She and Jaimie could end up dead. *Dead*, Rye!"

"They won't. It's going to turn out all right. I'm sure of it, Rafe. God wouldn't have brought them to you and allowed you to start loving them, only to snatch them away. You have to believe that. Have some faith."

Rafe's faith had taken a serious beating a little over two years ago on a stormy autumn night. "I'm trying, Ryan. But I'm scared to death."

The women's rest room was empty when Maggie entered. *Just my luck.* She could only pray another group of women would enter soon. She tossed down the diaper bag and turned on the water, talking loudly to Jaimie, trying to make all the sounds she might if she were actually changing his diaper. *Please, God. Please. Let someone come in.*

"Hey there, big boy," she managed to say in a relatively steady voice. "Are you Mama's little love?"

She jerked a paper towel from the dispenser. Turned the water off. Thumped the heel of her hand on the trash can. Pacing. Turning. Talking to her son.

Relief flooded through her when the door suddenly pushed open and three women filed in, one matronly and gray-haired, the other two younger. Maggie approached them, still carrying on a nonsensical monologue with her child as if she were changing his diaper. "Oh, yes, you're such a sweet darling. Mama's little man, and just look at the mess you've made!''

The women drew up and stared at Maggie as if she were nuts. Pitching her voice to an urgent whisper, she said, "I need your help. There's a man outside. He abducted me and my baby. He has a gun.''

Afraid that Lonnie would note the lack of noise, Maggie opened a stall door, kicked the flush handle of the toilet, and then let the door slam closed. Stepping to the sink, she wrenched on the water.

"Oh, my goodness!'' she said in a cooing voice. "I'm going to have to change you from the skin out, Jaimie!''

Turning back to the women, who were staring at her with appalled expressions, Maggie once again pitched her voice to a barely audible level. "Please, he'll kill my baby. I'm begging you. One of you take him. You can hide him under your coat, leave in a group.'' Tears filled Maggie's eyes as she searched each of the women's gazes. She jerked some paper towels from the dispenser, crumpled them to make noise, then shoved them into the trash receptacle. "Please! '' she whispered. "Just take him, get in your car, and drive away. Go to the nearest police station. Please?''

The older woman stripped off her blue parka and held out her arms for the baby. Maggie's legs nearly folded. She gulped back a sob as she handed over her child to a total stranger. She knew she was taking a risk. But Jaimie's chances were better this way than if she took him back to the car.

"Thank you.''

The older woman nodded as she cuddled the baby close. She draped the parka over her arm to hide Jaimie. "What's your name, honey?'' she whispered. Then, never taking her gaze off Maggie, she said in a loud voice, "Hey, lady? You got any paper on your side? The roll's empty over here.''

One of the younger women jerked from her seeming trance at the question and threw open a stall door to flush a toilet. "Yeah, hold on a minute. I'll hand some under to you!" she called.

At the noise, Jaimie began to wiggle. The woman holding him started to rock him. Maggie stared at her son, praying to God and all His angels that her son wouldn't start to cry as the woman left the rest room.

"My name's Maggie Kendrick," she whispered.

"Hey, lady," the younger woman standing in the stall doorway said loudly. "You want this paper or not?"

The older woman said, "Oh, thanks. I didn't see it. Sorry about that."

"Not a problem," the younger woman said.

The third woman stepped over to play with the water faucets and towel dispenser, her horrified gaze fixed on Maggie. "You'd think they'd keep these places stocked with paper. Where's our tax dollars going, anyway?"

"What's the man's name? " the older woman whispered.

"Lonnie Boyle."

"Make and model of the car?"

Maggie ran a hand into her hair, frantically trying to remember. "A red Honda, I think. A four-door sedan. Newer model, probably a '98." She closed her eyes and gulped. "Oh, you're such a good boy!" she said loudly.

"Cute kid," one of the younger women commented.

"Thanks. I think so," Maggie replied.

"Stall him," the gray-haired woman told Maggie. "I've got a cell phone. I'll call the cops. They can get here in only a few minutes."

She moved toward the door with Jaimie. The other two women flanked her, one stepping out slightly ahead and then hanging back to shield Jaimie from view with her body. Maggie gazed after them, her heart in her throat. At any second, she expected to hear Lonnie yell out. The door swung closed. She stood there alone in the rest room, so scared she could have sworn she heard the sweat oozing from her pores.

Two seconds, three. No yell from Lonnie. She

dragged in a shaky breath, slowly exhaled, grabbing frantically for her composure. "There you go!" she said in a wobbly voice. "I'll bet that feels better, huh, big boy? You be good now while Mama goes potty. All right?"

Maggie opened a stall door, shaking so violently that it was all she could do to walk in. She turned and struggled frantically to slide the bolt. Her fingers quivered, rubbery and unresponsive.

She heard a car engine roar to life outside. After finally managing to lock the door, she leaned weakly against it and closed her eyes. *Please, God. Let them make it safely away.*

"You gonna take all night in there?"

She jumped at the sound of Lonnie's voice. "I just got in here," she cried.

"Well, hurry it up!"

"I've been hurrying," she called back. "You think it's easy, managing to do this while I hold a baby? Think again. I've only got two hands."

She heard the sound of cars pulling out of the rest area. Even so, she knew Jaimie wasn't safe. If Lonnie realized she had handed him off to a stranger, she wouldn't put it past him to give chase. The man wasn't stupid. Without Jaimie, his hand was weakened. He would have nothing to hold over her head.

Tears streamed down Maggie's face. She stood there, using the door to hold herself up.

From here on in, she thought with giddy relief, *it's just you and me, you bastard.*

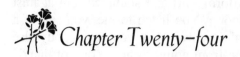 Chapter Twenty-four

"We just got a break!"

Rafe turned from gazing out the window to see Sergeant Hall stepping from the atrium into the kitchen sitting area. "What kind of break?"

"Some gal just called the state police on her cell phone. She says she ran into a young woman in a rest area just outside Jerico who claimed she'd been abducted. Asked this lady to sneak her baby out of the rest room and take him to the nearest police station." Hall made a circle with his thumb and forefinger, his broad face splitting into a grin. "Your baby is safe, and we've got the son of a bitch nailed to the wall. His location *and* a description of the rental car, in case he takes off before we can get there. Not likely, though. Cops are moving in on him from all directions."

Rafe wanted to shout. Only the joy no sooner surged through him than another wave of nearly paralyzing fear came in its wake. Maggie still wasn't safe, and when Lonnie found out she'd managed to get Jaimie away from him, he would probably go crazy.

"Which rest area?" Rafe demanded to know. The neighboring town of Jerico wasn't that far away. He could be there in twenty minutes. "Was the woman north or south of Jerico when she called in?"

Sergeant Hall shook his head. "I can't give you that information, Mr. Kendrick. You'd drive there and only get in the way. Let the police do their job.''

Rafe was on the man in a flash. He grabbed him by the front of his uniform shirt and slammed him against the sliding glass door. "You listen to me, you son of a bitch! That woman's my *wife!* Not you or anybody else is going to keep me from going to her. You got that?''

"Rafe!'' Ryan jumped in, grabbing his brother's arms. "Jesus Christ, have you lost your mind? You can't muscle a police officer around.''

Sanity returned. Rafe released the man and smoothed the front of his uniform shirt. "I, um ... I'm sorry. I, um ... lost my head there for a second.''

Sergeant Hall jerked at his shirt collar and stepped away from the glass. "I could throw your ass in jail. You know that?''

Rafe clenched his teeth, striving to control his temper.

Hall tucked his shirt back in and straightened his badge. "If it weren't for the fact that I've got a wife and kids at home myself and would probably react the same way in a similar situation, I just might do it!''

"He apologized. All right?'' Ryan put in. "He's upset right now. Not thinking clearly. Surely you can understand that.''

Hall nodded. "I realize he's upset. Anyone would be. But I can't be telling him which rest area they're at. It's against regs. If he went and caused a ruckus, or ended up getting himself or someone else killed, it'd be my ass hung out to dry.''

"We understand,'' Ryan assured him. "I do, anyway. And later, when my brother calms down, he will as well.''

Hall rubbed the nape of his neck. "I'll tell you what I *will* do for you, Mr. Kendrick. I'll go back out and stand near the police vehicles.'' He looked directly into Rafe's glittering eyes. "Those damned radios blast so loud, you can hear everything that comes over the air from several feet away.'' He smiled slightly and arched an eyebrow. "I'll keep an ear out and keep you posted on—"

Rafe shoved past him. "Thanks, Hall. I owe you, buddy."

The sergeant leaned out the sliding glass door. "I didn't say a word about those radios. You got it?"

Rafe never broke stride. "I got it."

Less than three minutes later, Rafe had heard the mile-post number of the rest area and was behind the steering wheel of Ryan's pickup. Such was his haste to reach the highway that he peeled rubber in the gravel of the drive, pelting the police cars with rock.

"Don't kill us getting there," Ryan warned, one hand gripping the dash. "We'll be there in fifteen minutes if you don't have a wreck first."

Rafe slammed on the brakes. "Five minutes, tops. If you're not up to the ride, get out now, Ryan."

"*Five?* Holy hell and high water." Ryan gripped the dash with both hands. "I'm going with you. Step on it."

Rafe did just that, grinding gears and peeling rubber as he shifted into fourth, then gunned the accelerator. "Buckle your seat belt and hang on."

Lonnie kicked the metal door, rattling the entire rest room stall with the force of the impact. Huddling on the toilet, Maggie stared under the partition at his wide-spread boots, remembering how he'd pummeled her with those steel-reinforced toes the morning he beat her up. Sweat ran in rivers down her face, trickled from there down her throat, and pooled in the cleavage of her breasts. She had been terrified of this man hundreds of times over the last seven years, but never more so than she was now.

"Lonnie, for heaven's sake," she said, barely managing to keep her voice steady. "I'll be done in just a minute. Just wait for us outside."

"You open this door, *now*, and get your ass out here," he ordered.

Maggie made a grunting noise. "I'm not finished yet. I can't."

"Don't tell me what you can or can't—"

"Oh!" a deep female voice rang out. "I'm sorry. I thought I was in the—I *am* in the ladies' rest room."

"I'm sorry," Lonnie said. "It's my wife. She's sick. No one else was in here, so I came to check on her."

Maggie grunted again. She could almost feel Lonnie's rage radiating through the metal door. She wouldn't be able to put him off for much longer. She could only pray the police came soon.

"Oh," she heard the woman say. "Would you like me to wait outside a second?"

"You okay in there, honey?" Lonnie asked.

"I'm all right," Maggie replied. "I'll be out as soon as I can. I'm sorry to make you wait like this, but I can't help it."

She watched Lonnie's boots step away. As the detested footgear disappeared from sight, she went limp with relief and hung her head.

The stall door next to her opened and clanked shut. She leaned down and looked at the other woman's smudged sneakers. She considered saying nothing, fearful that Lonnie might be lingering near the doorway and would be able to hear her. But she didn't want to put anyone else in danger.

In a stage whisper, she said, "That man who just left is crazy and dangerous. Please, don't stay to use the bathroom. Get out of here. If he goes over the edge and you're still in here, I'm afraid you'll get hurt."

The woman sighed. A second later, Maggie heard a rush of urine. "Have you ever wondered why men get so obnoxious when they're traveling? They're worse than kids."

Nonplussed, Maggie stared at the woman's shoe. Traveling? "No!" she whispered urgently. "You don't understand. He's—"

"Oh, I understand." The woman laughed softly.

"You think I'm hooked up with Prince Charming? If Pete yells at me one more time for having to stop and pee, I'm gonna shove his hot cigarette lighter up his ass. Chain-smoking. Can you believe it? I can barely breathe without my window down, and it's freezing out there. Would you believe he actually counts the cars that he's already passed while I'm using the rest room? They're all ahead of him again, he tells me. Like we're in some kind of race?"

Maggie felt as if she were trapped in a nutty dream. "No, you don't understand, lady. He abducted me! He's got a gun. The police may be on their way. If he hears sirens or sees cop cars, he'll go ballistic. I'm afraid he's going to kill me."

Long silence. Then: "You serious?"

Maggie grunted loudly, just in case Lonnie was listening. "He abducted me at gunpoint. He's already shot one woman tonight. Of course I'm serious. Get out of here, please."

She heard the woman stand up. "Oh, God," she whispered. "I just pissed down my pant leg." Maggie heard her zipper rasp. "Oh, Holy Mother. He's got a gun? I haven't made my Easter duty in six years."

Maggie stared at the puddle spreading over the floor in the next stall. She grunted again for Lonnie's benefit. "He's insane! I don't want anyone else getting hurt. Would you just get out of here?"

The woman made an odd little sound. The next instant, they heard the rest room door open again. Fearful that it was Lonnie coming back, they both stopped talking and listened.

Oh, God, oh, God. Maggie held her breath, praying mindlessly. Lonnie would shoot that woman if she got in his way, just as he had shot Becca.

The stall door to Maggie's right squeaked open and thumped shut. She saw a woman's red-laced hiking boots. Not Lonnie. When she had recovered enough to regain her voice, she leaned down and said, "Lady?

Don't use the bathroom. Just make a U-turn and get out of here. There's a man outside. He's got a gun. Your life may be in danger.''

"This is a joke. Right?'' the newcomer whispered. "Am I on *Candid Camera* or something?''

Candid Camera? Maggie accepted in that moment that the situation was so bizarre as to be unbelievable. Neither of these women was taking her seriously—one of them worrying about her Easter duty and the other thinking there was a hidden camera in her bathroom stall?

This was pointless. This rest area attracted a steady stream of visitors. No matter what she did, someone else was bound to be in here with her when Lonnie realized he'd been hoodwinked. Better that it be these two women than someone with small children.

Maggie rose to her feet, unbolted the lock, and pushed from the stall. She had to do something. Only what? She gazed at the door. No lock. If only she could think of some way to keep Lonnie from entering until the police arrived. She knew she wasn't strong enough to hold the door closed by herself if Lonnie was determined to get in, and there was nothing in the bathroom to barricade it shut. The trash receptacle would only tip over.

She stepped closer to the stalls. "Hurry. Both of you. If any of us are going to live through this, I'm going to need your help, and you'd better hustle before it's too late.''

Both women emerged from the stalls almost simultaneously, the deep-voiced woman in sneakers a stout, broad-shouldered individual, the owner of the hiking boots a thin, pale-faced blonde. Maggie looked them both in the eye.

"That man out there has already murdered one woman tonight, and the three of us will be next unless you help me. Do you understand? This is not a hoax. He's got a gun. We've got to hold that door closed to keep him out of here because he won't hesitate to shoot all of us. He's just that crazy.''

"My mom and kids are waiting out there for me!'' the blonde cried.

Maggie heard brakes squeal. Though she couldn't see outside, all her instincts told her a regular passenger car wouldn't be entering a rest area parking lot at such a high speed. She whirled, her heart pounding. In three running steps, she reached the door and threw her weight against it. Glancing back at the other two women, she cried, "That's probably the cops! Help me, damn it. Don't just—''

"You *bitch!*'' Lonnie yelled from outside. The next instant, he tried to open the door.

Maggie braced against him, using all her strength, but her sneakers merely slid backward on the tile. "Help me!'' she screamed. "Don't just stand there. He'll kill us!''

The sound of squealing tires came again. Maggie heard shouts and cries of alarm. "Freeze, Boyle!'' a man yelled.

A woman screamed. There came a loud crashing sound, as if someone had collided with a garbage can. The other two women rushed to help Maggie, the blonde crying, "Oh, dear God!''

The next instant, the deafening sound of gunfire erupted in the night. Maggie heard running footsteps, people shouting and screeching. The report of one of the guns was so loud that she knew it had to be Lonnie's. Trembling, she pushed against the door with all her might, thankful to have the heavyset woman beside her. The blonde was so slightly built and afraid, she wasn't much help.

At any second, Maggie expected Lonnie to open fire on the door. The bullets would penetrate the wood. She or one of her companions could be killed. With every report of a weapon, she flinched, expecting lead to plow into her body.

* * *

Rafe brought the pickup to a screeching stop and killed the engine, then threw open his door and bailed from the cab. *Maggie*. It was a scene out of his worst nightmare, the rest area crawling with people who were fleeing for their lives. Lonnie Boyle was crouched behind a rock drinking fountain in front of the rest-room block, shooting at the police officers. None of the lawmen could get a clear enough shot at the man to take him down.

Maggie. Where in God's name was she? Rafe scanned the crowd, searching frantically for her. He didn't see her anywhere. Ducking low, he ran toward the nearest police car, using parked vehicles along the curb for cover.

"I'm Rafe Kendrick," he said as he darted around the rear fender of the white bubble top. "It's my wife Boyle abducted. Where is she? Is she safe? I don't see her!"

Crouched behind the open door of his car, the cop glanced back over his shoulder. "Are you crazy, man? Get your ass behind the car."

"Where's my wife!"

The officer swore under his breath. "In the women's john, we think."

"Is she all right?"

"We don't know."

A bullet struck the front fender of the police car, which was parked at a slight angle to provide maximum cover. The state policeman flinched and ducked. "Damn. We've gotta take him out. He's gonna kill someone."

Crouching low, Rafe retraced his steps back to Ryan's pickup. His brother was crouched on the far side of the vehicle, watching the goings-on while protecting himself from the gunfire as best he could. "Where is she?" he asked when he saw Rafe.

"In the rest room, they think." Rafe hunkered next to his brother to take stock of their surroundings. Like most Oregon rest areas, the park-like lawns were bordered by timber and undergrowth. "I'm going to circle around and come in behind him. It's only a matter of time before he decides to storm that bathroom."

"You're gonna what?" Ryan grabbed Rafe's arm. "You can't do that. Are you nuts? The bastard'll shoot you." He gave a shaky laugh. "No way, bro. You don't even have a gun."

"I'm going. If she's still alive, she won't be for long if he goes in there. If something happens to her—" Rafe broke off and swallowed. He met his brother's gaze. In the light of the pole lights, Ryan looked pale and drawn, his eyes glittering with a mixture of anger and fear. "I have to do this."

"I'll go with you then."

"No." Rafe jerked his arm from his brother's grasp. "There's Jaimie and Heidi, Ryan. If something happens, I'm counting on you."

Ryan stared at him for a long moment. Then he finally nodded. No further words were necessary. Using the parked vehicles for cover, Rafe left the truck and ran in a crouch toward the south entrance of the rest area. From there, he would be able to enter the woods unseen, circle around from behind, and approach the rest-room block from the rear. With a little bit of luck, Lonnie would be so preoccupied returning the policemen's fire that Rafe could take him by surprise.

With a little luck. The words became a litany in Rafe's mind as he raced through the woods, thankful with every running step that he could see better than most people in the dark. He fell through the deep snow in places and pitched forward on the ice. He scarcely felt the impact. *Maggie.* He kept seeing her sweet face and her expressive eyes, the way her mouth curved when she smiled. He loved her. So very much. He couldn't let anything happen to her. He simply couldn't. Without her, his own life wouldn't be worth living.

When Rafe reached the rear of the rest room, he

pressed his back against the cement blocks and listened to the gunfire. *Shit*. When he ran out there, Lonnie's bullets wouldn't be the only risk factor. What if one of the cops accidentally shot him?

For a split second, Rafe stood there, weighing the odds, which weren't good. Then he decided he didn't care. He'd lost one family. He knew how it felt afterward—the pain that cut so deep you wanted to die yourself, the sense of hopelessness with no end in sight. He couldn't live through that again. Better to die trying to save her than to live without her.

Rafe pushed out from the wall, darted around the corner, and ran the length of the building in a crouch. The sound of the gunfire suddenly seemed muted, as if it came from a great distance. The pounding of his heart thrummed in his temples.

When he reached the front corner of the building, instead of slowing, he poured on more speed, angling right toward the stone drinking fountain as he burst into the open. *Running, running*. He felt as if he were pushing against a headwind, that every second lasted forever. A boiling rage narrowed Rafe's vision. He focused on Boyle's miserable, cowardly figure crouched behind the wide, tapering base of the stone-and-mortar fountain he used as a shield against the bullets.

Just before Rafe reached him, the other man jerked around, his eyes wide with fright. Rafe saw the gun come up. He tensed, expecting the bullet to rip into him as he leaped. The next instant, his body plowed into Boyle's, and the two of them rolled across the cement.

Ordinarily Rafe would have tried to come out on top. Not this time. Boyle could have that honor. As they rolled to a stop, Rafe shoved hard against the other man's shoulders, lifting him away from his body, hoping to give the police a clear target.

Rage contorted Boyle's features. "You bastard!" he cried.

Rafe felt the muzzle of Boyle's gun stab his ribs. He

tensed, expecting the man to pull the trigger. Before Boyle could, the deafening report of a high-powered rifle rent the air. Boyle jerked, and even in the eerie light, Rafe saw the stunned, disbelieving expression that crossed his face just before he went limp. Rafe shoved at the deadweight and rolled in the opposite direction, struggling to disengage his legs from the dead man's. When he finally managed to pull free, he just lay there on his side for a moment, feeling oddly separated from reality.

Over. It's over, Rafe thought. He had kept his promise. Lonnie Boyle would never lay a hand on Maggie again. He just prayed to God that he wasn't too late.

The thought jerked Rafe from his almost stupor-like trance. He stirred, pushed up on one elbow, and twisted onto his knees, swinging his gaze to the women's restroom door. Only vaguely aware of the cops who swarmed across the grass toward him, Rafe staggered to his feet, one thought repeating in his mind. *Don't let her be dead. Please, don't let her be dead.*

He couldn't feel his feet as he moved toward the door, couldn't feel the wood when he pressed his palm against it. "Maggie?"

When Rafe pushed, the door wouldn't open. He shoved a little harder, his voice ragged with fear when he called out again. "Maggie!"

Still bracing her weight against the door, Maggie didn't immediately recognize Rafe's voice. *Lonnie*, she thought. Then it hit her. Not Lonnie. She sobbed and reached for the door handle. But the two women on either side of her were still shoving with all their might to keep the door closed.

"It's all right," she cried. "It's all right! That's my husband."

The larger woman finally seemed to register what Maggie was saying. She stepped back. The blonde sobbed and stopped pushing as well. Maggie jerked the door open, glimpsed blue chambray and denim, and launched herself at the blur, confident that strong arms would catch her.

Rafe whooped with joy as he captured her in a fierce hug. "Maggie. Oh, God, Maggie."

He was shaking. Shaking horribly. Or was that her? Maggie couldn't tell for sure. Didn't care. It was the most wonderful feeling, having him hold her. He felt so big and solid and safe.

"I called his bluff. I didn't let him bully me. I took Jaimie with me to the bathroom." Maggie realized she was babbling and tried to stop talking, but she couldn't seem to stifle the words. "A lady covered him with her coat and sneaked him out. I did it, Rafe. I stood up to him, and it worked."

He clamped a big hand over the back of her head and pressed her cheek against the hollow of his shoulder. Maggie heard a man say in a furious voice, "What are you, mister, crazy? I damned near shot you! You have a death wish or something?"

Maggie tried to draw away from Rafe, but he tensed his arms to keep her face against his shoulder. "No, honey. Don't look."

As Rafe started to lead her away, Maggie said, "Don't look at what?"

"Lonnie. They shot him. He's dead."

Maggie laughed, the chortle high-pitched and sounding a little hysterical even to her. Dead? Of course he was dead. Otherwise the shooting wouldn't have stopped.

As Rafe drew her across the grass toward the parking area, a uniformed police officer ran up to them. Rafe came to a stop. "Hello, Sergeant Hall. Fancy seeing you here."

"That was a damned fool stunt to pull. You're lucky that sharpshooter didn't kill you!"

Rafe relaxed the arm at Maggie's waist, allowing her

to draw slightly away from him. "All's well that ends well."

For the first time, Maggie actually looked at Rafe. In the bluish-white lighting, she saw black splotches on his shirt. Her heart caught when she realized he was covered with blood. "Oh, my God. You're hurt!"

Rafe glanced down, touched one of the spots, and then shook his head. "No, honey. Not me. The blood is Lonnie's." He flashed one of those crooked grins she had come to love so very much, his gaze meeting the police officer's. "Like I said back at the house, Hall, I owe you. Thanks."

"I almost got you killed," the policeman said. "It's nothing less than a miracle that you're not dead."

"Yeah, well," Rafe said softly, "this time around, I had a miracle coming."

He guided Maggie around the cop, drawing her close as they walked, his lean thigh bumping her hip. She angled forward slightly to peer up at his dark face. "Rafe, how did you get Lonnie's blood all over your shirt?"

"It doesn't matter. What matters is that you're safe." He graced her with another of those fantastic smiles that always warmed her from the inside out. "So you called his bluff, did you? Tell me about it."

Maggie searched his gaze. "What did you do?"

"Nothing much." He jostled her with his arm. "I'm so proud of you, Maggie. Getting Jaimie out of there. Keeping your head. You're really something, you know it?"

Maggie had a feeling he was the one who was really something, but typically of him, he wasn't talking. "You saved me," she said accusingly. "I know you did. You did something crazy. What?"

He chuckled. "I didn't do anything crazy, I swear it." He leaned down to kiss her cheek. "Did the bastard hurt you?"

Maggie shook her head. "I pulled in here before he had a chance."

Ryan came loping across the grass to them. When he reached them, he said, "Jesus, Rafe. That was all right!"

Maggie dug in with her heels to stop. "That's it! I want to hear this. What did he do, Ryan?"

Ryan launched into an account of what had occurred while Maggie had been holding the rest-room door closed and was unable to see what was going on. When she learned how her husband had raced out into the line of fire to jump Lonnie from behind, she felt as if she might faint.

"Nothing much, you said. That's what you call nothing much? You might have been killed. How could you do something so stupid?"

Rafe released her as they drew up beside the truck. As he unbuttoned his shirt, peeled it off, and tossed it in the back, Maggie ran her gaze over him, thinking she'd never seen anyone so beautiful. It scared her half to death, thinking of how close she'd come to losing him. It also made her heart feel as it were breaking, for what he had just done gave testimony to how very much he loved her.

So much that he would lay down his life for her.

As he turned back toward her, his bronze upper body shimmered like lacquered teak in the dim light, the play of muscle in his shoulders and chest tempting her to touch him. Her gaze climbed slowly to his dark face. His hair lay in tousled, unruly waves of glistening ebony over his high forehead. The silvery glimmer of his eyes seemed to burn into hers, reminding her of the night when she'd first met him. His gunmetal-blue gaze had held her in its grip then, too, only now its searing intensity enveloped her with warmth.

She remembered how she'd once wished he were a toad who'd be magically transformed into a handsome prince who would rescue her and Jaimie. Many times since, she'd wondered if he were an avenging angel, sent down to her from God in answer to her prayers.

He was neither of those things, although she would always believe God had guided him to her. Not a prince, not an avenging angel. Rafe Kendrick was just a flesh-and-blood man—a boxcar cowboy in Wrangler jeans and riding boots.

As she stepped into his waiting embrace, Maggie kissed his shoulder, tasted the salt on his skin, and gloried in the hard, rugged length of him pressed against her. He felt as real, and solid, and enduring as the sun-warmed earth. Even better, he was all hers.

How could there be anything more magical than that?

Epilogue

Sunlight glanced off the water, making the calm lake look like a dark velvet blanket studded with diamonds. Tipping her head back, Maggie breathed in the fresh mountain air, her gaze fixed on the snowcapped peaks that ringed the small basin. She had grown to love this place, just as Rafe had once promised she would. Now it was home to her, a perfect world that was filled with all the people she loved most . . . her husband and child . . . her mom and sister . . . and all of Rafe's family as well. How could anyone be so lucky? Maggie didn't know, but she had finally come to believe this was going to be her reality from now on. Some magic didn't vanish in a puff of smoke . . . It was solid and enduring . . . and *hers*.

A distant shout drew her attention. She glanced up to see Heidi and Rafe emerging from the trees on horseback. Her little sister was laughing gaily, her smaller mount a gentle and well-trained sorrel, handpicked by Rafe to ensure the child's safety as she learned to ride. Heidi was clearly in her element, her erect but graceful posture in the saddle a promise of the expert horsewoman she was destined to become.

Maggie smiled and focused on her husband. He lifted a hand and waved. Even at a distance, she could see the love shining in his eyes and it enfolded her in warmth. Oh, how she adored him . . .

Tears of joy stung her eyes as she watched him ride toward her. He was mounted on Flash Dancer, the gorgeous stallion he'd once hated with such virulence that he'd threatened to shoot him, and seated in front of him on the saddle was Jaimie, who'd just turned nine months old.

In that moment, Maggie was reminded of the snapshot of Rafe and Keefer that she'd seen in the airplane hangar that long ago day when she'd first arrived at the ranch. Time and a wealth of love had restored her husband to his former self, she realized. Gone was the gaunt, tortured man she'd first met on a boxcar. He'd put on weight, every ounce of it well-toned muscle. Even as she gazed at him, the wind ruffled his black hair, and his laughter drifted to her on the breeze. He looked young again, and so very happy. It filled her with wonder to know her presence in his life had brought about the transformation.

As he rode closer, Maggie noted the careful way he held Jaimie, one big hand splayed over the baby's plump tummy to keep him from falling. She smiled again, recalling how she'd once worried about Jaimie being around horses. *No worries.* Rafe would lay down his life before he allowed anything to happen to his son.

"It's your turn, angel face," he called to her.

Maggie rolled her eyes. "No way! I'm not joining all of you in your insanity. I'm perfectly content here on the ground, thank you very much."

"Aw, come on, Maggie!" Heidi pleaded. "You can ride in front of Rafe. He won't let you fall. I'll stay here and help watch the baby!"

"Help who watch him? I'm the only one here. No thanks, sweetkins. I'll just stay put and let the three of you have all the fun."

"I'll watch him for a while!" a voice called from somewhere behind her.

Maggie glanced over her shoulder to see Becca ambling down the slope. She carried a wicker basket, and

Maggie was pleased to note that she bore its weight with her left arm, yet another sign that she was almost completely recovered from the gunshot wound to her shoulder.

Helen, Maggie's mother, trailed behind the housekeeper, her dark hair trailing like strands of silk in the wind, her blue dress molded to her slender body. "I can help take care of him, too!" she called. "Go ahead and go for a ride, Maggie. Rafe won't let anything happen to you." She cast her son-in-law an adoring glance. "Will you, Rafe?"

Rafe winked. "Never. I love her too much to let her get hurt." He glanced back at Maggie. "It's a question of trust. Everyone else has faith in me. Don't you?"

"What is this, a plot against me?" Maggie said with a laugh.

Becca grinned. "You bet. A body can't be living on this ranch in peace until she can ride a horse. Where's your courage?"

"I left it up at the house."

Becca set down the basket and stepped over to take the baby from Rafe. Flash Dancer snorted as she approached, but despite his apparent wariness of the housekeeper's flapping white apron, the stallion stood fast. Maggie suspected that the animal sensed he was carrying an easily unseated rider, for usually the horse lived up to his name, prancing proudly and throwing his head, for all the world as if he knew how beautiful he was and wanted to show off.

Sure enough, the instant Becca had Jaimie safely in her arms, the stallion sidestepped, his tail uplifted, his magnificent body rippling like varnished cherry in the sunlight.

"No excuses," Rafe said, swaying easily with the movements of his mount as he extended a broad palm toward her. "Come for a ride with me, Maggie girl."

The heated gleam in his eyes told Maggie that he had more than a short ride in mind. Her heartbeat skittered.

Surely he didn't intend to make love to her in the woods in broad daylight? *He did.* His firm mouth tipped into a challenging grin, and his gaze moved slowly over her with a burning intensity.

Like a marionette controlled by invisible strings, Maggie felt herself pushing up from the blanket and walking toward him. As much as she feared horses, a trip to heaven was worth dying for . . .

She took her husband's hand, and then, following his instructions, put her left foot in the vacated stirrup. He did the rest, lifting her with the brutal strength that had become her protection and constant sense of security. After some shifting and heart-stopping jostles, Maggie managed to get seated in the saddle in front of her husband.

"Oh, God!" The ground looked miles away, and Flash Dancer was tossing his head, his brown eyes rimmed with white when he looked back at her. "He hates me!"

Rafe laughed, the sound a low rumble that vibrated through her body as he hooked a muscular arm around her waist and drew her against him. "He's scared, Maggie. He smells your fear, and he's wondering where the threat is, that's all."

"I want off," Maggie cried, making tight fists in the stallion's mane. "I *knew* this wasn't for me. Oh, God. I'm going to die. He'll fall and land on top of us."

Rafe hauled sharply on the reins, turning the horse back toward the woods. "You're perfectly safe. Trust me."

"I trust you. It's the horse I have a problem—oh, my God! Don't go *fast!*"

If Rafe heard her shrill objections, he gave no indication of it. Leaning slightly forward, his hard chest pressing against her back like an immovable brick wall, he clicked his tongue, nudged at Flash Dancer's flanks, and urged the horse to a greater speed.

"Oh, God!" Maggie closed her eyes. "My butt. It hurts."

Rafe tightened his hold on her. "Put your feet on my boots and lever yourself up a bit so you don't bounce."

Maggie did as he told her, and the next instant, she felt as if she were floating. Rafe rode along the lakeshore for quite some distance, slowing the horse from a run to a trot only as they veered toward the forest.

"Where are we going?" Maggie asked.

"Someplace private."

She laughed, no longer feeling afraid. Flash Dancer moved with fluid power and surefooted grace. "You're out of luck. My fanny will never be the same. It'll be a week before you can touch me!"

"The hell it will. I'll kiss all the soreness away."

"Is that a threat or a promise?"

Rafe's only response was a mischievous chuckle. He slowed the horse to a walk and started nibbling on her ear. As always when he set his mind to seducing her, Maggie's blood began to heat. When she felt his hand moving from her waist to her breast, her breath caught and she leaned more heavily against him. This added an entirely new aspect to horseback riding.

"We can't do this," she protested weakly. "It's the middle of the day."

"Magic, honey. Come with me, and I promise you, it'll be pure magic."

Surrendering herself to the sensation of being set afire by his touch, Maggie could only moan.

He stopped the horse in a shady grove, far away from seeing eyes. When he dismounted and swept Maggie from the saddle into his strong arms, she went willingly, her reservations obliterated by the intoxication of his kisses.

He had promised her magic, after all.

And Rafe Kendrick was a man of his word . . .